PRAISE FOR AMY CLIPSTON

"This heartbreaking series continues to take a fearlessly honest look at grief, as hopelessness threatens to steal what happiness Allen has treasured within his marriage and recent fatherhood. Clipston takes these feelings seriously without sugarcoating any aspect of the mourning process, allowing her characters to make their painful but ultimately joyous journey back to love and faith. Readers who have made this tough and ongoing pilgrimage themselves will appreciate the author's realistic portrayal of coming to terms with loss in order to continue living with hope and happiness."

—RT BOOK REVIEWS, 4 STARS, ON ROOM ON THE PORCH SWING

"A story of grief as well as new beginnings, this is a lovely Amish tale and the start of a great new series."

—PARKERSBURG NEWS AND SENTINEL ON A PLACE AT OUR TABLE

"Themes of family, forgiveness, love, and strength are woven throughout the story . . . a great choice for all readers of Amish fiction."

—CBA MARKET MAGAZINE ON A PLACE AT OUR TABLE

"This debut title in a new series offers an emotionally charged and engaging read headed by sympathetically drawn and believable protagonists. The meaty issues of trust and faith make this a solid book group choice."

—LIBRARY JOURNAL ON A PLACE AT OUR TABLE

"These sweet, tender novellas from one of the genre's best make the perfect sampler for new readers curious about Amish romances."

—LIBRARY JOURNAL ON AMISH SWEETHEARTS

"Clipston is as reliable as her character, giving Emily a difficult and intense romance worthy of Emily's ability to shine the light of Christ into the hearts of those she loves."

—RT BOOK REVIEWS, 4½ STARS, TOP PICK! ON THE CHERISHED QUILT

"Clipston's heartfelt writing and engaging characters make her a fan favorite. Her latest Amish tale combines a spiritual message of accepting God's blessings as they are given with a sweet romance."

—LIBRARY JOURNAL ON THE CHERISHED QUILT

"In the first book in her Amish Heirloom series, Clipston takes readers on a roller-coaster ride through grief, guilt, and anxiety."

—BOOKLIST ON THE FORGOTTEN RECIPE

"Clipston delivers another enchanting series starter with a tasty premise, family secrets, and sweet-as-pie romance, offering assurance that true love can happen more than once and second chances are worth fighting for."

—RT BOOK REVIEWS, 4½ STARS, TOP PICK!
ON THE FORGOTTEN RECIPE

"Clipston is well versed in Amish culture and does a good job creating the world of Lancaster County, Penn. . . . Amish fiction fans will enjoy this story—and want a taste of Veronica's raspberry pie!"

—PUBLISHERS WEEKLY ON THE FORGOTTEN RECIPE

"[Clipston] does an excellent job of wrapping up her story while setting the stage for the sequel."

—CBA RETAILERS + RESOURCES ON THE FORGOTTEN RECIPE

"Clipston brings this engaging series to an end with two emotional family reunions, a prodigal son parable, a sweet but hard-won romance, and a happy ending for characters readers have grown to love. Once again, she gives us all we could possibly want from a talented storyteller."

—RT BOOK REVIEWS, 4½ STARS, TOP PICK! ON A SIMPLE PRAYER

". . . will leave readers craving more."

—RT BOOK REVIEWS, 4½ STARS, TOP PICK! ON A MOTHER'S SECRET

"Clipston's series starter has a compelling drama involving faith, family, and romance . . . [an] absorbing series."

—RT BOOK REVIEWS, 4½ STARS, TOP PICK! ON A HOPEFUL HEART

"Authentic characters, delectable recipes, and faith abound in Clipston's second Kauffman Amish Bakery story."

—RT BOOK REVIEWS, 4 STARS ON A PROMISE OF HOPE

". . . an entertaining story of Amish life, loss, love and family."

—RT BOOK REVIEWS, 4 STARS ON A PLACE OF PEACE

"This fifth and final installment in the Kauffman Amish Bakery series is sure to please fans who have waited for Katie's story."

—LIBRARY JOURNAL ON A SEASON OF LOVE

"[The Kauffman Amish Bakery] series' wide popularity is sure to attract readers to this novella, and they won't be disappointed by the excellent writing and the story's wholesome goodness."

—LIBRARY JOURNAL ON A PLAIN AND SIMPLE CHRISTMAS

A SEAT BY THE HEARTH

OTHER BOOKS BY AMY CLIPSTON

A SEAT BY THE HEARTH

An Amish Homestead Novel

AMY CLIPSTON

 ZONDERVAN®

ZONDERVAN

A Seat by the Hearth
Copyright © 2018 by Amy Clipston

Requests for information should be addressed to:
Zondervan, 3900 Sparks Dr. SE, Grand Rapids, Michigan 49546

ISBN 978-0-310-34909-9 (ebook)
ISBN 978-0-310-63655-7 (custom)

Library of Congress Cataloging-in-Publication
Names: Clipston, Amy, author.
Title: A seat by the hearth / Amy Clipston.
Description: Nashville : Zondervan, [2018] | Series: An Amish Homestead novel ; 3
Identifiers: LCCN 2018017484 | ISBN 9780310349082 (paperback)
Subjects: LCSH: Amish--Fiction. | GSAFD: Christian fiction. | Love stories.
Classification: LCC PS3603.L58 S45 2018 | DDC 813/.6--dc23 LC record available at https://lccn.loc.gov/2018017484

Printed in the United States of America

21 22 23 24 25 / LSC / 10 9 8 7 6 5 4 3 2 1

For editor Jean Bloom with love and appreciation.
Thank you for using your amazing talent to polish my books and
keep my characters and timelines straight. You're a blessing!

GLOSSARY

ach: oh

aenti: aunt

appeditlich: delicious

Ausbund: Amish hymnal

bedauerlich: sad

boppli: baby

bopplin: babies

brot: bread

bruder: brother

bruderskind: niece/nephew

bruderskinner: nieces/nephews

bu: boy

buwe: boys

daadi: granddad

daadihaus: a small house built onto or near the main house for grandparents to live in

daed: father

danki: thank you

dat: dad

Dietsch: Pennsylvania Dutch, the Amish language (a German dialect)

dochder: daughter

dochdern: daughters

Dummle!: Hurry!

Englisher: a non-Amish person
faul: lazy
faulenzer: lazy person
fraa: wife
freind: friend
freinden: friends
froh: happy
gegisch: silly
gern gschehne: you're welcome
grossdaadi: grandfather
grossdochder: granddaughter
grossdochdern: granddaughters
grossmammi: grandmother
gross-sohn: grandson
Gude mariye: Good morning
gut: good
Gut nacht: Good night
haus: house
Ich liebe dich: I love you
kaffi: coffee
kapp: prayer covering or cap
kichli: cookie
kichlin: cookies
kind: child
kinner: children
krank: sick
kuche: cake
kumm: come
liewe: love, a term of endearment
maed: young women, girls
maedel: young woman
mamm: mom

mammi: grandma

mei: my

Meiding: shunning

mutter: mother

naerfich: nervous

narrisch: crazy

onkel: uncle

Ordnung: the oral tradition of practices required and forbidden
  in the Amish faith

schee: pretty

schmaert: smart

schtupp: family room

schweschder: sister

schweschdere: sisters

sohn: son

Was iss letz?: What's wrong?

Willkumm: Welcome

Wie geht's: How do you do? or Good day!

wunderbaar: wonderful

ya: yes

zwillingbopplin: twins

AMISH HOMESTEAD
SERIES FAMILY TREES

Edna m. Yonnie Allgyer
|
Priscilla

Marilyn m. Willie Dienner
|
Simeon (deceased)
Kayla m. James "Jamie" Riehl
Nathan

Eva m. Simeon (deceased)
Dienner
|
Simeon Jr. ("Junior")

Nellie m. Walter Esh
|
Judah
Naaman

Laura m. Allen Lambert
|
Mollie Faith (mother—Savilla—
deceased)

Irma Mae m. Milton Lapp
|
Savilla

Florence m. Vernon Riehl
|
James ("Jamie") Riehl (mother—
Dorothy—deceased)
Walter Esh (father—Alphus
Esh—deceased)
Mark Riehl (Laura's twin)
(mother—Dorothy—deceased)
Laura (Mark's twin) m. Allen
Lambert (mother—Dorothy—
deceased)
Roy Esh (father—Alphus Esh—
deceased)
Sarah Jane Esh (father—Alphus
Esh—deceased)
Cindy Riehl (mother—
Dorothy—deceased)

Kayla m. James "Jamie" Riehl
|
Calvin

Elsie m. Noah Zook
|
Christian
Lily Rose

NOTE TO THE READER

WHILE THIS NOVEL IS SET AGAINST THE REAL BACK-drop of Lancaster County, Pennsylvania, the characters are fictional. There is no intended resemblance between the characters in this book and any real members of the Amish or Mennonite communities. As with any work of fiction, I've taken license in some areas of research as a means of creating the necessary circumstances for my characters. My research was thorough; however, it would be impossible to be completely accurate in details and description, since every community differs. Therefore, any inaccuracies in the Amish and Mennonite lifestyles portrayed in this book are completely due to fictional license.

ONE

PRISCILLA ALLGYER'S HANDS TREMBLED AS HER TAXI sped down the two-lane road. When the Allgyer's Belgian and Dutch Harness Horses sign came into view, her stomach seemed to twist.

She turned to her son, who'd nodded off in the booster seat beside her.

"Ethan." She nudged him. "Ethan, wake up. We're here."

"Already?" His honey-brown eyes fluttered open as he yawned. "But I just fell asleep." He peered out the window as the Prius steered up the winding rock driveway.

When they reached the top, she could see her father's line of red barns and stables. She'd been away for eight years, but all the buildings looked as pristine as if they'd just been painted. Perhaps they had. The white split-rail fence lining the enormous, lush, rolling green pasture where his beautiful horses frolicked looked the same. The large, two-story whitewashed house where she was born and raised seemed just as immaculate. Every building, every blade of grass on her father's horse farm was as impeccable as she remembered.

If only her childhood had been as perfect.

"This is where you grew up, Mom?"

"Yes." Her chest constricted as the taxi bumped over the rocks. She cleared her throat and tried to shake off the apprehension coiling through her. When she left all those years ago, she promised she'd never return.

But here she was with nothing but a few dollars to her name and a child she'd had out of wedlock.

"It's nice." Ethan pointed to the row of barns after unbuckling himself. "It's a horse farm?"

She nodded. Ethan lowered his window, and the humid July air mixed with the familiar aroma of moist earth and horses permeated the taxi and overpowered her senses.

"I can touch the horses?"

She shrugged. "I imagine so." *If my father even allows us to stay.*

She shoved that thought away. Aside from a few nights in a motel and then a homeless shelter, her parents were her only hope. Priscilla would do anything to give her son a safe home.

When she noticed movement in the corner of her vision, she turned toward her father's largest barn. The door had swung open, and a man stood with his back to the driveway. He looked taller than Robert Yoder, the farmhand who had worked for her father since she was a teenager. His shoulders seemed broader too.

The taxi came to a halt in front of the house, and Priscilla's attention was drawn to her childhood home. Her palms began to sweat as she studied the wraparound porch. Her father's harsh voice and biting criticisms echoed in her mind, and when she closed her eyes and rubbed her temples against a coming headache, she could still see his disappointed face.

This was a mistake. Her father would never forgive her. Maybe they should have stayed in Baltimore with Trent. Her left hand moved to her right bicep, hidden by the three-quarter sleeve of her purple shirt. The situation there might have improved if she'd tried harder to keep Trent happy.

But it wasn't safe to keep Ethan in that environment! It was her duty to protect her son.

"Miss?" The taxi driver turned to face her. "I think we're here."

Priscilla had just opened her mouth to respond when a tap near Ethan's open window startled her. She spun toward it and was surprised to find Mark Riehl peering in.

"Can I help—" He stopped, recognition sparkling in his bright-blue eyes. "Priscilla?"

"Mark. Hi." She tried to force a smile, but it felt more like a grimace.

"Your *dat* didn't mention you were coming home today." He glanced toward the house and then back at her.

"I didn't tell either of my parents I was coming." Her throat suddenly felt bone-dry.

"Oh." He smiled. "They're going to be surprised."

That was an understatement. "Yes, they sure are."

Mark turned his attention to Ethan and smiled. "Hi. I'm Mark." He extended his arm through the open window, and Ethan shook his hand.

"Hi. I'm Ethan. I'm six and a half. We're here to visit my grandparents."

"It's nice to meet you." Mark grinned as his eyes flickered back to Priscilla.

She swallowed a groan. Why did Mark Riehl, one of her schoolmates and an acquaintance from her youth group, have to be at her father's farm when she arrived? Coming home was difficult enough. Facing a peer from her past made it even more painful. News of her arrival would rage through the community like wildfire, and she was certain that judgment would follow.

"Miss?" The driver faced her again. "Are you going to get out of the car? Or do you want me to take you somewhere else?"

Priscilla hesitated as anxiety gushed through her. If she told the driver to take her to the nearest motel, she and Ethan could try this again tomorrow. But Mark had already seen her and—

"Let's go, Mom!" Ethan's insistence broke through her thoughts.

Mark stepped back from the door as Ethan wrenched it open, climbed out of the taxi, and started for the front porch. Mark bent down and leaned inside. "Do you have any luggage?"

"Yes, I do." She pointed toward the trunk. "We have two big suitcases."

"I'll get them for you." Mark tapped the roof to signal the driver to open the trunk, pushed the door closed, and then disappeared around the back of the car.

Priscilla paid the fare and thanked the driver before getting out. The stifling heat slammed into her like a brick wall as she turned to where Mark had both suitcases already sitting on the driveway.

"Ethan," Mark called as he closed the trunk, "why don't you come pull one of these suitcases to the bottom of those steps for me?"

"Okay!" Ethan jogged back down the porch steps and grabbed the handle of one of the suitcases before bumping it along the rock path.

Priscilla fingered the strap of her purse as the yellow taxi steered back down the driveway. She should have asked the driver to take them to a motel. Her mother might welcome her, but her father would most likely slam the door in her face.

"Priscilla?"

She looked up and found Mark studying her. He seemed taller than she remembered. While he'd always been taller than she was, as were most of her peers, he looked as if he towered over her five-foot-two stature by at least eight inches. Not only were his shoulders broader than she recalled, but his striking blue eyes seemed even more intelligent. He was more handsome than she remembered, too, with his light-brown hair, strong jaw, and electric smile.

He had an easy demeanor as well, and she bit back a frown. Mark Riehl had always been aware of just how attractive he was, and he enjoyed the attention of all the young women who followed him around, waiting for him to choose one of them to be his girlfriend.

Mark's twin sister, Laura, had been one of her best friends, but Mark had never seemed to notice Priscilla. No one did. She'd always felt as if she faded into the background with all the young men in their youth group. They noticed Laura and the other, prettier young women instead.

A smile turned up the corners of Mark's lips. "Are you ready to go into the *haus*?" He nodded toward the front porch. "Your *dat* walked inside a few minutes ago. I think your *mamm* is making supper."

"Mom!" Ethan's voice held a thread of whining as he called from the porch steps. "I'm hungry, and I need to use the bathroom."

"I'm coming." She started up the path with Mark at her side, and an awkward silence fell between them.

"What's that house for?" Ethan pointed toward the small cottage behind her parents' large farmhouse.

"That's called the *daadihaus*."

Ethan snickered. "The *what* house?"

"It's where my grandparents lived when I was little." Her heart felt heavy at the memory of her father's mother, who was widowed when Priscilla was still just a toddler. If only *Mammi* were still alive. She would've welcomed her and her son home. "My father's farmhand, Robert Yoder, lives there."

"He doesn't live there anymore." Mark lifted the suitcase he'd been pulling and carried it up the porch steps. "He quit a little over a year ago and moved to Ohio with his new *fraa*."

"What's a *fraw*?" Ethan scrunched his nose.

"*Fraa* means wife." Priscilla turned back to Mark. "Robert moved to Ohio?"

"*Ya.*" He set down the suitcase. "He met a woman who was here visiting relatives, and they fell in love. They married, and he moved to Ohio, where she was from." He went back down the steps for the second suitcase.

"Who's working for my father, then?"

"I am." When Mark reached the porch again, he opened the screen door and set each suitcase inside the family room. Then he held the door open for her and Ethan.

Questions swirled through her mind. Why would Mark work for her father when his own father owned a dairy farm? Wouldn't he be expected to help run the family business?

As she followed Ethan into the house, memories mixed with the smell of fried chicken wafted over her. She scanned the family room. It was just as she remembered. The two brown sofas her parents purchased before she was born still sat in the middle of the room, flanked by their favorite tan wing chairs. The two propane lamps and the matching oak end tables and coffee table were the same too.

The doorway at the far side of the room led to a hallway that led to her parents' bedroom and a bathroom. The staircase to the four upstairs bedrooms and another bathroom sat to her left. The stairs seemed to beckon her to venture to the second floor to see if her old room was still decorated the way it was when she'd snuck out of the house that night, leaving a note promising to never return.

Ethan took her hand in his and tugged. "Where are my grandparents?"

"Your grandmother is probably through there." Priscilla pointed to the doorway to her right.

Taking a deep breath, she steered Ethan into the large kitchen. Her mother stood at the stove, her back to the doorway, turning over pieces of chicken with a pair of metal tongs.

"Yonnie, I told you I would call you when supper was ready." She lowered the flame and half turned around. When her eyes focused on Priscilla and Ethan, she gasped and whirled. The tongs dropped to the floor with a clatter. "Priscilla?"

"Hi, *Mamm*." Tears stung Priscilla's eyes.

Mamm's mouth worked, but no words escaped.

"Hi." Ethan skipped over to her. "I'm Ethan, your grandson." He looked back at Priscilla over his shoulder. "How do you say grandson in Dutch?"

"*Gross-sohn*," Priscilla responded, her voice thick with raging emotion.

Mamm made a strangled noise and pulled Ethan into her arms. "My prayers have been answered!"

Priscilla wiped her eyes as guilt, hot and biting, nearly overcame her.

Mark leaned against the doorframe and folded his arms over his chest. "You haven't taught him Dutch." It was a statement, not a question.

"No." She shook her head. "His father didn't like me to speak it."

"Huh." Mark rubbed his clean-shaven chin.

"Priscilla." *Mamm* closed the distance between them and pulled her into a crushing hug, forcing the air from Priscilla's lungs. Then she stepped back and touched Priscilla's face. "You look tired."

"It's been a long day." Priscilla looked up at her mother, taking in her affectionate, dark-brown eyes and pretty face. Lines reflected the eight years that had passed.

"I can't believe you're here." A sheen of tears glistened in her eyes as she caressed the thick ponytail that cascaded past Priscilla's shoulders to the middle of her back. "Why didn't you call or write so I could prepare? I would have had your favorite meal ready for you."

"This wasn't planned. I mean, I had been hoping to come visit, but I ... Well, I wasn't sure when I was going to be able to ..." Her hand fluttered to her right bicep again.

There was so much she wanted to share with her mother, but she couldn't hurt her that way. Besides, they had an audience. Not only was Ethan there, but Mark Riehl, a man she'd never trust with her deepest secrets, was still watching them.

"I wanted to surprise you." Priscilla tried to smile, but her mother's eyes were assessing her. *Mamm* could probably sense she wasn't telling the truth.

"Are you back for *gut*?" *Mamm* touched Priscilla's cheek again.

"Possibly. Would that be okay?" Priscilla could hear the humiliating thread of supplication in her voice. She cleared her throat and glanced at Ethan, who had taken a seat at the long kitchen table where Priscilla had eaten all her meals while growing up.

"Of course it will be okay." *Mamm* nodded with emphasis. "This is still your home."

Will Dat *agree with that?* Priscilla felt her lips press together with apprehension.

"Would you like me to carry the suitcases upstairs for you?" Mark asked.

Priscilla spun toward the doorway. Mark shifted his weight on his feet as if he were eager to leave.

"No, I think I can handle them, but thanks for offering."

Mark lifted an eyebrow. "They're pretty heavy. I don't mind carrying them up for you before I go." He gestured toward the suitcases. "Just let me know where you want them."

"It's fine. Really," Priscilla said, insisting.

Mark nodded. "All right. It was nice seeing you. I'll head home now." He nodded at her mother. "I'll see you tomorrow, Edna. *Gut nacht.*" He turned to go.

"No, wait," *Mamm* called after him. "Stay for supper."

Priscilla studied her mother. Why would her mother invite Mark to stay? Did she think his presence might keep her father from lashing out?

"*Danki,* but I need to get home." He jammed his thumb toward the front door. "*Mei schweschder* and her family are coming over for supper tonight."

"Laura?" Priscilla asked, her heart swelling with affection for her best friend. How she'd missed both Laura and their mutual best friend, Savilla Lapp, over the years. Leaving them behind had been almost as difficult as leaving her mother.

"*Ya.*" Mark smiled. "She'll be *froh* to hear you're back."

"Oh. Tell her I said hello." Would Laura accept her back into the community after learning she'd had a child out of wedlock?

"I will."

A door clicked shut somewhere in the house, and then Mark looked toward the far end of the family room. "Hi, Yonnie. I was just getting ready to leave."

"Where did these suitcases come from? Is someone here visiting? Why didn't I know about this?"

Priscilla trembled at the sound of *Dat*'s voice. The moment had arrived. Her father might tell her and Ethan to leave. She held her breath and sent a silent prayer to God.

Please let him take pity on Ethan and me. I need to stay until I can earn enough money to rent a safe place for us. Please help me be the mother Ethan deserves.

"Yonnie!" *Mamm* called. "You have to see who's here! It's a miracle."

"Ethan." Priscilla held out her hand. "Come here and meet your grandfather."

Ethan crossed the kitchen to stand next to her, a smile spreading across his face. Surely her father wouldn't break her son's heart.

Dat appeared in the kitchen doorway, and although his dark-brown hair was now threaded with gray, he was the same tall, wide, overbearing man she remembered.

"Priscilla?" He seemed surprised, but then the look in his dark eyes turned fierce. "What are you wearing?" His eyes moved up and down her attire.

Her cheeks heated as she brushed her sweaty palms over her worn jeans.

Dat's face transformed into a deep scowl as his eyes trained on hers again. "Why isn't your head covered?"

His words seemed to punch her in the stomach.

"I'll get you a headscarf." *Mamm* hurried into the utility room off the kitchen.

"Yonnie," Mark called from behind her father. "I'm going to leave."

Priscilla had forgotten Mark was standing there until he spoke, and she longed to run and hide under the table. Why did he have to witness this painful and embarrassing conversation? When her father didn't respond, Mark stayed put. Why didn't he just leave? He'd already said good-bye.

"Who is this?" *Dat* pointed to Ethan.

"My son." Priscilla's voice was soft and shaky. Why did she allow her father to steal her confidence? She forced herself to stand a little taller as she addressed him. Then she turned to Ethan. She had to shield him from her father's festering anger and disapproval.

"Why don't you go use the bathroom in the hallway?" She pointed toward the family room. "Just walk through there. You'll see the door to the bathroom down on the right."

Ethan hesitated, dividing a look between Priscilla and her father. Then he nodded and hurried off.

"Didn't *Mamm* tell you about him? We exchanged letters."

Dat looked toward the utility room. "Your *mamm* didn't tell me she wrote to you. I told her any contact with you is forbidden because you're shunned." His icy voice seemed to bounce off the cabinets before seeping through her skin.

"Here you go." *Mamm* appeared beside her with a light-blue scarf. "Put this over your hair. I kept your dresses, so you can put one on tomorrow." She gave Priscilla a smile that seemed more forced than genuine.

"*Danki*," Priscilla whispered as she covered her hair with the scarf before tying it under her ponytail.

Dat frowned at her mother. "Why didn't you tell me our *dochder* had a *bu*?"

Mamm fingered her apron and looked between Priscilla and *Dat* as she'd always done when *Dat* criticized her. Couldn't *Mamm* ever stand up to him? It was obvious nothing had changed in this house. Anger, hot and explosive, heated her from the inside.

"I knew it would upset you," *Mamm* finally said.

"And you continued to write to Priscilla after I told you not to."

To Priscilla's surprise, *Mamm* lifted her chin. "*Ya*, I did. She's our *dochder*, and Ethan is our *gross-sohn*," she said. "They're our family."

"She's shunned," he repeated before turning his glare back to Priscilla. "Where's your husband?"

"I don't have one, and I left his father." Priscilla folded her arms over her waist, trying to calm her shaking body.

Dat's eyes widened, and she braced herself, awaiting the explosion.

Priscilla's gaze flickered to Mark, and she found his eyes

focused on her. Trepidation detonated in her gut. If only her father had waited to have this conversation until Mark was gone. Now before the next Sunday church service the entire community would buzz with the juicy gossip that Priscilla Allgyer had not only returned, but with a child born out of wedlock.

Mark nodded at her, adjusted his straw hat on his head, and slipped into the family room. She heard the front door shut behind him.

"You came back to *mei haus* with a *kind*, and you're not married?" *Dat's* voice rose.

"Yonnie," *Mamm* began, her voice trembling. "Please—"

"It's all right, *Mamm*. This was a bad idea." She ran to the front door and yanked it open, hoping she could catch Mark. When she spotted him walking toward one of the barns, she ran to the edge of the porch and leaned on the railing. "Mark!"

He spun and faced her. *"Ya?"*

"Would you please take Ethan and me to a motel?"

He hesitated, but only for a moment. *"Ya,* sure." He pointed toward the barn. "I just need to hitch up my horse."

"Thank you."

"No!" *Mamm* appeared on the porch, her eyes glistening. "Please don't go." She folded her hands as if she were praying. "I just got you back and met Ethan. My heart can't take losing you again."

"I can't stay here if *Dat* is going to criticize Ethan and me." Priscilla pointed to the open door behind her mother as her eyes filled with threatening tears. "I need a healthy and safe environment for my son."

"I understand, but please give me a chance to talk to your *dat.*" *Mamm* touched her shoulder.

Ethan appeared in the doorway. "I'm hungry."

Mamm gave Priscilla a hopeful look. "Will you please stay for supper?"

Priscilla hesitated as she glanced toward where Mark stood hitching his horse to his buggy.

"Please," *Mamm* said.

Priscilla glanced at Ethan in the doorway, taking in his sweet face. He looked confused at the idea that they might not be staying. She was grateful he hadn't heard her father's horrible words, but there might be times when she wouldn't be able to shield him. Could she risk that? And could she tolerate her father for the sake of both her mother and her son?

"Just give me a chance to talk to him," *Mamm* whispered. "I'll smooth things over with him, and everything will be fine."

"I'll give him one night," Priscilla said, lowering her own voice. "If he doesn't treat me better, especially in front of Ethan, we're leaving."

"*Danki.*" *Mamm* smiled as she took Priscilla's hands in hers. "I'm so *froh* you're here." Then she turned toward Ethan. "Do you like fried chicken?"

Ethan's face brightened, and he clapped his hands. "Yeah!"

"Will you help me set the table?" *Mamm* asked as she started toward the door.

"Yes," Ethan said.

Mamm touched his shoulder as they walked into the house together.

Priscilla turned toward the barn again.

"Priscilla?" *Mamm* stopped in the doorway. "Are you coming inside?"

"*Ya,*" she said, easily slipping into the language she now realized she'd missed. "In a few minutes. I need to tell Mark we're staying."

After her mother and Ethan disappeared inside the house, Priscilla descended the steps and folded her arms over her middle as she approached Mark. "Thank you for agreeing to help, but I've decided we're staying for now."

"Okay." Mark gave her a little smile. "I guess I'll see you tomorrow."

"*Ya*." She motioned toward the house as heat pricked at her cheeks and humiliation curled through her. "I'm sorry you had to witness all that back in the *haus*."

He waved it off. "Don't worry about it." He pulled open his buggy door. "Have a good night."

"You too. Be sure to tell Laura hello for me."

"I will."

As Mark's buggy disappeared down the lane, Priscilla wondered just how fast the rest of the church district would find out she'd come back to the community unmarried and with a child.

TWO

PRISCILLA STEPPED INTO THE KITCHEN JUST AS ETHAN set a basket of rolls on the table next to a platter of fried chicken and a bowl of green beans. She noticed a small folding table, set for one, in the far corner of the room.

She ground her teeth and looked at her father, who was sitting in his usual spot at the head of the table with a deep frown lining his face. Just as she'd suspected he would, he was carrying out her shunning as if he were the bishop of their church district. She wouldn't be able to eat with members of her community or exchange money with them. She was now a stranger even in her own home.

She rubbed the bridge of her nose as renewed guilt burned through her. She had no one to blame but herself. The shunning was her fault. She'd made the decision to run away and leave the community.

"Priscilla." *Mamm* smiled as she set a pitcher of water on the table. "Ethan is a great helper."

"*Ya*, he is." Priscilla mussed Ethan's thick, dark hair as he looked up at her. "What can I do to help?"

"I think we're all set." *Mamm*'s smile faded. "I put a table in the corner of the room for you."

"I see that." Priscilla lingered by the long table. She was grateful she had explained to Ethan that she might have to eat at a separate table because of religious beliefs about shunning.

"Let's eat," *Dat* said, growling out the words.

Ethan looked up at his *mammi*. "May I sit next to you?"

"I'd like that." *Mamm* touched his cheek and then looked over at Priscilla. "If it's okay with your mother—your *mamm*."

"*Ya*, of course." Priscilla's heart seemed to constrict as her mother gazed down at her son. She sank into the chair at the small folding table and bowed her head in silent prayer. Then she waited for her parents and Ethan to fill their plates before she carried her plate to the table and filled it with food.

"So you've already started school in Baltimore?" *Mamm* asked as she buttered a roll.

"I finished kindergarten," Ethan explained before forking green beans into his mouth.

"Do you like school?" *Mamm* asked.

"Yeah." He looked over at Priscilla. "How long are we staying? Will I go to school here?"

"*Ya*, depending on how long we stay." Priscilla picked up her glass of water.

"Will I go to an Amish school like you did?" Ethan asked.

Priscilla hesitated as she met her mother's curious gaze. "I'll talk to your grandparents about that." She looked at her father. He was still staring down at his plate just as he had since the beginning of the meal. If she and Ethan stayed here, would he continue to treat them as if they were invisible?

"Tell me about your friends in Baltimore," *Mamm* said to Ethan.

"Well, my best friend is Nico," Ethan began as he picked up a drumstick. "He's really great at playing video games." He took a bite of the drumstick, chewed, and swallowed. "This is good."

He looked over at Priscilla. "It's just as good as your fried chicken, Mom."

"Thank you. I use your *mammi's* recipe." Priscilla pointed at her mother.

Mamm's expression lit up as she turned toward Priscilla. "You do?"

Priscilla smiled. "It's the best."

"*Danki.*" *Mamm* gave her an affectionate look.

Ethan entertained Priscilla's mother with stories about his friends for the remainder of the meal. Then *Mamm* served chocolate cake and coffee. When they'd finished their dessert, Priscilla stood to help her mother clean the kitchen. She piled the dirty plates on the counter and then began to fill one side of the sink with hot, soapy water.

"I'm going to go out and take care of the animals," *Dat* said, still grumbling as he headed for the door.

"Can I help you?" Ethan trotted after him.

Dat stopped and turned, fingering his beard as he looked down at Ethan.

"Please?" Ethan folded his hands. "Please?"

Priscilla looked at her mother, who shook her head as if to tell her to remain calm.

"*Ya.*" *Dat* motioned for Ethan to follow as they headed through the mudroom and out the back door.

As Priscilla returned to washing dishes, she tried to ignore the angry knots in her shoulders. Coming here had been a mistake, but she'd had no choice. She just had to make the best of it.

"Ethan reminds me so much of you," *Mamm* said as she placed a handful of utensils on top of the plates on the counter. "He's so eager to help, talkative, and curious. You were just like him when you were six."

"This was a mistake." The words burst from her lips as she faced her mother.

"What?" *Mamm's* eyes widened. "No, no, don't say that. It wasn't a mistake."

"*Dat* doesn't want me here." She pointed to the table in the corner. "He's going to keep reminding me of all the mistakes I've made. He'd rather I just left."

"That's not true." *Mamm's* chestnut eyes glimmered with tears. "We both want you here. Let me work on him."

Priscilla swallowed a snort. "I don't think there's anything you can do to change him. He's just as tough on me as he was before I left." She looked out the small window above the sink as *Dat* and Ethan walked toward the pasture together. "I just hope he treats Ethan better than he treats me. If not, I'll have to go to a motel tomorrow and then find a job and a place to rent."

"He'll be fine." *Mamm* touched her shoulder. "Just give him time to adjust. Your coming home today was a shock. Let him process it."

"I'll give him a few days at most, but if he's still harsh with Ethan and me, we'll leave."

"I'll talk to him tonight, okay?" *Mamm's* eyes seemed to plead with her.

Priscilla nodded, and her thoughts turned to her dire financial situation. Even if she stayed here for a while, she needed income so she could save some money for a place of her own. "Do you still work as a seamstress and sell quilts?"

Even though her father's horses provided a bountiful livelihood, her mother enjoyed sewing as a side job. Her father had allowed *Mamm* to keep the money and spend it any way she pleased. Priscilla had often wondered if she primarily enjoyed working as a seamstress for the social aspect it provided. Her father had always been such a stoic man.

"*Ya*, of course. Why?"

"Could I help you and split the profits?"

Mamm's face lit up with a bright smile. "*Ya*, that would be nice. I left your sewing machine in your bedroom right where you had it."

"*Danki*." Priscilla moved on to scrubbing pots as she watched her father and Ethan lead a horse into one of the stables. She glanced over her shoulder at her mother. "So Mark Riehl has been working here for a year?"

Mamm stopped wiping down the kitchen table and rested her hand on her hip. "*Ya*, I guess it has been that long."

"Why does he work here when his father has that dairy farm?"

"He was looking for a job, and your *dat* needed the help when Robert left."

"Interesting." Priscilla mulled over the information as she washed utensils. "Why doesn't Mark live in the *daadihaus*?"

"He said he wanted a salary instead of room and board, but sometimes he eats supper with us if he's working late."

Why would Mark need a salary? Had his father's farm fallen on hard times? Or had his older brother taken over the farm and told him to find another job? It just didn't make sense. Both Riehl sons would need to help their father with the chores on a dairy farm that large.

"He's a *gut* worker," *Mamm* continued, oblivious to Priscilla's internal questions. "He's been a blessing to your *dat*."

As Priscilla turned her attention back to the dishes, she imagined Mark sitting at his parents' long kitchen table and telling his family all about her sins. She pressed her lips together. Somehow she'd have to find the courage to blend back into the plain community—at least for now.

"Look who finally made it home," Jamie, Mark's older brother, announced from the glider on the back porch of their father's house. His two-and-a-half-year-old son, Calvin, sat beside him and waved as Mark approached.

Mark's father, stepbrother, and brother-in-law laughed as Mark climbed the steps.

"Some of us actually have to work late and then make the trek home." Mark smirked at Jamie. "Unlike you, I can't just roll out of bed and be at work." He leaned down and gave his nephew a high five. "Hi, Cal. How are you?"

Calvin giggled and then leaned against his father. Mark had always thought he was the perfect mixture of his parents, with bright-blond hair from his mother and dark-blue eyes from his father.

"You're the one who made the decision to take the job on Yonnie's farm." Jamie rubbed his clean-shaven chin as he grinned. Although he was married, he hadn't grown the required beard. The bishop in their district made an exception to the rule for married volunteer firemen like Jamie because they had to wear custom-fit face masks. "You could've just stayed here and worked with Roy and me." He leaned forward and looked at their younger stepbrother. He was sitting on a rocking chair at the far end of the porch.

"Leave me out of this." Roy held up his hands. "You know I don't enjoy getting in the middle of your squabbles."

Mark leaned back against the railing. "I guess I missed supper, huh?"

"Cindy saved you a plate," *Dat* said, referring to Mark's younger sister.

"*Gut*, because I'm starved." Mark ran a hand over his flat abdomen. "I worked hard today. Although, if you work for Yonnie Allgyer, you work hard every day. That man is a slave driver."

"Laura was starting to worry that you'd been in an accident," Allen Lambert said from a rocker beside Jamie.

Mark smiled. His twin had been married to Allen more than three and a half years now, but she still worried about him. "I hope you assured her I was fine."

"I did, but she said she wouldn't be satisfied until you got home." Allen pointed toward the front door. "Go on and show her that her twin is healthy and safe."

"I will." Mark gave them a little bow and headed into the house, removing his work boots and straw hat in the mudroom before entering the kitchen.

"*Onkel* Mark!" A little blonde scampered across the kitchen and leapt into Mark's arms. Mark often thought about what a blessing it was when Laura adopted Mollie Faith after marrying her widowed father. Allen's first wife, Savilla, had been one of Laura's best friends. The whole family cherished this small version of her after she suffered a sudden and fatal illness nearly five years ago.

"Hey there, little one." Mark's heart swelled with love as he held her to his chest and kissed her head. "How was your day?"

"*Gut.*" Mollie touched his face and giggled.

"You're going to be five next month. How did you get so big?"

"I just get bigger and bigger!" She held her arms up straight and then giggled again.

He laughed. How he adored his sweet niece.

"You're finally home." Laura walked over and frowned as she looked up at him. "Florence said you didn't call and let her know you were going to be late."

Mark shrugged. "It was unexpected."

"You should have called anyway," Cindy quipped while drying a dish. Who was his twenty-two-year-old sister to tell him what to do? "I checked the voice mail," she added, "and all I found were messages from your girlfriends."

Mark rolled his eyes. "Franey and Ruthann are *not* my girlfriends."

"Have you bothered to tell Franey and Ruthann that?" Laura set her hands on her belly, where a small bump had started to form, revealing she was expecting a child. "At least Sally got *schmaert* and found a man who was willing to commit to just her."

"I've never made any of them promises," Mark responded as he rubbed Mollie's back. "It's their choice to spend time with me."

"*Ya*, but you still have supper with each of them at least once a week," Cindy chimed in again.

"And you told Jamie you tell them to call you because you like their attention," Kayla, Jamie's wife, added as she swept the floor. "It's none of my business, but that sounds like you're leading them on. They probably think you're going to ask one of them to marry you before too long. I'm guessing Franey is almost sure."

"I'm not ready to get married, and I've never said I was." Mark shook his head. "And why does Jamie tell you what I share with him?"

Kayla's cheeks blushed pink as her cornflower-blue eyes widened. She held on to the broom and touched her own belly. It boggled Mark's mind that his twin and Jamie's wife were both due to have a child within a few weeks of each other.

"I'm just kidding." Mark looked down at Mollie Faith, who had her thumb in her mouth as she rested her head on his shoulder. Then he met his twin's gaze. "I can't help it if the *maed* can't resist me."

"You're incorrigible." Laura folded her arms over her chest and rolled her eyes.

"No, sis, I just tell the truth. The *maed* have always loved me. I can't help that God made me irresistible," he said, joking. He looked down at his sweet niece again. "Right, Mollie Faith? You love me."

Mollie's head popped up, and she kissed Mark's cheek. "*Ich liebe dich, Onkel* Mark."

"See? I just have this effect on *maed*." Mark shrugged and then kissed Mollie's head. "I love you too," he whispered into her hair.

"We're twenty-six, Mark. It's time for you to grow up. Besides, you're going to wind up in trouble if you keep leading on Franey and Ruthann. One day one of them is going to get hurt." Laura held out her arms to Mollie. "*Kumm.* Let *Onkel* Mark eat his supper."

"No." Mollie buried her face in the crook of Mark's neck. He grinned.

"Don't encourage her." Laura's bright-blue eyes narrowed. "Mollie Faith. *Kumm.*"

"I want to stay with *Onkel* Mark." Mollie Faith wrapped her arms around his neck, and he couldn't stop grinning despite his twin's deepening frown.

"I think she's attached to him." His stepsister, Sarah Jane, chuckled as she set a stack of clean dishes in a cabinet. At least his stepsister, just a year older than Cindy, was nice to him.

Mark looked down at his niece. "Why don't you sit next to me while I eat my supper?"

Mollie nodded, and he set her on a chair before sitting down beside her.

"We kept your supper warm." Laura set a plate with steak, mashed potatoes, and corn in front of him.

"*Danki.*" Mark smiled up at his twin before bowing his head for a silent prayer.

"Mark, I'm so glad you finally got home," Florence said when she stepped into the kitchen. "How was your day?"

"Busy," he told his stepmother as he cut up his steak. "It went by quickly." He took a bite and nodded. "This is *appeditlich*," he said after swallowing. "Did you make it?"

"*Ya.*" Florence nodded at Cindy. "Cindy helped."

"*Danki.*"

"I'm going to go sit on the porch." Florence started for the mudroom. "Does anyone want to join me?"

"*Ya,* I will. The kitchen is clean and the dishes are put away." Sarah Jane caught up with her mother, and they disappeared.

"I need to get Calvin home." Kayla set the dustpan and broom in the pantry and then waved as she headed toward the back door as well. "*Gut nacht.*"

"I'm going to go upstairs and read for a while." Cindy wiped her hands on a dish towel as she looked at Laura. "Would you please tell me when you're heading out? I'd like to say good-bye to you, Mollie, and Allen."

"I will. I promise I won't leave without telling you."

"*Danki.*" Cindy left, and then Mark heard her footfalls echoing in the stairwell.

"Boy, I come home and everyone leaves," he quipped.

"You always knew how to clear a room." Laura filled a small plastic cup with water and then pulled a picture book out of a tote bag sitting on the floor by the entrance to the mudroom. She handed them both to Mollie before sitting down across from Mark and looking at him pointedly. "So how was your day? This is me asking now."

Mark wiped his mouth on a paper napkin. "I already said it was fine. Just busy." He spooned some mashed potatoes into his mouth.

"You don't normally work this late, do you?" Laura leaned back in the chair, and he saw her absently touch her abdomen.

"Sometimes I do." He made sure Mollie seemed engrossed in her book. "Did you have an appointment earlier this week?"

"I did." She tilted her head. "You're deflecting my questions."

He smiled. "I'll tell you what happened today if you tell me about your appointment." His smile faded. "I know you've been *naerfich*."

Laura's gaze moved to Mollie, who was flipping through the picture book and humming to herself. Then she looked at Mark again. "Everything is fine." Her words were measured and deliberate.

Mark nodded. *"Gut."*

"I know I shouldn't be nervous, but sometimes it's difficult after two miscarriages." Her eyes shimmered.

"They happened early on." He was careful to keep his tone mild. "Everything is going to be perfect this time. I can feel it."

"Danki." Laura began to draw circles on the tabletop as she frowned.

He could feel her worry as if it were his own. He needed to say something that would make her smile. "If it's a *bu*, are you going to name him Mark after your handsome twin *bruder*?"

"Like I said earlier, you're incorrigible." She groaned, and then there it was—her smile followed by a little laugh. He'd managed to erase her worry and replace it with laughter. Relief filtered through him. He always felt better when his twin was happy.

But then he pressed his lips together. During the ride home tonight, he kept visualizing the pain in Priscilla's eyes when her father criticized her for coming home dressed as an *Englisher* and with a child born out of wedlock. Priscilla's humiliation had been tangible, and it had touched him—more than he ever would have imagined.

"Mark, I've known you since before we were born." Laura pointed at him. "Something is on your mind."

He sighed.

"What is it?" Laura's eyes lit up. "Are you in love? Are you going to ask one of your girlfriends to marry you and you just didn't want us to know yet? Is it Franey?"

He swallowed a groan. "Please, Laura. You need to stop hoping for that. I have no plans to marry. I'm working for Yonnie so I can save money." He pointed toward the back of the house. "You know my goal is to build a *haus* of my own on this property. I'm fine if I never find a *fraa*."

Laura wrinkled her nose as if she smelled something foul. "That's really *bedauerlich*."

"Why?" He touched Mollie's shoulder. "I have *mei bruderskinner*."

Mollie smiled up at him and then looked down at her book.

"Who will do your laundry when you move out?"

Mark grinned. "I'll just bring it over here, and Florence will take care of it." He took another bite of steak.

"You're unbelievable," she said as she rubbed her temples.

Mark took a deep breath and moved the rest of his corn around. It was time to tell Laura her friend was home, but he debated how much to tell her. Priscilla's homecoming had been painful, and the story surrounding her son was her business. Would it be a violation of the Allgyer family's trust if Mark told Laura about what happened while he was there tonight? But Laura had been one of Priscilla's closest friends, and Laura was Mark's twin, his closest confidante. They'd always shared their deepest and darkest secrets. He had to tell her the whole truth.

Mark set his fork down and leaned back in his chair as he met his twin's gaze. "Priscilla came home this evening."

Laura clapped her hands over her mouth for a moment before speaking. "Why didn't you tell me as soon as you came home?"

"*Mamm?*" Mollie's blue eyes widened as she looked at Laura. "*Was iss letz?*"

"Nothing is wrong, *mei liewe. Onkel* Mark just told me my dear *freind* came home today. She's been gone a long time." She pointed to Mollie's book. "You can go back to your book, okay?"

Mollie nodded and looked down at the pictures of horses.

"Why did you keep that from me?" Laura frowned. "You know Priscilla was one of my best *freinden*. Priscilla, Savilla, and I were inseparable in school and youth group. I never understood why she left. She seemed okay, as if nothing was bothering her. I knew she argued with her *dat*, but she never made it seem like it was that bad."

"Maybe it was worse than you thought." Mark rubbed the back of his neck.

"What do you mean?"

"Her *mamm* was very *froh* to see her, but her *dat* wasn't welcoming. In fact, he was critical of her."

"Why?" Laura tilted her head. "I know she's shunned for leaving, but why wouldn't he be *froh* to see her?"

"She has a *sohn*. He's six and a half."

"Really?" Laura smiled. "That's *wunderbaar*."

"She's not married. She said she left his father, so I think there's a painful story there."

"Oh." Laura's smiled faded. "I'm sorry to hear that."

"*Ya*." Mark's thoughts swirled as his mind replayed Priscilla's strained reunion with her parents.

"Mark. I can feel your anguish." Laura touched her collarbone. "*Zwillingbopplin*."

"I know." He set the fork down again. "I just keep thinking that our parents would have welcomed us home no matter what. They would have rejoiced if you or Cindy had come home after so many years, even if you had a *boppli* out of wedlock."

"*Ya*, they'd just be *froh* we came home. *Mamm* would've always supported us. I miss her so much." Laura's eyes sparkled as she patted her middle again.

"I know." Mark's eyes stung as he thought of their mother. "I do too."

"But Yonnie has always been tough. You've told me he's not the easiest man to work for. He expects everything to be perfect, and he lets you know when it isn't."

He grinned. "*Ya*, but he pays well."

"I think he'll come around. Who can resist a *kind*, right?" She nodded toward Mollie. "I fell in love with Mollie the moment I first saw her, right after Savilla had her. I'm so grateful I can be a part of her life."

"I hope you're right, and that Yonnie comes around."

"He will." Laura smiled. "Tell me about Priscilla's *sohn*. I can't wait to see her and meet him."

THREE

Ethan snuggled into the double bed in the spare bedroom later that evening. "*Daadi* let me help with the horses, and he said he'll let me help tomorrow too."

"I'm glad you had fun." Maybe her father would continue to make Ethan feel welcome here. After all, he'd already taught him to call him *Daadi*.

"*Daadi* is kind of quiet. He seems sad."

Priscilla suppressed a scowl. *That's one way to describe him.* "He's always been kind of quiet. It's just how he is. Some people like to smile and tell jokes, and other people are quiet and more somber."

"Yeah." Ethan paused as if contemplating something. "It's funny not having lights or air-conditioning. It's kind of like when we went camping with Dad that one time." He pointed to the Coleman lantern on the nightstand next to the bed. "We had to use lanterns too, and there weren't any light switches."

"You're right." Priscilla smiled as she tucked the sheet around him. "It is sort of like camping." She kissed his forehead and then touched his nose. "You get some sleep, okay?"

"Okay. It's hot in here." He pointed to the open window on the far side of the room. "Will it get cooler?"

"Hopefully you'll get a breeze. You'll get used to it eventually." She flipped off the lantern. "Good night."

"How do you say good night in Dutch?"

"Gut nacht." As she crossed the room, she realized it was still decorated the same. Two dressers lined the far wall, and a simple mirror and a shelf with two candles adorned the other wall. Her mother had insisted on having a guest room, although Priscilla never recalled any guests coming to visit and enjoying the pretty room.

"Mom?"

"Yes?" Priscilla stood in the doorway.

"Will Dad visit us here?"

Priscilla's stomach dipped and then spiraled as her thoughts turned to Trent. "I don't know, sweetie. We'll see."

"I miss him."

She pressed her lips together as her shoulders tightened. She'd never told Ethan why it was necessary to leave his father behind. She'd merely explained it was time for Ethan to get to know his grandparents, and then she prayed they'd be accepted. She also prayed Trent would never find them and try to take Ethan away from her.

"I know you do. Don't forget to say your prayers. *Gut nacht,* Ethan."

"Gut nacht, Mom."

She began to pull the door closed but stopped when he called her back.

"How do you say I love you in Dutch?" he asked.

She smiled. *"Ich liebe dich."*

"Okay. *Ich liebe dich,* Mom."

Priscilla's heart seemed to turn over. Was she the mother Ethan deserved? "I love you too. Now get some sleep. You told me your grandfather said you can help with chores again tomorrow."

"I'm glad," he said before rolling over.

She closed his door and crossed the hallway, swallowing back raging emotions as she stepped into her former bedroom. Like the spare room, her bedroom hadn't changed. Her favorite trinkets still lined the long dresser. Her double bed was adorned with the pink and purple log cabin design quilt she'd finished shortly before she made the decision to leave her childhood home in search of a happier one.

She shook her head. She'd been eighteen, not a child. Why had she thought running away would solve her problems?

She opened her closet and found the dresses and aprons she'd left behind. She even found a pair of shoes on the floor.

"I kept everything in case you decided to come back."

Priscilla spun to face her mother. "I didn't hear you walking down the hall."

"I have your prayer covering too." *Mamm* crossed the room and opened the top drawer of the dresser. "I kept it in here."

"*Danki.*" Priscilla touched it. When she left the community, she adapted the *Englisher* way of dressing to blend in, abandoning the few dresses, aprons, and prayer coverings she'd packed. It would feel odd to put on her former clothing, but she felt a strange tug from her former life. Had she missed dressing this way?

"Your *dat* is going to talk to you in the morning."

She looked up into her mother's dark eyes. "About what?"

"His rules for you if you decide to stay."

"I expected that." Priscilla sank onto the corner of the bed. "He wants me to dress Amish, right?"

"*Ya*, he does, and he wants Ethan to dress Amish too." *Mamm* touched her shoulder. "Please tell me you'll agree to whatever he says. I don't want you and Ethan to leave."

"*Ya*, I will," she said, realizing she had made the decision to stay despite continued anxiety about being around her father. She forced a smile. "I'll make Ethan some clothes, and I'll see if my dresses still fit."

"They will. You look to be about the same size to me." *Mamm* touched her cheek. "I'm so glad you're here." Her eyes seemed to penetrate Priscilla's soul. "I suspect you wouldn't be unless something happened with Ethan's father. What was it?"

Priscilla swallowed as she debated how much to share. "He changed, and our home became an unsafe environment for Ethan."

Mamm's eyes sparkled with tears. "Did he hurt you?"

"I'm okay." Priscilla squeezed her mother's hand. "Ethan and I will be fine."

Mamm studied her. "Do you want to talk about it?"

Priscilla shook her head as a yawn overtook her. "Maybe later."

"All right. I'm always here."

"*Danki.*" Priscilla's heart seemed to swell. She was grateful for her mother.

"Get some sleep. *Gut nacht.*"

"*Gut nacht.*" Priscilla turned toward the doorway as her mother was leaving. "*Mamm?*"

"*Ya?*" *Mamm* swiveled to face her.

"*Danki* for allowing Ethan and me to stay here."

Mamm's eyes glimmered in the light of the Coleman lantern on her dresser. "Of course you can stay here. You belong here. You're our family. Sleep well." She closed the door as she stepped out into the hallway.

Priscilla walked to the closet and eyed a long-sleeved cranberry-colored dress. Since she'd left home in the summer, she'd left behind her long-sleeved dresses. She pulled the dress off the hanger and yanked off her purple shirt and jeans.

When she turned toward the mirror, her gaze fell on her right bicep and the scars that covered her arm. She touched the discolored and puckered skin, and her mind filled with memories of the night Trent had been so drunk and angry that he'd thrown a beer bottle at her.

Although Trent had never been violent toward Ethan, his drinking had put their son in danger. One day she arrived home from work to find Ethan home alone while Trent had gone out drinking with his buddies. At that moment Priscilla realized she had to get Ethan away from Trent before he wound up hurt.

That was the day she began planning her escape from Trent's drunkenness and abuse.

She closed her eyes to keep her tears at bay. She was strong, and she was determined to keep Ethan safe. She'd gotten away from Trent, and now she had to rebuild her life. If that meant living here and assimilating to the Amish life again, then she'd do it for her son's sake.

Priscilla slipped on the dress and studied her reflection in the mirror. The dress was a little snug, but she could let out the seams. She changed into her favorite nightshirt and shorts and then sat down at her sewing table. She was grateful her mother had left it and all her sewing supplies in her room. She set to work letting out the seams and shortening the sleeves to three-quarter length. Short sleeves were permitted during the summer, but she couldn't risk anyone seeing the scars on her arm. Her mind wandered as she worked, anxiety causing her stomach to roil as she imagined what her father would say to her in the morning.

When the dress was finished, she hung it back in the closet and went to her dresser. She touched the little wooden box where she'd kept her bobby pins since she was a little girl. Then she pulled out her prayer covering and ran her fingers over the organza. Tomorrow she would don her former clothing and try to find her way back into the Amish community. But would they accept her despite her transgressions?

The question lingered in her mind as she turned off the lanterns and climbed into bed. Turning to her side, she closed her eyes.

"Lord, give me strength," she whispered. "Guide me to where Ethan and I belong."

Then she closed her eyes and waited for sleep to find her.

"Gude mariye." Priscilla forced a smile on her lips as she stepped into the kitchen the following morning. The aroma of eggs, bacon, home fries, and fresh-baked bread washed over her, causing her stomach to growl.

"Gude mariye," *Mamm* echoed as she set a platter of bacon on the table.

Dat barely repeated the greeting from the head of the table.

"You look pretty, Mom," Ethan said as he sat beside her father.

"Danki. That means thank you." Priscilla touched her prayer covering. She'd put on the cranberry-colored dress and a black apron, and then she'd pulled her hair up before donning the prayer covering. The clothing felt oddly comforting. Perhaps she'd missed her former life.

Unwilling to go there, she turned toward her mother. "I'm sorry I didn't come down earlier to help you. What can I do now?"

"Don't worry. It's all done." *Mamm* handed her a plate and then gestured toward the small table in the corner. "Get yourself some food."

"Danki." Priscilla filled her plate and sat down. After a silent prayer, they all began to eat. With her stomach tied up in knots, she merely moved the eggs around as she waited for her father to

speak to her. Would he lay down his rules now? Or make her wait until later in the day?

"Are we going to work on chores after breakfast, *Daadi*?" Ethan asked between bites of home fries.

"*Ya*," *Dat* said. "Mark should be here soon, and you can help us outside."

"Yay!" Ethan cheered. "I saw your horses last night, but what kind are they?"

Dat answered Ethan's questions about the horses and the farm as they finished eating. Priscilla had gathered the empty dishes and was filling one side of the sink with water when her father finally addressed her. She was grateful Ethan had gone out to the porch to wait for him.

"Priscilla, I want to discuss your plans for staying here."

She turned toward him and nodded. "All right."

"If you stay under my roof, you and Ethan will dress Amish and abide by the rules of the *Ordnung*. Ethan will go to our Amish school." *Dat*'s expression could not have been stonier.

"I understand." Priscilla's hands shook as she dried them on a dish towel.

"You will also meet with the bishop and make yourself right with the church."

She swallowed. "I will."

"You'll do it today." *Dat* jammed his finger against the table. "As soon as the kitchen is cleaned up, you will call for a ride and go talk to him. With his agreement, you'll start your classes this Sunday."

"Okay." Priscilla kept back a biting retort. How she despised her father's caustic tone despite her agreeing to his rules.

"And one more thing." He narrowed his eyes. "After you're accepted back as a community member, you will look for a husband."

Her mouth dropped open. "What? Look for a husband?"

"*Ya*. Your *sohn* needs a father, and you need a husband. The sooner you find one, the better. You know how your situation looks to other members of our community. The best thing you can do is make it right. You know what I'm saying."

"No." Priscilla shook her head. "I will live like an Amish woman, and I will make myself right with the church, but I can't allow you to dictate my life beyond that. If that's how you're going to be, I'll find another place to live."

"No!" *Mamm* said. "Don't go."

Priscilla's body shook as she looked at her mother. "I have to go." She hurried up the stairs and into Ethan's room. She opened the closet and pulled out his suitcase before tossing his clothes into it.

Priscilla shook her head as anger and confusion warred inside of her.

"Please stay," *Mamm* pleaded as she stood in the doorway. "Your *dat* only wants what's best for you."

She spun toward her mother. "I can't let him push me to get married. When I'm right with the church, it means I'm forgiven. I can't be forced to marry. Ethan is *mei sohn*, no matter how he came into this world."

"Priscilla, calm down." *Mamm* took a step toward her. "Your *dat* is only thinking about your future. You can stay here and build a life for Ethan. Finding a husband isn't a bad thing."

"No, but it has to be my choice." Priscilla pointed to her chest. "I get to choose who's the best man to help me raise Ethan." What was she thinking? She could never let anyone hurt her again—or hurt Ethan. That was true. But even if she found someone she could trust, what decent man would have her? She would still be damaged goods.

"*Ya*, I know it has to be your choice, and your *dat* knows that.

He never said he would choose a husband for you. Why would he?" *Mamm* touched her arm. "Stop thinking about yourself and think about your *kind*. Where will you go if you leave here? Do you have enough money to provide a *gut* home for him?"

Priscilla's shoulders slumped. She didn't have enough money to rent an apartment, let alone a house.

"Stay here." *Mamm*'s voice cracked with emotion. "Just do what your *dat* wants, and I promise everything will be all right."

"Fine." Priscilla released the breath she hadn't realized she'd been holding.

"Go meet with the bishop." *Mamm* nodded toward the doorway. "I'll unpack Ethan's things, and I'll finish cleaning the kitchen. Then I'll start making Ethan clothes."

Priscilla nodded. "All right. I'll go see the bishop, but I'll help you with the chores first."

"Priscilla, I can—"

"No." Priscilla shook her head. "I'll unpack and clean up the kitchen. Then you can start making Ethan's clothes so he's ready for church on Sunday, okay?"

Mamm nodded.

Priscilla hesitated as doubt curled through her. Was making a commitment to the church the right choice? What if Ethan detested living on a farm after he'd been here a few days? Would he adjust to going to a one-room Amish school without the luxuries of electronics or the flexibility of his former clothes?

"Priscilla," *Mamm* said. "You need to do what's best for your *kind*."

"You're right." With her palms sweating, Priscilla headed down the stairs. She sucked in a surprised breath when she met her father at the bottom step. "I'm going to finish cleaning up the kitchen and then meet with the bishop."

"All right. Our driver's phone number is on the desk in the

phone shanty." *Dat* pulled out his wallet and held out a couple of bills. "This should cover the cost of the ride."

"I have a little bit of money."

"Take it." His tone was gruff.

"*Danki,*" she whispered as she took the money from him.

He gave her a curt nod before walking into the hallway.

As Priscilla stepped into the kitchen, she squared her shoulders. She reminded herself again that she was strong. She would find her way, for the sake of her son.

FOUR

"Do you need any help?"

Mark turned toward the entrance to the horse stall as he looked at Ethan. "Hi, Ethan."

"Hi." Ethan raised his hand in a wave. "*Daadi* told me to ask you if you had anything for me to do."

Mark grinned as he leaned on his pitchfork. "I see you're picking up Dutch pretty quickly."

"Yeah, my mom taught me a few words."

"You said you're six, right?"

He stood a little taller. "Six and a half."

"Uh-huh." Mark rubbed his chin. "So you're already in school, then. Don't *Englisher* schools start at five?"

"*Englisher?*" Ethan snickered and shook his head. "What does that mean?"

"An *Englisher* is someone who isn't Amish. So you're essentially an *Englisher.*"

"Oh." Ethan nodded slowly. "Yeah, I was in kindergarten last year. My mom just told me I'll start first grade here."

"Oh." *So Priscilla is planning on staying.* "Schools are different here. All the grades are in one classroom with one teacher." Mark lifted his straw hat and wiped his brow with the back of his hand. "I'm sure your school wasn't like that."

"No, it wasn't." Ethan seemed to study him. "Did you go to school with my mom?"

"*Ya*, I did. She was *gut freinden* with my twin sister, Laura."

"You have a twin sister?"

"*Ya*, I do, but we don't look alike. You can tell us apart because she's shorter than I am," Mark said. After a beat, Ethan laughed.

"Do you have any kids, Mark?"

"No, I can't say that I do. Do you?"

Ethan chuckled again. "I'm only six. Of course I don't." He shook his head. "You're funny."

"Well, looks aren't everything." Mark feigned disappointment with a shrug and a phony frown.

Ethan chuckled a third time. "Do you have any other brothers and sisters?"

"*Ya*." Mark leaned against the stall wall and set the pitchfork next to it. "Let's see. There's my older brother, Jamie." He counted everyone off on his fingers. "He's married to Kayla. They have a little boy younger than you named Calvin. He's really cool. You'll like him. Then there's my younger sister, Cindy. And I have two stepbrothers, Walter and Roy, and a stepsister, Sarah Jane. Walter is married, and he has two sons."

"Wow." Ethan's eyes grew wider. "You have a big family. I just have my mom and dad. My dad lives in Baltimore. I don't know when I'll see him again since my mom decided we should come here for a while."

"I'm sorry to hear that." Mark's thoughts spun with questions. Why had Priscilla left his father? And what drove Priscilla from the community eight years ago? Laura said Yonnie and Priscilla argued back then, and he certainly didn't welcome her back. But how bad could their relationship have been? "Do you like the farm?"

"Yeah." Ethan smiled. "The animals are fun. And it's like camping living in a house without electricity."

"It's like camping, huh?" Mark snickered. "That's a great analogy."

Ethan looked toward the entrance of the barn. "My mom went to see someone called the bishop a little while ago. I wonder when she'll be back."

"She went to see the bishop?" Mark felt his eyebrows rise. So Priscilla was going to rejoin the church. That meant she really was back for good.

"Yeah." Ethan tilted his head. "Who is he?"

"Well, have you been to a church before?"

"Uh-huh." Ethan nodded.

"He's like our preacher. He's the head of our church."

"Oh." Ethan looked confused. "Why would my mom go see him?"

Mark folded his arms over his chest as he considered an explanation simple enough for Ethan to understand. "I think she probably went to talk to him about becoming a member of the church again. She'll have to take classes and then be accepted back into the congregation."

"Oh." His brows furrowed. "So she has to ask permission to be a part of the church?"

"*Ya*, sort of."

Ethan nodded as if considering that. "Okay." Then he looked around the horse stall. "Are we going to stand here and talk all day? Or are you going to give me a chore to do?"

"Wow." Mark shook his head and sighed with feigned annoyance. "You're just as demanding as your *daadi*." Then he held out his pitchfork. "How about I teach you to muck the stalls?"

"Okay." Ethan rubbed his hands together before grabbing the tool. "I'm ready."

Priscilla climbed out of the van and paid her father's driver before walking up the rock path. She was back from meeting with the bishop, and her feet slowed with the weight of uncertainty as she climbed the front porch steps.

Although she'd made the commitment to rejoin the church, anxiety seemed to coil around her insides when she envisioned facing the congregation on Sunday. Would her former friends welcome her back into the fold? Or would they stare at her and her child and whisper about her promiscuity?

"Lord, give me strength," she whispered as she stepped into the foyer and dropped her purse on the bench by the door.

Voices rang out from the kitchen. She stepped through the doorway and found her mother clearing away dishes as her father, Mark, and Ethan sat at the table.

"Mom!" Ethan waved at her. "How was your meeting?"

Leave it to her son to get right to the point. She squared her shoulders and plastered a smile on her face. "It went just fine."

"Are you a member of the church now?"

"Ah. Well, not exactly." Priscilla's cheeks felt as if they'd caught fire as she met her mother's hopeful gaze. "But I will be soon."

"That's great." Ethan grinned.

"*Danki.*" Priscilla turned to her mother. "I can clean up if you have other things to do."

"Are you sure? You must be hungry." *Mamm* pointed to the table. "I made chicken salad, and we have the rolls I picked up at the bakery yesterday. Sit down and eat while I do the dishes."

"No." Priscilla touched her mother's arm. "You go on. I'll clean up after I eat."

"Okay. I'm working on a pair of trousers for Ethan. I'm almost done, and then I can start on a shirt."

"Danki."

Mamm left the kitchen, and Priscilla turned to the table as her father stood.

"It's time to get back to work." *Dat* dropped his napkin on his empty plate. "A couple of customers made appointments to come out this afternoon. I need to get ready for them."

He looked down at his plate and then headed for the door. As he walked past her, Priscilla's heart seemed to falter as she considered her father might never forgive her.

"Daadi, wait for me!" Ethan jumped up and followed his grandfather to the door. "Bye, Mom."

"Bye." Priscilla smiled as she gathered the last of the dishes. She turned to Mark, who was still sitting at the table. "Aren't you going with them?"

"I thought I'd have another sandwich." He plucked a roll from the basket in the center of the table. "Your *mamm* makes the best chicken salad. I think it's because she adds walnuts. They're *appeditlich.*"

She eyed him with suspicion. "I guess that means you eat here often."

He shrugged. "Your mom invites me to join them for lunch every day I'm here. I don't stay for supper often, but I do enjoy her lunches."

Priscilla carried the dishes to the counter.

"You look *schee,*" he said.

She leaned against the counter, squeezed her eyes shut, and swallowed a groan. Was Mark really going to flirt with her? Of course he was. This was how he'd always operated. He'd use compliments, quick wit, and his handsome face to win over the affection of the young girls in their youth group and then lead them on without any promise of commitment. She'd witnessed more than one friend or acquaintance falling under his spell, only to be heartbroken when he moved on to someone else.

But why would he be interested enough in her to flirt? Not only had he never noticed her before, but she certainly couldn't be desirable to him now. She was shunned and had a child from a failed relationship with an *Englisher*.

"What?" Mark asked. "Did I say something wrong?"

"No." She turned back to the table and picked up empty glasses. Mark scooped chicken salad from a bowl onto his roll and then added a piece of lettuce. "Why do you work here?" The question leapt from her lips without any forethought.

He shrugged. "*Mei dat* and I were here running an errand one day about a year ago, and your *dat* mentioned he needed a farmhand. We discussed a salary, and I took the job."

"But why here?"

"Why not here?" He grinned. "It's a great job."

"Why don't you live in the *daadihaus* here on the farm?"

"I want a paycheck so I can save money to build a *haus* on *mei dat*'s farm."

Priscilla considered his family, and a twinge of envy poked her. Mark had it all—loving parents and three siblings who would always be his close friends. She'd seen the Riehl family interact at church and whenever she visited Laura, and it was apparent how much they supported each other. She'd often wondered what it would have been like if her parents had given her siblings. Would a couple of brothers have taken off the pressure for her to be the perfect child? She moved to the sink to prepare for washing the dishes.

"How did it really go with the bishop?" His question broke through her thoughts.

"Oh, it was *wunderbaar*," she tossed over her shoulder. "I'm still shunned, and I need to be under the ban while I take three classes. Only then can I be accepted back into the church. The first class is this Sunday." She scraped crumbs from a dish with more force than necessary. But the chatter of her mother's sewing machine echoed from the second floor above them, and the sound was so familiar it was almost comforting.

"You haven't had lunch, right?" he asked.

"No, I haven't."

"Come eat with me."

She turned toward him and felt her brow pinch.

"Sit." He pointed to the chair across from him. "Please."

"You're going to eat with me?"

"Why not?"

She tilted her head and took in his pleasant expression and sky-blue eyes. What did he hope to gain by being nice to her? Had he told his family about her last night? Had his sisters instructed him to find out all her secrets so they could gossip about them at the next quilting bee? That didn't sound like the Laura she'd known, but she wasn't sure if she could trust anyone now.

His face broke out in his signature grin. "Why are you looking at me like I have an ulterior motive? It's lunch, Priscilla, not an invitation to share a bottle of liquor."

"You know I'm shunned, but you're inviting me to eat with you."

"But you have to eat, right?" He shrugged. "Sit and eat with me."

She hesitated, and then she turned back to the sink and shut off the faucet. It was just lunch, after all, and she would be careful not to share too much about her life in Baltimore.

She took a plate from the cabinet and utensils from the drawer before sitting down across from him. After a prayer, she began building a sandwich. He ate in silence across from her for a few moments.

"Ethan is a hoot," he finally said. "He helped me muck the stalls earlier, and he never stopped talking."

"He does like to talk." She took a bite of her sandwich, chewed, swallowed, and then wiped her mouth with a napkin. "Why are you working here instead of helping your *dat* with his dairy farm?"

"*Mei bruders* are plenty of help."

"*Bruders*?" she asked. "I don't understand. Did your parents have another child after I left?"

He shook his head, and his smile flattened. "No, I have three stepsiblings. Two of them live on the farm."

She gasped, her hand fluttering to her mouth. "You lost your *mamm*?"

His nod was solemn. "Five years ago."

"Mark, I'm so sorry." Tears stung her eyes. "I had no idea."

"It's been tough, but *mei dat* is *froh* again. He met Florence at the library, and they started dating. She has an older *sohn* who's married and took over her farm. Her younger *sohn*, Roy, is twenty-four, and Sarah Jane is twenty-three." He shook his head. "We're just one big, happy family now."

"Is that why you want to build a *haus*? You want some privacy?"

"I guess so. Also, I'm twenty-six and not married, so I think it's time I had my own place." He took a handful of chips and dropped them on his plate before handing her the bag.

"*Danki.*" She shook a pile of chips onto her own plate. "You mentioned Laura has a family now. How many *kinner* does she have?"

"She has a *dochder*, and she's expecting another *kind*."

"What about Jamie?"

"He's married and has a *sohn*. His *fraa* is expecting a *boppli* too."

"Wow." She popped a chip into her mouth while her mind spun with memories of her childhood. While her life was stressful at home, she'd always cherished time spent with her two best friends, Laura and Savilla. "How's Savilla? Is she married?"

Mark stopped chewing, and something unreadable flickered across his face.

"What?" She leaned forward, her curiosity piqued.

"Savilla passed away not long after *mei mamm* died."

Priscilla couldn't stop tears from filling her eyes. She couldn't believe her mother didn't tell her in one of her letters.

"I'm sorry. I didn't mean to upset you." He handed her another napkin.

"It's not your fault." She wiped her eyes and then her nose. "What happened?"

"She died unexpectedly as the result of a heart infection. It was terrible. Her husband, Allen, was just devastated. Their *dochder*, Mollie, was only two months old."

"*Ach.* That's so *bedauerlich.*" Priscilla sniffed.

"After Savilla passed away, her *mamm* helped care for Mollie. But then she broke her leg and hip and Laura took over with Mollie." His expression softened. "Laura and Allen fell in love, and they've been married almost four years now. Laura adopted Mollie, who's a sweetheart." It was apparent from the way he smiled that he was fond of his niece.

Priscilla shook her head as guilt stabbed her heart. Why had she stayed away for so long? Surely Laura needed her when she lost her mother and then Savilla. She wiped away more tears as she imagined Laura mourning her mother and then their best friend. Would Laura ever forgive Priscilla for leaving the way she had and not contacting her for eight years?

"I can't believe it." Priscilla's voice sounded thin and reedy. "Things have changed so much. I've been gone a long time."

"But you're back now." Mark raised his glass of water as if to toast her.

They ate in silence for a few minutes, and she allowed everything Mark told her to sink in. What else had she missed?

"Tell me more about how it went with the bishop." Mark's statement broke through her thoughts.

She shrugged while looking down at her half-eaten sandwich. "It went fine. He seemed *froh* to see me, and he was supportive of my decision to come back to the faith." She moved a chip around on her plate. "He made me feel welcome in his home. I thought he would since he'd always been pleasant, but the meeting wasn't anything unexpected. Like I said, I have to go to the classes on Sundays to relearn our faith. Then I have to confess in front of the congregation."

She tried to sound casual, even though the idea of standing in front of her congregation terrified her to the very depth of her soul. "So after I complete the classes I'll be a member of the community again, and life can go on for Ethan and me."

She looked up, and when she met his gaze, she found tenderness in his eyes that knocked her off balance for a moment. Was he pretending to care? Or did he truly want to be her friend?

"You don't sound so sure," he said.

"What do you mean?"

"Something is bothering you. Is your *dat* forcing you to make yourself right with the church?"

She swallowed. Was she that transparent? Or was he reading her thoughts? Maybe his suspicion was based solely on what he'd heard her father say the day she arrived.

"It's none of my business." He picked up another chip and tossed it into his mouth.

"Did you tell your family I'm back?"

He shook his head as he swallowed. "Only Laura."

She blinked. Her vision of Mark gossiping about her was entirely wrong, unless he wasn't telling her the truth. But she didn't find any evidence of a lie on his face or in his eyes.

"She's really excited that you're back. She can't wait to see you."

"I can't wait to see her," she admitted, ashamed she'd even considered Laura and Cindy gossiping about her. She ran her finger over the wood-grain tabletop as she felt the urge to share more with him. "I didn't come straight home today after I met with the bishop." The words seemed to leap from her mouth as if they craved someone's understanding ear. "I asked *mei dat*'s driver to take me to a coffee shop so I could just sit alone and figure out what I'm doing."

"What do you mean?" He leaned forward, his expression pensive.

"I just keep wondering if coming back here and rejoining the church is the right decision for Ethan. He needs a safe and stable home."

"Why would coming here be wrong, then?"

"What if the community rejects me? Sure, the bishop will tell them I'm a member of the church after I complete the classes, but what if people still treat me like I'm a sinner?"

"That won't happen. You know the entire community will forgive you. Besides, look around you." He gestured around the kitchen. "Your parents are *gut* Christian people. Ethan will have love and guidance here."

"*Ya*, you're right." She nodded, but doubt continued to taunt her. Still, this was too personal of a conversation for her to share with Mark. He wasn't her friend. Why did she feel the need to trust him?

She stood and started picking up their dishes. "I have chores to do, and I'm sure *mei dat* needs you outside. *Danki* for having lunch with me." She carried the dishes to the sink and set them in the water she'd drawn earlier.

When she turned, she almost collided with Mark's chest as he came to stand beside her.

"Here you go." He smiled as he set the utensils and their glasses on the counter. "I'll see you later."

"Danki." She looked up at him and took in his attractive face. Too bad he was a known flirt in her community. Not that she was remotely interested in another relationship.

"Don't doubt your decision to come home. People are going to be *froh* that you're back," he said. "Just wait and see when you go to church this Sunday."

"I hope you're right."

"You know I am." Then he winked before heading to the mudroom.

Priscilla rolled her eyes as she leaned back against the counter. Why would she ever consider Mark Riehl a friend? He had to be the most conceited man and worst flirt she'd ever known.

FIVE

PRISCILLA'S HEART POUNDED AS SHE WALKED WITH her parents and Ethan toward the Zook family's house.

"So I have to sit with *Daadi* during church because I'm a *bu*?" Ethan asked.

Priscilla looked down at him. Despite his short haircut, he looked Amish clad in his black trousers, white shirt, and black vest, the Sunday suit all male members of the community wore. "*Ya*, that's right."

Ethan touched *Dat's* arm. "Where do we sit?"

"In the barn." *Dat* nodded toward the structure. "I'll show you."

Priscilla looked at her father, and when their eyes met, he immediately turned away. She swallowed a sigh. When would he look at her and talk to her as if she were a valuable human being? She turned back to Ethan. Did he notice how her father acted toward her? Was it harmful for Ethan to witness how poorly her father treated her? Would *Dat's* example influence him to turn out like Trent?

As her thoughts turned to Trent, a shiver danced down her spine despite the humid air, and she absently rubbed her right bicep. She'd tailored two more long-sleeved dresses to give them three-quarter sleeves. Her mother asked why she didn't give them short sleeves, and she'd told her she'd learned to like longer sleeves best. She was relieved when *Mamm* let the subject drop.

She tried to dispel her doubt about moving back home as she smiled at Ethan and rubbed his cheek. "I'll see you after the service. Remember to be quiet and respectful."

"I will."

She squeezed his hand before he and her father took off toward the barn. Then she continued with her mother toward the Zook family's house. She stood up straighter as they approached the back porch.

"You have no reason to be *naerfich*," *Mamm* said as if reading her thoughts. "You have every right to visit with the women before the service."

"I have only a few minutes before I need to meet with the bishop." She fingered the skirt of her dress as she walked behind her mother up the steps.

"You have enough time to see your *freinden*." *Mamm* opened the back door.

Pressure clamped down on Priscilla's lungs as she followed her mother into the mudroom, where voices sounded from the kitchen. She closed her eyes and pressed her lips together for a moment before walking inside with shaking hands. The women in her congregation stood in a circle greeting one another, and she saw a sea of faces, most of them familiar.

"Priscilla!"

She spun as Laura came up behind her and then wrapped her arms around her shoulders.

"Oh, Priscilla." Laura's voice sounded thick. "Mark told me you were back, and I prayed you'd come to church today."

"Laura." Wetness gathered under her eyes. "It's been too long."

"*Ya*, it has." Laura touched her cheek. "You look great."

"You do too." It had always astounded her that Laura shared

coloring more like her older brother, Jamie, than her twin's. Laura had dark-brown hair, and Mark's hair was a lighter shade of brown. But all the Riehl siblings shared the same striking, bright-blue eyes.

"This is *mei dochder*, Mollie. Her *mutter* was Savilla." Laura nodded at the little blonde standing next to her holding a picture book.

Priscilla clicked her tongue as her eyes stung with more tears. "Mark told me what happened. I can't believe it."

"I know. I miss her so much." She touched Mollie's arm. "Mollie, this is *mei freind* Priscilla. Can you say hello?"

"Hi." Mollie waved at her and then hid behind the skirt of Laura's blue dress.

Laura laughed. "She's pretending to be shy."

"She's beautiful." Priscilla smiled at the girl, taking in her baby-blue eyes. She recalled Savilla's chocolate-colored eyes and surmised that Mollie's father must have blue eyes. Priscilla's eyes moved down Laura's body and stopped at her middle.

"I know Mark told you we're expecting." Laura touched her little belly and smiled. "I want to meet your *sohn*. Mark said he's a chatterbox and a *gut* helper."

"*Danki.*" Priscilla's gaze moved to a group of women approaching them.

"You must be Priscilla." A woman with golden-blond hair and blue eyes, and who looked about her age, stepped toward her. She was holding a toddler. "I'm Kayla, and this is *mei sohn*, Calvin."

"Kayla is Jamie's *fraa*," Laura explained before turning to a middle-aged woman. "This is my stepmother, Florence."

"It's nice to meet you," Priscilla said, shaking her hand and taking in Kayla's belly too.

When Priscilla felt a hand on her shoulder, she turned. A young woman smiled at her. "Cindy? Is that you?"

"*Ya*, it's *gut* to see you." Cindy hugged her.

"Oh my goodness. You're taller than I am!"

"Imagine how I feel," Laura quipped. "She's my little *schweschder*, and she towers over me."

"Laura!" *Mamm* joined them. "It's so *gut* to see you."

"Edna," Florence said. "We need to get together to sew again soon. It's been too long."

"*Ya*, it has," *Mamm* said, agreeing. "Did you finish that wedding ring quilt you were working on for that one customer?"

"I did."

As her mother and Florence continued to talk, Priscilla turned back to Laura. "I'm so sorry about your *mamm* and Savilla. If only I'd been here to help you through your grief. I feel terrible for not contacting you."

"I missed you so much, but it was even worse after I lost *mei mamm* and then Savilla." Laura touched Priscilla's hand. "I still can't believe they're both gone." She glanced down at Mollie, who was sitting on the floor and flipping through the pages of her book. "She reminds me of Savilla all the time. She has her smile. When I look in Mollie's eyes, I see Savilla, and it helps me cope with not having her."

Priscilla nodded. "She has her *schee* hair too. I think it's *wunderbaar* that Mollie has you."

"*Danki*." Laura smiled at her. "We have a lot of catching up to do. We need to get together soon."

"*Ya*, we do."

Laura's eyes glimmered. "It's so *gut* to have you back."

Priscilla swallowed against a lump swelling in her throat.

When the clock began to chime, announcing it was nine, Priscilla gestured toward the door. "I have to go meet with the bishop, but I'll see you soon."

"Okay." Laura gave her another quick hug and then whispered in her ear, "Promise me I'll see you soon."

"You will," Priscilla said.

Mark scanned the congregation as he sat on a backless bench next to Roy in the unmarried men's section of the barn and fingered his hymnal. He spotted Ethan sitting beside Yonnie. When Ethan met his gaze, the boy waved, and Mark grinned in response.

"What are you looking at?" Roy asked.

"Ethan is here." He nodded toward the boy.

"Ethan?" Roy's brown eyebrows shot up.

"He's Yonnie and Edna's grandson. He and his *mamm*, Priscilla, came to live with them this week. I went to school with Priscilla." He explained that Priscilla was best friends with Laura.

"Oh. You haven't mentioned that at home."

No, he hadn't. Mark had shared the news of Priscilla's homecoming with only one person—Laura. Her return seemed so personal, and for some odd reason, he felt the need to shield her from any community gossip.

That was crazy. He and Priscilla had never been good friends. He'd always considered her standoffish and unapproachable. The conversation he'd shared with her on Friday during lunch was the first meaningful discussion they'd ever shared.

The service began, and Mark joined in as the congregation slowly sang the opening hymn. A young man sitting two rows behind him served as the song leader. He began the first syllable of each line, and then the rest of the congregation joined him to finish each line.

Mark tried to concentrate on the hymn, but his thoughts kept turning to Priscilla. He imagined her meeting with the bishop and ministers in one of the upstairs rooms in the Zook house as they reminded her of their beliefs and the history of the Amish church. He remembered her story about visiting the coffee shop and what she'd told him about her doubts. Did she still think the community would reject her and Ethan?

During the last verse of the second hymn, he turned and moved his eyes to the back of the barn just as Priscilla stepped inside and walked up the aisle toward the front. She wore a red dress that had three-quarter sleeves, just like the dress she'd worn on Friday, and it puzzled him. It was a sweltering day, so why hadn't she put on a short-sleeved dress like the rest of the women in the community?

Priscilla kept her eyes focused on the floor of the barn as she made her way to the front row, where she sank onto the bench and then bent forward, her hands covering her face. A lump swelled in his throat. Why did he feel such a deep empathy for her?

The ministers entered the barn and placed their hats on two hay bales, indicating that the service was about to begin. They made their way to the front of the barn and sat in front of Priscilla. The chosen minister began the first sermon, and Mark did his best to concentrate on the words, but his eyes kept finding their way back to Priscilla. She remained frozen in place, her head bent and her hands covering her face as if she were pleading with God to forgive her transgressions. While it was tradition for a shunned member of the church to sit like that, it bothered him to see her that way.

The first sermon ended, and Mark knelt in silent prayer. After the prayers, the deacon read from the Scriptures, and then the hour-long main sermon began. During the second sermon Priscilla sat up, her back ramrod straight as if someone had poured steel down her spine. She kept her focus on the minister.

His gaze wandered toward the unmarried women, and he found Franey Herschberger's hazel eyes focused on him. A sweet smile turned up the corners of her lips. He returned the greeting with a nod. Beside her Ruthann King studied the lap of her pink dress.

While his siblings joked that he was dating them both, he

didn't consider his relationship with either of them serious. They were like special friends, with no promises of a future. The time they spent together was fun. They played board games and ate the delicious food they made for him. They talked for hours, but he'd never kissed either of them or even held their hands.

The arrangement didn't seem to bother Ruthann and Franey. They seemed to enjoy spending time with him and laughing at his jokes. Still, Laura insisted his relationships with them would someday lead to one of the young ladies nursing a broken heart. Mark disagreed. What was wrong with having a little fun?

When it was time for the fifteen-minute prayer, Mark knelt and focused on God. He opened his heart and began to pray.

Lord, danki for all the blessings in my life. Please keep my family healthy and safe. Danki for bringing Priscilla back to the community. I can tell she's struggling with her decision to rejoin the church. Please lead her and guide her heart. Protect her and Ethan and help her rebuild her relationships with her family and freinden.

After the prayer, the congregation stood for the benediction and sang the closing hymn. Mark's eyes moved back to Priscilla as she sang along with the hymn. Did she still feel like an outcast? If so, could he somehow help her find her way back into the community? Hopefully she would feel God's love wrapped around her like a cozy blanket, helping her feel welcomed back into the church, even if certain individuals should make her feel otherwise.

When the hymn ended, seventy-year-old John Smucker, his church district's bishop, stood and faced the congregation. "And now I invite all the nonmembers of the congregation to please exit and the baptized members to stay for a special meeting."

A murmur spread throughout the congregation as the young, unbaptized members filed out through the barn door, gathering the children as they went.

Priscilla walked to her father and whispered something to him before taking Ethan's hand and leading him toward the barn exit. When she walked past Mark, she met his gaze with a solemn expression. He nodded at her as Ethan gave him another little wave.

After all the nonmembers had left, Mark turned his attention back to the bishop.

"We're having a members-only meeting because one of our *schweschdere* has fallen into sin," John announced to open the meeting. "Priscilla Allgyer left the community eight years ago to live in Baltimore like an *Englisher*. She returned to her family this past Thursday and met with me on Friday. She's repentant, and she wants to return to the church. After her time under the *Meiding*, she can be received back into the church."

John paused a moment, and a soft murmur moved through the congregation once again.

Mark turned to the unmarried women's section and spotted Franey and Ruthann whispering. He pressed his lips together, and his shoulders tightened. He hoped his friends weren't gossiping about Priscilla.

His eyes moved to the married women's section, and when he spotted Edna wiping her eyes, an invisible fist seemed to punch his heart. He could almost feel Edna's joy over her daughter's return. He turned to the married men's section, where Yonnie sat stoically, his expression grave. Was he hiding his feelings? Or was he truly not overjoyed to have his daughter back in his life? He hoped Yonnie was simply talented at masking his emotions.

"The meeting is over," John said, and conversations broke out around the barn.

"Let's set up for lunch," Roy said, patting Mark on the shoulder.

"*Ya*, I'm hungry." Mark smiled as he picked up a bench and helped Roy set it into a stand so it could be used as a table.

"Mark!" Franey appeared beside him and fingered the tie of her prayer covering as she smiled up at him. "I was wondering if you'd like to come over and visit this afternoon. I made a couple of strawberry pies yesterday, and I know you like them a lot." She touched his bicep and tilted her head as her eyes pleaded for a positive response.

Although the strawberry pie was tempting, Mark wanted to spend the afternoon resting. He just wasn't in the mood for company outside of his immediate family.

"*Danki* for the invitation, but I think I'm going to just rest at home," he said with his best smile. "I'd love a rain check, though."

Franey groaned and stuck out her lower lip, an expression Laura referred to as Franey's "wounded puppy dog look" when she'd once witnessed it. Mark bit back a grin at the memory of his twin's comment. Although Franey was the same age as Mark and Laura, she sometimes acted a few years younger. But Franey was pretty with her bright-hazel eyes and medium-blond hair.

"We could set something up for next week." Mark hoped the vague offer of another time would suffice.

"Okay." Franey's smile was back. "I'll see you later." She turned and headed toward the barn exit.

"Why did you turn her down?" Roy asked as he sidled up to him.

Mark shrugged. "I'm just not in the mood."

"You could've told her I'm free this afternoon."

Mark gave a bark of laughter. "She's two years older than you."

"So?" Roy challenged him. "I like strawberry pie."

"I'll keep that in mind." Mark chuckled as they moved to lift another bench. But his thoughts were still with Priscilla.

SIX

"WHY CAN'T WE STAY FOR LUNCH?" ETHAN ASKED as he and Priscilla walked to her father's horse and buggy.

"I already told you. I can't share meals with the other members of the church until after my shunning is over." Priscilla opened the buggy's door for him. "I have to complete three classes with the bishop and ministers, before we can stay for lunch."

"What kind of classes?"

"It's sort of like Sunday school at the church we visited in Baltimore. The bishop and ministers are reminding me what our beliefs are."

"So you can't have lunch with everybody after church until your classes are done?"

"That's right."

Ethan rubbed his chin as he frowned. "But I want to eat lunch with *Mammi* and *Daadi*."

"Those are the rules." She pointed to the buggy. "Climb in."

Ethan climbed in and then turned toward her. "How are *Mammi* and *Daadi* going to get home if we take their buggy?"

"They're going to get a ride with one of our neighbors."

"Priscilla!" Cindy called as she rushed after them. "Wait a minute!"

Priscilla turned toward Cindy. "Why aren't you in the member-only meeting?"

"Because I'm not a member."

"What?" Priscilla felt her eyes widen. "But aren't you twenty-two?"

Cindy nodded, the ties of her prayer covering bouncing off the shoulders of her teal dress. "I am, but I haven't joined yet." Her expression clouded as a frown turned down her lips. "I'm sure Mark and Laura told you we lost our *mamm* five years ago."

"*Ya*, Mark did." She touched Cindy's arm. "I'm so sorry. Your *mamm* was a sweet, loving, and kind woman."

"*Danki. Ya*, she was." Cindy took a deep breath. "It's been tough since we lost her, and I just haven't felt like I'm ready to make a commitment to the community. I can't really explain it, but I guess I'm still a little lost without her."

"I understand." Priscilla's heart cracked open with grief at Cindy's loss.

"We didn't get to talk much earlier, and I want to tell you I'm really *froh* you're back. Laura told me she feels like a prayer has been answered. She really missed you."

Priscilla's heart warmed as tears stung her eyes. "*Danki.* That's really sweet of you to tell me that."

Cindy pointed to the buggy. "And I wanted to meet your *sohn*."

"That would be nice." Priscilla smiled as she walked over to the passenger side of the buggy. "Ethan, please come and meet *mei freind*. She's Mark's younger sister."

Ethan hopped out of the buggy and shook Cindy's hand. "Hi. I'm Ethan."

Cindy smiled, her pretty face lighting up. "It's nice to meet you. I'm Cindy Riehl."

"You're tall like Mark." Ethan pointed to Priscilla. "You and Mark are taller than my mom. She's short."

Priscilla and Cindy laughed.

"*Ya*, that is true," Priscilla said. "Most people are taller than I am."

Cindy turned back to Priscilla. "I'll let you get home. I hope I'll see you again soon. Florence sews with your *mamm* often, so maybe I'll see you at a quilting bee."

"That would be nice." Priscilla gave her a quick hug. "*Danki* for coming to talk to me."

"*Gern gschehne*," Cindy said. "Have a *gut* day."

Priscilla and Ethan climbed into the buggy and waved to Cindy as Priscilla guided the horse toward the road. The skill had come back to her immediately. At least her father hadn't questioned her abilities with a horse and buggy.

"The service was so different from our church back in Baltimore," Ethan began. "I didn't know what they were saying, and it was long, but I stayed quiet, just like you said."

"*Gut.*" Priscilla patted his leg. "You were very well behaved."

"You need to teach me a lot more Dutch," Ethan continued. "If you teach me how to speak it, I can understand better. Will the teacher speak Dutch in school?"

"No, they speak English in school."

"Oh good." Ethan glanced out the window. "I can't wait to go to school and meet other kids. Mark told me it will be a one-room schoolhouse. That's different from my school in Baltimore."

Priscilla stared out the windshield as Ethan talked on. Her thoughts spun with her worries about rejoining the community. Laura and the other women in her family had made her feel welcome, which was a relief. Maybe Mark was right. Maybe the members of the community would accept her back as one of their own. Still, she couldn't erase the feeling she got when all the eyes in the church were staring holes into her back during the service. Sitting in front of the bishop and ministers, she'd felt like a sinner on display.

If she didn't feel like she belonged in her own church district, how would she ever feel like she belonged in the community as a whole?

—◦✕◦—

Later that afternoon Priscilla came downstairs and found her parents sitting in the family room in their favorite chairs. *Mamm* was reading what looked like a devotional while *Dat* concentrated on a copy of *The Budget*.

Mamm looked up from her book. "Where's Ethan?"

"He's reading." She pointed to the stairs. "I told him to take a nap, but he said only babies nap."

Mamm snickered. "That sounds like something he'd say."

Priscilla lingered by the bottom step and watched her father as he continued to study the newspaper. Her heart cried for them to work out their differences and somehow build a loving relationship. But how could they if he wouldn't even look at her?

Mamm cleared her throat as she stood. "I'm going to go spend some time with Ethan." *Mamm* gave her an encouraging smile and nodded toward *Dat* before making her way up the stairs.

Priscilla fiddled with the skirt of her dress as she crossed the room and then sat down on the sofa across from *Dat*. She folded her hands in her lap and waited for her father to acknowledge her.

After several moments she took a deep breath. *"Dat."*

"Hmm?" he responded with his eyes still focused on the newspaper.

"Would you please look at me?"

He folded the paper, which rustled in loud protest, and then met her gaze over the top of his reading glasses. "What?"

What did she want to say? As soon as he'd met her gaze, her words evaporated like a puddle on a hot summer day.

With a frown he began to open the paper again.

"Wait." She held up her hand to draw his attention back to her. "I want to know if you're *froh* that I'm starting the classes." How she hated the desperation radiating in her tone. Why was she so eager for his approval?

Because he was her father, and he'd never shown an ounce of satisfaction or pride toward her. All she'd ever wanted was his love.

"That's what you were supposed to do." His voice was flat and emotionless as he opened the paper again. "After all, you're the one who left the community and went to live with an *Englisher*. You got yourself shunned, so now you have to face the consequences."

Her pain and sadness morphed into anger and then surged through her veins, pushing her to her feet. "Why can't you at least acknowledge that I'm trying to fit in again? Why can't you give me a chance to prove I'm going to complete the classes and make you proud?"

His eyes narrowed. "We'll see after the shunning is over. You haven't completed your classes yet or been accepted back into the community."

"So you think I'll fail?" Furious tears filled her eyes.

"I didn't say that."

"No, you didn't say it out loud, but you're thinking it." She pointed to him. "You've always expected me to fail."

"That's not true." He shook his head.

"*Ya*, it is true." Her voice shook. "That's why you wouldn't let me work on the farm with you. You didn't think I could handle training the horses."

"I never said that." He placed the newspaper on the end table beside him. "Training horses is a difficult job, and it's no place for a *maedel*."

"Right." She folded her arms over her middle. "Only *buwe*

should work on a horse farm, and you resented that *Mamm* could only give you a *maedel*."

"You need to stop talking like that." His loud voice echoed throughout the room.

"It's the truth," she continued, her body shaking with boiling emotion. "You were disappointed when the doctors told her she couldn't have any more *kinner* because you wanted an heir. You didn't want me. You wanted a *bu*, so you ignored me. All I could do was learn how to quilt, sew, and cook as well as *Mamm* to prove I wasn't as stupid as you thought I was. But nothing I did mattered, did it?"

"I never said you were stupid."

"No, you didn't, but your constant criticism has shown me over and over that I'm your biggest disappointment."

"I don't think this is an appropriate Sunday discussion."

"Why? Because the truth hurts?" She nearly screamed the words as tears trickled down her cheeks. She brushed them away. She couldn't let him see how much his disapproval cut her to the bone.

"I don't approve of your tone." He stood. "You need to stop this disrespect now."

"No." She pointed to the floor. "It's time for you to listen to me and respect what I have to say. You've never treated me like a *dochder*. You've only ever treated me like an annoyance."

He ran his hand down his face. "If you don't stop talking to me this way, you're going to have to leave. This is *mei haus*, and I won't stand for you to speak to me so disrespectfully."

"Really, *Dat*?" Her voice squeaked. "You'd throw out *mei sohn* and me?"

He hesitated, and then he scrubbed both his hands down his face. Was he restraining himself? Or did he feel guilty for considering putting her and her son out on the street?

When he didn't speak, she shook her head and started for the stairs.

"I give up," she muttered as she headed up to her room. When she reached the top step, she stopped and pulled in a quaking breath. She had to somehow let go of her resentment of her father and push past the pain and anguish his coldness and criticism caused. She had to be strong—not only for herself but for her precious Ethan.

"Priscilla?" Ethan's door opened and *Mamm* stepped out into the hallway. "How did it go?"

The hope in her mother's expression sent guilt spiraling through her. How could she tell her mother that she'd yelled at her father? *Mamm* would never approve of what she'd said. And her father was right—she had been disrespectful to him. But enduring years of his criticism had taken a toll.

"Not well." Priscilla moved past her mother and walked into her bedroom.

"Did you try to talk to him?"

"I did, but it was a disaster." She sank onto the corner of her bed. "He still acts like I'm the biggest disappointment in his life."

"You're not a disappointment." *Mamm* touched her shoulder. "I've been praying for your *dat* to realize he's always been too hard on you. I know God will work on him so he'll realize what a blessing it is that God brought you home. What matters now is that our family is back together."

"Right." Priscilla stiffened, hoping to keep her tears at bay.

Mamm stepped over to the door. "Are you going to come downstairs?"

"No, *danki*." Priscilla forced a yawn. "I think I might take a nap."

"Okay." *Mamm* lingered in the doorway but then disappeared into the hallway.

Priscilla's shoulders hunched as dread threatened to drown her. She wanted so badly to be strong. She had survived Trent's abuse, and she needed to stand firm in this house for her son's sake. She had to tolerate her father until she could save some money and find an affordable place for her and Ethan to live.

SEVEN

PRISCILLA SKIDDED TO A HALT WHEN SHE FOUND Mark standing at the kitchen counter Tuesday afternoon. He was drinking a glass of water.

"Hi." He grinned at her as he placed the glass on the counter.

"Hi." She looked down toward the floor and cleared her throat. She'd done her best to avoid him all day yesterday, seeing him only in passing when he came into the house. She'd hoped to avoid him again today so she wouldn't have to discuss her meeting with the bishop and ministers or how humiliating it had felt to sit in front of the entire congregation with her head bent and face covered. But now she was face-to-face with him, and he had turned that electric smile on her.

"*Wie geht's?*" He swiveled toward her and leaned his elbow on the counter.

"I need to call a driver." She jammed her thumb toward the door to the family room. "I'm out of material, and I'm making a couple of pairs of work trousers for Ethan."

Footsteps sounded in the family room.

"I can take you." Mark stood up straight. "I need to go to the hardware store for supplies."

"Oh no. That's okay. I'll just call a driver." The thought of being stuck in a buggy alone with Mark made her nervously shift her weight on her feet. What would she find to discuss with him during the ride to town and then back home to avoid his delving into her personal life?

"Save me some money and go with Mark," *Dat* chimed in from the doorway.

Priscilla gritted her teeth. Leave it to him to overhear her conversation.

"Let it go," Mark muttered under his breath. "Don't say anything."

Priscilla hesitated, surprised by Mark's interference. Then she nodded. "I'll get my purse," she said before hurrying out of the kitchen.

Mark gave Priscilla a sideways glance as he guided his horse toward the road. She stared out the window with her purse on her lap as if the passing traffic held all the secrets to the perfect life. The only sound was the *clip-clop* of the horse's hooves, the whirr of the buggy wheels, and the roar of passing cars. He was accustomed to his women friends talking his ear off when they spent time together, so the silence between them was unnerving, making his skin itch.

He racked his brain for something to say.

"How was your Sunday afternoon?" he asked.

Priscilla was silent for a moment, but then she turned toward him, her brow pinched. "What?"

"I asked how your Sunday afternoon was."

"Oh." She continued to look surprised. "It was quiet. I took a nap."

He nodded as he turned his attention back to the road.

"How was yours?" she asked.

Aha! He'd managed to start a conversation with her.

"It was *gut*. I just rested and spent time with my family." His glance missed hers as she turned back to the window.

Mark halted the horse at a red light, and out of the corner of his eye, he spotted Priscilla scratching her arm. Today she wore a purple dress that complemented her dark hair and chestnut eyes. Like her other dresses, this one had three-quarter sleeves.

"Why are you wearing longer sleeves when it's close to ninety-five degrees outside?"

An indecipherable expression flashed across her face, and then she shrugged.

"It's just comfortable." She quickly looked toward the passing traffic as if avoiding his eyes.

A horn tooted behind them, and Mark guided the horse through the intersection. A few awkward moments of silence stretched like a great chasm. Mark found himself wishing for a radio to at least fill the dead air with music.

"What do you need from the hardware store?"

Her question stunned him for a moment. "I have a list in my pocket. I need chicken feed and a new hammer since I managed to break one. Let's see. What else? A chisel, some batteries, and a box of nails."

"Oh." She folded her hands in her lap and stared out the windshield.

He tried to think of something else to say, but nothing came to him. Being with her felt awkward, and he'd never felt awkward around a woman before. Why was she different? None of the other young women in their community found him this dull. Was something wrong with him today?

When they reached the parking lot at the hardware store, Mark guided the horse to a hitching post. He tied it up and then turned, surprised to see Priscilla still sitting in the buggy.

He skirted around the buggy and leaned into the passenger window. "What are you doing?"

"I'm going to sit here and wait for you."

"But it's hot out here." He gestured toward the store. "Walk inside with me. I'll buy you a bottle of water."

"Okay," she said, climbing out of the buggy.

They walked side by side toward the store. When they reached the front door, he held it open for her, and she muttered a thank-you as she passed through.

Priscilla walked with him through the aisles as he gathered the items on his list. She lingered a step or two behind him, her arms folded over her waist as he shopped.

"You know, you're giving me a headache," he quipped with a smile.

"What?" Her dark eyebrows pinched together.

"Because you talk so much," he explained, grinning. "You're giving me a horrendous headache."

Her expression relaxed, and then she sighed.

"I'm just kidding." He hesitated, waiting for her smile to light up her face. But it didn't. Instead, she looked away. None of his methods were working on her. Did she truly find him uninteresting? The notion gnawed at his gut.

He made his way down the last aisle and added chicken feed to his cart. As he stepped into the main aisle, he heard someone call his name. Turning, he spotted Rudy Swarey walking toward him. Rudy was Laura's ex-boyfriend.

"Hi, Rudy!" Mark waved to him. "How are you doing?"

"I'm fine." Rudy shook his hand and then turned to Priscilla. "Hi, Priscilla. It's been a long time."

"It's nice to see you." She shook his hand, but her shoulders hunched and her lips flattened. She suddenly seemed skittish and unsure of herself. Was she uncomfortable seeing other members of the community?

"What are you two doing here?" Rudy asked, no doubt surprised to see them together.

Mark pointed to the shopping cart. "I'm just picking up supplies for the farm, and Priscilla needs some material at the fabric shop."

"You're still working for Yonnie?" Rudy asked. He was putting two and two together now.

"*Ya*, I am. I see you're staying busy." Mark gestured around the store. "The store looks great."

"*Danki*. It's going well. We have some new suppliers, and we're able to keep our prices competitive despite the chain stores in town." Rudy gestured toward the front of the store. "If you have everything, why don't I check you out so you can be on your way?"

Mark and Priscilla followed Rudy to the cash register, and Mark paid for the supplies, adding two bottles of water to his purchases. Then they headed out and he loaded up the buggy.

As he climbed in beside Priscilla, he turned toward her. Once again, she stared out the window as if she'd rather be anywhere else in the world. He couldn't take the silence between them any longer.

"Are you upset with me?" He heard the hint of desperation in his voice. What was wrong with him?

She faced him, her eyebrows careening toward her hairline. "Why would I be upset with you?"

"I don't know." He fingered the reins. "You're just so quiet. Did I do something to offend you?"

"No, you haven't done anything. I guess I just don't have much to say." She shook her head. "Let's get to the fabric store so I can get back home and finish making those trousers for Ethan."

"All right." He handed her a bottle of water. "Here. I got this for you."

"*Danki*." She opened it and took a long drink.

"Gern gschehne."

How was he ever going to figure out the puzzle that was Priscilla Allgyer?

The bell on the door chimed as Priscilla and Mark stepped into Herschberger's Fabrics. She gripped her list in her hand and took in the knot of women milling around the large store. Most of them were dressed Amish, but a few Mennonite and *Englishers* were shopping as well.

Priscilla's breath seemed to scorch a hole in her chest as she steeled herself against her growing anxiety at being seen in the community now that the bishop had announced her name during the church's members-only meeting.

"Mark!"

Priscilla turned toward the cashier counter, where Franey stood helping a customer. Her pretty face lit up with a wide smile as she waved at Mark.

"Hi, Franey." Mark returned the smile.

"It's *gut* to see you." Franey looked as if she wanted to leap over the counter.

"Hi, Mark." Sadie Liz, Franey's younger sister, approached them. "What are you doing here?"

Priscilla tamped down the urge to ask Sadie Liz if she were invisible. In all honesty she longed to be invisible these days.

"I'm looking for some material to make a few dresses," Mark said, teasing. "What color do you think would be best for me?"

Sadie Liz giggled. "How about blue to go with your eyes?"

"*Ya,* they are my best feature, aren't they?" he retorted, and then he pointed to a display of patterns. "Would I find the best pattern over there?"

73

"*Ya*, let me show you." Sadie Liz giggled again as they walked together toward the display.

Priscilla swallowed a groan and headed toward the bolts of material. She picked out what she needed and asked Franey's mother to cut the material for her.

As she took her place in line to pay, she spotted Mark in the corner still chatting with Sadie Liz, who was still giggling. Priscilla rolled her eyes. Did he ever stop flirting? Why were all the women in this community attracted to him as if he wore an invisible magnet?

Several women lined up behind Priscilla as she waited her turn. When she reached the counter, she placed her basket on it and pulled her wallet from her purse.

When Priscilla looked up, Franey's eyes were wide as she shook her head. "I'm sorry, Priscilla, but I can't accept your money."

Humiliation wafted over her as she leaned forward and lowered her voice. "You're joking, right?"

"No, I'm not." Franey's expression was serious, holding no hint of a joke. She also lowered her voice. "You're under the *Meiding*, so I can't take your money."

Whispers erupted behind Priscilla, and her legs began to shake with the weight of humiliation.

"Come on, Franey," Priscilla said, seething as her cheeks burned. "We went to school together, and you know me. I need this material so I can make clothes for *mei sohn*. Please just tell me what I owe you." She opened her wallet and held up a handful of bills.

"I can't. I'm not allowed." Franey pushed the material toward her. "Just take it."

"Please, Franey." Frustrated tears filled Priscilla's eyes as she felt the stares of the women in line behind her burning through her dress and into her clammy skin. "Take my money." Her voice sounded weak and unsure to her own ears.

Hold it together, Priscilla!

"I can't." Franey nodded toward the corner of the store, where her father was stocking shelves. "He won't let me."

A woman behind her clicked her tongue, and Priscilla could imagine her critical thoughts. How could these judgmental women even begin to understand what Priscilla had endured the past few years?

Priscilla's hand trembled as she pushed her wallet back into her purse. She prayed she wouldn't cry in front of Franey and the rest of the people watching her. She couldn't allow them to see her crumble. She was stronger than that!

"Hey, Franey." Mark appeared beside Priscilla and leaned on the counter. "How's your day going?"

"Hi, Mark." Franey's face brightened as she turned toward him. "My day has been fine. How's yours?"

"It's been great." He moved his finger over the counter. "I've been thinking about your offer on Sunday. Do you still have that strawberry pie?"

"I do." Franey nodded with enthusiasm. "I saved some for you."

"Wunderbaar. Maybe I could come over one night this week?"

"Of course!" Franey nearly squeaked. "How about Thursday?"

"Great." Mark smiled that electric smile that seemed to make Franey melt.

Priscilla's jaw locked so hard that her whole face ached. Was Mark really going to make a date with Franey now? Unbelievable! Did he think the world revolved around his dating schedule?

Mark pulled his wallet out of his back pocket. "Listen, I really need to get this material. How much do I owe you?"

Franey froze, and her gaze bounced between Priscilla and Mark.

"Come on, Franey." Mark's smile somehow seemed brighter as he nodded toward the long line of women behind them. "I'm certain these ladies are in a hurry, so why don't you just tell me what I owe you."

"Oh. Okay." Franey's smile was back. She added up the material, told Mark the amount, and he paid.

"*Danki* so much. I'll see you Thursday." Mark winked as he took his change from her.

Mortified, Priscilla snatched the bag out of Mark's hand and marched out of the store to his buggy, hoping to leave the accusing stares of the customers behind forever.

⸻

"I don't need you to fight my battles for me," Priscilla said as Mark climbed into the buggy beside her. "I had it all under control." She sat back in the seat and opened her purse.

"No, you didn't." Mark shook his head. "And I'm glad I was there to help you."

"I think you mean you were there to sweet-talk Franey." She pulled out a handful of bills and held them out to him. "Here."

He looked down at the money and then met her gaze. "I don't need your money."

She frowned. "And I don't need your charity. Take it."

He took the money and studied her for a moment, taking in the sadness that seemed to sparkle in her dark eyes.

"Consider the material a gift for Ethan." As he pushed his hand toward her with the money, she flinched before taking it.

"*Danki,*" she said as she slipped the bills back into her wallet and then focused on her black purse.

They both remained silent during the ride back to her father's farm, and, once again he longed for a radio.

When they reached one of her father's barns, he halted the horse.

Priscilla turned toward him, her expression more amiable this time.

"*Danki*," she whispered. "I appreciate what you did today."

He opened his mouth to respond, but she was already out of the buggy and marching up the path toward the house.

EIGHT

PRISCILLA DASHED INTO THE DOWNSTAIRS BATHROOM, closed the door, and leaned against it. Her arms hung at her sides as humiliation and anger gushed out like a raging river. She dissolved into tears. Franey's rejection had torn at her heart and solidified her reasons for being reluctant to return to this community.

After a few moments she leaned on the sink and stared at her image in the mirror. Her eyes were puffy and bloodshot, and tears had streaked her face.

"You're stronger than this," she whispered to her reflection. "And you need to show Ethan that courage."

Leaning over, she filled her hands with cold water and splashed it on her face. She couldn't allow her parents to see her fall apart like this.

As she dried her face on a towel, a new determination blossomed. She'd finish making Ethan's new clothes and then remind her mother about helping with her quilting and sewing business. She'd save all her money and then find a small place to rent and a job that would pay enough for her to live on her own. Once she left her father's house, he couldn't force her to marry an Amish man to support her and her son. She would make her own way. She had to. Her life depended on it.

Priscilla smiled at her reflection. Yes, she would make it on her own without the help of any man, including her father. She would show everyone just how resolute she truly was.

───※───

"Priscilla." *Mamm* stood in her doorway on Thursday afternoon of the following week.

"*Ya.*" She stopped sewing the quilt she'd been repairing for one of her mother's customers and turned toward her.

"Cindy Riehl left us a message and invited us over for an impromptu quilting bee. She said Laura will be there too." She beckoned toward the hallway. "It starts in a half hour, so let's go."

Priscilla hesitated. There was normally food at quilting bees, and she would have to eat alone, across the room from everyone else, which would humiliate her just as much as she'd been at Franey's store. Everyone would stare at her. She swallowed a groan at the thought.

"*Was iss letz?*" *Mamm's* brow furrowed.

"I don't know." She nodded toward the quilt. "I promised I'd have this done by the end of the day, and I—"

"So bring it with you and finish it there. You need to get out of this *haus.* You haven't left since you went to the fabric store last week. Let's go. Your *dat* and Mark already agreed to look after Ethan." Before Priscilla could respond, *Mamm* was gone, her footsteps echoing in the hallway.

For a brief moment Priscilla wondered if Mark had asked his sister to invite her to this quilting bee, but she dismissed that notion. Why would Mark worry about Priscilla, especially since she'd avoided him for more than a week? She'd said hello to him a few times, but otherwise she'd steered clear of both her father and him.

"Priscilla!" *Mamm* called from downstairs. "Our driver is here!"

"I'm coming." After gathering the quilt and sewing supplies she'd need, she hurried down the stairs and out to the waiting van.

"I'm so glad you're here." Laura smiled at Priscilla as they sat together on the glider on the Riehls' porch later that afternoon.

After sewing for more than an hour with Laura, Cindy, Florence, Kayla, Sarah Jane, and *Mamm*, Priscilla and Laura had slipped outside to talk alone. Mollie was inside helping Cindy work on a quilt for one of her customers.

"I am too." Priscilla picked up her teacup, sipped from it, and looked out across the meadow toward Jamie's house. "I want to say again that I'm sorry I didn't contact you after I left."

"It's okay."

"No, it's not okay, and I truly regret it." Priscilla touched Laura's hand. "*Danki* for forgiving me for disappearing without a trace. I'm grateful you've welcomed me back into your life."

Laura clicked her tongue and shook her head. "How could I not welcome you back? I've missed you so much. I'm grateful God brought you back to us."

Priscilla looked out across the gorgeous pasture again. She'd forgotten how beautiful the patchwork pastures were in Lancaster County.

Laura paused for a moment. "Tell me about Baltimore."

"What?" Priscilla spun toward Laura.

Laura lifted an eyebrow. "I hit a sore spot? I'm sorry."

"No, it's okay." Priscilla gripped the handle of her cup. "When I left I moved in with my cousin Thelma. She's a few years older than we are, and she left her community when she was nineteen.

We'd been writing letters for some time, and when I told her I was thinking about leaving, she invited me to stay with her."

Laura's eyes rounded, and she touched Priscilla's arm. "I had no idea you were so unhappy. If you'd told Savilla and me, we would've tried to help you."

"*Danki* for that." Guilt felt like a scratchy blanket that wrapped around Priscilla and tightened. "But it's not your fault. I was so confused, and I didn't know what I wanted." She looked down at her tea, too humiliated to admit that her father was the one who had driven her away. "Thelma worked at a restaurant within walking distance of her apartment, and I got a job there too, as a waitress."

"Was that where you met Ethan's *dat*?"

"*Ya.*" Priscilla kept her focus on her cup as she spoke. "He was a frequent customer, and he always asked to be seated in my area. One day he asked me out, and we started dating. About six months later, I moved in with him, and then I got pregnant." She flushed with shame. "Things were *gut* for a while, but then he . . . changed. I knew I had to leave, and that's why I'm here."

Laura rubbed her arm. "And I'm glad you came back no matter what happened."

Priscilla smiled and nodded as relief flooded her. She wasn't ready to share the details of her troubled relationship with Trent.

"What happened to your cousin Thelma?"

"She got married and moved to New Jersey. I haven't heard from her in a couple of months."

"Oh. How are things at home?" Laura asked. "I know you and your *dat* used to argue a lot."

"It's tolerable." Priscilla shrugged. "He insisted I make myself right with the church, which I'm doing. He also insists I need to find a husband, but I'm going to try to be on my own before he can enforce that demand."

"What do you mean?" Laura asked.

Priscilla lowered her voice to be certain her mother wouldn't hear from inside the house. "I'm saving the money I make helping *mei mamm* sew, and I'm going to find a place for Ethan and me. Then I'll find a steady job so I can be on my own. *Mei mamm* doesn't know my plan, so please keep it to yourself."

Laura seemed to search her eyes. "Tell me you're not going to leave the community again."

"I don't know."

Laura's expression clouded with something that looked like worry. She shook her head.

Priscilla needed to change the subject fast. "Tell me about Allen."

"Oh, he's *wunderbaar*." Laura got a faraway look in her eyes as she rubbed her belly and stared off toward the green rolling meadow. "I'm so *froh* with him. He's handsome, kind, and generous. And he's a *gut dat*. He loves Mollie so much, and I know he'll love our second *kind* just as much."

As Laura talked about Allen's carriage business and how hard he worked to support their family, Priscilla tried to imagine having a husband that wonderful. What would life have been like if Trent had married her, worked hard to support their family, and cherished her and Ethan? Heaviness settled over her heart, and she fought back threatening tears.

"Priscilla?" Laura leaned over and touched her shoulder. "Are you okay?"

"*Ya.*" She forced a smile. "I was just thinking about how blessed you are. I'm so *froh* you and Allen found each other."

Laura clicked her tongue. "I'm sorry. I didn't mean to brag or sound prideful."

"You didn't." Priscilla shook her head. "I just don't think a *gut* provider and *dat* for Ethan is possible for me."

Laura's eyes were determined. "Don't give up on our community."

Priscilla couldn't stop her snort. "What makes you think any man in the community would want to marry me, even if I was ready to trust another man?"

"Why wouldn't they?"

Priscilla turned toward her. "Laura, I'm shunned for leaving for eight years and then coming back with a *sohn* I had out of wedlock. Why would any man want to be with me?" She pointed to her chest. "I'm damaged."

"No, you're not." Laura shook her head. "You made a mistake, and you're doing what you have to do to make yourself right with the church. You're forgiven."

"I may be forgiven, but my sins won't be forgotten."

Laura sighed. "Stop being so hard on yourself. Give yourself time to readjust in the community. You're *schee* and sweet. Many men would love to have a *fraa* like you."

"*Danki.*" Priscilla shifted on the glider. She didn't believe Laura's insistence that any man would give her a chance after she'd had a child out of wedlock. She needed to change the subject.

"Laura, do you remember the time you, Savilla, and I went to that pond in Ronks in Mark's buggy, and we got stuck in a rainstorm? It was storming so hard we couldn't see out the windshield, so we had to pull over at a 7-Eleven and wait for it to pass. We just sat there and drank Slurpees until the storm passed."

"Oh my goodness!" Laura laughed. "I do remember that. That was so fun. Mark was so angry with me when I got home. He said I should have called and told him we were going to be late." She rolled her eyes. "He always worries about me."

"That's nice, though." Priscilla drained her tea as envy gripped her. What would it have been like if she'd had a brother to worry about her? "How about that time we went to Savilla's *haus* to bake *kichlin*, and we were so wrapped up in our discussion about the cute *buwe* in our youth group that we nearly set the kitchen on fire?"

Laura gave a bark of laughter. *"Ya!"* She wiped her eyes. "Her *mamm* was so upset with us. The kitchen was clogged with smoke!"

They shared more memories of their time with Savilla, and after a while the screen door opened. Cindy stepped onto the porch with Mollie close behind her, holding a tray of cookies.

"We brought you snacks." Mollie held up the tray.

"Ya, you're missing all the refreshments," Cindy added. "May we join you?"

"Of course." Laura patted the chair beside the glider, and Mollie hopped onto it. "We were just getting caught up. *Danki* for the snacks, *mei liewe.*"

As Cindy sat down beside Priscilla, Priscilla smiled. She was thankful for her wonderful friends who had welcomed her home despite her past mistakes.

Mark stepped out of the barn as the blue van parked in front of Yonnie's house. He hurried over just as Edna and Priscilla were climbing out of it. Ever since they'd been to the fabric store, he'd tried to talk to Priscilla, but all his attempts to draw her into a conversation had fallen flat. She gave him only one-word answers to any of his questions, and she still showed no interest in being his friend. It was driving him to the brink of madness.

While Edna paid the driver, Priscilla balanced a large bag containing a quilt, a sewing basket, and a plate of cookies as she walked toward the porch steps.

"Do you need any help?" he asked as he quickened his steps.

"No, *danki*. I'm fine." She teetered, and he grabbed the plate as it slipped from her hands.

"No, huh?" He grinned as he held up the plate.

"*Danki*." She reached to take it from him.

"Uh-uh." He shook his head. "Allow me." He made a sweeping gesture toward the porch.

She didn't protest.

"Hello, Mark." Edna carried two bags as she moved past them on the steps.

"Hi, Edna."

Edna disappeared into the house, and Priscilla turned toward the row of barns.

"Where's Ethan?" she asked.

"He and your *dat* are talking to a customer in the pasture. I've been working in the barn."

"Oh." She turned toward him, and for the first time in more than a week, she stood still as if she wanted to talk to him.

Relief flooded him. "How was the quilting bee?"

"It was nice. I enjoyed talking with your *schweschdere*." She eyed him with what looked like suspicion. "How was your date with Franey last Thursday night? Did you enjoy her strawberry pie?"

"The pie was *appeditlich*, but it wasn't a date."

"Really?" Her dark eyebrows rose. "The way you were flirting with her, it sure seemed like it would be."

"Wait a minute." He held up his free hand. "I wasn't flirting with her."

"Ha." She started up the steps. "You're unbelievable."

"What does that mean?" He charged forward, following her through the front door and into the kitchen. "I only did that so you could have your material."

"Oh really." She set her bag and sewing basket on the kitchen table and spun toward him. "So you used Franey, then?"

"Well, no." He stopped in the doorway and stared at her, speechless. No one had ever accused him of being a user. The word stung him as if it were an angry wasp.

"Mark, I've seen you in action." She stepped closer to him and wagged a finger just millimeters from his nose. "All you have to do is smile and you have most of the *maed* in our community eating from your hands. You know exactly how much power you have over them." She lifted her chin. "Just admit it. You love the attention, and you use the *maed* to make yourself feel powerful."

"Powerful?" He blinked. "Why would I want to feel powerful?"

"Never mind." She took the plate from his hand. "*Danki* for your help." She set it on the counter before retrieving her bag and sewing basket.

When she walked back to the doorway, he stayed planted where he was.

"Excuse me." When he didn't move, she sighed as she looked up at him. "I have work to do. I need to finish this quilt. I promised the customer she'd have it today."

"Are you angry with me?" He held his breath as he awaited her answer.

"No." Her forehead puckered. "I have no reason to be angry with you." She nodded toward the doorway. "I really need to finish this quilt, though. Please let me through."

He gave her his best smile, certain it would inspire her to stay and talk to him. After all, she was right. That was how he garnered most of the attention from the young ladies in their church district. Surely Priscilla couldn't resist his charms.

But her serious expression didn't melt into a smile. "Mark, I really do have work to do."

Rejection stabbed at his self-esteem. Was she immune to him completely? Or had he lost his touch?

Defeated, he took a step back, and she hurried up the stairs.

Her accusations echoed in his mind. Was he a user? The word made him cringe. Had it been wrong for him to ask Franey to get together with him? He had only wanted to help Priscilla and stop her humiliation. But maybe Priscilla was right. Maybe he had made a mistake.

Even though Priscilla insisted she wasn't angry with him, Mark was certain she didn't approve of him. And for some inexplicable reason, he wanted her approval more than ever. He had to find a way to prove to Priscilla that he was worthy of her friendship.

"I had so much fun at the quilting bee today," Kayla said as she sat beside Jamie in the glider that evening.

Jamie nodded as he rocked a sleeping Calvin in his arms.

"That's nice." Mark glanced out across the pasture toward Jamie's house as he sat on a rocker beside his brother. Someday soon his own house would stand beside it. He couldn't wait to walk through his front door after a long day at work and eat supper in his kitchen.

"It was great to see Priscilla again," Kayla continued. "I finally got to talk to her after meeting her at church last week. She's really sweet."

Mark's gaze swung to Kayla at the mention of Priscilla's name. "What did she talk about?"

"She didn't say too much to me." Kayla rubbed Calvin's back. "We mostly talked about sewing. She's really talented. She showed me how she was repairing a quilt for a customer. She sewed for a while, and then she and Laura came out here to talk. I think they wanted to get caught up in private. I didn't want to intrude, so I stayed inside."

Mark tried to hide his disappointment at Kayla's lack of

information. He wanted to know more about Priscilla's life in Baltimore, but it wasn't his business.

Kayla stood. "We should get Calvin home. I'm going to go say good night to everyone." She disappeared into the house, and the screen door clicked shut behind her.

Jamie looked down at his son. "I can't believe Cal is going to be a big *bruder* soon."

Mark smiled. "*Ya*, you're going to have two *kinner*. Can you believe that? We thought you'd never find anyone to marry you."

"At least I had enough sense to settle down."

"Excuse me?"

"You could have any *maedel* you want in this community, but you're still a bachelor." Jamie turned toward him. "What are you waiting for?"

"You know what I want." Mark gestured toward Jamie's house. "I want my own place, and that's my priority right now."

"Why?" Jamie asked. "You have your own room here. Besides, there's more to life than building a *haus*."

"That's easy for you to say." Mark pointed across the meadow. "You have a *schee* three-bedroom *haus* right there."

"You'll have one someday. Get married first, and then build your *haus*."

"No." Mark shook his head. "I'm not ready to get married."

"Why not?"

"Because . . . well . . . I'm just not."

"You know, Mark, it wasn't too long ago that you were giving me a hard time about being almost thirty and not married. You're twenty-six now. What are you waiting for?"

Mark paused and considered the question. "Maybe I haven't found the right *maedel*."

Laughter burst from Jamie's lips, and Calvin moaned and wiggled in his sleep before settling down again.

"What's so funny?" Mark deadpanned.

"You haven't found the right *maedel*? If that's true, then I don't think she exists. You've gained the attention of nearly every *maedel* in Lancaster County."

Priscilla's words from earlier in the day rang through his mind.

All you have to do is smile and you have most of the maed *in our community eating from your hands. You know exactly how much power you have over them. Just admit it. You love the attention, and you use the* maed *to make yourself feel powerful.*

Did his older brother think he was a user too?

Mark stood. "I'm going to bed." He touched Calvin's back. "*Gut nacht*, Cal."

"Did I say something wrong?" Jamie asked as Mark turned to go.

"Why would you say that?" Mark opened the screen door.

"Because you didn't give me a biting remark in response."

Mark tilted his head. "Look, Jamie, when I'm ready to get married, you'll be the first to know."

Jamie shook his head. "I'll be more like the third. First you'll ask your future *fraa*, and then you'll tell your twin."

"Fine. You'll be the third." Mark tapped the doorframe. "*Gut nacht.*"

As he stepped into the family room, a question filled his mind. Would he ever feel the urge to be married? If not, he might spend the rest of his life living alone in the house he built on his father's farm. Was that what he wanted?

NINE

"HOW DID YOUR CLASS GO?" LAURA ASKED AFTER the service on Sunday.

"It went well." Priscilla shrugged. "You remember how the classes went before we were baptized. They're about the history of our beliefs. Just a refresher." She glanced around the barn as the men began to set up the tables for lunch.

"You have one more class, and then you'll be accepted back into the church." Laura's smile widened.

"*Ya*, I know." Although Priscilla should be relieved that her shunning was almost over, a niggle of worry started at the base of her neck. Was she ready to become a member of the church? Did she even deserve to be a member?

"I'm hungry," Ethan whined as he rubbed his abdomen. "Can't we stay for lunch today?"

"I'm hungry too," Mollie agreed as she stood beside him.

"No, Ethan, you know we can't stay," Priscilla said, trying to keep her temper at bay. "We've discussed this."

Laura bent down and smiled at Ethan. "You'll be able to stay and eat with us soon." Then she stood up straight and touched Priscilla's arm. "I hate that you have to leave."

"Like you said, I'll be helping you serve the noon meal in a couple of weeks." Priscilla's heart seemed to turn over at her friend's words. She looked across the barn and spotted Franey and Ruthann standing with Mark, smiling and gazing up at him as if he were the most interesting person in the room.

"Will he ever pick just one *maedel*?" The question burst from Priscilla's mouth without any forethought. Why did she even care that Mark flirted with more than one young woman—or any women? It wasn't her business. When Mark met her gaze and smiled, Priscilla felt a strange zing of electricity flowing through her veins, taking her by surprise. She quickly turned away, focusing on Laura again.

Laura frowned. "I keep praying he'll choose one and settle down."

"I doubt that will ever happen. Mark has always loved being the center of attention."

Laura chuckled. "That's the truth."

"Priscilla," *Dat* said when he appeared at her side. "You know you can't stay to eat with the rest of the congregation. You need to go."

"*Ya*, I know." Priscilla's mood deflated at her father's stern eyes and curt warning. After he walked away she turned back to Laura. "I'd better go. Take care."

Laura's expression seemed filled with sympathy. She gave Priscilla a quick hug and then touched Ethan's head. "I'll see you both soon."

New humiliation mixed with anger pricked Priscilla's skin as she took Ethan's hand and steered him out of the barn. Why did *Dat* feel the need to remind her she wasn't welcome to stay for lunch? Priscilla didn't need to be reminded that she was shunned and unwelcome at her community's table. He seemed to enjoy shoving her state of affairs down her throat any chance he could. Each night he reminded her to sit at the separate table for supper as if she hadn't eaten her meals there for more than two weeks.

Priscilla swallowed a sigh. She'd always dreamt of having a loving father. So many times she'd witnessed Laura's father hugging her and encouraging her. She even recalled Savilla's father consoling her after she'd fallen and skinned her knee. But Priscilla had no memories of her father showing her affection or telling her that he loved her. She just wanted his love, his emotional support. Why did some fathers dole out love and affection in abundance and others offer only dribs and drabs?

She bit her trembling lower lip as they approached the waiting horse and buggy.

Ethan looked up at her, his eyebrows pinched together. "Are you okay, *Mamm*?"

Priscilla felt her face relax as she took in her son's innocent face. She touched his nose and then smoothed his thick, dark hair. "*Ya*, I'm fine. I was just thinking about all the chores I need to do tomorrow."

"Oh." He smiled. "Can we have peanut butter and jelly sandwiches for lunch?"

She stopped and cupped his cheek. "That sounds *appeditlich*."

"Apple what?" he asked, his nose scrunched as if he smelled something foul.

She laughed at his adorable expression. "*Appeditlich*," she repeated. "It means delicious. We need to work on your Dutch."

"Teach me more words," he said.

"Okay." As they climbed into the buggy, Priscilla did her best to dismiss her frustration about her father. All that mattered was that she and Ethan had each other. She'd never let Ethan wonder if she loved him. She'd be sure to show him every day.

"Ethan?"

"What?" He looked at her.

"Ich liebe dich, mei liewe."

He grinned. "I love you too, *Mamm.*"

Her heart swelled with affection for her son. He was the only man she needed in her life.

Mark's eyes lingered on Priscilla as Franey talked about how busy her father's fabric store had been. When Priscilla met his gaze, her cheeks reddened. Then she quickly looked at his twin. Why would she avert her eyes so quickly?

"Did you hear a word I said?"

"Huh?" Mark turned to Franey's narrowed eyes, and he fixed his best grin on his face. "I'm sorry. Go ahead."

"I asked you if you'd like to have supper at *mei haus* this week." Franey jammed her hand on one small hip.

"Oh." Mark rubbed his chin. "I'll have to check my schedule."

"Your schedule?" Ruthann's brow furrowed. "I thought you said you had time for each of us this week."

"Right." He cleared his throat. "I'll let you know." He turned back toward Priscilla just as her father said something to her. When her shoulders hunched, alarm surged through Mark. What was her father saying to make her so upset? The urge to protect her flooded his veins, taking him by surprise. Why would he want to take care of someone who had no interest in even being his friend?

After her father walked away, Priscilla said something to Laura, who hugged her. Then Priscilla and Ethan headed out through the barn doors.

Mark turned his attention back to Ruthann and Franey, but their words were only background noise to his swirling thoughts.

"Mark?" Ruthann asked after a few moments. "Is something wrong?"

"*Ya*. I mean, no." He divided a smile between them. "I really need to start moving the benches, and you should get started serving the meal. I'll talk to you later, okay?"

"Oh," Franey said before sharing a confused look with Ruthann.

"Okay," Ruthann added.

"Let me know about supper, okay?" Franey asked.

Without responding, Mark headed over to Laura. She and Mollie and Cindy were heading toward the barn exit.

"Sis," Mark called, quickening his steps as he approached them. "Laura! Wait a second."

"Hey, Mark!" Roy called from the other side of the barn. "Are you going to help with the benches? Or are you going to chat all afternoon?"

Mark held up his index finger toward his younger brother. "One minute."

Roy shook his head and then said something to Jamie beside him.

Laura and Cindy had spun to face Mark, and Mollie yanked on Laura's hand.

"We need to go serve the meal," Laura said. "What do you need?"

"I want to talk to you."

"I'm hungry!" Mollie whined.

Cindy took Mollie's hand. "I'll take her to the kitchen and feed her."

"*Danki*," Laura said with a sigh. "I'll be right there." As Cindy and Mollie walked away, she pivoted back to Mark. "What's this about?"

Mark gestured for Laura to follow him to a corner.

"What did you and Priscilla discuss before she left?"

Laura raised her eyebrows. "Just girl stuff. Why?"

"She seemed upset when her *dat* spoke to her, and I was wondering what happened. What did he say?"

Laura grinned as she leaned forward. "Why are you suddenly so interested in Priscilla?" She wagged a finger at him. "Do you like her?"

"Sure I do. She's our *freind*, right?"

"Uh-huh." Laura shook her head. "It's more than that. You really like her."

He swallowed a groan. "Please, sis. We're not sixteen anymore."

Laura studied him, and he could almost hear her thoughts clicking through her mind. She was drawing conclusions about his interest in Priscilla, and that sent annoyance hurling through him.

"If you're so interested in what Priscilla's *dat* said to her, you can ask her yourself."

"Fine." He gave her a curt nod. "I will."

Priscilla yawned as she descended the stairs the following afternoon. Her eyes were tired from staring at her sewing machine all day. She'd finished two sewing projects for customers and had started a third when she decided she needed a break.

She'd skipped lunch, and her stomach felt hollow as it growled. A turkey sandwich and a couple of her mother's peanut butter cookies would hit the spot.

When her shoe hit the bottom step, she turned toward the kitchen and stopped in her tracks. Mark came around the stairwell. She gripped the banister as she looked up at him. She'd hoped to avoid another awkward conversation with him today, but he always seemed to have a sixth sense about when she was on her way to the kitchen. How did he manage to anticipate her every move?

"Hi." He smiled. *"Wie geht's?"*

"I'm fine." She did her best to sound chipper despite her rising anxiety. "How are you?"

"I can tell you're not fine." His gaze was penetrating, and she hugged her arms to her chest.

Was she so transparent to everyone? Or to only him?

"What's bothering you?" he asked.

"I'm just busy. I had hoped to finish four sewing projects today. I'm only on the third one, and I'll have to start supper in another couple of hours." She started toward the kitchen doorway. "I'm on a quick break to eat some lunch."

"Nope, that's not it. You looked unhappy after church yesterday."

"What do you mean?" She squinted her eyes as she tried to recall what he might be talking about.

"I saw your *dat* say something to you before you and Ethan left the barn. You looked upset. What happened?"

"It was nothing." She went to step toward the kitchen, and as if predicting her attempt to flee, he slipped in front of her and leaned against the doorframe.

"Really, Mark?" She jammed her hands onto her hips. "You're going to block me from walking into the kitchen, just like that day you blocked me from getting out of it?"

"I do what I have to, to make you talk to me." He tilted his chin, and he somehow looked taller and more attractive than usual. It was as if his blue eyes were brighter and his jaw was more chiseled.

What was it about Mark that made him so desirable when he'd never shown any interest in her?

Then his mouth turned up in that electric smile, the one that reduced women like Franey, Sadie Liz, and Ruthann to giggling nitwits.

But it wouldn't work on Priscilla. She'd already been fooled by one attractive man's deception, and she would never fall for that again. Trent had seduced her, and then he'd betrayed her.

Lifting her chin, she stood taller and looked up at him. "Does that usually work for you?"

He blinked as if he was surprised. "Does what work for me?"

"The flirting." She gestured at his face. "The cocky attitude and smile."

He shrugged. "*Ya*, I guess it does."

"Well, I'm immune to your charms, Mark, so you can knock it off." She pointed toward the kitchen. "Please move out of my way."

"Not until you tell me what happened yesterday."

"Fine. I'll tell you." She gestured widely. "I was talking to Laura, and *mei dat* came over and reminded me I had to go. As if I would forget I'm not welcome at meals. He reminds me here every day when he points to my sad little table in the corner. But this time he had to embarrass me in front of *mei freind* and the entire congregation." She pointed at him. "There. Are you *froh* now? You know how pathetic my life is."

His smile faded, and his face clouded. Bitterness, resentment, and hurt boiled in her belly at the tenderness and concern she saw in his eyes. How could it be real? Trusting him would be a mistake, and he'd already gotten her to reveal too much personal information.

"I'm hungry," she muttered. "Would you please let me by?"

He took a step to the side, and she slipped past him. As she began to make her sandwich, she felt his eyes still watching her every move from the doorway. She tried to ignore him despite her flaming cheeks. She finished making her sandwich and put away the supplies before grabbing a few cookies from the jar on the counter.

"Why didn't you eat lunch with your family and me today?" he finally asked after several moments.

"Because I don't like having to eat at another table." She immediately regretted revealing another truth to him. How did he always manage to pull her deepest feelings out of her? She kept her eyes focused on her lunch to avoid his gaze.

"I'll eat with you." He walked over to the table and dropped into a seat.

"I appreciate your concern, but I don't need your pity. I'm just fine on my own."

He flinched, and she tried to ignore the guilt chewing on her stomach.

"I just want to be your *freind*, Priscilla."

"*Danki*, but I'm fine. Really."

He opened his mouth to speak but then closed it as if he thought better of wasting more breath on her.

She bit back a grin. She'd reduced Mark Riehl to silence, something she'd been certain was impossible.

She gathered her lunch and headed up the stairs to her bedroom to eat alone.

Mark stowed his horse and buggy, and then he headed up the path to his father's house. Confusion weighed heavily on his shoulders. For the past two days, he'd continued to try to encourage Priscilla to talk to him, but she either responded to his questions with one-word answers or ignored him. Nothing had changed.

Bewilderment was his constant companion, and he was at the end of his rope. It was apparent that no matter how supportive and kind he tried to be to Priscilla, she didn't want to be his friend. A sane person would most likely have given up by now, but he couldn't convince himself to give up on her. It was as if an invisible force pulled him to her, and he couldn't rest until she gave him a chance to prove he could be a genuine and trusted friend to her.

As he stepped into the mudroom, voices echoed from the kitchen. He paused, ran his hand down his face, plastered a smile on his lips, and then marched into the kitchen where his entire family sat around the table, including Laura and her family. The aroma of pork chops filled his senses, causing his stomach to growl as he crossed to the sink and washed his hands.

"The prodigal *sohn* has returned," Jamie announced.

"No, he's the prodigal twin," Allen quipped, and everyone laughed.

"How was your day, Mark?" Florence asked.

"*Gut.*" He faced the table as he dried his hands with a paper towel. "I didn't realize everyone was going to be here for supper tonight."

"I told you this morning, but you never listen to me," Cindy responded.

"What?" He held his hand to his ear. "Did you say something, Cindy?"

"Ugh." Cindy groaned, rolling her eyes.

"He's incorrigible," Laura chimed in. "I tell him that all the time."

"No, he isn't." Mollie shook her head as she sat beside Laura. "He's *mei zwillingboppli onkel.*"

"That's right." Mark crossed the room as everyone laughed. He stopped by Mollie's chair and kissed her head. "Did you save this seat for me?" He patted the back of the empty chair beside her.

"*Ya*, of course." Mollie grinned up at him, and his heart seemed to swell. He adored her.

"She wouldn't let anyone else sit there," Sarah Jane said. "Jamie tried."

"*Ya*, he did." Roy laughed. "Mark is clearly the favorite *onkel*."

"Well, I am the best-looking *onkel*," Mark said, joking as he sank into the chair beside Mollie. Then he leaned over and rubbed his nose against hers as she giggled.

Everyone groaned, and Mark bowed his head in silent prayer before filling his plate high with food from the platters at the center of the table. Florence had made breaded pork chops, mashed potatoes, broccoli, and rolls. His stomach gurgled with delight as he buttered a roll. It was still warm. He hadn't realized how hungry he was until he breathed in the delicious aromas.

While he ate, he tried to concentrate on the conversations swirling around him, but his thoughts kept turning to Priscilla. Why was it that most of the single young women in the community enjoyed his company but Priscilla repeatedly pushed him away? What was he doing wrong?

"Are you done?"

"What?" Mark looked up as Cindy stared down at him.

She raised her eyebrow before gesturing around the table. "Everyone else is done, and the men have already gone outside to talk. You've been sitting here moving around the mashed potatoes on your plate for almost five minutes. *Was iss letz?*"

"Nothing, nothing." He took a drink from his glass of water.

Cindy didn't look convinced. "You're never quiet during supper, Mark."

"That's for sure," Laura chimed in from the sink, where she was scrubbing a pot.

"You normally guide the conversation," Kayla added as she dried a dish.

Mark tried to think of something witty to say in response, but he came up empty. Maybe there *was* something wrong with him!

"I'm done. *Danki*." He pushed back his chair and turned to Mollie as she struggled to sweep the floor. "That broom is twice your size. Do you need help?"

"No, *danki*. I've got it." She pushed the ties of her prayer covering over her shoulders and then stuck out her tongue as if concentrating on her task.

He grinned as he stood. "*Danki* for supper, Florence. It was *appeditlich*."

"I'm glad you liked it." Florence gathered up his utensils and Cindy took his plate.

He looked at Laura as he started toward the mudroom. She was studying him. By the expression on her face, he was certain she was going to try to get him alone to ask him what was wrong. How was he going to explain that for the first time in his life, he had no idea how to get a woman to pay attention to him?

Leaning against the back porch railing in front of Jamie, he tried to join the men's discussion about how quickly the harvest season would arrive. But he was lost in thought when Laura stepped onto the porch holding Mollie's hand.

"We should get going," she told Allen. "It's almost Mollie's bedtime."

"Time flies when you're having fun." Allen stood and scooped Mollie into his arms. "Say *gut nacht*, Mollie."

Mollie reached for Mark, and he pulled her into his own arms for a hug.

"*Gut nacht, Onkel* Mark," she said before kissing his cheek. "*Ich liebe dich*."

Mark melted at the sound of her little voice. "*Ich liebe dich, mei liewe*." After another quick hug he handed Mollie back to her father.

As Mollie addressed each of her uncles and grandfather, Laura rested her hand on his forearm. "I want to talk to you." She nodded toward the steps. "Walk with me."

Mark complied, following her toward the barn.

"*Was iss letz*?" she asked.

"Nothing." He shrugged as he glanced out toward Jamie's house.

She stopped and spun toward him. "You know I can feel your worries, right?" She touched her collarbone.

"*Ya*, I know." He stuffed his hands in his pockets and looked at the sunset. The sky was streaked with such intense reds and oranges, it looked like fire.

"You were so quiet at supper that I wondered if someone else had taken your place."

When he laughed she grinned.

"There's my twin." She tilted her head. "So what is it? Are you tired of Yonnie's moods and ready to quit the horse business?"

"No, that's not it." He glanced out toward the pasture. "I'm just worried about Priscilla."

"Did something happen to her?"

"No, no. She's fine. It's just that I've tried to be her *freind*, and she won't talk to me. I can see the sadness in her eyes, and I want to help her. But every time I try to get her to talk, she rebuffs me." He looked down and kicked a stone with his toe. "I've tried really hard to show her that my friendship is genuine."

Keeping his gaze focused on the ground, he shared how he'd convinced Franey to sell him the material Priscilla needed and then how Priscilla had avoided him ever since.

"I just don't get it, sis. It's like she has no interest in talking to me. I feel like I bore her, and I've never had anyone react to me that way. I have no idea what to do." When he looked up, Laura grinned at him. "Why is this so funny?"

"You don't just like Priscilla. You care about her." She jammed a finger into his chest.

He shook his head. "Not in the way you're implying."

"*Ya*, you do." She clapped her hands. "It finally happened!"

"What finally happened?"

"You're falling in love."

"No, no, no." He held up his hands. "I'm not—"

"My prayers have been answered! You're finally going to get married."

"Whoa. Sis, you've got it all wrong."

"No, I'm exactly right." She rubbed her middle as she spoke. "You can't stop thinking about her, and you can't stand that she won't give you the time of day. That's love, Mark."

He groaned and looked at the emerging moon. Why had he confided in her? He wanted advice, not an incorrect analysis of his feelings. "I don't like her like that. I'm just worried about her. Can you help her?"

Laura tapped her chin with her finger and then snapped her fingers. "I think she still feels she won't be included and loved by the community, and that's what's weighing on her. Why don't I invite her over for supper one night? I know we're just one family, but that should help."

"But the shunning isn't over for another two weeks."

She waved off his words. "I'm not worried about that. She's welcome at my table."

He nodded slowly. "But you know you're breaking the rules, right? You're not supposed to eat at the table with her until the shunning is over."

Laura raised her eyebrows. "Are you going to tell the bishop?"

He shook his head. "No."

"Then I think we'll be fine. *Ya*, I'm breaking the rules, but I'm doing it for my best *freind*. I think most people in the community would understand."

"Okay." He nodded as the idea took root. "That just might work."

"*Ya*, it will work." She clapped her hands. "I'm so *froh*. You've finally met your match." When he frowned she touched his arm. "Your secret is safe with me."

"Laura," Allen called from the driveway. "We need to get going."

"I'll be right there," she called back. "I'll see you soon, Mark."

"*Danki*," he said before she hurried down the path to her family.

As Laura climbed into their buggy, hope lit in Mark's chest. His twin would fix this.

TEN

"I HAD SO MUCH FUN TODAY," ETHAN SAID AS HE SWEPT the kitchen floor. "Mark and I mucked the stalls, and then he let me help him fix the henhouse."

"You're a *gut* helper." Priscilla looked over her shoulder at him as she stacked clean dishes in a cabinet.

"That's nice," *Mamm* said as she wiped off the table. "You like Mark, don't you?"

"Oh *ya*." Ethan bent and swept the crumbs into the dustpan. "He's really nice to me."

Priscilla bit back the bitter taste of guilt as she remembered how she'd avoided Mark earlier in the week. It had been two days since she'd rejected his invitation to eat lunch with him. He'd seemed to still want to talk to her when he approached her in the kitchen on Tuesday and then again out on the porch on Wednesday. But she'd dismissed him both times.

Why did he continue to try to win her over with friendship? Most men would have given up by now. What did he hope to accomplish by befriending her? She wasn't worthy of his constant attempts, but he didn't seem to be planning on giving up anytime soon.

"There! All done." Ethan dumped the crumbs into the trash can and then set the dustpan and broom in the utility room.

"Are you ready for your bath?" *Mamm* asked.

"*Ya.*" Ethan started toward the stairs.

"I'll get him ready if you want to finish the kitchen," *Mamm* said, offering her help.

"*Ya,* that would be fine. *Danki.*"

Priscilla finished stowing the utensils and wiping down the counters.

Once the kitchen was clean, she went into the family room. Her father was sitting in his favorite chair reading *The Budget.* She wiped her palms down her apron as her stomach seemed to flip.

How she longed for her father's approval, for his love. She still felt like a stranger in the home where she'd been born.

Her thoughts turned to the small swing set *Dat* and Mark set up for Ethan last week. She'd watched Ethan play on the swings and slide more than once since then, and the smile on his face had made her happy. It was clear *Dat* loved his grandson, which was a step in the right direction. Perhaps she could use the swing set as a bridge to a truce.

Taking a deep breath, she squared her shoulders. "*Dat.*" Her voice trembled as she took a step toward him.

He peered at her over his reading glasses, his lips making a flat line.

She stared at him, her words caught in her throat and her thoughts a jumbled mess.

When he looked back down at the newspaper, her shoulders tightened with anger.

"I want to thank you for building the swing set for Ethan," she began. "He really enjoys it."

Dat mumbled something that sounded like "*gut*" while keeping his eyes on his newspaper.

"*Dat,* look at me," she pleaded. She nearly faltered at the thread of desperation in her voice.

He kept his focus on the newspaper as if she were invisible.

"Don't ignore me," she insisted. "I'm your *dochder*."

His eyes snapped to hers, and his face clouded with a scowl. "You stopped being *mei dochder* the day you left this community."

His words speared her, like a knife piercing her heart.

He returned to reading as if he hadn't just inflicted pain.

"Did you ever consider that you could be the reason I left?" she snapped. Swallowing back a burning knot of sobs, she fled up the stairs. When she reached her bedroom, she stepped inside, closed the door, and wilted against it as tears streamed from her eyes.

"There's a voice mail message for you."

Priscilla looked up from her sewing machine the following morning. She faced her mother in the doorway as dread washed over her, locking her muscles. Had Trent found them?

"Why are you looking at me like that? You should go listen to it." *Mamm* nodded toward the hallway. "You're going to be excited."

"Who is it?" Priscilla held her breath.

"Laura."

"What did she say?"

"Just go listen to it." *Mamm* grinned and then disappeared from the doorway.

Breathing a sigh of relief, Priscilla finished the stitches on the quilt she'd been repairing and then headed outside.

She breathed in the humid air as she descended the back porch steps and trekked toward her father's office in the largest barn. She looked over at the pasture and spotted Mark leaning forward on the split-rail fence as he stood beside Ethan and gestured toward where her father was training a horse. Mark smiled as he said something to Ethan, who nodded in response, his face serious as if he were concentrating on what Mark told him.

Ethan looked over his shoulder at Priscilla, and his face broke into a smile as he waved. "Hi, *Mamm*!"

"Hi, Ethan!" Priscilla waved in response.

Ethan stood up straighter and pointed to Mark. "Mark is teaching me about horse training!"

Mark glanced at her, smiled, and shrugged. "Your *dat* is really the expert. I'm still a student."

"That's nice. *Danki*, Mark." She smiled.

Something in Mark's smile changed, and it seemed more genuine and tender. She took in his attractive face, tall stature, and broad shoulders, and heat infused her cheeks. He truly was a striking man, and she appreciated his kindness and patience toward her son. If only her life were different, maybe she could consider him a trusted friend. But how could she trust another man? She couldn't take that risk with Ethan or with her heart.

Mark nodded before he and Ethan turned back to the pasture, and she hurried into the barn, its aromas greeting her as she walked to the office. She picked up the phone's receiver, dialed the voice mail number, entered the code, and retrieved Laura's message.

"Hi." Laura's voice sounded through the receiver. "This is Laura Lambert. I'm calling for Priscilla. Priscilla, I want to invite you and Ethan to join my family and me for supper tomorrow night. It will be a lot of fun, and we'd love for you to come. We'd like to eat around five thirty. I hope to see you both there. Let me know if that works. *Danki!*" She left her phone number, and then the line went dead.

Priscilla sank onto a stool as she considered her response. While she'd love to join Laura and her family for supper, she also didn't want to be subjected to eating at a separate table. Laura hadn't isolated her at the quilting bee, but a family dinner would be different. How embarrassing would it be to go to supper at a friend's house and be ostracized because she was still shunned? No, now wasn't the time to socialize with friends. As much as she wanted to spend time with Laura, she'd have to wait.

She dialed the number and, feeling like a coward, hoped to get voice mail so she wouldn't have to hear the disappointment in her friend's voice when she turned down her invitation.

After a couple of rings, Allen's voice came through the phone. "You've reached the Bird-in-Hand Carriage Shop. We sell, restore, and repair buggies. The shop is open Monday through Friday, eight to five, and Saturdays, eight to noon. Please leave a message, and I will call you back as soon as I can. Thank you."

After the beep Priscilla began to speak. "Hi, this message is for Laura. This is Priscilla. Thank you so much for your invitation, but we're not going to make it for supper tomorrow night." She picked up a pencil and absently drew circles on a notepad. "I'm backed up with sewing projects, and I need to get them completed so the customers can have them. *Danki* for inviting me, but maybe Ethan and I can come another time. Talk to you soon. Bye!"

When she walked by the pasture, Ethan and Mark waved again. She entered the house, climbed the stairs, and took her place at the sewing machine.

She was finishing up the quilt repair when *Mamm* came and sat on the chair beside her table.

"Did you call Laura back?" *Mamm* asked.

"*Ya.*" Priscilla turned toward her. "I turned her down and said maybe some other time."

"Why?" *Mamm*'s eyes searched hers for an explanation.

"I don't want to go to Laura's *haus* and feel like an outsider." She shrugged and looked down at the quilt.

"An outsider? What do you mean?"

"I don't want to go to supper with her entire family and have to eat at a separate table. I know that's the rule, but it's humiliating for me. It's bad enough Ethan and I can't stay for lunch after the services. Being singled out there would be even worse." Priscilla turned and began sewing again.

"Wait." *Mamm* placed her hand on Priscilla's shoulder, prompting her to stop working and turn toward her. "Laura wouldn't invite you over just to exclude you. You should go. You need to get out of this *haus* and be with your *freinden*."

"No, not until the shunning is over."

"But Priscilla, you need to—"

"Please, *Mamm*." Priscilla held up her hand to stop her from speaking. "I'm fine." She gestured toward the pile of sewing projects stacked on her dresser. "I'm busy, and I'm *froh*. I'll worry about seeing *mei freinden* after I'm caught up on my projects and I can sit at the same table to eat with them. Okay?"

Mamm nodded, but she continued to study her.

Priscilla's stomach tightened as she anticipated a lecture from her mother. She turned her attention back to the quilt and hoped *Mamm* would leave without instructing her on how to live her life.

"What happened with Trent?"

Priscilla stilled at the question, her eyes trained on the quilt as her stomach soured.

"When I asked you the first night you were back if he'd hurt you, you said you were okay. I told you I'm ready to listen if you want to talk, but you haven't opened up to me. I'm worried about you. What happened?"

Priscilla's hand flew to her bicep as she considered her response. "He was loving and attentive when I first met him, but he changed, especially after I had Ethan."

"How did he change?" *Mamm* prodded.

Priscilla rubbed the back of her neck as she considered her

words. "He had a short temper, and he expected me to work harder and make more money while he stayed home and drank. He couldn't keep a job, and I had to take care of everything. I grew tired of his moods."

Mamm clicked her tongue and shook her head. "He should have been taking care of you and Ethan. Was he cruel to Ethan?"

"He never physically hurt him, but he yelled at him."

"I'm sorry to hear that. I'm glad you were strong enough to leave him and come home to us." *Mamm* rubbed her back. "Just don't let Trent's behavior hold you back from moving on with your life. Don't let Trent define your relationships with others."

Priscilla nodded. "Okay."

Mamm stood. "I'm going to get back to work. Let me know if you need any help."

"I will." Priscilla forced a smile as she looked up at her. *"Danki, Mamm."*

After her mother left the room, Priscilla turned her attention back to the quilt and tried not to allow her thoughts to linger on Trent.

Mark tried to keep his focus on his work as he hammered a nail into the barn door, but his thoughts kept drifting to how pretty Priscilla looked in the rose-colored dress she was wearing when he saw her walking from the house to the barn. He'd been mesmerized when she smiled at him and waved. Was she going to give their friendship a chance?

"Mark?"

He tented his eyes with his hand and looked up at Edna standing over him.

"Hi, Edna." He set the hammer on the ground and stood, wiping his hands down his dusty trousers. *"Wie geht's?"*

"I need your help."

"What can I do for you?"

Edna glanced toward the house and then looked up at him. "Laura left Priscilla a message inviting her and Ethan to supper tomorrow, and Priscilla refuses to go. She says she doesn't want to feel like an outsider with her *freinden*."

Disappointment pulled at his lips. His sister's plan wasn't going to go as smoothly as he'd anticipated. "How would Laura make her feel like an outsider?"

"She says she doesn't want to have to sit at a separate table during supper and feel ostracized."

"Laura would never do that."

"I know." Edna folded her hands as if she were praying. "Would you please convince her to go?"

Mark couldn't stop a smile. "What makes you think I have the power to change her mind?"

"I just have a feeling she might listen to you. Would you please talk to her?"

"Ya." Mark shrugged. "I'll give it try."

"Danki." Edna patted his arm. "You're a *gut* man."

As Edna walked away, Mark racked his brain for a new approach that would convince Priscilla to go to his sister's house tomorrow night.

"Did you have a *gut* day?" Priscilla sat on the edge of Ethan's bed and tucked the sheet under his arms later that evening.

"Ya." Ethan nodded. "Mark told me all about training horses, and *Daadi* says he's going to teach me how to do it when I'm

bigger. Are we going to stay here long enough for *Daadi* to teach me how to train horses?"

"*Ya*, I was thinking that we might stay here longer than we planned. Would you like that?" Priscilla pushed a strand of his thick, dark hair off his forehead and kissed it. She hoped her father would keep that promise and maintain a close and healthy relationship with Ethan.

"Yeah, it would be fun to stay longer. I think Dad would love to see the horses, though," Ethan continued. "Do you think we can invite him to come visit us?" He patted the empty side of the bed beside him. "He could sleep with me if you want."

Priscilla's belly churned as a wall of panic at the thought of seeing Trent slid into her. "I guess we'll see."

"Please, *Mamm*?" Ethan whined.

"I'll have to think about it." She touched his nose to distract him. "Get some sleep. Don't forget to say your prayers."

"*Gut nacht, Mamm. Ich liebe dich.*"

She rubbed his arm. "You're doing well with your Dutch." She stood. "Good night, and I love you too." She stepped out of his room and closed the door behind her.

Someday she'd explain why she had to take him away from his father. When she did, maybe her son would understand and forgive her.

ELEVEN

MEMORIES OF HAPPIER TIMES SPENT PREPARING MEALS with her mother rained down on Priscilla as she flipped through a cookbook. She paused when she reached her mother's recipe for chicken and dumplings. She already had the chicken thawed. That had always been her father's favorite meal. If she made it, would he thank her? Would he acknowledge that she was a good cook?

She bit her lower lip as she read the directions. She had to check the pantry and make sure she had—

"When will you be ready to go?"

Priscilla spun toward the doorway where Mark stood. "Go where?"

"To *mei schweschder's haus.*"

She shook her head. "I'm not going."

"*Ya*, you are going. So get ready." He jammed his thumb toward the front door. "I want to leave in about an hour, after I've cleaned up. Meet me outside."

So Mark is going to be there. She looked down at the cookbook. "I'm going to make supper here, so just go without me."

"No, you're going with me. We have to be there at five thirty."

"No, I'm not." She shook her head again. "I already left Laura a message telling her that I'm not."

114

"Well I told her that you are."

"She understands I have things to do." She opened the pantry door and waited to hear his footsteps heading away from her, but instead his footsteps came closer.

"Priscilla," he said. "Priscilla, please look at me."

Out of the corner of her eye, she saw him reach for her, and without thinking, she flinched, blocking her face as his hand came closer.

"What have I done to scare you?" His voice was next to her ear, and heat cascaded throughout her body.

"Nothing." She ignored him and moved a few items around on the pantry shelf.

"That's the second time you've flinched from me." His voice changed, and it seemed to hold an edge of earnestness she'd never heard from him before. "Why are you so skittish?"

"I'm fine. You just caught me off guard." She could hear the thickness in her voice as she waved him off.

"I'm sorry. I didn't mean to startle you." He was still speaking close to her ear, and his nearness sent more warmth pouring through her.

What was wrong with her?

She looked at the floor and tamped down the sudden urge to tell him the truth—to unload all the dark, painful secrets she'd carried for the past few years.

No! Don't trust him! He's a user! He'll only hurt you!

"It's okay. I'm fine. Really, I am," she whispered as a swelling knot of anguish grew into what felt like a lump of ice in her chest. "I really need to get back to my cooking."

After a beat, his footsteps started out of the pantry. Her hands trembled as she returned to searching for all the ingredients she needed.

"Your *mamm* asked me to take you and Ethan to Laura's, so

I'm going to." His voice sounded from the family room. "Can you both be ready in an hour?"

Priscilla sagged as all the fight drained out of her. "Fine. We'll be ready."

"*Danki*, Priscilla."

She nodded while keeping her eyes focused on the pantry shelves. After the front door clicked closed, she covered her mouth with her hand and swallowed her surging anxiety. The anxiety wasn't so much about how she'd be treated at Laura's anymore. It was about how she was going to navigate a life where Mark Riehl appeared at every turn.

Priscilla gripped a plate of cookies as Mark knocked on Laura's back door. She glanced around the property, taking in the big brick farmhouse and the large three-bay workshop. Laura had a good life with Allen, the kind of life Priscilla knew she'd never have.

The back door swung open, revealing Laura with a bright smile turning up her lips.

"You made it!" Laura hugged her twin and then pulled Priscilla in for a tender embrace. "It's so *gut* to see you." She shook Ethan's hand. "How are you?"

"Fine. *Danki*." Ethan smiled up at her.

"Come in." Laura beckoned Priscilla to follow her into the house.

Mark smiled as he made a sweeping gesture, indicating that Priscilla should go first.

Priscilla's heart stuttered as she made her way through the mudroom and into the large kitchen where Cindy and Kayla worked at the counter and the men already sat around the table.

"Priscilla!" Cindy called. "I'm glad you came."

"How are you?" Kayla asked.

"I'm doing well. *Danki*." Priscilla smiled as relief uncoiled the knots in her shoulders. She took a deep breath. It felt so good to be part of a community again. How she'd missed having real friends. She looked up at Mark and smiled. Her mother and Mark had been right—she needed this tonight.

"*Onkel* Mark!" Mark swept Mollie into his arms, and she wrapped her arms around his neck.

"How's my girl?" Mark asked before kissing her head.

"Ethan." Jamie patted the chair beside him. "Come sit with me. How are you?"

As Ethan sat down beside Jamie, Priscilla turned to the other women. "Can I help you with anything?"

"*Ya*." Laura pointed to a cabinet. "Would you like to put glasses on the table?"

"Of course." Priscilla set the plate of cookies on the counter. "I brought some chocolate chip *kichlin* to share."

"I love chocolate chip," Mollie announced as Mark set her on the floor.

"That's great." Priscilla grinned as she reached for the glasses.

"Mollie," Ethan called. "Come sit by me."

"Okay!" Mollie scampered across the kitchen and hopped onto a chair.

"They get along great," Laura whispered as she rested her hand on Priscilla's arm. "I'm so glad you decided to come."

Priscilla smiled. "I am too." And she was.

—⟨∘⟩—

"How are your sewing projects going?" Laura asked as she sat beside Priscilla during supper. "You sounded busy when you left me the voice mail message yesterday."

117

"They're going well." Priscilla glanced over at Laura. "I finished four projects between yesterday and today."

"I'm so glad you finished them so you could have supper with us tonight," Kayla chimed in from Priscilla's other side as she turned to Calvin and handed him a roll. He was squirming in a booster seat.

"Danki." She looked across the table where Mark had ended up next to Ethan and Mollie.

Ethan scooped a spoonful of peas into his mouth before whispering something to Mollie, who smiled.

"This is delicious, Laura," Priscilla said.

Laura looked toward her husband sitting at the other end of the table. She grinned. "Allen just loves my hamburger casserole. Right, *mei liewe?*"

"What's that?" Allen raised his eyebrows.

"You just love my hamburger casserole, right?" Her grin widened as if there was an unspoken private joke passing between them. "He loves casseroles."

"That's right." Allen raised his glass to her. "Your casseroles are my favorites."

Envy became a heavy rock in the pit of Priscilla's belly. She'd never have that kind of connection with a man.

"What kind of sewing or mending repairs do you do for your customers?" Kayla asked.

"I do just about anything," Priscilla said. "I've repaired a few quilts, shortened trousers, and even altered a wedding gown for a young woman who's going to wear her grandmother's."

"Wow!" Laura said. "That sounds like difficult work."

"Not really." Priscilla looked over at Cindy, who sat by Jamie. "You're an expert seamstress, right?"

Cindy shook her head and blushed. "Not really."

"She's being modest," Laura said. "Cindy is the best seamstress in the family."

"I learned everything from *Mamm.*" Cindy looked down at her plate.

"*Ya,* you did." Laura nodded.

A hush fell over the sisters, and Priscilla's heart felt the pain of their loss.

Priscilla turned to Kayla. "How have you been feeling?"

"*Gut.*" Kayla nodded. "I had a doctor's appointment yesterday, and everything looks great."

The family talked about the new additions coming to their family for the remainder of supper. When they were finished eating, Priscilla helped Laura bring two apple pies and a shoofly pie to the table while Kayla made coffee.

"Oh, I am stuffed," Mark said as he leaned back in the chair and rubbed his flat waist. "Sis, you make the best pies."

"*Danki.*" Laura stacked the empty dessert plates. "I'm so glad you all could come."

"*Mamm,* may I show Ethan my swing set?" Mollie asked.

"*Ya,* of course." Laura waved her off. "Have fun."

Mollie looked at Mark. "*Onkel* Mark, would you please go with us?"

"Of course." Mark stood, and Mollie took his hand. "Let me guess. You want me to push you on the swing."

"Yay!" Mollie sang as she, Mark, and Ethan headed toward the mudroom.

"Ready to go sit on the porch?" Allen asked Jamie as they stood.

"*Ya,* let's go."

"Take your *sohn,*" Kayla instructed as she began filling one side of the sink with hot water.

"*Ya, Mamm,*" Jamie said, teasing her as he removed the tray from Calvin's booster seat and wiped his face with a wet cloth Kayla handed him.

Priscilla joined Kayla at the sink and dried dishes, making small talk about recipes as they worked. When she spotted movement outside the kitchen window, she peered out to where Mark pushed both Ethan and Mollie on the swings, one with each hand. He talked and laughed, and Priscilla shook her head as a smile turned up the corners of her lips. The children loved Mark, and he loved them.

Why hadn't Mark settled down with one of the eager women in the community? Priscilla had to admit he would make a wonderful father—and a handsome one too.

She swallowed a groan and returned to drying the dishes. Was she becoming one of his eager *maed*? She hoped not! What good would that do?

But the question haunted her as she worked. She couldn't allow herself to fall for Mark Riehl. Giving her heart to any man, especially him, would only lead to disaster.

"You seemed like you had fun tonight." Mark peeked at Priscilla as he guided his horse down Laura's driveway.

"*Ya*, I did." She gave him a half shrug and then turned toward him and smiled. "*Danki* for making me go." The smile lit up her whole face and made her even more attractive.

"*Gern gschehne.*" He turned back toward the road, and they rode in silence for several minutes. When snores sounded from the back of the buggy, he glanced at her again. "Did Ethan fall asleep?"

She looked over her shoulder and then grinned. "*Ya*, he did. You wore him out on the swings."

"No, those *kinner* wore me out. My arms are sore."

She seemed to relax in the seat, and a comfortable silence sat between them.

After several moments she turned to him once again. "Why haven't you married?"

The question stunned him silent for a beat. "I don't know. I guess I've never found the right *maedel*."

"But you flirt all the time. Do you have feelings for any of the *maed* you attract?"

Once again her question caught him off guard, and Priscilla waited as he took a moment to consider his response. "They're all nice, and I consider them *mei freinden*, but I don't want to marry any of them."

"Do you ever want to get married?"

He halted the horse at a red light and then smirked at her. "Are you proposing to me? Because I have to be honest with you. I really like you, but I'm not sure I'm ready to make a commitment to you. I mean, maybe we should at least go on a date first."

"Mark Riehl, you're hopeless."

He laughed as he guided the horse through the intersection. "I'm just *froh* you had fun tonight. You seemed at ease with my family, and I was grateful to see that."

"Did you plan this evening for me?"

He paused as dread exploded like buckshot. *Caught, red-handed!* "No."

Out of the corner of his eyes, he spotted her wagging a finger at him.

"You hesitated."

"Look," he began, his words measured, "I just wanted you to see that you're not an outsider."

"What do you mean?"

"You act like you think you don't belong to this community, but you do. I think coming back here was the best choice you could've made for both you and Ethan."

"That's easy for you to say, but you don't know everything about me." Her voice was soft as she looked out the window.

"Priscilla, you can talk to me if you need someone to listen." He held his breath, hoping she'd share whatever was bothering her. But she didn't. She kept facing the road as headlights zoomed past them.

He sighed. They were back to square one. Why hadn't he kept his mouth shut instead of trying to tell her how much the community cared about her? Perhaps he should mind his own business. But that seemed impossible when he cared about her and Ethan too.

The *clip-clop* of horse hooves and the sound of passing cars filled the buggy once again as he did his best to analyze her feelings for him. It seemed that one moment she trusted him and liked him as a friend, but then the next he was invisible and insignificant. If only he could convince her that he wanted to be her friend, maybe she would trust him.

"Why do you dislike me?" His question broke through the suffocating silence.

She swiveled toward him. "I don't dislike you. I just don't know why you keep expecting us to be such *gut freinden*. I'm not the kind of *maedel* you seek out. When we were younger you were interested only in the *schee maed*, the exciting *maed*. You never noticed me when we were younger, so I don't expect you to particularly notice me now."

"Are you kidding?" He snorted. "I noticed you. You're *mei schweschder*'s best *freind*."

She blew out a heavy sigh that seemed to bubble up from her toes. "That's not what I mean."

"So what do you mean, then?" He longed to understand her, but her words just confused him.

"Just forget it, okay? It doesn't matter."

"It matters to me."

She turned toward him, her pretty lips turned into a frown. "I'm not the kind of *maedel* you like. Why would you waste your time on me?"

"Waste my time on you?" He shook his head.

"That's what I said. I've always been part of the background, not the kind of *maedel* you wanted to—and still want to—spend time with, like Franey and Ruthann. Why don't we leave it that way, okay? It will keep life uncomplicated." She waved him off, as if he didn't matter.

The gesture gutted him. So she didn't want to be his friend. He had to let it go, but the dismissal burned him like a hot knife to his soul. He kept his eyes focused on the road ahead as he guided the horse onto the road leading to her father's farm.

Mark clamped his teeth together so hard that his jaw throbbed as the farm's driveway came into view. Confusion churned in his stomach. He wanted to be Priscilla's friend, but all his efforts were met with a polite dismissal. What could he possibly do to earn her friendship?

And why was he so determined to win her over? Why couldn't he just let it go?

When he halted the horse near the house, she turned toward him, her eyes seeming to glitter with sadness.

"*Danki* for taking me to Laura's tonight," she said, her voice thick. Then she leaned over the seat and shook Ethan. "Get up. We're home."

"Okay." Ethan yawned and rubbed his eyes. "*Gut nacht,* Mark."

"*Gut nacht.*" He opened his mouth to ask her what he could do to close the great chasm that seemed to continually widen between them, but Priscilla had already climbed out of the buggy and started toward the house.

There had to be a way to earn her trust. He'd try harder, and maybe, just maybe, she'd give him another chance.

TWELVE

Mark's thoughts swirled like a tornado as he sat next to Roy in the barn during the service. As the congregation sang the last hymn, the humid August air felt like a constricting blanket hovering over him.

Today was the day Priscilla would be forgiven and rejoin the congregation. Her shunning would be over, and she would be welcomed back as a sister in the faith. It was a momentous day, and he longed to be by her side after the service to welcome her personally. But he was certain he wouldn't be the first person she'd seek after her acceptance.

He'd spent the entire service staring at the back of Priscilla's prayer covering and analyzing the past week. He'd tried different approaches for trying to encourage her to open up to him, but none of his lame conversations had resulted in more than a half-hearted smile or the one-word responses he couldn't get used to. Still, each rejection had made him more determined to win her friendship. He wasn't going to give up, no matter how many times she dismissed him with an uninterested wave of her hand.

When the hymn ended, the bishop stood and faced the congregation. "And now I invite all the nonmembers to please exit and the baptized members to stay for a special meeting."

A murmur spread over the barn as the children and nonmembers of the church exited. When Priscilla stood, her gaze moved toward the unmarried men's section, and her eyes flickered over to his. He tried to smile at her, but she looked down and then headed out of the barn, her eyes focused on the barn floor.

Roy leaned over and whispered, "This is it. She's going to be a member again."

"I know." Mark nodded. "I'm glad for her."

Roy's eyes narrowed as he studied Mark for a moment. "Do you have feelings for Priscilla?"

"What?" Mark sat up straighter. "Why would you say that?"

"I don't know." Roy tapped his clean-shaven chin. "You just seem totally focused on her when she's around."

"That's ridiculous." Mark turned his attention back to the bishop.

"As you know, Priscilla Allgyer has returned to the community after eight years. She moved to Baltimore to live like an *Englisher*, but as of today, she has completed her time under the *Meiding*, and she is ready to be received back into the church."

John paused and looked around the congregation. "She told me she's ready to confess. The ministers and I agree if you vote to accept Priscilla today, we're going to immediately welcome her back into the fold. Now I need to know if each of you agrees she's repentant and ready to be received back into the church." John pointed to the side of the barn where the men sat. Then he pointed to the minister. "I will ask the men, and Abner will ask the women."

Mark sat up taller as John walked over to his section of the barn. On the opposite side of the barn, Abner went to the women. Mark heard each woman take turns saying "*Ya*," and he silently asked God to encourage every member to echo that response.

"Do you believe Priscilla Allgyer is repentant and ready to be received back into the church?" John asked the unmarried men.

"*Ya*," Mark said when it was his turn.

"*Ya*," Roy echoed.

Each man after Mark gave the same response, and the muscles in his back eased.

When John moved to the married men's section, he again asked if they agreed. Each of the men responded with "*Ya*."

Mark swallowed a deep breath of relief.

Then John moved to the center of the barn. "We will invite our *schweschder* back in to confess now."

Mark gripped the bench and sucked in a deep breath. He prayed Priscilla would be strong as she stood in front of their congregation to repent for her sins.

Priscilla wrung her hands as she stood at one corner of the barn and watched the children play on Mary Glick's elaborate wooden swing set. Ethan and Mollie swung next to each other while teenage girls leaned on a nearby fence and talked.

Priscilla's heart felt a mixture of fear, excitement, and relief. She was finally going to be accepted back into the church. But uncertainty still plagued her. Was she making the right choice for Ethan's future? Did he belong in this community after being born in the *Englisher* life?

It's only temporary! I'll be out of here and on my own soon, and then I can go back to the Englisher *life!*

Maybe this wasn't about Ethan as much as it was about her.

Closing her eyes, she opened her heart in prayer.

God, please lead me down the path you've chosen for me. Help me figure out what's best for mei kind. *Is he supposed to remain in this community? Is this the right choice for Ethan's future? Help me make the right choice and be a gut mutter. I'm so confused, and I never know if I'm doing the best I can for mei sohn, even though I try. Help me, God. I need you more than ever—not just for Ethan's sake, but for mine too.*

"Priscilla."

She jumped with a start at the sound of her name.

"I'm sorry." Cindy came up behind her. "I didn't mean to startle you. I wanted to see if you're okay. You looked pretty terrified when you walked out of the barn."

"That's an accurate description for how I feel right now."

"Everything will be fine." Cindy rubbed her arm. "You made it through the hard part. Now the bishop will tell you you're forgiven, and you can stay for the noon meal and shop at Amish stores."

"I know." Priscilla looked out toward the swing set again. It seemed like only yesterday that she was playing on a swing set without a care in the world. How had her life become so complicated?

"Do you want to talk about whatever is bothering you?"

Priscilla turned toward Cindy's pretty face. "Do you ever wonder where you belong?"

Cindy nodded. "All the time. Why do you think I haven't joined the church?" She fingered her white apron. "When *mei mamm* died I felt like I was lost, just floating through life without a destination. I thought it would get easier with time, but it's been five years and I still feel like I'm straddling a line between the Amish church and the outside world. It's not that I don't want to be Amish, but I'm not sure I belong here."

Priscilla studied Cindy's bright-blue eyes. How was it that she was only twenty-two years old but understood how Priscilla felt?

Cindy gave her a sheepish smile. "You're looking at me like I'm *narrisch*."

"No." Priscilla shook her head. "I understand exactly how you feel."

"But you came back, so I thought you figured out you belonged here." Cindy pointed to the ground. "If you didn't feel that way, why are you confessing?"

Priscilla shook her head. "It's not that simple." She gestured toward the swing set. "I had to find the safest home for *mei sohn*. Coming home was my only option."

Cindy seemed to contemplate her words for a moment. "What would you have done if you hadn't had Ethan to consider?"

"I don't know."

"So how do you know if you truly belong here?"

"I don't."

"I see." Cindy looked past her. "Jamie and Laura are settled and *froh*, and I believe Mark will settle down soon, even though he says he's not interested in getting married. Sometimes I think I'll be alone for the rest of my life. I keep waiting to wake up and realize I'm in the right place, but it hasn't happened. I've prayed about it, but I don't think God is ready to answer me."

"You're so young, Cindy. It will happen for you."

Cindy smiled at her. *"Danki."*

Just then the bishop came around the corner, his brow furrowed and his frown serious. "We're ready for you. You can repent now."

"Okay." Priscilla smoothed her hands down her apron and cleared her throat.

John's expression was serious but also caring. "Priscilla, are you ready?"

"I think so." Panic chewed at her insides, and she stood on shaky legs. Where was the courageous woman who had packed all her worldly possessions and snuck out of the townhouse she rented while Trent was out with his friends?

John gestured toward the barn doors. "Let's go. The congregation is waiting."

She squared her shoulders and followed the bishop, her steps bogged down with the heavy apprehension pressing her heart.

When she reached the barn's entrance, her lungs seemed to seize. Would the congregation accept her confession as she knelt before them? Would they believe her intentions were sincere?

John stood inside the barn and swiveled toward her. "Are you going to come in?"

Unable to speak, she nodded. She followed him up the center aisle, between the sections with unmarried men and unmarried women. When her eyes locked with Mark's, her hands trembled. The intensity in his gaze caught her off guard, stealing her breath for a moment. While she'd tried her best to ignore and dismiss Mark since they'd had supper at Laura's house, she sensed a tiny flare of what felt like attraction for him growing. Why was she wasting her time thinking about Mark Riehl? He would never love a woman as plain as she was.

She looked toward her father, and when she met his impassive expression, dismay stirred inside her once again. No, this wouldn't be as simple as confessing. The congregation wouldn't be satisfied with her honesty. How could the whole community forgive her if her own father, who was supposed to love her, couldn't even do it?

"Our *schweschder* Priscilla has completed her instruction classes, and she is ready to repent for her sins." John's words slammed Priscilla back to reality as they stood in front of the congregation. John's wife, Naomi, came to stand beside him as he turned to Priscilla.

"Please go down on your knees," John instructed her.

As she knelt, Priscilla's stomach clenched, and bile rose in her throat.

Please, God, give me strength.

"Priscilla," John announced. "Are you truly repentant and sorry?"

"Ya." Her voice quavered with anxiety as she felt the weight of the congregation members' stares. Were they all silently judging how she'd spent the last eight years?

"Is it still your desire to join the church again?"

"Ya." Her voice was tiny and unsure, sounding more like a terrified little girl than a grown woman.

"Do you promise to renounce the world and the devil?"

"Ya." Her hands shook, and her body shuddered like a leaf in a windstorm. Was she strong enough to do this? Did she deserve to be a member of the church after all the mistakes she'd made? Was this right when deep in her heart she was just contemplating leaving once she had the resources she'd need?

"In the name of Jesus," John continued, "I give you my hand."

She clasped his right hand with hers, and he helped her up. She took a shaky breath as her eyes stung with tears and, keeping with tradition, Naomi kissed her cheek.

"Priscilla," John continued, "stand up and be a faithful member of the church."

Priscilla nodded.

"I am *froh* that Priscilla has made the decision to come back to the church," John said. "I know I can speak for her parents and say they are *froh* and grateful God led her home. Today is a joyous day."

Priscilla glanced at her mother and found her wiping her eyes. When she looked at her father, his expression remained grave, his lips pressed in a thin line. Her thoughts turned to his cruel words from the night he said she was no longer his daughter. Would this day change his mind?

"It's always a blessing when one of our *bruders* or *schweschdere* makes the decision to return. We welcome Priscilla back into our congregation." John smiled at her. "We welcome you back into the fold."

Priscilla wiped away her tears and nodded. *"Danki."*

"The meeting is over," John announced.

Priscilla folded her shaky arms across her waist while a flurry of conversation started around the congregation and the men began converting the benches into tables for the noon meal.

"I'm so *froh.*" *Mamm's* voice sounded thick with emotion as she came up from behind Priscilla and pulled her into a hug. "My prayers have truly been answered."

"Danki," Priscilla whispered into her mother's neck as tears pricked her eyes.

Laura hugged her next. "Welcome back. I know I keep telling you this, but I'm so very thankful God brought you back."

"Danki." Priscilla wiped at the tears streaming down her cheeks. *"Danki* for welcoming me. I'm so grateful for you."

"We're so *froh* you're back," Florence said before she, Sarah Jane, and Kayla took turns hugging her.

"It's time to go help the other women." Sarah Jane gestured toward the barn exit, and her mother started toward it.

As Florence and Sarah Jane walked away, Laura looped her arm around Priscilla and smiled at her. "Promise me you won't leave again."

Priscilla opened her mouth to agree, but then she held back the words. It was a sin to lie, and she did still feel the pull of the *Englisher* community. Yet if she left and then returned, she'd have to go through the same process—the shunning and meetings with the bishop and ministers. Could she endure all that again?

"Come on," Kayla said. "The others are expecting us."

Priscilla followed her friends to the door. When she strode past Mark, Jamie, and Roy lifting a bench, her eyes met Mark's, and an unexpected tremor shimmied down her back. He nodded at her, and she quickened her steps.

"Laura is so *froh* Priscilla is back," Allen said as he sat across from Mark during lunch. "She was in tears last night talking about what a blessing today is for her and the rest of the community."

"*Ya*, it is." Jamie lifted a pretzel from his plate. "Kayla said something similar on the way here this morning."

Mark cleared his throat and glanced toward the other side of the barn where Priscilla filled coffee cups and smiled at the men seated along the long table. She looked gorgeous in the hunter-green dress she wore today. He'd longed to pull her into his arms and hug her, just as his twin had done after the members-only meeting.

What was wrong with him?

Jamie leaned toward him. "You're awfully quiet. What's on your mind?"

"Nothing." Mark forced his lips into a smile. "I'm just tired. It was a long week at the farm. We're training some horses, and Yonnie asked me to repaint one of the barns. I feel like I can't get caught up." He shrugged and swiped a pretzel from his plate. "You know how it is."

"*Ya*, I do." Jamie nodded toward Roy, who was engrossed in a conversation with their *dat* and Allen. "Roy and I have been working on a few projects too. They never seem to go as quickly as you imagine."

"*Kaffi?*"

Mark craned his neck and glanced over his shoulder as Priscilla appeared holding a carafe. Her chestnut eyes focused on him, and his mouth dried as they stared at each other. For a moment it felt as if the rest of the congregation faded away and they were the only two people in the barn. His heart hammered, and his pulse spiked. What was happening to him?

"Would you like some *kaffi*?" she repeated, breaking their connection.

"*Ya, danki.*" He handed her his cup, and she filled it.

After she filled the cups of the men surrounding him, Mark angled his body and watched her move down the line. He studied her beautiful profile and admired how her eyes sparkled and her rosy lips curved up as she worked her way toward the end of the table.

When he realized he'd been staring at her too long, Mark swiveled around and picked up his coffee cup. He glanced beside him and found Jamie watching him. His eyebrows were lifted, and his expression flickered with something that resembled surprise—or maybe curiosity.

Jamie had caught him watching Priscilla, but Roy, Allen, and *Dat* were still engrossed in a conversation about Allen's carriage business. A thread of relief wove its way through Mark.

As he sipped his coffee, Mark braced himself, waiting for Jamie to make a biting comment, but Jamie remained silent for a beat.

"So, Priscilla, huh?" Jamie picked up another pretzel and popped it into his mouth.

"What do you mean?"

"Please, Mark." Jamie grinned. "I'm not blind."

"You're not blind to what?"

"You've finally fallen in love."

"Love?" Mark shook his head. "No, no, no. That's not it at all."

"So what is it?"

"I'm determined to be her *freind* because I think she really needs one. I've tried everything, but it's not working. She won't talk to me, and I don't know what to do to fix it." He turned toward her as she filled another cup. He couldn't stand the irritating distance between them. It was slowly chipping away at his insides.

Jamie's lips twitched.

"Why is that funny?" Mark's irritation flared.

"Mark, let me tell you something." Jamie leaned toward him. "The only *maedel* who could make me so insane that I'd nearly lose my mind was Kayla. If you're frustrated because Priscilla won't talk to you, then you're in love." He nodded toward Priscilla. "Find a way to tell her how you feel about her."

"How I feel about her?" Mark blinked as he struggled to comprehend Jamie's hidden meaning.

Jamie pointed at Mark's chest. "You're crazy about her. You're just too blinded by frustration to see it. But trust me, little *bruder*, it's written all over your face."

"Mark," Roy began, "when are you going to start building that *haus* you keep talking about? Your room is bigger than mine, and *Dat* just said I can have it when you move out—unless Cindy wants it."

"What?" Mark placed his hand over his heart as if he'd been stabbed. "You're trying to kick me out? What kind of *bruder* are you?"

As everyone laughed at his joke, Mark pretended to join in, but his mind remained stuck on Jamie's words. He needed to construct a plan to convince Priscilla to talk to him. If she would just open up to him, maybe he could sort through all his confusing feelings for her.

⁓⁀⁓

Priscilla hated how her body trembled as she approached her father in the family room later that afternoon. Her first attempt to navigate through their painful and rocky relationship and find a peaceful solution had failed. But now that she was accepted back into the church, she hoped she could make some headway toward a normal, loving, father-daughter relationship with him.

"*Dat.*"

"What do you need?" He kept his eyes trained on his newspaper.

She looked toward the windows and spotted her mother and Ethan sitting together on the glider on the front porch. Then she squared her shoulders and lifted her chin. She wouldn't allow her father to get to her. "You haven't said anything about how I've made myself right with the church. I thought you'd be *froh.*"

"I am." He peered at her over his reading glasses. "Now you need to find a husband."

She bit her lower lip to stop the furious words that threatened to escape. She longed to give him a piece of her mind, explaining that she didn't need a husband for redemption. She was already forgiven by God and the church, but she stifled her rant. Arguing with him hadn't helped before, and she was certain she'd come up empty again today.

"Is there anything else?" he asked.

"No, that's it." She turned toward the front door, and the urge to flee gripped her again. She'd already saved up a good amount of money, but it still wasn't enough to pay the first month's rent on an apartment in a nice area, let alone put down a deposit.

As she stepped onto the porch, she found *Mamm* sitting with her arm around Ethan as he leaned against her shoulder. Guilt squashed her anger. She didn't want to hurt her mother again, but she also didn't want to live in a home where her father made her feel unwanted and unworthy of his love.

"Isn't it nice out here?" *Mamm* asked as Priscilla sank onto the rocker beside them.

"*Ya*, it is." Priscilla moved the chair back and forth. She would give her father more time to forgive her, but if he continued to hurt her, she'd find another place to live as soon as she had enough resources. She couldn't live in a place that continued to break her heart.

THIRTEEN

Irritation built in Mark's gut as he stood by the barn door and looked toward the back porch. Priscilla was hanging a load of laundry. He swiped his hand over his sweaty brow and ground his teeth as he took in her serene expression. She was clipping a pair of Ethan's trousers onto the clothesline that spanned the distance between the porch and one of her father's barns.

Despite the stifling August heat, she wore another longer-sleeved dress today, this one blue. He hadn't seen her wear a short-sleeved dress since she arrived at her parents' house nearly two months ago, and it puzzled him.

He'd been trying so hard to talk to her, going as far as offering her a bouquet of wildflowers he'd picked in her father's meadow and an ice cream sundae he'd picked up while in town one day for supplies. Not one of his tactics had earned him any more than a smile or a murmured "*Danki*." She still refused to have an in-depth discussion or treat him like a trusted friend. Instead, she continued to avert her eyes whenever he approached her and frown at him when he offered a silly joke.

But Mark wasn't a quitter. He'd try until he ran out of words. For some unknown reason, he couldn't give up on Priscilla.

He started up the path to the house, glancing over his shoulder once to make sure Yonnie and Ethan were still in the pasture talking to the bishop, John Smucker. John had come to discuss purchasing a horse for his teenage grandson.

Only a few clouds dotted the sky, but the smell of threatening rain filled his nostrils.

When he reached the porch, he stopped and gazed up at Priscilla. She gave him a sideways glance and then hung another pair of Ethan's trousers.

"Can we talk?" he asked.

She shrugged. "Sure."

"I've been trying to pull you into a conversation for weeks now. Would you please give me a chance?"

"*Ya*, of course you can talk to me." She kept her focus on the wash instead of meeting his eyes, and it caused his frustration to burn hotter.

"Look at me."

She looked at him, her eyes hesitant. Did she really not trust him?

"Why can't we be *freinden*?" He blew out a sigh.

"We are *freinden*. I never said we weren't."

He gave a wry bark of laughter. "That's pretty funny, because you're much more attentive toward your other *freinden* than you are to me."

She folded her arms over her waist and studied him as if he were a confusing puzzle. "Mark, I don't know what you want from me."

"I just want to be a real *freind*—someone you trust and talk to about meaningful things."

"You are *mei freind*." She turned her back to him and dug in her laundry basket, indicating the discussion was over.

Her dismissal sent white-hot fury roaring through Mark's veins, and he saw red.

That does it!

"You know what, Priscilla?" His voice was louder than he'd anticipated, and he heard the tremble in it.

She turned toward him, her brow pinched as she studied him.

"I officially give up," he continued, his voice growing louder. "If my friendship isn't *gut* enough, then so be it. I don't need your friendship anyway. I have plenty of *freinden* who treat me with dignity and respect."

Then he spun on his heels and stalked into the barn. Grabbing a pitchfork, he began to muck the first stall, slamming the tool through the hay to ease the wrath that bit into his back and shoulders.

Confusion and anger swarmed through Priscilla as she tossed the pair of Ethan's trousers she held in her hands back into the basket. Why was Mark angry with her for not being the friend he'd expected her to be? She didn't owe him anything. In fact, she had done her best to be pleasant to him, although she wasn't about to encourage him. Was he upset that she didn't follow him around and fight for his attention like Franey and Ruthann did?

She had to find out why he felt he had the right to talk to her that way when she hadn't done anything wrong.

She hurried down the back porch steps and stalked toward the barn. When she stepped inside, she marched over to where he mucked a stall and pointed her finger toward his face.

"Why did you just yell at me?" she demanded. "Are you angry I don't follow you around and compete with the eager *maed* in our church district for your attention? Besides, you're the one who always has to be the center of attention. I just want to be left alone."

"Really?" He tossed the pitchfork against the stall wall with a clatter and smirked at her. "If you wanted to be left alone, you wouldn't be living with your parents. You'd be off on your own."

"I have no choice. I had nowhere to go. I'm stuck here until I can earn enough money to rent a place for Ethan and me."

He blanched. "So you're going to leave? You're going to break your *mutter's* heart again? Do you know how selfish that is?"

"Selfish?" His words shot across her nerves like shards of glass, cutting and fraying them. "You don't know anything about me. And I don't owe you an explanation for the choices I've made."

"Then why are you standing here trying to prove to me that you're not selfish?" His gorgeous eyes challenged her, and a heartbeat passed as they stared at each other.

"Forget it," she muttered.

When she turned to leave, she tripped on a stone, stumbled, and staggered forward as she tried to right herself. Losing her footing, she slammed into the barn wall, pain radiating from her shoulder to her elbow. She shut her eyes and took deep, cleansing breaths to avoid yelping at the pain.

"Priscilla!" he called as he hurried over to her. "Are you all right?"

"Ya." Her face burned with a mixture of embarrassment and frustration. She tried to move away from the wall, but she couldn't. Her right sleeve was snagged.

"Wait." He reached for her. "Let me see."

"I'm fine."

He blew out a sigh, his eyes narrowed. "For one second, would you not be so stubborn?"

"Fine."

"Danki."

He leaned forward and touched her sleeve, and his nearness sent her senses spinning. She breathed in his scent—earth and soap mixed with sandalwood. The aroma sent heat coursing through her veins. She closed her eyes and took a trembling breath. What was wrong with her? This was Mark, the man who could have any woman he wanted in their community and would never give her the time of day, at least as anything more than a friend. And she didn't even want him as more than a superficial friend. She had to protect the wall she'd erected between them.

"I can't get it." He jiggled her sleeve. "It's stuck on a nail."

"Let me." She gave her arm one hard yank, and the sound of ripping fabric filled the air as her arm broke free. She teetered and fell backward into a sitting position. She looked down at her arm and then blew out a puff of air when she found it was bare. The ugly, purple, puckered skin was exposed for the world to see, her sleeve hanging tattered by her side.

"Priscilla." Her name left his lips in a murmur that sounded almost reverent as he dropped to his knees beside her. "Who did this to you?" He cradled her battered bicep in his hands as he examined it.

"Please don't touch me," she hissed through her teeth. She tried to dislodge her arm from his hands, but he kept her cemented in place.

He moved his fingers over the scars with a gentle touch, like the whisper of butterfly wings. She stopped breathing and tears stung her eyes.

"Did he do this to you? Ethan's father?" he asked again.

She sniffed and then tried once again to remove her arm from his grasp.

"Please tell me the truth."

She shook her head and looked down at the barn floor. "Just let me go."

"No, I want to know the truth once and for all." He looked down at her arm once again and moved his finger over the scar.

His touch almost drove her crazy as shivers moved up and down her entire body. "Did he hurt you often?"

She shook her head. "Only when he was drunk."

"What?" The expression in his eyes was fierce as they met hers. "How often was he drunk?"

"He wasn't like that when I first met him." She shook her head again, trying to breathe normally. "When I left here I lived with my cousin Thelma and got a job in a diner near her apartment. Trent was one of my regular customers. He liked me, and he used to ask to sit in my section."

She looked down at the floor. "He asked me out, and we started dating. After a while I moved in with him. In the beginning he was kind and attentive, and I enjoyed how he made me feel. When I was with him, I felt loved. I got pregnant with Ethan, and I thought he was going to marry me. I thought we were going to be a family, and that was what I wanted. That was what I craved." She kept her eyes focused downward.

"The day after he hurt me he apologized and brought me flowers. He promised he'd never do it again, and I believed him because I was blinded by my love for him. But he hit me again only a week later. I wanted to leave him, but I was terrified, and I had nowhere to go. I was stuck with a boyfriend who hit me, but I had a *kind* to protect."

A weight lifted off her shoulders as she finally shared her deepest and darkest secret. And then she shattered, like spun glass. A choked sob escaped her lips, and her tears broke free.

"*Ach*, Priscilla." Mark pulled her against him and wrapped his arms around her as she sobbed into his chest. "It's okay. You're safe now. I won't let him hurt you ever again." He whispered his gentle words into her prayer covering, and they were a balm to her battered soul.

She held on to him, and for the first time in so long she felt safe and protected, and she didn't want to let go. When her tears finally stopped, she sat back and wiped her face.

"When did he do this?" He touched her arm.

"About six months ago." The memory came on so fast, it left her head spinning. "When I got home from work, he grabbed my purse and pulled out my tips. It had been a slow night, and he was furious I hadn't brought home more money." She shivered as she remembered the maliciousness in Trent's dark eyes. "He started screaming at me. He was drunk, more drunk than I'd seen him in a long time. I told him to go sober up, and he threw a beer bottle at my head. The bottle missed me, but it hit the wall and exploded just above me. Glass landed in my arm, and I had deep gashes. He wouldn't let me go to the hospital."

A muscle ticked along Mark's jaw.

She looked down at her arm. "I bandaged it up as well as I could, and it healed like this. Now I'm disfigured, and I can't ever wear short sleeves." She shook her head as a hole opened in her heart and sadness flooded in. "I made so many mistakes. If only I hadn't gotten involved with him."

She looked up into Mark's blue eyes. "But I don't regret having Ethan. He's *mei sohn*, my heart." She placed one palm over her chest. "If I could have changed anything, it would be that he had to live with that monster." Her lower lip trembled.

"Stop blaming yourself." Mark cupped her chin with his hands and leaned down, his mouth close to hers. "Trent was the evil one, not you."

She nodded as she lost herself in his eyes.

"No one has the right to hit you. No one." He leaned even closer, only a fraction of an inch from her mouth. "And I will never let anyone hurt you again."

The intensity in his eyes stole her breath, and for a moment she was certain he was going to kiss her. She stilled, waiting for the feel of his lips against hers.

"Mark! Priscilla!" *Dat* bellowed. "What's going on here?"

As Mark jumped to his feet, Priscilla covered her bare arm with her opposite hand.

Her father and the bishop stood at the entrance to the barn, and their stern stares seemed to burn a hole through her.

Mark held out his hand, and she took it before he lifted her to her feet as if she weighed nothing. When he released her hand, she fought the urge to grab his hand once again. She yearned for the strength and solace his touch had provided.

A heavy ball of dread invaded Priscilla's body as she hugged one arm to her waist. She glanced at Mark, who stood up straight and swallowed, his Adam's apple bobbing.

"What's going on here?" *Dat* repeated as he turned his menacing glare on Mark. "What were you doing to *mei dochder?*"

"Nothing inappropriate was going on here." Mark held up his hand. "We were just talking."

Her father sneered as he glanced at the bishop and then back at Mark. "Nothing inappropriate? I'm not blind, Mark. What do you think you're doing? You're here to work, not this."

"We weren't doing anything inappropriate." Mark's voice remained calm and even, and she marveled at his confidence. "I would never disrespect Priscilla or you, Yonnie. You know me."

"What do you have to say for yourself, Priscilla?" *Dat* demanded.

"Mark is telling the truth." She despised the tremor in her voice. "We were only talking."

"You were talking while sitting close together on the floor of the barn." He pointed to her arm. "With a ripped dress!"

"It was innocent, Yonnie," Mark insisted.

"Go get changed," *Dat* barked at Priscilla, his eyes steely.

With her eyes focused on the floor, she left the barn and then almost ran to the house. A light misting of rain kissed her cheeks, and a rumble of thunder growled in the distance. She didn't recall a forecast of rain for today, but dark clouds clogged the sky.

As she climbed the porch steps, her thoughts swirled with worry and fear. Would the bishop shun her again? If so, would it be worse and more humiliating this time? What would the community say about her if they heard she was doing inappropriate things with Mark Riehl in the barn?

Oh no.

She did a mental head slap as she walked into the house and started up the stairs. How could she have allowed herself to pour her heart out to Mark? She'd promised herself she would never tell anyone what Trent had done to her, but once she started opening up, the truth flowed out of her like a river.

Priscilla crossed her bedroom and stood at the window. Its panes were peppered with raindrops. More thunder rumbled as she looked out toward the barn and her conversation with Mark echoed in her mind. She glanced down at her arm and touched her scar. Her heart seemed to trip over itself, and her skin heated as she recalled the gentleness of his touch and the intensity in his eyes. The attraction between Mark and her felt real, palpable. But surely he was an expert at creating those feelings.

Priscilla cupped her hands to her hot cheeks as she recalled the electricity that had sparked between them. She could feel to the depth of her soul that he was going to kiss her. And she'd *wanted* him to kiss her! She'd held her breath and waited for the contact, but her father and the bishop had interrupted them before their lips could collide.

Swallowing a groan, she dropped onto the corner of her bed. She was doomed. Although she'd tried her best not to fall victim to his charms, she'd let Mark into her heart. Why had she allowed herself to trust him? But his empathy seemed so genuine. Now she would be nothing to him but another eager *maedel* fighting for his precious attention.

Yet she'd felt cherished and safe in his strong arms, and it was exactly what she'd craved for years. The feeling had been wonderful, almost like a dream. What would it be like to have someone in her life who really cared about her and loved her?

What was she thinking? Mark Riehl wasn't capable of loving and caring for just one woman. Even if he were, she was kidding herself if she believed she could be the one woman for him.

Priscilla pushed the notion away and changed into a fresh dress. As she looked at her reflection in the mirror, she touched her prayer covering, and that familiar apprehension rolled over her. Her father and the bishop had caught Mark and her in an intimate conversation, which was forbidden for unmarried couples. Her father would most likely punish her, and the bishop could shun both her and Mark. Her heart couldn't stand the idea of being ostracized during another shunning and then confessing in front of the congregation yet again.

Then an even worse punishment occurred to her, rocking her to her core. What if her father demanded that she and Ethan move out, leaving them homeless and destitute? What would she do then?

FOURTEEN

"She's telling the truth." Mark glared at Yonnie as Priscilla ran out of the barn. Fury was a bitter taste in his mouth. "We weren't doing anything wrong. We were having a private conversation."

Yonnie shook his head and turned to the bishop. "It looked inappropriate to me. There's no telling what would've happened if we hadn't decided to walk in here."

Mark took a step toward him, his hands balled into fists at his sides as his heart hammered against his rib cage. "Yonnie, nothing inappropriate would've happened if you hadn't walked in. I would never take advantage of Priscilla that way. I'm more honorable than that, and you can trust me around Priscilla." He nodded toward the barn exit. "You need to have faith in your *dochder*. She may have made mistakes in the past, but we've all had lapses in judgment. Stop using her past against her."

While John's expression remained impassive, Yonnie's grave expression suddenly brightened with a strange gleam in his eyes.

Mark gritted his teeth as confusion and suspicion mixed with his burning anger. Rain beat a steady cadence on the barn roof above them.

Yonnie turned to the bishop. "Why don't we take our discussion outside, John?"

"Ya." John started for the door.

Yonnie leaned toward Mark and lowered his voice. "I suggest you remember who owns this farm. If you want to keep this job, you'll mind your own business when it comes to my relationship with my family. Now, if you know what's best for you, you'll get back to work."

Mark took a deep, shaky breath as Yonnie followed John out of the barn. Once his boss was gone, Mark turned toward a wall and kicked it with all his might. Pain exploded in his foot, and he hopped and grunted in response.

When he came to a stop, he leaned back against the wall and scrubbed his hand down his face as his thoughts spun.

What had just happened?

In less than an hour, he'd gone from being frustrated with Priscilla to longing to console her and take away all the pain her ex-boyfriend had caused her. And then he found himself caught up in holding her, touching her, and being close to her. And if Yonnie and John hadn't walked in, he would've kissed her.

He groaned and stared up at the barn ceiling as thunder rolled. How could he have allowed himself to lose all control with her? What was it about Priscilla that brought out his most confusing and fervent emotions?

He padded over to the barn exit and looked out toward the doorway of another barn where Yonnie stood speaking to John out of the rain. His arms flailed about as if he were engrossed in a heated discussion. Was he complaining about Priscilla and calling her cruel names?

This is your fault! If you hadn't held her in your arms and almost kissed her, this never would have happened.

The voice crept in from the back of Mark's mind, leaving guilt and regret in its wake. He turned toward the house and fought the urge to walk in there and ask to speak to Priscilla alone to apologize.

But that would only make things worse for the two of them. He had to wait for the situation to defuse before he could speak to her. The plan was simple, but the idea of staying away from Priscilla felt like pure torture.

What was happening to him?

Stepping back into the barn, Mark picked up his pitchfork. Yonnie had told him to get to work, and he didn't want to risk losing this job. As he began to muck the stalls, Priscilla's words about how Trent had treated her echoed through his mind, causing him to work harder and faster. He had to burn off some steam before he drove himself crazy.

As he continued to work, the scars on Priscilla's arm and the tears in her gorgeous eyes haunted him. He would do everything in his power to be the friend she deserved, no matter how she tried to reject him. He couldn't give up on her. Her father and her ex-boyfriend had failed her, but he would never fail her. No matter what the cost.

Priscilla jumped with a start as a clap of thunder ripped through the air. She pulled the last pair of her father's trousers from the clothesline and placed them in the basket as the unexpected rainstorm continued to drum the roof and splatter on the porch. She'd have to hang the clothes on a line in the utility room.

When she heard footsteps, she turned and sucked in a deep breath as her father and the bishop came up on the porch. She gripped Ethan's shirt in her hands and pressed her lips together. Now she'd learn her fate after the incident in the barn.

The strangely satisfied look displayed on her father's face sent alarm slithering through her veins.

"We'd like to speak with you inside the *haus*, Priscilla." *Dat* pointed to the door. "Now."

"*Ya, Dat.*" She hurried inside to the utility room with the basket of clothes she'd have to deal with later. She peeked out the window and spotted Ethan sitting on the porch playing with a toy car. He looked so happy, so adjusted to this new life. But her decision to open her heart to Mark in the barn may have changed everything. She had to be strong now for Ethan's sake.

She went into the family room, glad to hear her mother still at her sewing machine upstairs. Her father and the bishop stood by their wood-burning stove.

"I've discussed this at length with John, and we've decided you need to marry Mark." *Dat* said the words as if they were mundane and not life changing, earth shattering.

"What?" Priscilla divided a look between her father and the bishop as her pulse galloped. Had she heard her father correctly? He expected her to marry Mark?

No, no, no, no! He was the last person she'd ever marry!

"You need to marry Mark," *Dat* repeated. "Your behavior in the barn suggests that you and Mark have been involved in an intimate relationship for some time, and this is both sinful and disappointing. The only way to make this right is to marry him as soon as possible." He turned to the bishop. "Right, John?"

"*Ya.*" John gave a curt nod. "You and Mark can decide on the wedding date. And there should be no more physical contact between you until you're married."

"But we haven't had any—"

Dat shot Priscilla an icy glare, and she stopped speaking.

"It's settled, then. You'll marry him." *Dat* turned to John. "*Danki.*"

John nodded. "I'm going to go talk to Mark." Then he turned and disappeared through the front door.

"What's going on?" *Mamm* came down the stairs, her dark eyes wide.

"John and I caught Priscilla and Mark kissing in the barn." *Dat* folded his arms over his wide chest. "John and I spoke and agreed she should marry him as soon as possible."

Mamm blinked, and her gaze settled on Priscilla. "Is that true? Were you kissing Mark?"

"No." Priscilla grasped the edges of her apron, and she felt a surge of confidence that seemed to rise from deep within her battered soul. "It's not true at all. We were talking, and he was sitting close to me. *Dat* has decided to use this as an excuse." She glared at her father. "This is just what you wanted. You wanted me to find a husband, and since I haven't, you arranged one for me. You want me to marry so I'm no longer an embarrassment."

"Mark is perfect for you." He gestured out the window. "He can have half of my business. I'll give you both land and even build you a *haus*. You can live in the *daadihaus* until your new *haus* is built."

Disgust roiled in Priscilla's stomach as she studied her father. *Dat is getting what he wants. And although Mark might do this to avoid being shunned, he won't want to turn down every man's dream—land, a successful business, and a* haus.

Mamm stepped over and touched Priscilla's arm. "Mark is a *gut* man, and he cares about you and Ethan. He will be a *gut* husband and *gut* provider."

"That's all that matters, right?" Priscilla yanked her arm away from her mother's grasp. "No one cares how I feel or what I want." She wagged a finger at her father. "It's all about what's best for you. Now everyone will see Priscilla as a *gut* woman. I've confessed my sins and I'm forgiven. And now I just have to legitimize *mei sohn*."

"If you want to stay here, you need to marry him." *Dat* barked the words at her. "If not, then you and Mark will be shunned for your inappropriate behavior. You both know we have a strict rule of no touching before marriage, and I can't take another shunning in my family."

Priscilla's knees wobbled as she realized the truth. She was trapped in this situation. She had to do what her father and the bishop said. She couldn't allow her father to evict her and Ethan. They'd have to go to a homeless shelter because she couldn't ask anyone in the community—not even Laura—to take them in if she was shunned again. She had to succumb to their demands, even if it meant marrying a man she hadn't chosen, a man who would never have chosen her. She had to make this work for her son's sake.

Priscilla turned back to her father. "What makes you think Mark will agree to this?"

"Trust me," *Dat* said, insistent. "He will."

Mark's arms and back ached as he set the pitchfork aside and started toward the barn exit. He had mucked all the stalls in record time. His stomach growled, indicating it was time for him to head home for supper, but he longed to stay and talk to Priscilla. He needed to know that she was okay, but he had to force himself to leave.

Tomorrow was Friday. Maybe her father would realize he'd been wrong about what he'd witnessed in the barn and would allow Mark to talk to Priscilla.

"Mark." John Smucker appeared in the barn doorway. "I need to speak with you."

"John, I didn't realize you were still here." Hope sparked

within Mark. This was his chance to make things right! "I want to talk to you too. What you saw earlier wasn't what it seemed. We were only talking, and I would never have tried to do anything inappropriate with Priscilla. She's *mei freind*, and I care about her."

"I realize that." John fingered his long, graying beard. "It's apparent how you feel about her, which is why you need to marry her."

"Marry her?" Mark took a step back as if the words had punched him.

"*Ya.* The damage has been done, and only you can make things right." John's tone was even, despite the weight of his words. "It's what's best for her and the *kind*. Only you can repair her reputation."

Renewed fury boiled through Mark's veins. "Whose idea was it for Priscilla to marry me?"

John paused as if caught off guard by the question. "Well, Yonnie and I agreed on it."

"Really?" Mark lifted his chin. "Did Yonnie suggest it to you?"

"That's not important."

"*Ya,* it *is* important." Mark's voice rose. "And rather than keeping this innocent incident to yourself and counseling Yonnie to do the same, you're going to go along with what he wants?" He stared at the bishop for a few moments as the truth dawned on him. "Tell me you're not blind. Tell me you see what's really going on here, John. Yonnie treats Priscilla terribly, and he's forcing her to marry me as some sort of punishment."

John's look became steely. "You've got it all wrong. Yonnie is a *gut daed*, and he's only doing what's right. Priscilla needs a stern hand because of her past behavior."

"Priscilla's sins were forgiven when she repented."

John's eyes narrowed as he studied Mark for a moment. "Mark, it's obvious you care for Priscilla, which means you'll do what needs to be done. If not, then you'll both be shunned for the inappropriate and intimate behavior before marriage I saw with my own eyes. Besides, you've earned yourself quite a reputation with the young women in this community. I think this marriage will be *gut* for you too."

"My reputation?" Mark exclaimed. "Are you serious?"

"*Ya*, I am. Everyone knows you enjoy the company of the *maed* in the community, and you're nearing thirty. I think it would be a *gut* decision for you to finally settle down." He paused. "It's up to you what happens now. How would your *dat* feel if you were shunned?"

Mark's throat constricted. He couldn't allow the bishop and Yonnie to humiliate Priscilla again, but was he ready to get married?

"What's your choice?" John asked.

"I'll speak to Priscilla, and we'll decide together."

"Fine, then. But Yonnie and I have already spoken with her, and I believe she sees what's right. I need to get home to *mei fraa*. I'm sure supper is ready." John nodded and started toward the door. "Tell your *dat* hello for me."

John disappeared from the barn, and Mark stilled as if his boots were glued to the barn floor.

Shock rippled through him as all his hopes and dreams dissolved. He felt as if he were dreaming. This couldn't really be happening! How could his entire future be decided for him in a matter of a few hours? He felt as if he couldn't breathe as the bishop's words echoed through his mind. If he married Priscilla, he'd never build a house on his father's farm. He'd never come home to his own kitchen, his own bedroom. He'd never have the freedom he'd envisioned in that little house he'd hoped to build next to Jamie's. Instead, he would have a wife and a child to support, which meant he'd have to consider their wants and needs before his. Was he ready to be responsible for a family?

But if he wasn't ready, then he and Priscilla would be shunned. Priscilla had already told him she wanted to leave the community, and another shunning would be just the catalyst to shove her away. His lungs constricted at the thought of her leaving their community forever.

Closing his eyes, he sent a fervent prayer up to God.

God, please lead me down the right path. I'm at a crossroads, and I'm so confused I feel like I can't breathe. I feel like the world is closing in on me. I have to make the right decision or I could jeopardize the lives of two other people. I don't want to force Priscilla to marry me, and I'm not sure I'm even ready to be married. But I also can't stand the thought of losing her. Show me your will. Show me the way.

With a deep, shaky breath, he stepped out of the barn. The rain had stopped, but dark clouds still dotted the sky and the smell of rain remained in the air. He strode through the mud and up the back porch steps, and then he knocked on the storm door. The door opened and Yonnie stepped out on the porch.

"I thought you were gone," Yonnie said. "It's almost six."

Mark jammed his hands in his pockets to stop himself from wiping the smug expression off his boss's face.

Calm down! You don't want to be shunned!

"I want to talk to Priscilla. Is she available?"

"She's making supper with her *mutter*." Yonnie lifted his chin. "What do you want to discuss?"

"You know what I want to discuss, Yonnie." Mark fought to keep his voice calm despite his raging anger. "It's about our future."

"I'd like to discuss that with you, actually." Yonnie nodded toward the barns. "If you agree to marry *mei dochder*, I'll give you half my business, plus half my land, and I'll build you any size *haus* you want."

Mark pressed his lips together as his stomach soured.

This is bribery! This is more sinful than if I'd kissed his dochder *in the barn!*

"What do you think, Mark?" Yonnie held up his hands. "I think that's a fair payment for marrying my *dochder.*"

"Priscilla can't be bought and sold like one of your horses," Mark said, seething as his entire body vibrated with sudden, white-hot anger. "I'm not going to force her to marry me. I'm going to let her make that decision."

"Fine." Yonnie pointed toward the door behind him. "Would you like to come in?"

"No." Mark shook his head. "I'd like to speak to her out here. In private."

"I'll get her for you."

Mark spun toward the porch railing and leaned forward on it while he waited. His thoughts were moving so fast that he felt queasy. There had to be a way to stop this ridiculous mandate. But how?

When the door clicked open, he glanced over his shoulder at Priscilla. She fingered her black apron as she gave him a shaky smile.

"Hi." He stood up and faced her.

"Hi." She pushed the ties of her prayer covering over her shoulder. "I guess the bishop spoke to you."

"*Ya.*" He lifted his straw hat and pushed back his thick hair. "I wanted to talk to you about it in private. I think that if we talked to the bishop, we could—"

She put her finger to her lips as if to shush him and then pointed to the open windows behind her. "*Kumm.*" She reached for his arm and then pulled her hand back. "This way."

He followed her down the porch steps, and then they walked side by side on the path leading to the *daadihaus,* the small, one-story brick house just past the empty swing set.

They walked up the porch steps, and she sank onto a glider and nodded toward the spot beside her.

"How are you?" he asked as he sat down and angled his body toward her.

She shrugged. "I guess I'm okay."

"I'm sorry." He heard the quaver in his own voice. "This is all my fault."

"No, it's not." She shook her head. "It's my fault."

"No, if I hadn't been kneeling on the barn floor so close to you, then we never would've wound up in this mess."

She looked up at him, and her lower lip trembled. "No, *mei dat* would've found another way to make you marry me. He wants the stigma of his *dochder's* illegitimate *sohn* taken off his family."

Mark glowered and shook his head. "What if we go talk to the bishop? He's always been a reasonable man. If we explain exactly what happened and I take the blame, then maybe he'll change his mind." He jammed a finger into his chest. "He can shun me since I'm the one who got too close." *And almost kissed you.*

Her expression grew grave. "I have no choice. I'm trapped, and there's no way out unless I want to be homeless. *Mei dat* won't let me stay unless I marry you. I don't have enough money saved to find a place to rent, and I can't afford day care for Ethan if I have to work outside of school hours. You're my only option for giving *mei sohn* a decent home. He's innocent in all of this. He didn't choose this life." She looked out toward her father's house. "I guess marrying you is better than being out on the street or living in a shelter."

Mark flinched at her biting words, but then he worked to make his expression serene.

"I should have realized when I decided to come home that *mei dat* would punish me for sinning." She looked over at him. "Would you rather go through with the marriage or be shunned?"

He frowned as disgust rolled through him. "I can't allow your *dat* to throw you and Ethan out on the street, and I can't stomach the idea of you both living in a shelter. What if I talk to Jamie and Laura? They both have plenty of room in their homes. What if you and Ethan lived there?"

She gave him a sad smile. "That's sweet, but it would never work. I'd still be shunned, and so would you."

"But isn't that better than having to marry me?"

She sighed and turned away from him. "I think we're both trapped unless you want to be shunned. But if you're shunned, *mei dat* can't pay you until the shunning is over."

Mark snorted. "He'd probably fire me anyway. I'd have to go back home and work on *mei dat's* farm."

"But that's not what you want."

"I don't want you and Ethan to be homeless. I don't think we have a choice."

They were silent for a moment, and he longed to hear her thoughts.

"What about your girlfriends?"

"Girlfriends?" He raised an eyebrow as he angled his body toward her again.

"You know." She gave him a sardonic smile as she counted them off on her fingers. "Let's see. Franey and Ruthann. And Sadie Liz seemed to really like you that day at the fabric store."

"I've told you, they're *not* my girlfriends."

"Do they know that?"

"You sound like *mei schweschdere.*" He had to change the subject. "Priscilla, we can make this work if we have to. We've known each other our entire lives. Surely we can find a way to live together."

"*Ya.*" She nodded. "I guess it could be worse. At least you're not a stranger."

Mark tried to pretend the insult didn't cut him to the quick. "All right. I guess it's settled, then."

She sighed. "*Ya*, I guess so."

"So." Mark smiled. "Will you marry me?"

She rolled her eyes and then laughed, and he enjoyed the sound. "You already know the answer to that question."

"Are you going to tell Ethan?"

She pursed her lips. "*Ya*, but I need to find the best way to tell him."

"Now we need to meet with the bishop and pick a date, right?"

She nodded.

"We can go see him tomorrow after I get here in the morning."

She nodded again, and then they stared at each other. Once again, he longed to know what she was thinking. Was she disappointed, scared, anxious? Did she care about him at all?

She stood. "I guess I should get inside and help serve supper."

"*Ya*, and I need to get home."

Mark followed her down the porch steps, and they walked side by side up the path toward her parents' house.

When they reached the house, she looked up at him once again. "*Gut nacht.*"

"*Gut nacht,*" he echoed. He started toward the barn and then spun toward her once again. "Priscilla!"

She pivoted toward him, her eyes questioning his.

"For what it's worth, I'm sorry for all of this," he said.

She seemed to wilt a little, her slight shoulders hunching. "It's not your fault. I'm sorry you've been tangled up in my mess."

He smiled at her. "We'll get through it."

She nodded. "Be safe going home."

"I will." But he wasn't planning on heading home right away. He was going to go see Laura and beg her to help him make sense of this crazy day.

FIFTEEN

MARK HALTED HIS HORSE AT HIS TWIN SISTER'S back porch, and then he jumped out and tied the mare to the fence before loping up the steps. His mind had raced with bewilderment and anger as he'd made the trek to her house.

When he reached the back door, he knocked and then glanced up at the now cloudless sky, taking deep breaths to calm his zooming heart.

The screen door clicked open, and Allen smiled at him. "Mark. Laura had a feeling you might stop by. Come in." He made a sweeping gesture. "We were just finishing supper. Are you hungry?"

"*Ya.* I mean no." The thought of eating caused Mark's sour stomach to roil even more. "I was wondering if I could talk to Laura."

"Of course. Come on in."

"Who is it?" Laura called from the kitchen.

"Your twin," Allen responded.

"*Onkel* Mark!" Mollie called.

As Mark stepped into the mudroom, Mollie slid around the corner and skidded into him, her little arms outstretched. He grinned as he knelt and hugged her.

"Hey, Mollie girl." He kissed the top of her blond hair. "How's my big girl? I can't believe you're five now."

"I'm *gut*." She smiled up at him, and he touched her nose before hanging his straw hat on a peg by the door. "I love the doll you gave me for my birthday last week. *Mamm* is going to make me clothes for her. I named her Savilla after my other *mamm*."

Mark's lungs squeezed, but he kept a smile on his face. "That's really nice."

He followed her into the kitchen, and the aroma of country-fried steak and baked potatoes wafted over him, causing his stomach to growl.

"Mark." Laura stood up from her chair at the table. Her face clouded with a frown, and her eyes narrowed. "Something is wrong. You've been on my mind all afternoon." She pointed to the tray of steak in the center of the table. "That's why I made your favorite meal."

"I need to talk to you." He rubbed the back of his head.

"It's serious." Her tone was grave as she turned to Allen. "Would you please give Mollie a bath?"

Allen looked at each of them and then nodded. "*Ya*, of course." He turned to Mollie. "Let's go, kiddo. It's bath time."

"But I want to see *Onkel* Mark." She threaded her fingers with Mark's and held on tight.

"You can see him after your bath." Allen's face seemed to question if that were true, and Mark nodded. "You can play in the tub for a while, and then we'll come back down."

Mollie considered this and then nodded. "Okay." She looked up at Mark again. "Don't leave before I see you. Pinky promise?" She held up her pinky, and he threaded his own with it.

"Of course I won't." Mark leaned down and whispered in her ear. "I would never leave before saying good night to my twin niece."

Her smile brightened, apparently pleased. Then she scampered over to Allen and took his hand before he steered her through the family room toward the stairs.

Laura touched his arm. "Have you eaten?"

Mark shook his head. "I came right here after leaving Yonnie's."

"Sit." She pulled out her chair and pointed to the seat. "I'll get you a plate."

He pinched the bridge of his nose as the beginning of a headache stabbed at the back of his eyes. He had to sort through the events of the day and figure out how to explain it all to Laura. But how could he even explain it when he was so confused? It all felt like a bad dream—more like a nightmare.

Laura cleared away the used plates and utensils. After placing them in the sink, she set a glass of water, a clean plate, and utensils in front of him, and then she sat down beside him. "You need to eat."

He shook his head. "I don't think I can."

Her blue eyes shimmered. "I've never seen you like this." She swallowed. "At least, not since we lost *Mamm*. What happened today?"

He rested his elbow on the table. "I'm still trying to make sense of it." He turned toward the platter of steak again.

"Eat." She pushed the dish toward him.

After a silent prayer, he filled his plate with steak, a baked potato, and string beans. He ate a bite of the steak and nodded. "You still make the best country-fried steak."

"*Danki.*" Her expression grew impatient. "Now, tell me what happened."

Between bites he shared his story, starting with the discussion he and Priscilla had in the barn earlier and ending with their conversation on the porch of the *daadihaus*. He told her every detail, not holding back anything despite his swelling guilt and frustration. When he finished speaking, he angled his body toward his twin and held his breath, awaiting her sage assessment and advice.

When she stared at him wide-eyed, he placed his fork beside his plate and gave her a palm up. "Well, sis? What do you have to say?"

"I-I don't know." She shook her head. "I'm a little over-whelmed. I'm trying to get my brain around the fact that Trent hurt Priscilla, you almost kissed her in the barn, and the bishop and her *dat* are forcing you two to get married. It's a lot to take in, Mark."

He gave her a grave nod. "I know."

"When I asked her about Trent, she didn't share that he'd hurt her. She just said she had to leave."

"Really?" Mark asked. "You're her best *freind* and she didn't tell you?"

"No, but she confided in you."

Mark puzzled over that for a moment. Why would Priscilla trust him and not Laura? Of course, he'd seen the evidence when the sleeve of her dress ripped. That made the difference. She couldn't hide that scar from him any longer.

"I could feel your confusion and anger all day." She touched her collarbone. "But I never in my wildest dreams imagined you would tell me this." She pressed her lips together, opened her mouth, and then closed it again.

"What?" He leaned forward. "Don't hold back. What were you going to say?"

"I'm surprised John is being so forceful about this. When Rudy's *mamm* talked to him about how I was staying over here to take care of Mollie, John was reasonable. He told Allen I shouldn't stay here, and he trusted Allen and me to make the right decision." She rubbed her belly as she settled back in her chair. "I guess he feels that it would be best for the community if Priscilla is married. It's *bedauerlich* to hear that, but I guess I can see his point of view. I just think it should be Priscilla's choice and your choice who you want to marry."

"Exactly. He also said it would be *gut* for my reputation if I were married since I seem to enjoy spending time with the young women in our community. I know the family teases me, but I never thought other people were judging me because I like to have more than one female *freind*." Mark nearly spat the word. "And not only are Yonnie and John blackmailing me with the threat of shunning, but Yonnie is trying to bribe me as well by offering me half of his business, land, and a *haus*. It's not right."

"No, it's not. I'm very disappointed in Yonnie." She looked down at the table.

"So what do you think I should do?"

Her gaze snapped to his. "What do you *want* to do?"

"I can't let Yonnie throw Priscilla and Ethan out on the street, and I can't allow John to shun her again and ruin her name in the community. She's been through enough."

"Huh." A smile seemed to tug at the corner of her lips.

"What?" He groaned. "Please just say what you're thinking."

"I find it interesting that you're thinking only of Priscilla. You haven't said much about how this will affect you."

"That's not an answer I was hoping you'd give me. What do you think I should do?"

"I don't know." Laura shook her head. "This is your decision."

"You're not helping." Mark rubbed at his eyes as his headache flared. "I need your advice. I need you to be *Mamm* and tell me what to do."

"I miss her so much."

"I know. I do too." Mark slumped in his chair. "She would

know what I should do." He picked up his fork and moved the remaining string beans around on his plate. "I can't stop thinking about the pain in Priscilla's eyes when she told me what Trent had done to her. I've never been so angry in all my life. I wanted him to feel that same pain, but I also wanted to take her pain away. I've never felt anything like that."

Laura snapped her fingers. "I was right! You *are* in love with her."

"What?" Mark shook his head. "No, no, no. Just because I care about her doesn't mean I'm in love with her."

She smiled. "You love her, Mark. Just admit it."

He sighed. "I came over here to get your help, sis. This isn't helping."

She glanced toward the doorway. "You want my honest opinion?"

He rolled his eyes. "You're really going to ask me that?"

"Fine, fine." She waved him off. "I think you should pray about it and then follow your heart. If you truly care about Priscilla and you can see yourself building a life with her, then you should marry her."

"You think I'm capable of being a *gut* husband?"

"Why not?"

"Sis, no one knows me better than you do. You know just how spoiled, self-centered, and cocky I am. How can I possibly be capable of taking care of a *fraa* and a *sohn*?"

She gave him a cheeky grin. "*Ya*, but you've got me as your twin, so at least you have something going for you."

He guffawed. "That's something I would've said. I'm proud of you." His smile faded. "But seriously. I'll let Priscilla down from day one. This will never work. She's better off without me."

A pleasant smile curved up his twin's lips as she touched his bicep. "That is the most humble statement I've ever heard you make. If you keep striving every day to be a *gut* husband and *dat,* then you will be."

He stared at her.

She pushed back her chair and stood. "You need to finish your meal. I have a surprise for you."

"What?"

"I made your favorite dessert too." She opened the refrigerator and pulled out a chocolate cake.

"That's *wunderbaar.* You just made my day so much better. *Danki,* sis."

"I *said* you were on my mind today." With a smile she carried the cake to the table. "We can have it when Allen and Mollie come back down." Then she returned to the counter where she gathered a knife, four cake plates, and forks. "Mark, just open your heart to God, and he'll lead you down the right path for you and Priscilla. He did the same for Allen and me."

Mark nodded as he chewed another piece of steak. He swallowed and took a drink of water. "If I marry her, I want you to promise to keep all this a secret. I don't want anyone to know we were forced to marry. I don't want to risk her reputation in any way. I need to protect her and Ethan from the gossips in this community."

Laura gave him a knowing smile. "You know your secret is safe with me."

"*Danki.*" He was so grateful for his twin.

"I need to talk to you about something." Priscilla tucked Ethan's sheet around him.

"Okay." Ethan's dark eyes focused on her with interest. "What is it?"

"Mark and I have decided to get married."

"Oh." Ethan nodded. "So that means he'll live with us, right?"

"That's exactly right. We're going to stay in the *daadihaus* until we build another *haus*."

"Will he be *mei daed*?"

"*Ya*, he'll be your stepfather. Do you know what that means?"

He nodded. "My best friend, Nico, has a stepfather. So he has two fathers."

"Right." She rubbed his arm. "How do you feel about that?"

Ethan shrugged. "It's okay." He paused for a minute as if contemplating something. "Can I call Mark *Dat* since he'll be my Amish dad?"

"*Ya*, I think that would be fine." She smiled as relief flooded her. He seemed to be taking it better than she thought he would.

"My friend Sammi back in Baltimore said people fall in love and then they get married. Does that mean that you and Mark are in love?"

"Ah, well, no, not exactly." Priscilla rubbed at a knot in her shoulder. "Mark and I are friends—*freinden*. Sometimes *freinden* decide to get married." She stilled, hoping her son would accept that answer.

"Okay." He nodded again. "So if two people really like each other, they can get married."

"Right."

"And that means you, me, and Mark will live in a *haus* together just like a family?"

Priscilla smiled as an unexpected warmth rolled through her. "That's exactly right."

"Nico has a half brother and a half sister. Will I get a brother and sister too? A *bruder* and *schweschder*?"

Her stomach lurched at the unexpected question. How was she going to address the intimacy issue with Mark? They weren't in love, but would he still expect her to fulfill her wifely duties? She shivered at the notion.

"Are you okay, *Mamm*?"

"*Ya*, I just don't know the answer to that question. I guess we'll see."

"Okay." He snuggled down under the sheet and yawned. "*Gut nacht.*"

"*Gut nacht.* I love you." She kissed his forehead and then stepped out of his room, closing the door behind her.

As she walked into her bedroom, Ethan's question rolled around in her head, and the muscles in her shoulders tightened. Tomorrow she and Mark would visit the bishop and decide on a wedding date. Then her new life with Mark Riehl would be set in motion.

She dropped onto her chair and stared at her sewing machine, which she'd believed would be her ticket to freedom from the Amish community. But now she was trapped here and heading into a marriage she'd never wanted. When she married Mark she'd be yoked to him for the rest of her life since divorce wasn't permitted. She'd be forced to marry a man she didn't love, which meant the marriage would be a sham. She'd never know what it was like to fall in love with a man who loved her in return.

Could she stomach seeing Mark every day, thinking of everything she'd given up to marry him? Would she resent him, and would that resentment morph into hate? If so, would Ethan sense her animosity toward his stepfather? How could that be healthy for her son?

Marrying Mark also meant she'd have to give up any chance to leave the community. Unless she was strong enough to leave and never look back, the decision to marry Mark would keep her trapped on her father's farm and stuck to Mark's side for eternity. This was a path she'd never envisioned or wanted. But how could she not offer her son the safety and security of a real home?

She held back threatening tears and ran her finger over the cool metal machine. Tomorrow she would have to choose a color and begin creating her wedding dress and the dresses for her attendants. And after they were married, she'd have to pack up her things and move into the *daadihaus* with Mark. How would she ever survive this?

With prayer.

The answer came from deep in her heart. She closed her eyes and opened herself to God.

I don't know why you've chosen this path for me, but I have to trust that you're in control. Please help me make the best decisions for Ethan, and please guide Mark to make the best decision for him. I'm scared, but I know you'll keep Ethan and me safe.

Then she got ready for bed, climbed in, snuffed out the lantern, and stared at the ceiling.

SIXTEEN

"DID YOU CHANGE YOUR MIND?" PRISCILLA TURNED toward Mark as he guided the horse out of her father's driveway and wiped her sweaty palms down the skirt of her rose-colored dress.

"Change my mind about what?" Mark kept his gaze focused on the road ahead.

"About marrying me? Did you decide to be shunned instead?"

"No." He shook his head without taking his eyes off the windshield. "I'm not going to back out on you."

"Oh." She chewed on her lower lip. "So you're going to go through with it?"

"*Ya*, if you are." He peeked over at her.

"I was planning on it. Did you tell your family last night?"

"I told only Laura. I went to see her after I left here."

"Oh." Priscilla's stomach writhed as she envisioned Mark telling Laura he was going to marry her. "Did you tell her what happened yesterday?"

He nodded, still looking straight ahead.

"Did you tell her *everything*?"

"*Ya*, I did." He gave her a sideways glance. "We can trust Laura."

As his words echoed through her mind, she found herself stuck on the word *we*. She and Mark were a couple now. But would he think of Priscilla before he thought of the other women he'd been seeing in the community? Could he ever truly love and cherish her the way a husband should? Did she want him to?

"I mean it," he added. "Laura and I have always shared our deepest secrets. She won't tell anyone about the bishop insisting we marry or be shunned. When we tell the rest of the community, they only need to know that I asked you to marry me. The rest is our business."

"Okay." She nodded. "What did she say about what happened?"

"She was surprised John was so forceful with his demand for us to marry. She said she was disappointed in him and your *dat*."

"And she's not disappointed in me?"

Mark halted the horse at a red light and angled his body toward her. "Why would she be disappointed in you?"

"Because you're her *bruder*, and you're being forced to marry me."

"Laura would never blame you for any of this." The tenderness in his eyes hummed through her. "You're her best *freind*. Why would she be disappointed in you?"

"Because this wasn't your choice. You're her twin, her closest relative, and your future has been decided for you."

"Laura has been pressuring me to settle down for a long time. She'd be the last person to be upset about it. Besides, like I said, you're her best *freind*. She told me to pray about it last night and then follow my heart."

"And?" Priscilla held her breath.

"I prayed about it, and, well, here I am. We're on our way to see the bishop and make plans for the wedding."

They rode in silence for several minutes. Priscilla's thoughts swirled in her mind. She was going to marry Mark Riehl. Never in her wildest dreams did she imagine she'd become Priscilla Riehl.

"Did you tell Ethan?"

The question took her by surprise. When she looked at Mark, she found him studying her as the horse sat at another red light.

"*Ya*, I did."

"And . . . ?"

"He took it well." She smiled. "He wants to know if he can call you *Dat* since you'll be his Amish dad."

A cryptic emotion flashed in his eyes. Was it affection, fondness, surprise, or something else?

"Would that be okay with you?" she asked.

"*Ya.*" His voice sounded thick. "That would be just fine."

When a horn tooted behind them, Mark guided the horse through the intersection and turned onto the road that led to John Smucker's dairy farm.

Tiny balls of anxiety formed in Priscilla's belly as Mark guided the horse up the short driveway to the *daadihaus* located behind the main farmhouse where John's son lived with his family. She gathered all her courage from deep within her. She could go through with this for her son.

"Are you ready?" Mark asked as he halted the horse.

"I think so." She climbed out of the buggy and met him by his horse as he tied it to the fence. "Have you given any thought to a date?"

He smiled. "I assumed you'd be in charge of that. You just tell me what date and time, and I'll be there."

She nodded. "All right. I was thinking the fourth Thursday in September. That gives me five weeks to make dresses and all the preparations."

"That sounds *gut* to me." He made a sweeping gesture toward the front steps. "I'll follow you."

Priscilla's heart thudded so fast she thought it might rip through her rib cage as she climbed the steps and knocked on the door. Mark stood directly behind her, his body heat mixing with hers. Why did his nearness drive her crazy?

The door swung open and Naomi, John's wife, smiled at her. "Priscilla. Mark. It's so nice to see you."

"Hi, Naomi." Priscilla forced her lips into a smile. "We were wondering if we could speak with John."

"Oh. Was he expecting you?" Naomi's gaze bounced between them.

"No, not really," Mark chimed in. "Does he have a few minutes to talk?"

"*Ya*, of course." Naomi motioned for them to enter. "Please have a seat. I'll tell him you're here."

Priscilla stepped into the small cottage and scanned the room, finding a small sitting area with a sofa, two wing chairs, two end tables with propane lamps, and a coffee table.

Mark moved past her and touched her arm. "We can sit." He sank onto the sofa and patted the cushion beside him.

She swallowed and then sat down beside him. When her leg brushed his, she felt a flutter in her chest as her pulse took on wings. Had she lost her mind?

"Priscilla. Mark." John stepped into the family room and gave them a big smile, as if this were a joyous occasion. "How nice to see you."

Priscilla swallowed the acidic words that threatened to leap from her tongue. He was the bishop, and he could convince the other ministers to shun her. She had to keep her tongue in check.

"Hi, John." Mark stood and shook his head. "Do you have a few minutes to talk?"

The sounds of dishes clinking and water running came from

the kitchen. Was Naomi truly cleaning up? Or was it an excuse to listen in on their conversation with her husband?

John sat on a wing chair across from them and smiled. "What brings you here today?"

Priscilla gave Mark a sideways glance, and Mark's expression seemed to warn her to not say anything acerbic.

"We've decided to get married." Mark gestured toward her. "Priscilla has picked a date, so we'd like to discuss arrangements."

"That's *wunderbaar.*" John clasped his hands together and sat forward. "I think you've made the best choice."

Priscilla held back a frown.

Mark's expression grew serious, and he lowered his voice. "We want everyone to know that we came to the decision to marry on our own. I don't want any rumors floating around that we were forced into this decision. Do you understand?"

Priscilla's eyes rounded as appreciation snuffed out her anger. Was Mark defending her reputation?

"*Ya*, of course." John's expression was solemn. "Our conversation yesterday has been kept confidential. I haven't shared it with anyone."

Priscilla felt her body relax slightly.

John's expression suddenly brightened. "What date have you chosen?"

For the next ten minutes, Mark and John discussed their wedding plans while Priscilla listened, her head swimming with the gravity of it all. This was really going to happen. She hadn't dreamed the bishop's ultimatum. She was going to marry Mark Riehl and live with him in the *daadihaus* on her parents' farm. She was trapped in a life she'd considered leaving after she earned enough money.

How was she going to adjust to being someone's lawful wife? Would the marriage really work? Could she and Mark build a harmonious life together? What if they didn't get along? Would it be a healthy environment for Ethan?

But more than that, she couldn't envision herself living with another man. How was she going to ever trust Mark after the way Trent treated her? Would Mark one day turn to drinking alcohol and hitting her the way Trent had? The Amish didn't permit divorce, so she would be stuck with this marriage for the rest of her life, no matter what. Was she prepared to make this life commitment to a man she didn't even love?

Her head ached and her neck stiffened as she considered the reality of what was happening.

"Priscilla?"

"*Ya?*" She turned to Mark. He was studying her.

"Do you have any other questions for John?" Mark's brow furrowed as if he were asking her if she was okay.

"No, *danki.*" She smoothed her hands down the skirt of her dress. "I think we're all set."

"Fantastic." John stood, and they followed suit. He leaned forward and lowered his voice as he shook Mark's hand again. "You've made the right decision, and I'm convinced you won't regret it."

I pray you're right. Priscilla shook his hand. "*Danki.*"

Priscilla was in a daze as she climbed into Mark's buggy to start their journey back to her father's farm. She had to gain control of this situation.

"We need to set some ground rules," she blurted as Mark guided his horse toward the road.

"Ground rules?" He raised an eyebrow.

"*Ya.*" She sat up taller as unexpected confidence surged past her inner turmoil. "This is going to be a marriage in name only. We're going to live like two *freinden*, not husband and *fraa*."

He nodded slowly as if understanding her implications. "Agreed."

"When *mei daadi* built the *daadihaus*, *mei mammi* had two requests. She wanted a fireplace and hearth like ones she'd seen at an *Englisher* bed and breakfast, and she wanted an extra bedroom as a sewing room. After she died my parents put a spare double bed in that room. I'll sleep there with Ethan." She clasped her hands together while awaiting his response. Would he agree to her not being with him at night?

"Okay." He kept his eyes focused ahead. "I respect that."

"*Gut.*" Her heartbeat slowed to a more normal pace. "So I guess now we have to tell our families?"

"*Ya*, I guess so." His gaze flickered to hers. "Yours first?"

"*Ya*, although since they both already know everything, I'm sure the conversation will be mostly about wedding plans— especially in front of Ethan." She sucked in a deep breath. "How's your family going to take the news?"

"They're going to be surprised." His words were slow, measured.

"Will they approve of me?"

He halted the horse at a red light and faced her. "Sweetheart, they're going to be so shocked and delighted that I'm settling down that they will shower you with love and affection." He smiled. "And, *ya*, they already approve of you. You're one of Laura's dearest *freinden*. You're already family."

She rubbed her forehead. What if she let his family down? What if she let Laura down?

"So we have five weeks to make your dresses." *Mamm* clapped her hands as a bright smile spread across her lips. "How many attendants will you have?"

Priscilla drew a blank. She turned to Mark as he sat beside her at her parents' kitchen table. When they arrived home, her mother already had lunch prepared for them—platters of rolls, lettuce, lunch meat, and cheese sat by a bowl of macaroni salad and jars of condiments. She'd begun peppering Priscilla with wedding questions as soon as she and Mark walked in the door.

"We haven't talked about attendants yet." Priscilla set her ham sandwich on her plate and turned toward Mark. "I suppose you'd like to have your *bruders*?"

Mark nodded and swallowed. "Jamie, Roy, and Walter." He looked over at Ethan. "And Ethan too."

"So I could have Laura, Cindy, and Sarah Jane." She turned to her mother. "We need to make four dresses."

"What color?" *Mamm* asked.

"Red," Mark said.

Priscilla spun toward him. "Red?"

He pointed toward her. "It looks great on you with your dark hair."

Priscilla studied him, confusion filling her mind. He'd noticed what color looked best on her?

"I think you look good in red too!" Ethan said between bites of macaroni salad.

"They're right," *Mamm* said. "So we need to get to the store."

"Let me ask his *schweschdere* first," Priscilla said.

"They'll say *ya*," Mark chimed in.

"Have you told your family yet?" *Mamm* said.

"Only Laura," Mark said. "And she was supportive. We should go to *mei dat*'s for supper tonight and tell them."

"*Ya*, you should," *Mamm* said. "You know how news flies through this community. Once it gets out, everyone will know. You want your family to hear it from you."

"That's a *gut* point." Mark took a drink of water from his glass.

"Can I come?" Ethan asked.

"Of course you can," Mark said. "You're family too."

Priscilla's stomach churned as she imagined facing Mark's large family when he told them they were going to get married. Would they believe she and Mark had fallen in love in only two months? Or would they see right through Mark's façade?

"We need to start working on the biggest barn," *Dat* said. "We'll want it to be clean and painted for the ceremony. Some of the floorboards need to be replaced as well."

Priscilla's gaze snapped to her father's face as he looked across the table at Mark. Her father was smiling, and while he was admitting the barn wasn't already in perfect shape too. Was he happy that she was getting married? Or was he happy he'd gotten his way? It was probably a mixture of both. She frowned.

"I'll help paint the barn." Ethan held up his hand as if he were volunteering at school.

"And we should plant flowers," *Mamm* added. "We should plant your favorites, Priscilla—daisies."

"I love the idea." Priscilla smiled. "I've missed working in the garden. I couldn't do that when we lived in Baltimore. It's my favorite hobby."

"I'll help!" Ethan's expression brightened.

"*Danki*, Ethan," Priscilla said.

"We need to get to the nursery too, then. I have to make a list." *Mamm* took a notepad and pen from the counter and began writing a shopping list, announcing each item they'd need for the wedding.

"We have to clean out the *daadihaus* too," *Dat* added. "We should probably paint the inside. When do you think you'll move in, Mark?"

"I don't know. Maybe the night before the wedding?" Mark asked.

"No, that will be too chaotic." *Dat* shook his head. "How about a couple of weeks before the wedding?"

"That sounds *gut*." Mark picked up his turkey sandwich. "What do we need for the *haus*?"

"It's furnished," *Dat* said. "It just needs to be cleaned."

Priscilla's lunch suddenly felt like a lead ball in the pit of her stomach. Everything was happening so fast. When was it all going to slow down?

The conversation swirling around her faded as she stared down at her plate and imagined her life marching by. She was about to embark on a new journey—a new but loveless marriage in a new home. How was she going to cope?

She turned toward Mark and took in his handsome profile— his chiseled cheekbones, strong jaw, and bright-blue eyes. He would be her husband, living with Ethan and her, but he would never truly love her. Further, he'd never have the opportunity to fall in love with anyone else. She was robbing him of his future just as much as he was stealing hers. Maybe she should've agreed to be shunned.

Her gaze moved to Ethan as he grinned at Mark. She had to agree to marry Mark for Ethan. He deserved a safe home, and Mark would be a good provider and role model for her son.

She could do this. After all, she'd survived living with Trent for almost seven years.

"We have a lot of work to do." *Mamm* beamed as she looked around the table. "This will be a family effort. We'll get it all done in time." She turned her smile to Priscilla and whispered, "I'm so *froh*. You made the right decision."

Priscilla forced a smile. If only she had the same confidence in her future.

SEVENTEEN

"WE HAVE AN ANNOUNCEMENT TO MAKE." MARK glanced around the full table in his father's kitchen that evening. He was standing near his *daed*, Priscilla at his side.

For some reason, he had decided to wait until they were finished eating before he told everyone the reason he'd called and requested a last-minute family supper. They'd been patient as they shared the delicious chicken and egg noodles Florence made, but he could tell they were all bursting with curiosity—especially since he'd invited Priscilla and Ethan to join them.

Poor Ethan had squirmed in his chair the whole meal, dying to tell his secret. But Priscilla had given him strict instructions to keep quiet.

Now the whole family was staring at Mark. He turned toward his fiancée, and her brown eyes widened with something that looked like fear sparkling in them. He looped his arm around her shoulders and yanked her to him, causing her to stumble awkwardly before grabbing his waist to right herself.

"Priscilla and I are getting married." His voice sounded too loud and slightly wobbly.

The room went silent and someone muttered, "What?"

"Yeah! Mark's going to be my stepdad!" Ethan said.

Then Florence stood and clapped. "That's *wunderbaar!*" She hurried over and hugged Mark and then Priscilla. "Oh, what a blessing! When is the wedding?"

Priscilla shared the date, her voice quiet and unsure.

"Oh my goodness!" Kayla jumped up from her seat. "That's not too far off." She turned to Laura and Cindy. "We need to help Priscilla get ready. There's so much to do."

The women gathered around Priscilla. After each one took a turn hugging her, they immediately began to discuss wedding plans. Mark stole a glance at Ethan. He and Mollie seemed fascinated by the commotion among all the adults.

Dat and Jamie appeared beside Mark. They shared a confused look and then turned to face him.

"Is this a joke?" *Dat* whispered, and Mark shook his head, his throat suddenly dry.

"This is a shock." Jamie eyed him with suspicion. "You sure acted like you weren't ready to get married the last time we talked."

Dat patted Mark's back. "I never saw this coming. You really kept it quiet that you were dating."

"Well, you know how it is." Mark grinned and hoped he sounded convincing. "We couldn't wait. I was just so excited that she came back to the community, and I couldn't wait to ask after she became a member again."

Priscilla turned toward Mark and gave him a look that said, *Knock it off,* before turning back to his sisters. "We're going to keep it small, only family and *freinden,* but I'd love for you three to be my attendants."

Cindy squinted her eyes as she studied Priscilla. "Why are you going to keep it small? Everyone is so *froh* you're back."

"*Danki,*" Priscilla began, "but I'm not sure *everyone* is glad I'm back."

"Why would you say that?" Sarah Jane asked.

When a wry smile turned up Priscilla's pretty lips, Mark braced himself for her sardonic comment.

"Well, I don't think the other young *maed* from my youth group will be cheering when they learn Mark asked me to marry him instead of any of them." Priscilla turned toward Mark. "I might have some hecklers."

Laura and Jamie burst out laughing, and Mark glowered at them.

"What are you going to tell Franey and Ruthann?" Laura asked.

"I think they'll be fine," Mark said.

Cindy shook her head. "I'm not so sure. Franey seems pretty determined to be your *fraa*."

"Let's celebrate!" Florence moved to the counter and picked up a chocolate cake.

"Oh," Mark said, nearly groaning. "My favorite."

Jamie smacked Mark's back and then leaned up close to his ear. "We're going to talk later. Come by *mei haus* after you take Priscilla and Ethan home. I'll wait up for you." Then he walked over to the chair where Calvin sat on a booster seat and patted his head before sitting down beside him.

Mark swallowed. How was he going to convince his older brother that this marriage was genuine?

He turned to Priscilla as she continued to discuss plans with the women in his family. She looked beautiful with her cheeks flushed pink and her eyes sparkling in the light of the Coleman lanterns hanging above them. His heart swelled when he imagined living with her in the *daadihaus*. Could they make this marriage work? Would she ever have any affection for him?

Oh no. Was he falling for her? He couldn't allow himself to feel anything but friendship for her. Her heart wasn't in this marriage, and her ground rules proved how disconnected she felt from him. She didn't want to truly be with him, and she'd never give him her whole heart. She didn't desire to have children with him. She'd made it apparent that she craved only the stability of the marriage for the sake of her son.

Was she only biding her time until she could afford to move out? When he gave her access to his bank account, would she take his money and leave him alone in the *daadihaus*? What would he do then? He'd never be permitted to remarry while Priscilla was still alive.

"Who wants *kuche*?" Florence announced as she set two chocolate cakes on the table.

"Eat some *kuche*," Laura whispered in Mark's ear. "Everything is going to be fine."

Hoping his sister was right, Mark sat down, looked up at Priscilla, and patted the seat beside him. She sat down, and he smiled as his family continued to embrace his future wife.

It seemed that his family would accept his announcement as genuine—as long as he could convince Jamie that it was.

"What's on your mind?"

Priscilla swiped her hand down her face and contemplated how to put all her churning thoughts into words as Mark guided the buggy back to her father's farm later that evening.

She glanced into the back of the buggy where Ethan slept and thought about Mark's family. They had seemed surprised but supportive of their decision to marry.

Soon she'd be a member of the Riehl family, and her heart warmed at the idea. Even Ethan seemed to fit in as he played with Mollie and Calvin. But if marrying Mark was so right, why did it feel so wrong? She wouldn't have a real marriage, but it would be the next best thing. Didn't that make it acceptable in God's eyes? Wasn't this what God wanted her to do for her son?

"I can smell the smoke from your thoughts all the way over here." Mark grinned at her. "Why don't you just share what's bothering you?"

"Nothing. I was just thinking about how your family is so supportive."

He snickered. "Yeah, they sure are. Sometimes they're too interested in my business."

"That's because they love you. You're blessed to have their love and support."

His smile faded as he gave her a sideways glance, but he remained silent.

She shifted in the seat. "I am wondering why you didn't tell your family the truth."

"The truth about what?"

"About why we're getting married. They can't possibly believe we're in love."

Mark rubbed his chin as if considering his answer. "I didn't think they needed to know."

"Because you're embarrassed. You don't want them to know the bishop found us sitting close together in the barn, right?"

"No. Because we didn't do anything wrong. They don't need to think we were having an inappropriate relationship. Like I told you earlier, only Laura knows, and I intend to keep it that way."

Was he truly protecting her reputation? Or his own? The question took hold of her mind as they approached her father's farm.

But was it fair to expect him to keep it a secret if her family knew the truth? No, it wasn't. He was in this as much as she was.

She turned toward him. "Mark, if you want to tell your family the truth, then you should. I trust you to explain what happened, and I trust your family too."

He raised his eyebrows. "Okay. But I don't think I will."

When Mark halted the horse in front of her father's porch, Priscilla woke Ethan, and they all climbed out of the buggy.

Mark walked them to the steps, and after saying good night to Mark, Ethan hurried into the house.

Priscilla looked up at Mark, and a fist-size ball of unease formed under her ribs. "So I guess I'll see you tomorrow . . . and then at church."

"I have to run some preplanned errands for the farm all day tomorrow, but I'll pick up you and Ethan for the service on Sunday."

"Why?"

"We're engaged now, so we should ride to and from church together."

"Right. We have to make sure everyone believes this is real."

"So I'll see you Sunday." He started down the steps.

"Mark," she called after him, and he spun toward her. "Are you ready for the community to find out about us?"

He rested his hand on the railing. "*Ya*, I am. Are you?"

"*Ya*." She nodded. "*Gut nacht.*"

"*Gut nacht.*" He strode down the steps.

As his horse and buggy started down the driveway, she glanced around her father's vast property. Of course Mark was ready for the community to find out he was marrying Priscilla. After all, he hadn't turned down her father's offer of half his successful horse breeding and training business and land. He was set financially for life. Besides that—and not wanting to be shunned—why else would he want to marry her?

But was his desire for acceptance and wealth enough to sustain a commitment to her for a lifetime?

The question lingered in her mind as she stepped into the house. She locked the front door and then walked into the kitchen, where a yellow lantern glowed. She stepped into the doorway and expected to find her mother there, but she bristled as her gaze collided with her father's.

"How did his family take your wedding announcement?" *Dat* lifted a glass of water and took a drink.

"Fine." She folded her arms over her waist. "They actually believe we're in love."

The twinkle in her father's eyes caused the angry knots in her shoulders to tighten.

"Everything will work out just fine." *Dat* stood and set the glass on the counter. "Mark will have the *haus* he's always wanted and eventually my farm. You'll have a husband, and Ethan will have a proper *dat*. Plus, my farm will finally have an heir since Ethan is here."

She shook her head as irritation churned in her stomach. "Have you ever considered what I want?" She jammed her finger into her collarbone. "You act as if my opinion doesn't matter. You never once have thought about my happiness."

His eyes narrowed. "That's not true. I'm doing what's best for you and *mei gross-sohn*." He pointed toward the ceiling. "Your *bu* needs a *gut* role model for a *dat*. Mark Riehl is a *gut*, solid Christian man."

"But shouldn't marriage be based on mutual love and respect?" Her voice thinned. "Didn't you marry *Mamm* because you loved her?"

He waved off her comment. "Love and respect will come later."

"What if it doesn't?" She raised her arms for emphasis. "What if I'm trapped in a loveless marriage for the rest of my life? Doesn't that matter?"

"What matters is that you and your *sohn* have a *gut*, stable home." He took a step toward her, his lips forming a deep scowl. "Isn't that better than living on the street?"

"I don't know." She shook her head. "I thought my happiness mattered for something."

"Maybe you should have thought of that before you ran off and got pregnant," he snapped.

His words were a kick to her stomach, and she gasped as if the statement had caused her physical pain. Reeling from the cruelty in his dark eyes, she left the kitchen and mounted the stairs.

She stopped short in the hallway when she heard her mother's voice. It sounded as if *Mamm* was reading Ethan a story in his room. Priscilla leaned back against the wall and closed her eyes.

"Please, God," she whispered. "Give me strength. Help me find my way through this confusing mess."

Then she fought back threatening tears and stepped into her son's room. She'd get through this somehow—for him.

Mark stowed his horse and buggy in his father's barn and then headed down the path to Jamie's house. He found his older brother sitting on his porch, a lantern on the floor illuminating him as he rested his elbows on his thighs and leaned forward. A look of suspicion had overtaken his face.

"I was wondering if you were going to stand me up," Jamie said as Mark climbed the porch steps. "Just weeks ago you told me you weren't ready to get married. You also told me I'd be the third to know when you got engaged. How could you not let me know you were planning to make this announcement?"

"I'm sorry to disappoint you." Mark dropped into the rocker beside Jamie and gave it a gentle push. "I wanted to tell everyone at the same time."

Jamie turned toward him, raising a dark eyebrow. "So what's really going on here, little *bruder*?"

Mark brushed his hands down his thighs and stared out toward the dark pasture. How was he going to lie to his older brother? But he made a promise to Priscilla, and he intended to keep that promise. She was going to be his wife, and their marriage needed a good, solid foundation based on trust.

Who was he kidding? This was a marriage of convenience, arranged as punishment, thanks to the bishop.

"Wow. I've never seen you be so secretive. This must be a *gut* story."

"No, not really." Mark plastered a smile on his face. "Priscilla and I have fallen in love. I wasn't expecting it, but it just happened."

Jamie's loud laughter sliced through the air.

Mark swallowed a groan.

"You fell in love?" Jamie wiped his eyes. "Please, Mark. How gullible do you think I am?"

Mark sighed and tipped his head back. Why hadn't he just gone straight home and to bed?

"What really happened?"

Mark gripped the arms of the chair.

Jamie's smile faded. "You know you can trust me, right?"

Mark nodded. "*Ya*, I do know that, but I made a promise."

"Wait a minute." Jamie's expression grew more serious. "Is she—do you *have* to get married?"

"What?" Mark sat up straight. "No, no, no. It's nothing like that." He shook his head. "This is why I don't want to tell you the truth. I'm afraid people are going to make assumptions about her and about us that aren't true. I want people to believe that she came back after all these years, we fell in love, I proposed to her, and she said *ya*."

"So if that's not what happened, what is the truth, Mark?"

"I'll tell you the truth, but you and Laura are the only ones who'll know, other than Priscilla's parents and the bishop. I want it to stay between us. Do you understand?"

Jamie nodded. "*Ya*, I do. Now tell me."

Settling back against the rocking chair, Mark explained how Priscilla's father and the bishop had found them when she opened up to him in the barn. He explained the bishop's ultimatum, their decision to marry, and their meeting with John.

When he finished speaking, Mark moved the rocker back and forth and stared out toward the pasture again, his stomach in knots while he waited for his brother's opinion of it all.

"Wow."

"Really?" Mark deadpanned. "All you can say is 'wow'?"

Jamie held up his hand. "Give me a minute to process this."

Mark rubbed his temples as that familiar stress headache began behind his eyes.

"Do you love her?" Jamie asked.

Mark hesitated. "She's a *gut freind*."

"You shouldn't marry her if you don't love her. It will never work if you don't have that foundation of love."

"I can't confess to something I didn't do, and she shouldn't have to either. Plus, Yonnie offered me land and half the business, I'll have a place of my own, and our siblings will have more room in the *haus*. It just makes sense."

"I understand, but that's not a reason to get married."

"It's a great reason." Mark pointed to the porch floor. "I'll have stability, and so will Priscilla and Ethan."

"You need to really think about this. Marriage is for life. You and Priscilla will resent each other if you marry for the wrong reasons. You deserve happiness too."

Mark shook his head. "You don't understand. I've already made the commitment to Priscilla, and we've spoken to John. I can't go back on my decision. I can't disappoint Priscilla like that.

All the men in her life have let her down. Her father treats her terribly, and Ethan's father abused her. If I change my mind, I'll be just as bad as they are."

"Mark, please just listen to me." Jamie leaned forward and held up his hand as if to calm Mark. "You will regret this. You need to talk to the bishop again. Tell him you think there should be another solution other than shunning or getting married. You and Priscilla weren't doing anything inappropriate in the barn, and this has all been blown out of proportion. Make him understand that this isn't right."

"I think it's more complicated than that. I think Yonnie pressured the bishop to make us get married. I think he's embarrassed by Priscilla and he wants to legitimize Ethan." He glowered. "He only cares about how Priscilla looks to the community."

A strange expression flickered over Jamie's face as he was silent.

"What are you thinking?" Mark asked.

"Nothing."

"Jamie, just say it. I can feel your criticism."

"It's not criticism. I think you care about her more than you're willing to admit."

"No, I don't. I care about her like I care about a *freind*. I just think this can be *gut* for both of us. She needs a husband as well as a father for Ethan. Besides, like I said, I'm getting land and a business."

"It might sound like a *gut* idea, but if you're marrying her for what Yonnie will give you, the marriage is going to fail."

Anger whipped through Mark. "That's easy for you to say. You have it all right here." He gestured toward the house. "You have the farm, Kayla, Calvin, and a *boppli* on the way."

"I thought you didn't want those things," Jamie said, challenging him.

Mark pressed his lips together. Jamie was right. When did Mark start wanting those things?

They sat in silence for a beat.

"Did you pray about it?" Jamie suddenly asked.

"*Ya*, I did last night."

"What was the answer?"

"The answer was *ya*, that I should marry her. Will you support me?"

"Of course I will." Jamie smiled. "And I think Priscilla is perfect for you."

"What makes you say that?"

"When she teased you about Franey and Ruthann tonight, I could tell she's not intimidated by you. She's not afraid to challenge you or speak her mind. Kayla is the same way with me. She challenges me just about every day. In my opinion that makes Priscilla a *gut* match for you. I just hope you two can find your way together."

A tangle of emotions expanded deep within Mark. "I do too."

EIGHTEEN

"So Mark." Ethan leaned over Mark's buggy seat Sunday morning. "When you marry *mei mamm*, does that mean Mollie and Calvin will be my cousins?"

Mark tilted his head while keeping his eyes focused on the road ahead. "*Ya*, I guess they will be your cousins."

"Awesome. I've never had cousins before."

"Sit down," Priscilla scolded him. "Stop hanging over the seat like that."

Ethan sat back, but he kept his attention on Mark. "Mom says we're going to live in the *daadihaus* until *Daadi* builds us a bigger *haus*, and you'll be my stepdad."

"Right." Mark gave Priscilla a sideways grin.

"I'm sorry," she muttered as her cheeks heated. "We talked about this again last night, and he has a lot of questions for you."

"It's fine. This is a big adjustment." Mark looked over his shoulder at Ethan. "What do you want to ask me?"

"Can I call you *Dat* since you'll be my Amish dad?" Ethan tapped his chin. "Or should I call you Mark since you're not my dad yet?"

"You can call me whatever you want, but just don't call me late for dinner." Mark grinned, and Ethan hooted with laughter.

"Oh, Mark." Priscilla shook her head, but she couldn't stop herself from chuckling.

"In all seriousness," Mark began with a sentimental smile, "you can call me *Dat* or Mark. It's up to you."

Ethan rubbed his chin. "I think I'll go with Mark for now and then *Dat* after you marry *mei mamm*."

"That sounds *gut* to me." Mark glanced over at Priscilla and winked.

The gesture touched Priscilla's heart.

Don't allow him to lead you on. He'll never truly love you!

The voice startled her and cooled the warmth.

When they arrived at the Yoders' farm for the church service, Ethan hopped out of the back of the buggy.

"*Daadi* is here," he announced as he ran around to Priscilla's door. "He said I can sit with him again today."

Priscilla nodded. "Okay."

"See you later!" Ethan waved as he hurried off.

Priscilla climbed out of the buggy and watched Ethan meet her father near the barn. Then she turned to Mark as he sidled up to her. "I find it fascinating that *mei dat* isn't *froh* to have me back, but he loves *mei sohn*."

Mark nodded toward her father. "You know how he is. Just give God time to melt his heart."

She turned toward him and studied his pleasant expression. "Are you sure you don't want to change your mind about this?"

"About what?"

"About us." She gestured between them. "This marriage. Becoming a stepfather and husband."

His expression hardened. "No, I don't want to change my mind. Do you?"

She hesitated and then said, "No."

He pursed his lips, his blue eyes gleaming in the morning light. "What are you thinking right now?"

"The community is going to be shocked when they find out you're marrying me."

"So?" Mark shrugged. "Let them be shocked. It's our business."

She laughed. "No, that's not how gossip works."

"Gossip is a sin."

"*Ya*, but it's alive and well."

He took a step toward her and lowered his voice. "Are you okay?"

The tenderness and concern she found in his face touched her deep in her soul. Was it genuine? No, it couldn't be—at least not beyond being a friend. He was just trying to convince her this relationship would somehow last.

"*Ya*, I will be."

"*Gut.*" He rubbed her arm, and the sudden, unexpected contact caused her to flinch. "I'm sorry," he said. "I just wanted to tell you it will be fine. I'll see you after the service."

"Okay." She drew in a deep breath and watched him saunter to the barn, where he greeted the men in his family.

"Priscilla!" *Mamm* waved as she walked over to her. "It's a *schee* day, *ya*?" She pointed to the cloudless, bright-blue sky.

"*Ya*, it is."

"Let's go inside." *Mamm* gestured toward the house.

Priscilla strode beside *Mamm* and entered the kitchen, where the women in the congregation were gathered in a circle greeting one another.

Her mother walked over to Florence, and when Priscilla's gaze fell on Laura, Sarah Jane, Cindy, and Kayla, she waved and walked over to them.

"*Gude mariye,*" Priscilla said. "How are—"

"There she is!" Florence announced. "There's Mark's bride!"

All conversation around the kitchen ceased, and Priscilla saw every set of eyes focus on her. She felt as though their curiosity was burning into her skin. She tried to swallow against her suddenly arid throat as she hugged her arms around her waist.

Florence smiled and held her hand to her chest. "I'm just so grateful Mark is finally going to settle down."

Priscilla stilled as a flush crawled up her neck to her face. *Oh no, no. Please be quiet, Florence!*

"Mark Riehl is getting married?" a voice asked.

"Really?" someone across the room said. "Mark is going to settle down?"

Priscilla longed to crawl under the kitchen table and hide from the inquisitive crowd of women.

"That's right," Florence continued. "They're getting married in five weeks."

"It's fine." Laura's voice was close to Priscilla's ear. "Once the announcement is out, it will get easier."

Priscilla met her best friend's kind eyes. "You think so?"

"Of course." Laura rubbed her arm.

When Priscilla turned to her right, she found Franey's eyes wide and glistening as she studied her. Then Franey turned and made a hasty exit out the back door.

Embarrassment spread through Priscilla as a group of women huddled around her.

"Congratulations," Ruthann said as she hugged Priscilla. "I always hoped Mark would pick me, but I never really felt his heart was in our friendship." She smiled, but her dark eyes were wet with unshed tears.

"*Danki,*" Priscilla said as shock surged through her.

"How did you get Mark Riehl to want to settle down?" a woman who looked to be her mother's age asked.

"You must have stolen his heart quickly," another quipped.

"Did you date when you were teenagers?" a third asked. "I don't recall that he dated you."

"Your wedding is coming quickly. You have to get started on your dresses soon," a fourth said.

Priscilla took a deep breath and began trying to respond to the questions as quickly as they were thrown at her.

Mark nodded at a couple of friends as he made his way through the knot of people milling around the barn after the service. His mind had been swimming with thoughts of his upcoming wedding as he tried but failed to concentrate on the sermons.

His eyes had also kept gravitating to the unmarried women's section, where Priscilla sat between Cindy and Sarah Jane. She looked radiant today in her pink dress, yet she also seemed lost in thought as she stared down at her lap. Had she been focused on their upcoming nuptials too?

He stepped out of the barn and walked the path toward the house while recalling their conversation in the buggy this morning. He'd enjoyed his conversation with Ethan. For the first time in his life, he looked forward to becoming a father. He hoped and prayed he'd be a good one—like his father and Jamie were.

Why was he changing so quickly? He felt like a new man, a different person since he'd decided to get married.

"Is it true?"

Mark spun and came face-to-face with Franey. Her pretty face featured a deep frown as her eyes trained on his.

"Is it true?" she repeated as she took a step toward him.

"Is what true?" Who was he kidding? He knew exactly what she wanted to know.

"You're marrying her, aren't you?" Her voice shook as her lower lip quivered.

Oh no. Please don't cry. Not here.

He nodded. "*Ya,* I've asked Priscilla to marry me."

"Why?" Her eyes glittered. "I've waited five years for you. Five years!" Her voice broke as tears spilled down her pink cheeks.

"*Ach,* no." Guilt, hot and searing, sliced through Mark as he pointed to the far corner outside the barn, away from the curious crowd that turned toward them. "Why don't we walk over there?"

"Why?" Franey's voice grew louder. "You don't want everyone to hear how you've hurt me?"

Mark's shoulders hunched.

"Five years, Mark!" She nearly spat the words at him. "I've invited you over for hundreds of meals. I've sat on my father's porch and talked to you for hours. I've welcomed you into my home. Yet she's back barely two months, and you propose to *her.* What does she have that I don't? Am I not *schee* enough? Am I not *schmaert* enough? What is it, Mark? What's wrong with me?"

"It's not that at all. There's nothing wrong with you." He reached for her arm, and she stepped away from him. "Franey. *Kumm.*" He took her arm and steered her away from the barn door as questioning eyes locked on them. "It's not you. You're a *wunderbaar maedel,* and you'll make a husband very *froh* someday."

She gave a cry. "Apparently not. I thought you cared about me. I was blind."

"I do care about you—as a *freind.*"

She groaned and wiped at her tears.

"Franey, listen. I never meant to hurt you." He tried to smile. "I'll cherish the time we've had together. This wasn't anything I planned. Love is just unpredictable sometimes. Priscilla and I have a deep connection I never expected."

"I thought we had a connection."

"Look, I'm sorry."

"How could you?" Her eyes narrowed. "How could you lead me on like that for so long?"

"I didn't lead you on."

"*Ya*, you did." She pointed at him. "You called me twice a week and you even invited yourself over some nights. Why would I not think someday you'd propose to me?" Then she turned her finger toward herself. "I knew you were seeing Ruthann too, but I thought you and I had something special."

"I never made you any promises." But Mark did a mental head slap. Laura was right. What he'd done was wrong.

"No, you didn't make me any promises, but you kept me hanging on for years. You acted like you liked me."

"You're right, and I'm sorry."

"No, *I'm sorry* I ever believed in you." Franey shook her head. "I meant nothing to you. I was just someone to pass the time with until you met your true love."

"No, you're a *freind*, a *gut freind*."

She shook her head, and then her expression darkened. "You know, I had a feeling something was going on between you and Priscilla the day you brought her to the fabric store."

He blinked. "Why would you say that?"

"It was the way you acted when you purchased the fabric for her. I should have known then that you had fallen in love with her."

Mark tried to hide his surprise at her comment.

"You were seeing her before her shunning was over?"

He shook his head. "No, of course not."

"Well, it doesn't matter now." She lifted her chin. "I wish you many blessings in your marriage." She pushed past him and headed back into the barn.

Mark leaned his back against the barn wall and rubbed his forehead. How could he have been so blind? Why had he allowed his relationship with Franey to get so complicated? Guilt was a snake slithering around his insides.

Closing his eyes, he blew out a deep breath.

———∞———

Priscilla's heart pounded as she stood on the back porch of the house. Mark and Franey were standing close together and talking by the corner of the barn. She couldn't hear what they were saying, but it was obvious that the conversation was emotional and intense.

Mark reached for Franey's arm and leaned in closer to her, and Priscilla tried to swallow back the jealousy that rolled through her. So he *did* still have feelings for Franey. Would he cheat on Priscilla with Franey after they were married?

Acid churned in her stomach. Priscilla wanted a marriage in name only, but she cared if he had feelings for Franey because she didn't want any more humiliation than she'd already had to endure since she returned. How would it look to the community if they found out Mark was seeing Franey behind her back? They'd both be shunned.

Another thought gripped Priscilla. What if Mark told Franey the truth about their marriage? Surely Franey would tell her friends, and then the entire community would know Mark was marrying her not only to avoid being shunned, but to get half of her father's business and some of his land. That was worse than his having an affair.

"Priscilla?"

"*Ya?*" Priscilla turned toward Cindy's curious expression.

"Could you please help me serve the *kaffi*?" Cindy held up a carafe.

"Of course." Priscilla plastered a smile on her face.

"Are you all right?" Cindy asked.

"*Ya*, I'm fine." Priscilla stepped into the house. "Do you want me to take this carafe or fill a second one?" As she busied herself with the task of helping to serve the food, her worries about Mark and Franey taunted her.

—⟨⟩⟨⟩—

"Have you thought about table decorations?" *Mamm* asked as she and Priscilla sat on the back porch later that evening.

"No, not really." Priscilla pushed the glider to life with her toe as she looked toward the swing set where Ethan was going down the slide.

"What's on your mind?"

"Nothing." Priscilla shrugged and cradled her mug of warm tea in her hands.

"Priscilla, I can tell when you're upset. It might help if you talk about it."

"It's *gegisch*, really." Priscilla averted her eyes by studying her plain white mug.

"Why don't you let me be the judge of that?"

Priscilla sighed. "I saw Mark talking to Franey today. They were having what looked like an intimate conversation outside the barn before we had lunch. And, well, it bothered me."

"Why did it bother you? Mark is marrying you, not Franey."

Priscilla pressed her lips together. "You know the truth of why he's marrying me. He's avoiding being shunned. And he's also going to be well off, thanks to *Dat*'s business and land."

Mamm looked unconvinced. "I think he cares about you."

Priscilla gave a sardonic smile. "*Mamm*, I hope you realize nothing happened in the barn that day when *Dat* and John say they 'found' us doing 'inappropriate' things." She made air quotes with her fingers. "We were talking. That's it. Mark and I weren't dating in secret. He doesn't love me."

"But you're *freinden*." *Mamm* patted her leg. "That's a great foundation for a *gut* marriage."

Priscilla clicked her tongue. "We're not close *freinden*. We're just acquaintances trapped together now."

"That's not what I see." *Mamm* gave her a knowing smile. "He cares about you."

"No, he doesn't." *But if only he did . . .*

"Just give it time. It will all work out. The Lord works in mysterious ways."

As Priscilla took a sip of tea, she longed for her mother to be right. But instead, she was certain their marriage was headed for disaster.

NINETEEN

"Sis." Mark approached the van as Laura climbed out of it the following Thursday afternoon. "I didn't know you were planning to visit today."

"Hi. I came to help Priscilla with her dresses for the wedding. She doesn't have long to make them." Laura balanced a cake saver in her hands as she hoisted her purse onto her shoulder.

"Give me that." Mark took the container, and she paid the driver. "That's nice that you offered to help her."

"That's what family is for, right?" Laura smiled up at him. "I'm so glad you're marrying Priscilla. You're going to be perfect for each other."

"*Ya*, we are." He gave a wry smile. "Where's my favorite niece?"

"She's playing at Irma Mae's today. I thought it would be easier if she went there so I could concentrate on helping Priscilla." She pointed to the cake saver. "I just might have brought over a chocolate *kuche* for you."

"Really?" He grinned. "For me?"

"Maybe. But you have to promise me something."

"I'll do anything for your chocolate *kuche*." He shrugged as they walked up the porch steps.

"You have to be extra nice to Priscilla and supportive of her while she makes the wedding plans. You know how stressful wedding planning can be. You've seen me go through it."

He opened the front door, and she stepped through. "Okay."

"*Danki.*" She smiled up at him. "You seem different since you made the decision to get married."

"Oh. Do I?" He lifted his chin and posed. "Am I more handsome? Funnier? Less resistible?"

"Ugh." She swatted his arm, and he could feel her irritation. "You're hopeless."

"That's why you love me. Priscilla is probably upstairs since I hear the sewing machine going. Her *mamm* is in the utility room doing laundry." He pointed toward the kitchen. "Would you like me to put the *kuche* in there for you?"

"*Ya. Danki.*" She gave him a little wave. "I'll see you later."

As Mark set the cake carrier on the counter, his twin's words rattled through his brain.

I'm so glad you're marrying Priscilla. You're going to be perfect for each other.

He shook his head. How could his twin be so blind? This marriage was doomed to fail, but he'd make the best of it. At least Ethan seemed to like him. Ethan was a blessing for certain.

"I'm here to help." Laura slowly sat down in a chair across from Priscilla and rested her hands on her belly, which looked like it already protruded a little more than it had the day before. "Put me to work."

"I'm so *froh* you're here." Priscilla pointed to the notebook on her bed. "I have everyone's measurements there. Do you want to start cutting out Cindy's dress?"

"I'd love to."

Priscilla gathered supplies for Laura and then returned to working on her own dress.

"How are things going for you?" Laura asked. When Priscilla met her gaze, Laura added, "With your *dat*?"

Priscilla shrugged. "Okay, I guess. He still doesn't talk to me much at all, but he's kind to Ethan, which I appreciate."

Laura seemed to study her, and Priscilla looked down at the dress.

"Did Mark tell you I know the truth about why you're getting married?"

"*Ya.*" Priscilla nodded, keeping her eyes focused on the dress. Was Laura going to try to talk Priscilla out of marrying her twin? If she succeeded, what would she say now that the announcement had been made to the community? How could she ever face the bishop again?

"I'm not upset, Priscilla."

"Really?" Priscilla looked up, shocked to find her best friend's smile.

"Why would I be upset? I've been praying for years that Mark would settle down, and he's finally going to. You're a blessing."

"A blessing?" Priscilla shook herself. Had she heard Laura right? "How is being forced to marry me a blessing?"

Laura set the scissors on the desk beside the sewing table. "God has a reason for everything that happens, and he has the perfect plan for each of us. There's a reason why your *dat* and the bishop found you both in the barn."

Priscilla grimaced. "It sounds so bad when you say it that way."

Laura chuckled. "Mark told me what happened, and I know it was innocent."

But I wanted him to kiss me . . .

Priscilla dismissed the unwelcomed thought. "But I'm ruining his life."

"What?" Laura shook her head. "No, you're not. You're forcing him to grow up, and it's about time."

"We should get back to work." Priscilla turned her attention to the dress, and they worked in silence for several minutes.

"You know," Laura began, breaking through the quiet, "Mark is a *gut* man, and he'll take *gut* care of you and Ethan."

Priscilla glanced at her.

"He uses humor and arrogance as a defense mechanism. Deep down, he's just as humble as Jamie. And he's a hard worker."

Priscilla nodded. "I've seen how hard he works here, and he's very kind to Ethan."

Priscilla's thoughts swirled as they turned their attention back to their work.

"I think he cares about Franey," Priscilla blurted.

"What?" Laura's forehead furrowed.

"I saw them talking at church yesterday." Priscilla described their body language. "It was intense."

Laura shook her head. "I don't think he cares about her as anything more than a *freind*. When he told me he was going to marry you, he didn't mention Franey or Ruthann. He talked only about you."

Priscilla was unconvinced.

"What are you thinking right now?" Laura asked.

"I'm wondering how we're going to adjust to living together. How can we be a *gut* example for *mei sohn* if we don't love each other?"

"Give it time. It will all be fine. Just pray about it and ask God to guide your heart and give you patience."

Priscilla nodded and turned back to her sewing machine.

"So what are you considering for table decorations?" Laura

asked. "I was at the market yesterday, and I saw the most gorgeous red candles that would match this material."

They talked about the wedding, and then Laura gave her updates about people they'd both known in school and youth group.

Later they took a break and had cake with her mother and Ethan in the kitchen before Priscilla walked Laura outside to call her driver.

"I had a great time," Laura said as they stood in the driveway waiting for the van.

"I did too." Priscilla hugged her. "*Danki* for helping with the dresses."

"*Gern gschehne.*" Laura grinned. "Soon we'll be *schweschdere.*"

Mark jogged up behind them, his dark trousers and gray shirt speckled with white paint, evidence that he'd been working in the *daadihaus.* "You're leaving, sis?"

"*Ya.* I need to get home and start supper. Irma Mae is going to bring Mollie home soon." Laura pointed to the house. "I left you chocolate *kuche.*"

"*Danki.*" He rubbed his hands together.

Laura turned toward Priscilla. "I have to warn you. You'll probably find yourself baking a lot of chocolate *kuche* after you're married."

"Please." Mark gave Priscilla an adorable smile. "I promise I'll work hard to earn it."

Laura snickered as her driver steered his van up the rock driveway. "I'll see you two soon."

"*Danki* again," Priscilla said. "I'll return the *kuche* saver."

"No hurry." Laura climbed into the van and waved before it headed down the driveway.

"Well, back to work," Mark said when the van was out of sight. "The *daadihaus* isn't going to paint itself." He turned and started up the path to the small house.

"Mark," Priscilla called after him, and he spun toward her. "Would you like to stay for supper?"

He studied her for a moment, and then his lips curved into a smile. "Only if I can have a piece of *mei schweschder's kuche.*"

"Of course."

"Great. Then I'll stay."

As he strode toward the house, she tried to imagine their marriage. Would it ever be filled with laughter and love as well as chocolate cakes?

No. A marriage had to be built on a foundation of love. How could love come later? That wasn't how it worked.

With a frown, Priscilla walked back into the house and tried to put the negative thoughts out of her mind, but they lingered there, mocking her as she returned to her sewing project.

"Was *mei schweschder* any help today?" Mark asked as he sat on a rocking chair beside hers on the front porch later that evening.

"*Ya*, she started on Cindy's dress while I worked on mine."

"*Gut.*" Mark looked off toward the row of barns, and she longed to read his thoughts.

They had chatted about the wedding and Ethan's day at school during supper, and then he'd helped her father and Ethan take care of the animals while she and her mother cleaned the kitchen.

"How is the painting at the *daadihaus* coming along?" she asked.

"I'm almost done with the first coat." He rested his hands on the arms of the chair. "I'm hoping to finish the second coat before the end of the week. The walls look *gut.*"

"Great." She moved the chair back and forth as her thoughts

turned to Franey. While she longed to ask him what they had discussed on Sunday, she didn't want to seem clingy or reveal the jealousy she'd felt. Instead, she stared out toward the barns and hoped he'd say something to kill the awkwardness between them.

"What's bothering you?" he finally asked.

She strangled a moan. That wasn't what she'd hoped he'd say. "Nothing." She forced a smile. "I was thinking about the *daadihaus*."

"No, you weren't." He swiveled toward her and smiled. "You were thinking about something much more interesting than my painting skills." He sat up a little taller. "By the way, I am talented with a paintbrush, in case you were wondering."

Her thoughts moved to Laura's comment earlier that day. Did Mark use humor and arrogance as a defense mechanism? No, she doubted it. He truly believed he was talented and handsome, and he was right.

"*Gut nacht*, Mark." Ethan appeared in the doorway, looking proud. "I said that right, didn't I?"

"You certainly did." Mark grinned at him.

"*Mammi* said I have to take a bath. I'll see you tomorrow when I get home from school." Ethan waved and then disappeared into the house, the storm door clicking shut behind him.

"I need to get going. *Danki* again for supper." Mark stood and held out his hand. Not sure what else to do, she gently shook it. When his skin touched hers, she felt an electrical current zing up her arm. Had she imagined it? If not, had he felt it too?

"*Gern gschehne.*" Priscilla stood as Mark started down the steps, surprised she was reluctant to let him go.

TWENTY

A WEEK LATER THE RUMBLE OF A TRUCK ENGINE sounded nearby, and Mark stepped out of the largest barn. The September sun warmed his arms as he walked toward the faded red, late-model Chevrolet pickup bouncing up the driveway.

Confusion sparked as Mark quickened his steps to catch up with the driver. Mark didn't recall Yonnie's mentioning that a customer had made an appointment to come see a horse. In fact, Yonnie and Edna had gone to town for supplies an hour ago, and already home from school, Ethan had tagged along for the promise of ice cream. Yonnie never would have left the farm if he were expecting a customer.

When Mark reached the truck, he tapped on the window.

A man who looked about Mark's age lowered the window and nodded. "Hi." He had dark hair and eyes, and he seemed nervous as he cleared his throat.

"May I help you?" Mark asked.

"Is this the Allgyer family farm?"

"*Ya.*" Mark pointed behind the truck. "The name is on the sign. Are you looking for a horse?"

"No." The man shook his head. "I'm trying to find Priscilla Allgyer. Does she live here by any chance?"

A dark foreboding grabbed Mark by the shoulders. "She might."

"Well, if she does, thank goodness!" The man slapped his hands together. "I've been searching for months. All I knew was her last name and that her father was Amish and sold horses. I can't believe I finally found her. Do you know how many Allgyers there are around here?" He gave a chuckle that sounded forced as he pointed at Mark. "Sure you do, since you're obviously Amish."

"What do you want?" Mark barked the question as alarm burrowed into his gut.

"I need to see her." Trent climbed out of the truck and stood next to it.

"Who are you?"

"I'm Trent Parker." Trent held out his hand in an offer of a handshake, but Mark remained in place, unmoving. "I was hoping to see her. Is she home?"

Mark stiffened as his eyes narrowed. "What are you doing here?" He ground out the words. "You have no right to come here. You're not welcome."

Trent held up his hands as if in surrender. "I'm just here to apologize."

"Don't bother." Mark pointed in the direction of the road. "You need to leave, or I'm going to call the police and have you escorted off this property."

Trent shook his head. "I won't leave until I see Priscilla and my son."

"You don't have the right to call Ethan your son." Mark gripped the truck's door handle. "You need to leave now. I mean it."

"Trent!" Priscilla jogged over to the truck from the house. "What are you doing here?"

Mark's body quaked as he turned toward her. "I just told him to leave. Stay away from him."

"No." She shook her head as she reached for Mark's arm. "Just give me a minute to talk to him."

"Please don't." Mark took her arm and gently steered her away from the truck. "I saw what he did to you. I will not allow him to hurt you again."

"I'm fine." She placed her hands on his biceps as she stared up into his eyes. "I will stand right here and talk to him, but I want you to leave, okay?"

He shook his head. "I can't bring myself to leave you alone with him."

"Mark." She spoke slowly as if he didn't understand the language. "I promise you I will be fine. He's not going to hurt me here, especially in front of you." She nodded toward the barn. "Just go back to work. I'll be only a few minutes, and then I'll make him leave. I'll yell for you if I feel threatened, okay?" She touched his hand, and he enjoyed the feel of her soft skin against his. "I need you to trust me on this."

"Fine." He gave her a curt nod and then glanced past her to where Trent had climbed out of the truck. "If he hurts you . . ."

"Go. I promise you I will be fine."

With fury pumping through his veins, Mark headed toward the barn. When he reached the barn door, he turned, crossed his arms over his chest, and watched Priscilla approach Trent.

He stood ready to jump into action if Trent even reached for her.

"What are you doing here?" Priscilla hated the thread of worry in her voice. She couldn't let Trent know how nervous he made her. At least she wasn't as afraid as she thought she'd be if he ever showed up on the farm. Mark's presence made the difference.

"I'm here to apologize." He pointed toward her scarred arm. "I'm sorry for everything that happened. I got help, and I stopped drinking. I want to tell you and Ethan that I'm ready to be a family. I'm better, and I will be the father and boyfriend you both deserve."

If only he'd said those words months ago.

No! How could she ever trust him after the way he'd treated her? She deserved better, didn't she?

She shook her head. "It's too late."

"No, it's not." He took a step toward her, and she stepped back, away from him. "I want to make it up to you. I have a steady job now, and I'm looking for a better place for us to live. I'm ready to provide for you. If you and Ethan come with me, you won't even have to work. You can go back to school or stay home. It's up to you." His desperation covered her like a silky, slimy substance.

"No." She lifted her chin and made her voice strong and forceful. "We're not going anywhere with you."

Trent looked around the farm. "Is Ethan in the house?"

"He's not here."

Trent's dark eyes seemed to study her. "You look different. You seem more confident."

She nodded. "I am."

"And you're Amish now, huh?" He grinned. "You looked better in jeans and T-shirts. That bonnet looks uncomfortable. I like your hair down."

"It's a prayer covering." She touched the ties. "You need to go. You've said what you came to say. Get out of here before Mark calls the police." She glanced past him to where Mark stood watch by the barn, his expression unmoving. She'd never seen him look so serious or so angry. It sent uneasiness swirling through all the cells in her body.

Trent turned and stared at Mark. "Is he your new boyfriend?"

He'd raised his voice as Mark took a few steps toward them. Did Trent want Mark to hear?

"He's a family friend." She matched her tone and volume to his, not wanting him to believe he was gaining the upper hand.

Trent studied her for a moment, and her skin felt as if it were crawling. "Where's Ethan?"

"He got home from school early today, so he went to the store with my parents."

"When will he be back?" Trent asked.

"I don't know."

"I want to see him." Trent's expression softened as he lowered his voice. "Please. I really want to see him. I've missed you both so much."

"You should have considered that before you did this to me." She pushed up her sleeve, revealing the puckered skin. "And before you neglected our son. You need to go now."

"But I want to see Ethan."

She shook her head. "Now is not a good time."

"If now isn't a good time, then when is?"

"I don't know." She shrugged. "Let me think about it. I'll call you."

Trent's eyes narrowed, and his jaw tightened. "I have a right to see him. He's my son."

"No, you don't, actually." She lifted her chin again as a sudden surge of confidence swept through her. "Remember how you disappeared just before Ethan was born? You weren't at the birth, and I didn't know if you were ever coming back. Your name isn't even on the birth certificate. That means you have no legal rights to him at all." She pointed to herself. "Besides, if you were so concerned about your son, you would have treated me with respect."

"I've changed. I'll make up for my mistakes." Trent held up his hands. "I told you. I got help and found a decent job."

"Good for you." She nearly spat the words at him.

He pulled his wallet from the back pocket of his jeans. "What if I gave you money? How much do you want?"

"You can't be serious!" Anger flooded her. "You want to buy your way into your son's heart?"

"No." He pulled out a wad of bills. "But I owe you for child support. How much do you want?"

"I don't want any of your money."

"Sure you do." Trent held out the cash, desperation lining his face. "How much?"

"You need to go." Mark sidled up to him.

Priscilla had been so focused on Trent that she hadn't even noticed Mark as he approached.

"You need to go right now." Mark opened the truck door and gestured for Trent to climb in. "Does Priscilla have your number?"

Trent nodded as he put the money back in his wallet. "My number hasn't changed."

Mark nodded. "Good. She'll call you if she decides to allow you to see Ethan. Now go before I make you go."

Trent climbed into the truck and slammed the door. Then he looked between Priscilla and Mark, his gaze finally landing on Mark. "You'd better watch out for her. She's not stable. She'll turn on you too." Then he started the engine and drove away.

Once the truck was out of sight, Priscilla released the breath she'd been holding.

Mark turned toward her, his eyes narrowed. "*Freind?* You told him I'm your *freind*?" Bitterness and frustration radiated off him in waves.

"Mark, please." She held up her hands. "I didn't want him to know any of my personal life."

"Why?" His scowl deepened. "Do I embarrass you?"

"No." She shook her head. "That's not it at all."

"Why didn't you tell him we're engaged?" He gestured toward the road. "Do you still love him?"

She paused, considering her feelings for Trent Parker. "No, but it's complicated."

"You hesitated." He wagged a finger at her. "So you do love him. You love the man who hit you, cut you, and scarred you."

"No, it's not that, but we have a *kind* together. We'll always be tied by Ethan. That's why I couldn't just send him away. You have to understand—"

He held up his hand. "Save it."

As Mark stomped off toward the barn, Priscilla felt frozen between two men and two worlds.

Mark's arms and shoulders throbbed with pain as he hammered another new board into the barn floor with all his might. His jaw ached as he continued to clench it.

The vision of Priscilla talking to Trent filled his mind as anger, raw and raging, drowned him. Why did she tell him Mark was only her friend? Was she hoping Trent would offer to take her and Ethan with him? If he had, would she have gone? Didn't their friendship and her promise to marry Mark mean anything to her?

"Mark!" Ethan scampered into the barn. "I brought you a present. I hope you like chocolate peanut butter ice cream." He stood tall as he held out a little bag.

The anger seemed to dissolve as Mark looked down at the little boy's proud smile. "*Danki.* That's my favorite flavor." He set the hammer and nails on the floor.

"I thought so. Here. Take it." Ethan shook the bag. "It might be melting."

Mark took the bag and opened it. He found a cup of ice cream with a lid and a spoon. "*Danki* for thinking of me."

"Of course I thought of you." Ethan scanned the barn. "Can I help you with the boards? You can show me how."

"You don't have to." Mark took a bite of ice cream, and it melted in his mouth.

"I thought I saw my dad's truck earlier." Ethan picked up the hammer as he spoke. "We were driving toward the farm, and I saw a red truck that looked just like my dad's. It was ahead of us, so I couldn't see who was driving it."

Mark stilled for a moment and then took another bite.

"I told *Mammi* and *Daadi* that it looked like his truck, but they didn't say anything." Ethan swung the hammer around.

"Don't do that," Mark said, warning him. "You might hit yourself in the head or drop it on your foot. Trust me. It hurts when you do that."

Ethan stopped swinging the hammer. "I was thinking about my dad. I wonder if he misses me. It's been a long time since I've talked to him."

"Do you miss him?" Mark took another bite of ice cream.

"Yeah, sometimes I do." Ethan nodded.

"Do you want to go back and live with him?" Mark knew he was probably overstepping his bounds, but he so wanted the boy to say no.

Ethan shook his head. "No, I like it here with you, *Mammi*, and *Daadi*."

"Why don't you want to live with him?"

"Because he's not nice to *mei mamm*. I don't like how he . . . talks to her." Ethan set the hammer on the floor and then looked at Mark again. "Will you be nice to her when we live with you?"

Mark nodded, hoping with all his heart that Ethan had never

seen his father physically abuse his mother. He didn't think so. "I promise I'll always be nice to your *mamm*."

"Good." Ethan picked up two nails. "Show me how to put the new boards on the floor."

"Let me finish my *appeditlich* ice cream first." Mark held up the spoon. "You want a taste?"

"I already tasted it." Ethan smirked.

"Did you really?"

"No, but I made you believe me!" Ethan cackled.

Mark grinned and pointed the spoon at him. "That was a *gut* one. You're learning." Then he poked Ethan's arm. He prayed Priscilla would never take Ethan away from him.

Priscilla stood by the entrance to her father's large barn. She fingered the skirt of her green dress and chewed her lower lip as she watched Mark kneel on the floor and hammer a new board into place.

His face was lined with frustration and maybe sadness as he worked. The pain in his eyes had haunted her as she and her mother planted flowers in the remaining hour or so before they had to start making their evening meal. She'd hoped he would come out of the barn and talk to her, but she hadn't seen him. The distance between them was tearing her apart, and she'd felt worse and worse as she'd made a meat loaf.

"Mark." Her words were muffled by the loud banging of the hammer echoing through the empty barn. "Mark!"

He stopped working, sat back on his heels, and looked up at her. His handsome face hardened with a frown as he lifted his straw hat and wiped his hand over his brow.

"Are you hungry?" She took a step into the barn. "It's almost suppertime."

"No, Ethan brought me ice cream a little while ago." He turned back to the floor and picked up more nails.

"Wait. I want to talk to you."

His shoulders hunched as he stared down at the floor.

"Please look at me." She walked over to him.

He kept his eyes focused on the floor. "What do you want?"

"I want to apologize and explain myself."

"There's nothing to explain. It's obvious you still love Trent, despite all he did to you." He looked up at her, and the disappointment in his eyes sent guilt spiraling through her.

"That's not true." Her voice sounded strained to her own ears. "When I met Trent, I was lonely, and I was desperate for someone to care about me. I was never *gut* enough in *mei daed*'s eyes, and Trent was the first man who paid attention to me. When we were in youth group, the *buwe* always looked at Laura and Savilla, but none of them gave me a second look. Maybe because I've always been so short or maybe because I wasn't as outgoing and *schee* as your *schweschder* and Savilla. It was as though I was invisible next to them."

Mark's eyebrows drew together as he scowled. "That wasn't true."

"No, it was true. I never felt special, and aside from *mei mammi* and *mei mamm*, I'd never felt anyone love me."

"I'm sure your *dat* loves you, even though he doesn't always treat you well."

She frowned. *You have no idea.*

"He does, Priscilla. He's your *daed*." Mark stood and brushed the dust off his dark trousers. "I know that with the bishop's help, he's forcing you to marry me, but you have to give him time. He's—"

She waved off his comment. "Please, let me finish. Trent

showed up at a time when I was at my lowest and feeling hopeless. He knew what to say to convince me that he cared about me, and I quickly fell for it."

Mark's expression darkened as his eyes locked with hers.

"I felt affection for him, but looking back, I'm not sure it was ever true love. He said he would take care of me, and I was too weak to take care of myself. And then I had Ethan. No matter what, I'll always be connected to Trent because of Ethan."

"Do you want to go back to Trent?" Mark asked, his voice sounding thin and reedy.

Priscilla was almost certain she heard a hint of worry in Mark's voice. Was he jealous of Trent? No, that couldn't be possible. Why would Mark be jealous of Trent when he didn't love her?

"No." She shook her head. "I would never go back to Trent. I don't love him, and I could never trust him after what he did to me." She opened her mouth and then closed it.

"What are you not telling me?"

"I don't know what to do. I don't trust him around Ethan, but he is Ethan's father."

"I don't want him around Ethan at all. If you're asking for my opinion, my answer is no." Mark's concern for Ethan warmed her heart. "Why don't you want Trent to know you're going to marry me?"

"I don't want him to know anything about my life since he's not a part of it anymore."

Mark looked unconvinced.

"That information felt too personal." She reached for him and then pulled her hand back. "I'm not embarrassed by you, Mark. I'm sorry if I hurt you."

He studied her for a moment, and then his frown waned. "I'm not perfect, but I will never hurt you or Ethan."

Her chest swelled with affection at the comment. He was burrowing in, digging in deep, and carving out a piece of her heart. But she didn't feel worthy of a man as good as he was.

"*Danki.*" She looked deep into his blue eyes. Had he forgiven her? "Why don't you come in and eat something? Ice cream is not a healthy meal, and you skipped lunch earlier because you were working so hard."

"No." He shook his head and pointed toward the far end of the barn. "I have plenty of boards to replace. I'll eat something later."

"Okay." She studied his face, hoping he would smile at her. A smile would let her know everything was okay.

But he didn't smile as he picked up the hammer and set to work. She watched him for a few beats and then headed back to the house.

TWENTY-ONE

"HOW'S THE SEWING GOING?" MARK LEANED AGAINST the doorframe of Priscilla's bedroom on Tuesday afternoon of the following week.

She looked up, and her breath stalled in her lungs. Mark's eyes seemed to be a brighter shade of blue, and he somehow seemed taller and more attractive. How did he do that?

She longed to tell him to leave so she could hold back her growing attraction to him. That was the reason she'd been using their conversation about Trent as an excuse to act cool around him.

"I'm sorry." He stepped inside her room and grinned. "Did I startle you?"

"No." She shook her head. "I'm just surprised to see you."

"Why?" He laughed. "You know I work here." He walked over and pointed to the half-finished dress on her sewing table. "So how's it going?"

"Pretty well." She shrugged. "I finished my second one yesterday." She held up the dress. "This will be Sarah Jane's."

"Nice." He touched the material. "You're talented."

"*Danki.*" She hoped he couldn't see her blushing. "Do you need something?"

"That's what I came to ask you." He sat on the chair across from her. "I have to go out for supplies. Do you need anything?"

She paused, and then said, "Would you mind stopping at the Bird-in-Hand Bake Shop?"

His eyes lit up, as if he were happy for the task. "No, not at all. What do you need?"

"I've been craving a large pretzel. Ethan likes them too."

"Okay." He nodded toward her sewing table. "Anything else? Like material or something else you need for the dresses?"

Her eyes moved to her material. She was running low, but did she want to risk sending him to Franey's store without her?

"What is it?" He leaned forward, resting his forearms on his thighs. "I can find it if you write it down. I'm not a complete moron. Just a partial one."

She turned toward him, and his smile widened. "Are you certain you're only partial?"

To her surprise, he laughed.

"What do you need?" he asked again.

"Material and a few more spools of thread. And a few other things. I need to make Ethan a new pair of church trousers since he fell and ripped his only pair." She picked up her notepad and began writing a list. "Everything will be on here."

"Okay." When she was done, he took the list and stood. "I'll be back soon with pretzels and supplies."

"*Danki.*"

He started toward the door.

"Mark."

"*Ya?*" He faced her in the doorway.

"Are you having second thoughts?"

"No, but if you keep asking me, I might develop some."

She gaped at him.

He laughed, and relief threaded through her.

"I'm kidding, so stop looking so worried." He waved at her. "I'll be back soon."

As he disappeared from the doorway, she hoped she hadn't made a mistake sending him off to Franey's father's store alone.

⸺ ᏩᎦᎵ ⸺

Mark stepped into the fabric store and glanced at the front counter.

When Sadie Liz spotted him, she lifted her hand and waved. "Hi, Mark! I'll be right with you." Then she turned back to the customer in front of her.

Mark wandered around, glancing at Priscilla's list and wondering how he was going to find all the items without help. Asking Priscilla if she needed anything had seemed like a great idea, but he was lost here. He'd rather pick up groceries than try to find his way around a fabric store.

But he'd had an ulterior motive when he went upstairs to check on her earlier today. Priscilla hadn't spoken to him longer than a few minutes since she'd asked him to stay for supper last Thursday and he'd declined. After their conversation in the barn, she'd been cool again, and the atmosphere between them had been strained. It was his fault. He'd had no real reason to assume she would ever go back to Trent.

But the damage had been done. Just yesterday he walked up on the porch while she hung out laundry and chatted about how nice the *daadihaus* looked with the fresh coats of paint. But she only nodded in response. The day before, he'd mentioned how excited Cindy and Sarah Jane were about the wedding, and Priscilla only smiled.

He'd never before had to work so hard to get a woman to talk to him, and this was the woman he was going to marry. That was why he'd used the offer of running errands as a lame excuse to spend a little bit of time with her. He was grateful she hadn't just given him a one-word response—"No."

"How may I help you?" Sadie Liz appeared beside him with a wide smile on her face.

"I need to get these supplies for Priscilla, but I have no idea where to begin." He handed her the list.

Sadie Liz examined the list and then nodded. "I can find all of this for you. I'll be back in a jiffy."

"*Danki.*" Mark spun the display of patterns a few times and then walked over to a wall of quilts.

After a few minutes he walked toward the back. When he heard Franey say his name, he stilled and listened to the conversation taking place in the next aisle.

"Oh *ya*," Sadie Liz said just loud enough for him to hear. "Mark is so handsome. He could have married any *maedel* in our community."

"That's true," Franey said with a sigh. "I thought for certain he was going to choose me."

"Why do you think he chose Priscilla?" Sadie Liz asked.

A beat went by, and Mark held his breath.

"Go ahead," Sadie Liz encouraged her. "Say what you're thinking. I can tell you want to."

"Well, she already had one *kind* with a man," Franey said. "Maybe they're expecting one together."

"You think she's pregnant?" Sadie Liz exclaimed.

Mark's blood boiled. Clenching his fists at his side, he forced a pleasant expression on his face and headed to the counter at the front of the store. Anger and disappointment swirled in his gut as he waited for Sadie Liz to appear with Priscilla's supplies.

When Franey emerged from a nearby aisle, she smiled, and he nodded a response as he shoved his hands into his pockets.

"Hi, Mark," Franey called as she approached.

"Hello." He hoped he sounded pleasant.

"I have all your supplies," she said as she stepped behind the counter. "You had quite a list."

"Well, Priscilla is busy working on the dresses for the wedding, and Ethan needs a new pair of church trousers." He pulled his wallet from his back pocket as she began ringing up the items.

Sadie Liz appeared beside Franey and began putting the items into bags.

"How's your day going?" Franey asked him.

"Fine. It's been busy." He rested his wallet on the counter. "There's a lot to do on Yonnie's farm. I just finished painting the *daadihaus* earlier this week. Now I'm cleaning the barn and replacing its rotten floor boards for the wedding."

"Oh." Franey's smile grew tight. She rang the last item and told him the price.

Mark handed her the money, and she gave him his change. "Well, I'd better get back to the farm." He smiled. "Priscilla is expecting me to bring her supplies and then a pretzel. She and Ethan love pretzels, and I'm *froh* to bring my future *fraa* the things she loves."

Franey's smile faded.

Sadie Liz nodded. "Oh, I'm certain you are."

"*Danki* for your help." Mark slipped his wallet into his back pocket.

"*Gern gschehne.*" Franey gave him a little wave.

"See you at church," Sadie Liz said.

Mark turned to go, and then he stopped and faced them. "Oh, and by the way, Priscilla and I *are* expecting."

The two women's eyes grew so wide he feared they might fall out of their heads.

"Well, aren't we all *expecting* a cold winter?" He narrowed his eyes. "You do know it's a sin to spread rumors, right? Especially when they're not true."

Franey's mouth dropped open.

Before they had a chance to respond, he stalked out of the store.

"Danki!" Ethan announced as Mark handed him the large pretzel in the kitchen. "This is the perfect afterschool snack."

"Gern gschehne." Mark placed the two bags of supplies on the counter.

"Danki so much." Priscilla came up behind him. "How much do I owe you?"

Mark rolled his eyes. "Please. We're going to share a bank account soon."

"I guess that's true." She turned to Ethan as he sat at the table and ate the pretzel. "How is it?"

"Wunderbaar," he responded with a mouthful.

"You need to swallow before you talk."

Ethan nodded and continued chewing.

"Here's yours." Mark handed her a large pretzel in a wrapper. "I hope it's still warm."

She took the pretzel and smiled. *"Ya,* it is. *Danki."*

He nodded, and she noted the tightness around his mouth. Something was bothering him. Had he seen Franey and regretted his decision to marry Priscilla?

"Is everything okay?" She braced herself for his response and possible rejection.

He nodded. *"Ya."*

"Did you see Franey at the store?"

A strange expression flashed over his features, and it stole her breath for a moment.

"*Ya*. She sends her regards." He jammed his thumb toward the door. "I need to finish unloading the supplies from my buggy. I'll see you later."

"Do you need help?" Ethan asked, his mouth full again.

"Ethan!" Priscilla snapped.

Ethan's shoulders hunched, and he looked down.

"No, but *danki*, Ethan. I've got it." Mark disappeared out the door, leaving her with doubts he'd told her everything there was to tell.

TWENTY-TWO

MARK TOOK A PAPERBACK FROM HIS BOOKSHELF AND ran his fingers over the cover the following Monday night. It was the last book *Mamm* gave him before she died. His eyes stung as he turned it over in his hand. She'd stopped at her favorite bookstore before grocery shopping one day, and when she saw the mystery novel sitting on the end of a display, she thought of Mark. She passed away only a week later, before he'd had a chance to start reading it.

He'd held on to the book since the day she gave it to him, but he couldn't bring himself to even open it. It was as if reading it would somehow erase her memory. It was a silly notion, but he couldn't push it out of his mind.

A knock drew his attention to the doorway of his bedroom where he found Cindy standing with an unsure expression on her face.

"May I come in?" She bit her lower lip.

"*Ya*, of course." He dropped the book into a nearby box. "I was just packing."

"I can't believe you're moving out tomorrow." She gestured at the sea of boxes.

"*Ya*, I know." He grinned. "I bet you thought this day would never come."

"No, I knew it was coming. You've been talking about building your own *haus* for a long time, and I had a feeling you'd wind up getting married first."

"Huh." He set two more books from the shelf into the box. "Why did you assume I'd get married first?"

She shrugged and picked up a softball from one of the boxes. "It was just a feeling I had. I guess since you kept saying you'd never get married, I assumed God had a different plan for you. It seems like his plans always take us by surprise."

"What do you mean?" Mark sat on his desk and faced her.

"It's difficult to explain." She turned the ball over in her hands as she spoke. "Jamie wasn't expecting to meet Kayla and fall in love with her when he did, and then Laura fell in love with Allen when she was trying to make things work with Rudy. God seems to know what's best for us when we think we already have it all figured out."

He nodded as her words soaked through his mind. "What about you?"

"What about me?" Her cheeks flushed. Cindy never seemed to enjoy being the center of attention.

"What do you think God has in store for you?"

"I don't know." She shook her head and looked down at one of his boxes as if avoiding his eyes. She dropped the softball into the box and then turned to the box of books beside it.

"Do you think you'll fall in love and get married like the rest of us, Cindy?"

"I don't know."

"Why not?"

She kept her eyes focused as she fished through the contents of the box.

"Cindy?" He stood. *"Was iss letz?"*

"Nothing's wrong." She looked at him and offered a forced

smile. "I'm just *froh* for you and Priscilla. You're a great couple, and you'll be *gut* together." Her fake smile disappeared. "I'm going to miss you. I'm going to be the last Riehl sibling here."

He sighed. "I know, but I won't be far, and neither is Laura. Jamie and Kayla are just down the path too. We're still family, and we'll see each other all the time." He studied her blue eyes, which seemed to sparkle in the glow of his lanterns. Was she going to cry? His shoulders tightened. He needed to lighten the mood—quick!

"Besides, you get my room since Roy decided to stay in his." He made a sweeping gesture. "You'll finally have your own space, and it's much bigger than the room you share with Sarah Jane."

She shook her head. "It won't be the same without you here." She swiped her fingers over her eyes. "You and Priscilla better come and visit often."

"We will." He paused for a beat as the question he'd longed to ask for years surfaced in his mind. "Do you think you'll ever join the church?"

Her eyes rounded for a fraction of a moment and then returned to normal size. "I don't know."

"It's because we lost her, right?"

She took a step back toward the door. "I should let you finish packing."

"Wait." He reached for her arm. "I didn't mean to upset you. Please don't leave."

She stilled, but her eyes seemed to glimmer with uneasiness.

"I miss *Mamm* too. She's always in the back of my thoughts," Mark admitted. "But you need to remember that she'd want us to move on."

"How?" Cindy's voice was tiny, as if she were six years old again.

"I don't know." He shrugged. "I guess we just keep praying for strength and then put one foot in front of the other. Our family has changed and grown, but we're still here. I'm going to marry Priscilla, but I'm still your *bruder*. Just like Jamie and Laura are still your siblings. You're never going to lose us."

"How do you know that?" A single tear traced down her pink cheek. "We lost *Mamm*."

Mark winced as if she'd rammed a stake into his heart. "I know, Cindy, but you can't live in fear. We have to just live." He touched her arm. "I'll be only a phone call away, okay?"

She nodded.

"Come here." He gave her a quick hug. "You're still my favorite youngest *schweschder*."

She laughed. "I'm your only youngest *schweschder*."

"Exactly." He grinned, grateful to see her smile.

She moved toward the door and then turned back. *"Gut nacht."*

"Gut nacht." He lifted his chin as if to wave. "Take *gut* care of my room."

"I will."

As she disappeared into the hallway, Mark hoped Cindy would someday feel comfortable enough to join the church and settle down. It broke his heart to see her still clinging to their mother's memory, but he understood the depth of her grief.

Only God could heal his baby sister's heart, and he prayed that someday soon God would.

"For a single guy, you sure have a lot of stuff," Jamie quipped as he set a box on the floor of the small living area of the *daadihaus* the following day.

"I don't have that much stuff. You just like to whine." Mark glanced around the room, taking in the sofa sitting in front of the fireplace hearth.

Across the room was a small kitchen area, including a table with four chairs. The two bedrooms, a utility room, and a bathroom were all just off the living area. This tiny house would be the home he'd share with Priscilla and Ethan until he and Yonnie began building a larger house. Somehow it already felt like home, which didn't make any sense. Perhaps it was because this would be *his* house. His first house with his new wife.

Mark swallowed against his suddenly parched mouth.

"You're going to be a husband and a *dat* in a little more than two weeks." Jamie looped his arm around Mark's shoulders. "Are you ready for this, little *bruder*?"

Mark rubbed his chin as anxiety filtered through him. "Sure I am. How hard can it be?"

Jamie's laugh was loud, and it annoyed Mark. He shook off his older brother's arm and stepped away from him.

"Can you two quit hugging and get the door?" Roy called as he stood outside the screen door with another box.

"Whoops! Sorry!" Mark rushed over and opened the door. *"Danki."*

"Where does this go?" Roy scooted past him.

"The bedroom." Mark skirted around him and opened the door to the larger bedroom with two dressers. A nightstand sat beside a queen-size bed. He had to ask Priscilla if she had sheets the right size since his sheets would only fit the bed in the other bedroom.

He kneaded the back of his neck as he surveyed the boxes scattered on the floor.

"Is there anything else in the trailer?" Jamie asked.

"No, that's about it." Roy held out his arms. "Do you want us to help you unpack?"

"Are you guys hungry?" Priscilla appeared in the bedroom doorway. She looked beautiful in her gray dress. She scanned the room. "You have a lot of stuff, Mark."

"See?" Jamie exclaimed.

"Don't encourage him," Mark snapped, and they all laughed.

"Come on." She beckoned them. "I made BLTs." Then she disappeared from the bedroom, and Mark heard the screen door close behind her.

"Let's unpack after we eat." Roy rubbed his flat abdomen. "I'm hungry." He headed out the door.

"I am too." Jamie followed him.

Mark sat on the corner of the bed, and it creaked under his weight. Tonight he would spend his first night in this house, a house that would be considered his.

His life was about to change. He shivered. Was he ready to be a husband and father? Did he have the strength and courage to care for a family?

"Hey, Mark!" Roy bellowed from outside. "I'm going to eat your BLT!"

"I'll be right there," Mark called.

He glanced around the bedroom one last time before heading out to meet his younger brother.

Priscilla bit into her BLT sandwich as she sat across from where Mark was sitting between his brothers.

Everyone laughed as Jamie shared a story about a cow named Sassy that learned how to open the gate and trot down the street to visit the neighbor's German shepherd.

"I think she believes she's a dog," Roy chimed in.

"*Ya*, I agree." Jamie chuckled.

Dat and *Mamm* laughed, and Priscilla smiled. It was good to see her father smile.

Priscilla's gaze locked with Mark's, and when he smiled, heat crawled up her neck to her cheeks. She'd never felt that kind of intensity when she was with Trent. Did it mean her feelings for Mark were more genuine and deep? No, that wasn't possible. She didn't know Mark as well as she knew Trent. She was only imagining the depth of her feelings for him.

"I have to meet this cow," Priscilla told Mark. "Would you please take me over to your *dat*'s farm sometime?"

"Sure." Mark picked up his glass of water. "That would be fun. I think Ethan would enjoy meeting Sassy too."

"How's the move going, Mark?" *Mamm* reached for another roll from a platter in the center of the long table.

"He has a lot of stuff," Roy quipped.

Mark groaned. "I'm so tired of hearing that. As if you didn't have a hundred boxes when you moved into *mei dat*'s *haus*."

"That wasn't just my stuff," Roy retorted. "If you remember, *mei mamm* and *schweschder* moved in too."

"So Cindy and Sarah Jane will have their own rooms now, right?" Priscilla asked.

Mark nodded. "Cindy is going to take my room. She's moving in today. That's why *mei dat* stayed home. He's helping her."

"She must be excited to have her own room," *Mamm* said.

Mark's expression darkened as he and Jamie shared a look.

"Oh. Did I say something wrong?" *Mamm* said.

"No." Mark shook his head. "Cindy just has conflicting feelings. I think she misses Jamie and Laura, and now I'm leaving . . ."

Priscilla's eyes stung as she thought of Mark's mom.

"Oh, I understand." *Mamm*'s expression was solemn. "I know you've all had a tough time since you lost your *mamm*. I'm sorry."

Mark looked down at his plate, and an awkward silence filled the kitchen. Priscilla longed to push back her chair, hurry around the table, and hug Mark to take away his pain.

Where had that come from?

"So," Jamie suddenly said, "are we going to help you unpack your boxes and organize your clothes too?"

Mark lifted an eyebrow. "You really want to organize my sock drawer?"

"Well, it's better than mucking stalls," Roy responded.

Everyone laughed, and the tension in the air dissolved.

When the bacon, lettuce, and tomato platters were empty, Priscilla and *Mamm* hopped up from the table and began clearing it.

"I made a chocolate *kuche* too," Priscilla announced as she filled one side of the sink with soapy water.

"You did?" Mark's face lit up. "For me?"

"Well, it's for everyone, Mark." She gave him a feigned pointed look. "You have to share."

He stuck out his lower lip. "Next time, just make one for me."

"If you eat the whole cake by yourself, you'll get fat," Roy said, and everyone laughed again.

"Let me help you." Mark stood. "I'll put on the *kaffi*."

"No, sit." Priscilla waved him off.

"I'm capable of putting on *kaffi*." He came up behind and reached over her head for the percolator.

"I can do it." She turned and bumped into his chest. She breathed in his familiar scent—earth and soap mixed with sandalwood—and his nearness sent a shivery wave over her skin.

Behind him, her father and Jamie became engrossed in a conversation. Trying to concentrate on anything but Mark, she caught something about training horses and how perhaps the techniques could help with the unruly cow.

Mark leaned down to her. "You need to realize I'm not going

to sit on my rear end and let you wait on me." His voice was close to her ear, and heat flooded her senses. "Got it?"

Unable to speak, she nodded.

"*Gut.*" His lips twitched. "So show me where the *kaffi* is."

"Okay." She pointed to the cabinet, and he withdrew the can before setting up the percolator.

As she turned toward the counter to get the cake saver, she looked at her mother, who gave her a knowing smile. Priscilla felt her brow furrow. What was *Mamm*'s expression supposed to mean?

"So about that *kuche.*" Mark rubbed his hands together. "Let's see if it's as *gut* as Laura's."

"What?" Priscilla snapped, and he laughed.

"If it's not, then you'll have to make me another one." Mark took the cake saver and set it on the table.

"We'll see about that." She smiled as she gathered plates, utensils, and a knife to cut the cake.

As she set everything on the table, her thoughts moved to Trent once again. She couldn't recall a time when she'd felt so comfortable joking around with him the way she and Mark teased each other. Perhaps this marriage would be easier than she'd imagined.

Still, doubt made her ask a question she couldn't let go. How would they adjust to living together if they weren't in love?

Priscilla balanced a plate of chocolate chip cookies as she descended the porch steps and walked toward the *daadihaus* later that evening. Above her the sunset painted the sky in canary yellow and tangerine.

Ethan's laugh filled the air as she started up the path. Priscilla turned and spotted Mark and Ethan playing catch with a softball.

"That's right." Mark pointed. "Just toss it a little higher."

Ethan stuck out his tongue as if in deep concentration before tossing it to Mark, who caught it with ease.

"Perfect!" Mark smiled, and it lit up his handsome face. "*Gut* job. Try it again." He tossed it back, and Ethan caught it. "Great! You're getting the hang of this."

Priscilla's heart felt like it tripped over itself. She couldn't recall a time when Trent had showed Ethan how to play any sport, aside from sitting in front of a video game console.

"Cookies!" Ethan announced when he spotted Priscilla. "Are those the oatmeal raisin ones you made earlier?"

"Oh no." Mark shook his head as he held up the ball. "She made those for me." He pointed to himself.

"No." Ethan laughed. "She made them for me."

"Actually," Priscilla chimed in, "I made them for everyone, but you have to wash your hands before you can have any." She waved toward the *daadihaus*. "Go on. Wash your hands."

Ethan jogged through the grass and into the house as Mark sidled up to her.

"Just admit it." He swiped a cookie from the plate. "You made them for me."

"You need to wash your hands." She swatted his arm, and he laughed before taking a bite.

"Oh, Priscilla." He groaned. "These are fantastic. You can make them for me every day for the next twenty years."

"Remember what Roy said." She wagged a finger at him. "You'll get fat."

"I don't care. I'll be fat and *froh*." He took another bite.

She couldn't stop her laugh. "That's nice of you to teach Ethan how to play catch."

"He said he likes school, but he's a little intimidated with how much softball they play. You remember how much softball we played in school." He slowed when they reached the porch steps. "I thought I'd give him a few pointers on throwing and catching. We'll work on hitting the ball later. I don't want him to feel embarrassed."

She smiled as Mark went inside, and appreciation filled her. Mark truly cared about her son.

"I want a cookie!" Ethan charged out of the house and grabbed one from the plate.

"Slow down." Priscilla said, warning him. "You'll get a stomachache."

Ethan took a bite and then pointed toward the field behind her parents' house. "*Daadi* said that's where he's going to build our *haus*."

Priscilla nodded and turned to Mark when he came back and took another cookie from the platter. She tried to imagine a two-story brick house standing behind her parents' house. It seemed like a foreign concept. When she left, she never imagined coming home and living on her parents' farm.

"Do you want to see my room?" Ethan grabbed her arm.

"What?" Priscilla asked.

"We talked about living in the *daadihaus* earlier," Mark explained. "He helped me finish unpacking."

"Oh," she said before Ethan yanked her toward the porch steps, causing her to teeter.

"Don't knock your *mamm* over," Mark said with a smile. "I don't want her to drop *mei kichlin*."

"They're not all yours," Ethan said, and Mark laughed.

Priscilla followed Ethan into the house, and she spotted a mountain of empty boxes sitting by the hearth.

"I'm going to take all those out tomorrow," Mark said, appearing behind her. "I was just storing them there overnight."

Ethan pulled her into the spare bedroom, which included

a double bed, a dresser, and a nightstand. "This is going to be my room."

"Wow." She forced a smile while wondering how to tell him he wasn't going to sleep alone here. "It's very nice."

"When can I move in?" The smile on his face was as wide as she'd ever seen there.

"Not until after the wedding."

"Oh." His smile faded.

"It's only a couple of weeks away, though." Priscilla held out the plate of cookies. "Why don't you take another one?"

"Okay." Ethan swiped a cookie from the plate and then headed back outside.

"If you'd like to see more of the other bedroom, too, go ahead," Mark told her.

Priscilla put the tray of cookies on the kitchen counter and then stepped into Mark's room. The bed was made with the blue sheets she'd given him, along with a gray, white, and blue lone star quilt. She ran her fingers over the quilt, silently marveling at the beauty and skill sewn into it. Who had made this for him—perhaps his mother or grandmother?

"Cindy gave it to me last Christmas."

She gasped and turned toward the doorway.

"I didn't mean to startle you." Mark stepped into the room.

"It's so *schee*." She touched the quilt again. "She's talented."

"She is."

Priscilla's gaze moved to the corner of the room, where she spotted a box with pieces of wood sticking out of it. She stepped over and picked up a flat piece of wood with a carving of a tree on it. She ran her fingers over the tree and silently marveled at the detail. The tree had leaves and a complete root system under the trunk. It was beautiful.

"I meant to leave that box in *mei dat*'s attic," Mark said. "I'm going to take it over there when I go back."

She looked up at Mark. "Did you make this?"

He shrugged. "*Ya*. It's not very *gut*."

"It *is* very *gut*." She took in his sheepish expression. "When did you start carving wood?"

"I've always done it as sort of a hobby. *Mei daadi* showed me how when I was little. He gave me a set of tools before he passed away, but I've lost a few of the chisels. One of these days I might buy another set, but I really don't have time to carve anymore."

She looked down at the box and flipped through more of his creations, finding a carved picture of a barn and one of a bird. Each one was so detailed, they were lifelike.

"These are incredible. You're so talented." She ran her fingers over the image, as admiration for him rolled through her. "You need to make time to keep doing this. Don't take the box to your *dat*'s."

"Why?"

"These are great. You should keep them, and maybe someday you can teach Ethan how to carve. I think he'd like that."

"Okay."

She set the carvings back into the box and then turned toward him.

He sank onto the corner of the bed and ran his hand over the quilt. "*Danki* for the sheets."

"It's no big deal. I'm glad I found a set that fit this bed." She glanced around the room and suddenly wondered where she would keep her clothes. Would she change in Ethan's room or in here? No, in the bathroom. She trembled at the thought of their wedding night. She'd already told him she would sleep in Ethan's room, but would he insist otherwise?

"What's on your mind?" he asked.

She hoped her expression wouldn't betray her private thoughts as she met his curious eyes.

"You can have this room," he said. "The sofa isn't all that uncomfortable."

"I don't expect you to sleep on the sofa after working hard on the farm all day." She shook her head. "I just have to figure out how to tell Ethan that I'm staying with him." *And then pray he doesn't tell everyone I'm not sleeping with his stepfather.*

"That's why it would be easier if I slept on the sofa and then got up before he did."

She shook her head. "You deserve the bed in here. I'll make do until our new *haus* is built."

He lifted his eyebrows. "Have you always been this stubborn?"

"You know the answer to that." She looked out the window to avoid getting lost in the depths of his gorgeous blue eyes. "I'll just have a talk with Ethan the night before the wedding and explain to him that sometimes *freinden* get married and have separate bedrooms." She hoped Ethan wouldn't ask why she didn't have a separate bedroom when they lived with Trent.

"If that's what you want." Mark sounded resigned.

No, it wasn't what she wanted in a marriage, but it would have to work. Doubt threatened to drown her.

"Mark," she began as she turned to him. "Are you sure—?"

"Really, Priscilla?" He stood. "Do you know how furious *mei bruders* will be if I have to ask them to move all this back to *mei dat's haus*? You heard how much they complained about all my stuff."

She laughed.

His expression became tender. "You have a great smile. I wish I could make you smile more."

She gaped as he turned and left the bedroom.

TWENTY-THREE

THE NEXT DAY MARK HEARD THE PHONE RINGING in Yonnie's office as he stepped into the barn. He hurried in and picked up the receiver.

"Allgyer's Belgian and Dutch Harness Horses," he began. "This is Mark. How may I help you?"

"I'm trying to reach Priscilla Allgyer," a woman's voice said. "Do I have the right number?"

"*Ya*, you do. May I ask who's calling?"

"My name is Tammy Larson, and I'm a social worker at Lancaster General Hospital." The woman hesitated, and dread pooled in the pit of Mark's gut. "I have her son, Ethan, here."

"What?" Mark gripped the receiver with such force that he thought it might break in his hand. "Why is Ethan there?"

"May I ask your relationship to the child?"

"I'm going to be his stepfather," Mark explained. "I'm engaged to his mother. My name is Mark Riehl."

"You're Mark," she said, recognition sounding in her voice. "Ethan mentioned you. Ethan has been in an accident, but he's going to be okay."

"I don't understand." Mark heard his voice echo around the room as it raised a notch. "How was he in an accident?"

"Ethan was walking home from school, and a Mr. Parker, who says he's Ethan's father, convinced him to get into his truck with him."

"Trent." Mark spat out the name as fury burned through his veins.

"Mr. Parker has admitted he'd been drinking. He hit a parked car. Someone called an ambulance, and it brought them both here."

"How is Ethan?" Mark asked, his anger mixing with worry for the boy.

"He's sore." She hesitated. "He seems to have hurt his arm, and I think he's going to need some stitches. Also, I think he'll be bruised from the seat belt. Is his mother home?"

"Yes, she is," Mark said. "Tell Ethan we'll be there as soon as we can."

"Thank you," Tammy said.

Without another word, Mark hung up the phone and ran toward the house.

⟡

"Priscilla!" Mark yelled.

Priscilla stilled, and the sewing machine stopped. She took in the frantic thread in Mark's voice as his boots clomped their way up the stairs to her bedroom.

"What?" She jumped up from her sewing table and met him in the hallway.

"We have to go." His eyes were wide as he worked to catch his breath. "We have to leave now."

"Where are we going?" She searched his face for an explanation as her heart began to thump. Something was wrong.

"Everything is going to be fine, but we have to leave for the hospital. Your *dat*'s driver is on his way."

"I don't understand. Why are we going to the hospital?"

He hesitated.

"Tell me!" she begged him.

"Ethan is fine, but he was in an accident." His words were measured.

"What?" Her voice broke as her pulse galloped with fear. "What happened?"

"Just come with me." He took her hand and tugged her toward the stairs.

"Tell me what happened." She squeezed his hand and yanked him back.

"I'll tell you in the car." Mark held on to her hand and led her down the stairs.

Tears began to pour from her eyes as visions of horrible accidents swirled through her mind. Had he been hurt on the playground or been hit by a car while walking home from school? The possibilities were endless, and the anticipation was quickly eating away at her soul.

"What happened to Ethan?" Priscilla demanded when they reached the bottom step. She tugged at his hand and pulled him toward her. "Mark, tell me!"

Mamm appeared in the kitchen doorway, her dark eyes wide with concern. "What's going on?"

"Ethan is fine," Mark began slowly, "but he was in an accident, and a social worker called from the hospital. Your driver should be here soon to take us there."

Mamm clutched her chest. "What happened?"

Mark took a deep breath, and his body shook. He was visibly upset, and that knowledge sent alarm spiraling through Priscilla. She gripped his hand tighter.

"Apparently Trent lured Ethan into his truck when he saw Ethan walking home from school." Mark's expression grew stony as Priscilla gasped. "Trent had been drinking, and he hit a parked car. Ethan is fine according to the social worker, although he's going to be sore. She said he might have hurt his arm and he needs some stitches. He's also bruised from the seat belt, but he's okay." He peered out the window. "Warren is here. Let's go." He nudged Priscilla toward the door.

"I'm coming with you," *Mamm* insisted. "Let me just tell your *dat*."

Priscilla hurried into the hospital room behind the nurse, her heart feeling as if it might beat out of her rib cage. She'd spent the drive to the hospital vacillating between fury at Trent and worry for Ethan's well-being.

When they finally arrived at the hospital, she had practically run to the front desk and asked for Ethan. She was grateful that a nurse took her, Mark, and her mother back to see him immediately instead of forcing them to worry in the waiting room.

She blew out a puff of air when she found Ethan sitting on the edge of an exam table, staring up at cartoons on a television set as a young woman sat in a nearby chair. His right arm was in a sling, and a large bandage, stained with bright-red dots, covered his little forehead.

"Mamm!" Ethan exclaimed.

"Ethan!" Priscilla hurried over to him. "How are you?"

"My arm hurts, and my head hurts too."

"I'm Tammy, the one who called you," the young woman said as she walked over and shook Priscilla's hand. She looked to be in her midtwenties. "You must be Miss Allgyer."

"Ya." She pointed to Mark. "This is my fiancé, Mark, and my mother, Edna."

Tammy said hello to them.

Mark shook her hand. Then his expression clouded with a frown. "Where's Trent?"

"He's in another room." Tammy nodded toward the doorway. "He's receiving treatment, and the police are going to interview him. They'd like to talk to you as well, Miss Allgyer."

"What happened?" Priscilla turned toward Ethan.

Ethan grimaced. "I was walking home with *mei freinden*, and Dad pulled up next to us. He said he had permission from you to pick me up and take me out for ice cream."

Mark came to stand beside Priscilla, and she could feel the rage coming off him in waves.

Priscilla shook her head. "I never gave him permission to pick you up." Her voice vibrated with anger. She felt a hand on her back and turned toward Mark, who gave her a reassuring expression, as if to calm her.

"I didn't know," Ethan said, his voice cracking. "I thought it was okay."

"It's not your fault." Mark's voice remained even despite his deep frown. "Go on."

"Well, Dad seemed kind of weird," Ethan continued. "His words sounded funny, like they used to sometimes. I asked him if he was okay, and he said he was."

"He was drunk," Priscilla whispered.

"Well, he smelled funny like when he used to drink beer. Then he couldn't drive very well. He was swerving, like this." Ethan pretended he was steering a car with his left hand, and he leaned a little to the right, grimaced, and then leaned to the left. "I started getting scared because he wasn't staying on the right side of the road." His lower lip quivered, and his dark eyes filled with tears.

"It's okay." Priscilla rubbed his back, her heart breaking when he sniffed. "Keep going." She glanced at Mark, and he shook his head. Beside him, *Mamm* sat in a chair and wiped her eyes with a tissue.

"And then he hit a car," Ethan continued, his voice shaking. "The crash was so loud, and I was so scared. My arm hit the door hard, and then the window broke and glass flew into my head."

Ethan shouldn't have even been in a truck without a child's seat to restrain him, let alone in a front seat. When he dissolved in tears, Priscilla gathered him into her arms and fought back her own tears.

"It's okay, Ethan," Priscilla whispered into his dark hair. "You're safe now, and I won't let anyone hurt you again."

"I won't either." Mark was beside her in an instant, and he patted Ethan's left arm. "I'll keep you safe."

Priscilla looked up into Mark's sky-blue eyes and felt such appreciation. He was the father Ethan needed, no matter how make-believe their marriage was.

Mark turned to Tammy. "Will the police charge Trent?"

Tammy nodded toward the doorway. "Could I please speak to you outside?"

Mark gave her a nod, and then turned to Priscilla. "I'm going to step outside with her."

"I want to come with you," she said.

"Go." *Mamm* stepped over to her with a box of tissues. "I'll stay with him." She stood beside Ethan and wiped his eyes with a tissue. "You're safe now, Ethan. We're with you, okay?"

Ethan nodded. "Yeah. I know."

Priscilla walked out into the hallway with Mark and Tammy. Tammy pulled the curtain closed, giving Ethan privacy and blocking his view of them. Then she pointed to a treatment room across the hall. A tall police officer stood outside of it.

"The police are going to ask if you want to bring charges

against Mr. Parker," Tammy said as she looked at Priscilla. "No matter what, he'll be charged with driving under the influence and child endangerment. Pardon me for asking this, but does he have any legal rights to Ethan?"

"No." Priscilla shook her head. "His name isn't even on Ethan's birth certificate."

"Okay. I'm glad to hear that because of his past behavior. In my opinion Mr. Parker is not a safe person. He should never be alone with Ethan."

"How do you know about his past behavior?" Priscilla asked.

"Ethan admitted he's aware that his father drinks and that he's been violent with you. He told me what Mr. Parker did to your arm."

Priscilla gaped. "I never told him about my arm, and I always try to keep it covered."

Tammy offered her a sad smile. "Miss Allgyer, children are more observant than you realize. He probably heard a conversation, saw your arm at some point, and then connected the dots. Plus, he mentioned to me that Mr. Parker made you cry often. He's aware of what went on in your home."

Priscilla nodded as a crippling guilt rained down on her. Her attempts to protect Ethan from his father's abusive behavior had failed.

"It's up to you if you want to bring charges against him since he didn't have permission to take Ethan," Tammy continued. "He has no legal right to the child, and it's evident that he's been abusive to you and harmful to Ethan."

Priscilla nodded as confusion nearly overcame her. Should she ask the police to charge Trent even though it was against her church's beliefs to bring charges against someone? But this was her son. Trent had clearly put Ethan in danger, and the consequences could have been much worse. What if Trent had hit another vehicle head-on? Ethan could have been hurt much worse or even . . .

She swallowed a sob as it bubbled up in her throat.

"Hey." Mark's voice was close to her ear. "I want to talk to you before we see Trent."

"Okay." She took a deep breath and pulled herself together.

Mark turned to Tammy. "I need a minute with Priscilla before we see Trent."

"Okay." Tammy nodded and motioned to the treatment room across the hallway, where the police officer continued to stand guard.

"As I indicated, Mr. Parker is in there," she said. "I'll give you a few minutes to talk to him. Also, the doctor needs your permission to treat Ethan. She wants to take an X-ray of his arm to be sure he has no fractures, and she also needs to stitch his forehead. I'll get her for you."

"Thank you," Priscilla said before she walked away. Then she turned to Mark. The seriousness in his expression caught her off guard for a moment. His face had contorted into a deep frown, and his blue eyes shined as if they were full of tears. His posture was straight, and his hands were balled into fists. He looked as if he might snap into a rage or cry at any second. She'd never seen him so emotional. "What do you want to discuss?"

"Tammy said it's your choice if you want to bring additional charges against him." Mark glanced around the hallway and then lowered his voice. "What if you tell Trent you won't press charges if he promises to stay away from us from now on, and if he doesn't try to stop me from adopting Ethan?"

Speechless, Priscilla stared up at Mark for a moment. "You want to adopt Ethan?"

"*Ya*, if you'll allow me to." His expression held what looked like hope or longing. "I meant it when I told Ethan I would protect him. I want to be his father, for real."

Her heartbeat sputtered. "*Ya*, he needs you." *And I do too.*

"*Gut*." His gaze moved to the treatment room where Trent was and then back to her. "Do you want me to do the talking? Or do you want to handle it?"

She swallowed. "I think we can both talk. We'll see how it goes."

"Are you okay?" His gaze seemed affectionate as he touched her cheek. She leaned into the gentle caress and pulled strength from him.

"*Ya*, I think I will be. I'm glad you're here." The words tumbled out of her mouth without any forethought.

"I promise we'll get through this," he said.

Mark threaded his fingers with hers, and together they walked to the treatment room. Priscilla squared her shoulders as they approached the officer, who held up his hand to stop them.

"May I help you?" the officer asked.

"My name is Priscilla Allgyer. I'm Ethan Allgyer's mother." Priscilla motioned toward Mark. "This is my fiancé, Mark Riehl. I want to speak to Trent Parker about what he did to my son."

The officer looked between Priscilla and Mark and then nodded. "Go ahead."

"Thank you." Mark released her hand and then touched her back. "We won't be long."

Priscilla pushed back the curtain and stood up taller as her gaze fell on Trent. He sat on another exam table with a bandage above his right eye. An angry, purplish bruise trailed down the right side of his face.

Trent looked at her and Mark, and his lips pursed. He hit a button on a remote control, muting the sound on the television, and then he turned toward them. "I guess you're here to yell at me." He blew out a deep sigh. "I was wrong, and I'm sorry."

Priscilla marched over to him as fury boiled inside her. "That's all you have to say?" She gestured widely. "You lied to my son, told him you had permission to take him, and promised him ice cream. And then you drove drunk with him in your truck and hit a parked vehicle?" Her voice rose. "Now he needs an X-ray on his arm because it could be broken, and he needs stitches on his forehead. There's no excuse for this! I'm thankful he's here to tell me the story."

"I have the right to see him." Trent's eyes narrowed. "He's my son too."

"No, you have no legal right to him," Priscilla snapped. "You're not legally his father. He doesn't have a legal father."

"But that will change soon enough." Mark joined her at the bed, his expression grave.

Trent divided a look between Priscilla and Mark. "What does that mean?"

"It means we have a proposition for you," Mark said. "You're in a lot of trouble. Not only did you drink and drive, but you hurt a young, innocent boy. The social worker told Priscilla she has a right to bring more charges against you."

"Is that so?" Trent snorted. "How can you charge me?"

"You didn't have permission to take Ethan. The police know you've been abusive in the past to both Ethan and Priscilla, and apparently, that's enough to charge you with kidnapping and child endangerment." Mark turned to Priscilla. "Do you want to tell him?"

Priscilla nodded. "If you agree to stay away from Ethan and us from now on, and you don't challenge Mark's plan to adopt Ethan, we won't press charges."

Trent swallowed and then paused for a moment as if

contemplating their offer. Then his eyes focused on Priscilla. "So I guess this means you're marrying this guy?"

"*Ya*, I am." She raised her chin. "We're getting married next week. Mark wants to adopt Ethan, and he'll be the best father Ethan could ever ask for. You're a danger to my son, and I want you to stay away from him."

Trent's expression fell. "I did make a huge mistake. I never should have gotten behind the wheel today." He looked toward the television, and his eyes seemed to mist over. "Can I write to him later? Maybe in a few years?"

Priscilla looked at Mark. "What do you think?"

Mark shrugged. "You can keep the letters for him, and then Ethan can decide when he's older if he wants to read them and respond." His eyes narrowed. "But Trent can't have any other contact with him. No phone calls and no visits."

Priscilla nodded. "I agree." She turned back to Trent. "Will you agree to this?"

"Yeah." Trent nodded. "I won't stand in Mark's way to adopt him."

"Thank you." A weight lifted off Priscilla, and she touched Mark's arm. "We'll be in touch."

"All right," Trent said.

Priscilla and Mark started toward the doorway.

"Priscilla," Trent called, and she looked over her shoulder at him. "For what it's worth, I am sorry."

"Maybe so, but you'll never have another chance to do something like this again," Mark snapped before pushing back the curtain and gesturing for Priscilla to step through the doorway first.

As she and Mark stepped out into the hallway, she could feel to the depth of her bones that Mark would be the father Ethan needed and deserved.

—◦✕◦—

"How's Ethan?" *Dat* asked as Priscilla stepped into the kitchen later that evening. He was sitting at the table eating a cookie with a glass of milk.

"He's fine. He's sleeping," she said as she filled a glass with water. "Like *Mamm* told you, he didn't break his arm, but he sprained it, and he has to wear the sling for a couple of weeks. He says the stitches in his forehead are tender, but the doctor said the pain should subside in a few days. He's going to be sore for a while, but all in all, it could have been much worse. I'm grateful God protected him."

Every bone in her body ached after spending the rest of the afternoon at the hospital. She was grateful to have Ethan home and fed. After a bath and a story, he'd fallen asleep.

She was also grateful he'd at least worn a seat belt, and she was even more grateful to have Mark with her during the harrowing experience. He never left her side when they met with the social worker and police or when they brought Ethan home. He'd stayed until Ethan finished his supper, and then he'd gone to the *daadihaus* and promised to see him the next morning.

As soon as they were married, they'd obtain the paperwork for Mark to adopt Ethan. Then they would be a family for real. The notion sent a strange heat through her. Mark seemed to truly love her son.

"How could you allow that to happen to Ethan?"

Priscilla spun toward her father. "What?"

"How could you allow Trent to put Ethan in danger like that?"

"Why are you blaming me for Trent's behavior?" She set her glass on the counter and then stared at him with disbelief. "Trent is the one who lured Ethan into his truck with the promise of ice cream. He lied to Ethan and told him I approved of the visit. I don't see how that's my fault."

Something inside her shattered, and she rolled up the sleeve of her dress to reveal her ugly scars. "Would you like to see what Trent did to me?" She stepped over to him and held out her arm. "He did this one night when he was drinking. He didn't think I'd brought home enough money in tips, and he threw a beer bottle at me."

Dat's eyes rounded as his mouth dropped open.

"Would you like to know why I finally left him?" she asked, her voice sounding more confident than she felt.

He nodded.

"I decided it was time to get *mei sohn* away from him when I came home from work and found Ethan alone. Trent had gone out drinking with his buddies." She pulled her sleeve down over her arm. "That was when I knew it was time to leave, before Trent's behavior became even more erratic and Ethan was in even more danger. So tell me how Trent's behavior is somehow my fault. I was the one who got Ethan away from him."

She took a deep breath as her confidence blossomed and surged through her. "Do you know why I left here and wound up with Trent?"

"Because you couldn't stand to be Amish," *Dat* scoffed.

"No. It was because of you." She wiped away a furious tear. "It was because of how you constantly criticized me and belittled me. I thought I had to get away from here before you broke me. But you didn't break me, and neither did Trent. Neither of you was able to suffocate my spirit despite everything you put me through."

Dat blinked.

She nodded in the direction of the *daadihaus*. "Did Mark tell you he's going to adopt Ethan?"

Dat shook his head. "He didn't."

"*Ya*, he is. He's going to be Ethan's legal father. Trent's name isn't on Ethan's birth certificate, so he has no legal right to him. Still, we told Trent that if he agreed to stay away from us forever and not interfere with the adoption, we won't press charges against him."

"That was a *gut* decision," *Dat* said, and Priscilla bit back her shock at his compliment.

"I thought so too." She set her glass in the sink. "I'm going to bed. *Gut nacht.*"

Before her father could respond, Priscilla dragged herself up the stairs to her bedroom. The weight of her fatigue pressed down on her shoulders as she changed into a nightgown and crawled into bed.

As the events of the terrifying day echoed through her thoughts, she opened her heart and prayed.

Thank you, God, for keeping Ethan safe. Please continue to keep him safe in the days to come.

Then she closed her eyes and allowed exhaustion to pull her into a deep sleep.

TWENTY-FOUR

MARK PUSHED THE PORCH SWING INTO MOTION WITH his toe and breathed in the warm September evening air a week later. Tomorrow his life would change forever. He'd become a married man, and Priscilla would take his name. Soon after that Ethan would officially be his son. Just a short time ago, he'd told Jamie he wasn't ready for marriage or children, and now he would have both.

How had life changed so quickly?

When a horse and buggy came up the driveway, Mark stopped the swing. Were Priscilla or her parents expecting company?

The horse halted, and when his father climbed out of the buggy, Mark felt alarmed. Did *Dat* need help? But why would he come all the way over here when Roy and Jamie both lived on his farm?

Mark hurried down the porch steps and up the path, thankfully noting that his father didn't look worried or upset. "Hi, *Dat*. Do you need something?"

"*Ya*, I need to visit you." *Dat* smiled as he tied the horse to a hitching post.

"Oh." Mark pointed toward the *daadihaus*. "Come on over."

"Great." *Dat* patted Mark on the shoulder as they walked together. "You look *gut*."

"*Danki.*" Mark raised a curious eyebrow. "You haven't seen *mei haus* yet. Come on in."

They climbed the steps together, and Mark welcomed *Dat* into his home.

"So this is it." Mark gestured around the small family room. "This is the *schtupp* and the kitchen." He pointed to the doors. "We have two bedrooms and a small bathroom. And there's a utility room over there for the wringer washer. Yonnie is going to build us a bigger *haus*. He said we can break ground in the spring."

"This is *schee.*" *Dat* walked over to the hearth and touched one of the candles Priscilla had put there as a decoration last week. "A fireplace."

"*Ya.* Priscilla said her *mammi* wanted one." Mark smiled as he thought of the surprise gift he planned to give her tomorrow after the wedding.

"Very nice and homey." *Dat* smiled at him. "It's a *schee* night. Why don't we sit on the porch?"

"Okay." Mark gestured toward the kitchen. "Would you like a glass of water?"

"No, *danki.* I'm fine."

On the porch Mark sat on the swing and *Dat* sat beside him in a rocking chair.

"How's Ethan doing?" *Dat* asked.

Mark's body tensed as he recalled the ordeal Ethan endured the week before. "He's better. The stitches were removed from his forehead on Monday, and the doctor said the scar won't be noticeable. His arm is much better. He wants to stop using the sling, but the doctor says he'll need to wear it at least another week. His bruises are looking better, and he seems to be okay emotionally."

Mark paused before going on. "We've talked about it, and he understands that he didn't do anything wrong. Trent was wrong to lie to get him into the truck, and to drink and then get behind the wheel." He gritted his teeth. "I can't fathom how Trent thought that was okay."

Dat shook his head. "Sometimes people make really stupid decisions. We just have to pray Trent gets the help he needs and never hurts anyone again."

"*Ya.*" Mark nodded and settled back on the swing. A comfortable silence fell between them for a few moments.

"It's not supposed to rain before Sunday," *Dat* finally said. "I think tomorrow is going to be the perfect fall day."

Mark turned toward his father as curiosity gripped him. "Okay, *Dat.* Why are you really here?"

Dat smiled as he looked over at him. "I was surprised when you announced you were getting married. I was certain you'd be a bachelor until you were at least forty."

Mark guffawed. "So you didn't think I'd marry one of my eager *maed*, as Priscilla calls them?"

Dat shook his head. "I knew all along they weren't the *maed* for you."

"Okay." Mark nodded. "And Priscilla?"

Dat leveled his gaze, the humor evaporating from his face. "I know the truth."

"Jamie told you." Mark frowned.

Dat nodded.

Mark sighed as his shoulders deflated. "I should have known," he muttered. Why had he trusted his older brother? He should have trusted only his twin.

"Don't be angry with Jamie. I had suspected something more was going on. I asked him, and he told me the truth." *Dat's* expression filled with concern. "I wish you had told me."

"So you think I'm making a mistake, and you came over here to try to talk me out of it."

"No, but I'm concerned."

"Why?" Mark hated the thread of doubt that still coiled low in his gut.

"Do you love her?"

Mark rested his elbows on his thighs as he threaded his fingers together. "I'm not sure."

"*Sohn*, I'm not going to lie to you or sugarcoat it," *Dat* began. "Marriage takes patience and compromise. Some days are easier than others. Your *mamm* and I had some challenging times. When the farm had a tough year and money was tight, we took our frustrations out on each other. Some days we hardly spoke, and your *mamm* was so angry with me that she locked herself in our bedroom while she cried."

Dat got a faraway look in his eyes, as if he were clearly seeing those days with Mark's mother. "At times we argued about the *kinner*. She'd tell me I was too tough on you and your *bruder*, and then I'd tell her she spoiled you both." He turned toward Mark and smiled. "Do you remember the time you and Jamie went fishing and came home soaked and covered in mud?"

Mark laughed. "*Ya*, I do. I think I was eight and Jamie was twelve. I had fallen into the pond, and Jamie came in after me. He was afraid I was going to drown."

"You two came into the *haus* and got mud all over the kitchen. Your *mamm* was furious about the mess." *Dat* grinned. "She was even angrier with me because I laughed."

They both broke into cackles, and Mark wiped at his wet eyes.

"Oh, we had some *gut* times." *Dat* sighed. "And we had some tough times, but we got through it because we loved and respected each other." He shook his head. "Florence and I are older, and we've both been married before. So we're more patient than you young folks tend to be. But we disagree at times too."

Mark looked toward Yonnie's house as he tried to imagine what his marriage would be like.

"You have to learn to compromise," *Dat* continued. "A *gut* marriage takes work. The marriage will be *froh* only if you respect Priscilla and are patient with her. Sometimes you won't agree." He paused. "Normally I would have told you all this shortly after you announced your engagement, *sohn*, but I think my suspicions held me back. When Jamie told me the truth today, I decided to come. You and Priscilla have a unique challenge."

Mark rubbed his chin, which would soon be covered in a sprouting beard.

Dat wagged a fat finger at him. "The most important advice is don't go to bed angry. If you do that, your anger will fester overnight, and it will be much worse the next day. Believe me."

"Okay."

Dat's expression softened. "And cherish Priscilla. Show her how much you care about her and Ethan."

Mark heaved a sigh as he worked to memorize all his father's advice.

Leaning over, *Dat* rubbed his shoulder. "You're a *gut* man with a *gut* heart. You'll be a *wunderbaar* husband and *dat*. Just give yourself time to adjust. And remember, all that matters at the end of the day is love."

Mark nodded.

Dat stood. "Well, I suppose I should let you get some sleep."

Mark walked his father to his horse and buggy. "*Danki* for coming to see me."

Dat shook his hand. "I'm proud of you, Mark."

"Why?"

Dat leaned against the buggy. "John was wrong to force you to marry Priscilla when you hadn't done anything wrong."

Mark nodded.

"But Jamie told me you couldn't allow Priscilla to go through more humiliation. You're standing up for what you feel is right, and you're putting Priscilla's reputation and well-being above your own. That shows how mature and selfless you are, and that will make you an even better husband and *daed*." *Dat* gave him a quick hug. "I'm proud of all of *mei kinner*, and your *mamm* would be too."

Tears stung Mark's eyes as he thought of his mother.

"*Gut nacht*," *Dat* said. "I'll see you tomorrow."

"*Gut nacht*."

As his father's buggy disappeared down the driveway, Mark wondered how he would ever live up to the task of being the husband and father *Dat* was certain he could be.

Priscilla pulled up her green window shade and peered toward the *daadihaus*. When she spotted Mark and his father sitting on the porch and laughing in the waning light of evening, she smiled. Had Vernon come to wish Mark well the night before the wedding?

She watched them for a few moments. And then she climbed into bed. She needed to get some extra sleep—if that were even possible. She stared at her dark ceiling, and her heart raced as she imagined the wedding tomorrow. The past five weeks had rushed by at lightning speed.

Although she'd wanted to keep the wedding small, it seemed their entire church district would be there, and of course everyone would stare at her and Mark as they sat at the front of her father's barn. The benches had been delivered on Monday, and Mark, Ethan, and her father finished setting them out last night. The food was prepared and the table decorations were made. Now she just had to make it through the actual wedding.

How was she going to go through the ceremony without trembling?

Her thoughts moved to the pair at the *daadihaus*. She was going to marry Mark Riehl. He'd always been the handsomest boy at school and youth group, and she was going to be his wife. How had that happened?

Rolling to her side, she groaned. She wasn't ready for this, but she didn't have a choice. It seemed she hadn't had a choice in any decision since she'd come back to this community.

"I can do this," she whispered. "I can be strong for Ethan."

She tried to imagine Ethan and Mark together, playing softball and talking on the porch. This was the right decision for her son. Mark would be the father Ethan needed. But what kind of husband would he be to Priscilla?

The question echoed in her mind, but she couldn't expect more than friendship from Mark when she'd made it clear he couldn't expect more than friendship from her.

"I don't think I can do this." Priscilla sat on the corner of her bed and hugged her middle as her stomach soured. She looked up at her mother and shook her head. Tears pricked at her eyes. "I can't."

"You can, and you will." *Mamm*'s dark eyes narrowed. "More than a hundred people are in the barn right now. This wedding is going to happen. It's time for you to stand up and go marry Mark Riehl as you planned and promised."

Priscilla's lip quivered. She'd spent nearly the entire night staring at the ceiling and trying to imagine her life with Mark. It all felt surreal—and wrong.

"I can't do it." Priscilla's voice vibrated with her anguish. "I'd rather be shunned. I just can't do it. I can't live a lie."

"It's not a lie. He's already moved into the *daadihaus*, and yesterday I heard your *dat* and him discussing plans for your new *haus*." *Mamm* motioned for her to stand. "Get up. The bishop is going to wonder where you've gone. Do you want rumors to start in the community?"

Priscilla gave a humorless laugh. "You don't think they already have?"

Footsteps echoed in the stairwell, and Priscilla braced herself. Was her father coming to yell at her? She'd cry for sure if he did.

"Priscilla?" Laura looked beautiful as she stood in the doorway clad in the red dress Priscilla made for her. She touched her extending abdomen as she studied Priscilla. "Are you okay?"

"*Ya.*" Priscilla sniffed.

"She's *naerfich*," *Mamm* said, and Priscilla shot her a look.

"Laura, I don't think I can do it." Priscilla shook her head. "I can't be the *fraa* Mark needs or deserves."

Laura clicked her tongue as she sat down beside her and took her hand. "*Ya*, you can, and you will. Mark is blessed to have you."

Priscilla shook her head and rubbed her eyes with her free hand. "No, he's not. I'm a mess, and he should have a better *fraa*."

Looping her arm around Priscilla's shoulders, Laura pulled her in for a hug. "You and Mark are going to have a *wunderbaar* marriage."

"Not if Priscilla refuses to leave her bedroom," *Mamm* snapped before pointing at the clock. "You need to get out to the barn now." She waved her arms in the air and hurried out of the room, muttering something about giving up.

"Priscilla, listen to me," Laura began. "We're all *naerfich* on our wedding day. I saw Mark earlier, and he looked just as nervous as you do."

"Really?" Priscilla looked up at her.

"*Ya.*" Laura smiled and rubbed her back.

"Were you nervous when you married Allen?"

"Oh *ya*." Laura gave a little laugh. "I was a mess, but Cindy and Mark calmed me down."

That knowledge eased something inside of Priscilla.

"Everything will be fine." Laura stood and held out her hand. "Come on. Let's go before the bishop comes looking for you."

Taking a deep breath, Priscilla stood and allowed Laura to thread her fingers with hers. Then she headed toward the stairs and her future as Priscilla Riehl.

TWENTY-FIVE

PRISCILLA FOLDED HER HANDS, TRYING TO STOP them from shaking as she sat at the front of her father's barn. The stale air was nearly unbearable, causing beads of sweat to pool on her temples. She'd do anything for a breeze. If only the barn had windows.

She swiped her hand across her forehead before resting it on the lap of her red dress. Then she glanced across the aisle to where Mark sat next to his attendants—Ethan, Jamie, Walter, and Roy. Mark wore his Sunday best—a crisp white shirt, black vest, black trousers, and black suspenders.

They'd sung a hymn, and then the minister launched into a thirty-minute sermon based on Old Testament stories of marriages. Mark's bright-blue eyes were fixed on the minister as if he were hanging on his every word.

Priscilla, however, couldn't focus or stop her body from trembling. She felt as if she were stuck in a dream. Today her name would change, and she would move into the *daadihaus* later this evening.

Everything in her life was about to change.

She smoothed her quaking hand over the skirt of her red dress as her thoughts turned to the uncertainty of what her future would hold. Was it possible she and Mark could develop affection for each other? Or would their marriage forever remain one of convenience—merely giving Mark a stable future and her a place in the community?

Priscilla shifted in her seat, and the overwhelming awareness of eyes studying her overtook her senses. Glancing to the side, her gaze collided with Mark's. His lips turned up in a tender smile, and she tried to mirror the gesture, but she couldn't. Mark seemed happy, but that could be a ruse. After all, his twin sister said he used humor and arrogance to mask his insecurity. Why had she ever trusted his smiles?

Yet her relationship with Mark had changed from being distant to forging a close friendship. She *had* gained a level of trust in him, and she was so grateful that he loved her son. But they had no foundation of love or trust necessary for a real marriage between them, and they couldn't force those either.

It had seemed to make sense to marry Mark to avoid shunning and to give her son a home, but now reality hit her like a ton of hay bales crashing down from the loft in one of her father's barns. She had to stop this wedding. She had to stand up and tell the bishop that she changed her mind and would face the shunning instead.

And allow Dat *to kick you and Ethan out of his house and off his land forever?*

The voice came from the very back of her brain. No, she couldn't allow that. And she couldn't break her promise to Mark either.

She glanced over at Ethan as he sat beside Mark. Her son looked happy and proud. Was he proud to be part of the Riehl family? He was gaining a stepfather who seemed to cherish him and cousins who loved him. Maybe this was the best choice.

Oh, she was losing her mind! When would she stop feeling so off-kilter?

Laura touched her arm, and Priscilla looked up at her. Laura lifted her eyebrow as if asking if she was okay, and Priscilla nodded. Looking satisfied, Laura turned back toward the minister. Thankfully, he continued to talk, oblivious to their silent conversation.

Beside Laura, Cindy and Sarah Jane looked beautiful in their matching red dresses. They would all be her new sisters.

Priscilla glanced at Mark again when she thought she felt his stare, and he gave her another smile. This time she smiled in return, but her smile faded as fear washed over her once again. She had to make this marriage work for her son's sake, but she didn't know how to be Mark's wife. She only knew how to be Ethan's mother. She breathed around the razor-edged knot of anguish that lodged in her throat.

When the sermon was over, Priscilla bowed her head as the rest of the congregation knelt for silent prayer. When the prayer ended, the bishop stood and began to preach the main sermon. His words were only white noise as the undercurrent of worries that had been rippling inside her continued to grab her attention. She'd packed all her and Ethan's belongings yesterday, and her father and Mark carried the boxes and suitcases to the *daadihaus*, leaving behind only what she and Ethan needed for today.

She still didn't know how she was going to explain to Ethan why she was sleeping in his room.

Suddenly the sermon was over, and Priscilla's body began to shudder anew. She tried to swallow, her throat feeling like sandpaper rubbing together. She glanced up just as the bishop looked between her and Mark. It was time for her to stand with this man so they could declare their desire to be married. She didn't know if she was strong enough to go through with this after all. If she backed out now, would Mark and his family ever forgive her?

Would *Dat*?

"Now here are two in one faith," the bishop said. "Priscilla Elizabeth Allgyer and Mark Abraham Riehl." The bishop asked the congregation if they knew any scriptural reason for the couple not to be married. After a short pause he continued. "If it is your desire to be married, you may in the name of the Lord come forth."

Priscilla turned toward Mark as fear crawled onto her shoulders and dug its claws into her. With a smile, Mark held out his hand. She took it, and he lifted her to her feet. His hand was warm and strong, and when she swayed with dizzying doubt, he held her fast. She peeked up at him as he watched the bishop intently. His face was serious as they took their vows.

Priscilla's heart pounded as the bishop read "A Prayer for Those About to Be Married" from an Amish prayer book called the *Christenpflict*.

Priscilla and Mark sat down for another sermon and another prayer, and she willed herself to concentrate on anything but her doubts. She was safe. Ethan was safe. Their families and the community would be satisfied. That was all that mattered.

After the bishop recited the Lord's Prayer, the congregation stood, and the three-hour service ended with the singing of another hymn.

And then it was official—Priscilla and Mark were married. She thought she might choke on the lump forming in her throat.

The men began rearranging furniture while the women prepared to set out the wedding dinner. Priscilla tried to remember what they were serving. Oh yes. Chicken with stuffing, mashed potatoes with gravy, pepper cabbage, cooked cream of celery, cookies, pie, fruit, Jell-O salad . . . Maybe if she concentrated on the mundane, she'd be okay.

Priscilla stood, and Mark held out his hand again.

"Are you ready?" he asked.

Priscilla stared at him before blinking. Mark Riehl was now

her husband and partner—forever. There was no going back. No changing her mind. She was stuck with Mark, and he was stuck with her. The idea stole her breath.

When will this feel real?

"Are you ready?" His smile drooped as he repeated the question, his hand still held out to her.

"I don't—"

"Priscilla!" Laura came from behind her and hugged her. "Congratulations!"

Cindy was next to offer a hug. "I'm so *froh mei bruder* has finally settled down."

Priscilla glanced at Mark. He was engrossed in a conversation with Jamie and Allen as his father stood beside him and laughed.

Mamm arrived and hugged her as she whispered in her ear. "You made the right decision. You'll be *froh* with Mark. Trust me."

"Welcome to the Riehl family," Kayla said as she squeezed Priscilla's arm. "They are a blessing."

"But no one can spell your name when you're in the *Englisher* world. Just wait until you see a doctor. They think it's spelled R-E-A-L," Florence said. Everyone around her laughed.

"Let's eat!" Ethan said.

Priscilla forced a smile as Ethan tried to tug her toward the food the women were beginning to deliver to the tables. She felt as if she were spinning out of control, and she was ready for the world to slow down and let her off.

"Congratulations, *sohn*." *Dat* patted Mark's back.

"*Danki*." Mark glanced at Priscilla, who looked stunning in her red dress as she spoke to his sisters. She was his wife. He had a wife! And a son!

"Pretty soon you'll be welcoming a little one too." Jamie smacked Mark on the back.

"What?" Mark looked at his older brother, and everyone laughed.

"You'll have a *boppli* too," Jamie said, explaining slowly as if Mark were a dolt.

"I knew what you meant," Mark said, grousing.

"Don't worry." Allen's smile widened. "*Kinner* are fantastic. I thank God every day for my Mollie." His gaze turned to where Laura stood holding the little girl's hand. "*Kinner* are a blessing. Don't let anyone tell you any differently."

Mark's heart warmed at the thought of having a child with Priscilla. But then he remembered Priscilla's rules from the day they'd met with the bishop.

This is going to be a marriage in name only. We're going to live like two freinden, *not husband and* fraa.

He swallowed back his gripping regret. Any hope for having a real marriage fizzled.

"Don't look so terrified." Allen chuckled. "You'll be a great *dat*."

"Sure he will." Jamie looped his arm around Mark's shoulder. "If I can be a *dat*, then anyone can."

"Oh, it's not so bad." Walter, his stepbrother, joined their circle. "You just have to have patience and remember that as much as you want to send your *kinner* back, you can't."

Everyone chuckled.

"That's the truth," *Dat* chimed in. "There are days when you'd like to."

Mark laughed and then glanced over at Priscilla. She'd looked terrified during the wedding, and he'd longed to hold her hand and comfort her. He'd prayed she'd relax. Hopefully tonight he could talk to her and promise her that everything would be okay.

While his brothers continued to make jokes, his mind wandered to how he'd stayed awake for hours last night mulling over his father's wise words. He'd concluded that he would do his best to be patient with both Priscilla and Ethan. He'd allow Priscilla to take the lead in their relationship. He'd let her come to him for affection when—and if—she was ready. Until then he'd bide his time and be the best friend he could be without crossing any intimacy lines—even if that meant her having her own bedroom when they moved into the new house next year.

As much as he loathed the idea of living like two friends, he couldn't force her to do anything. He wouldn't abuse her the way Trent had. He would respect her, just as his father advised.

While this marriage hadn't been their choice, he'd do everything possible to make it work. He just prayed Priscilla would do the same.

"*Gut nacht!*" Priscilla waved as Laura and her family climbed into a van.

As the vehicle bounced down the driveway, Priscilla cupped one hand to her mouth to stifle a yawn. The day had been long, and she was ready for bed.

"Ethan is fast asleep," *Mamm* said as she came down the path from the *daadihaus*. She held a Coleman lantern in her hand. "He was worn out from playing with his cousins."

"*Ya*, he was." Priscilla hugged her sweater to her chest. The night air had cooled as soon as the sun set. "Cindy, Sarah Jane, and I cleaned up most of the food from the barn."

"We'll finish it tomorrow." *Mamm* waved off her worry. "Go on to bed. I'll see you in the morning." She looked past Priscilla and smiled. "There's your husband."

Priscilla's heart seemed to trip over itself at the word *husband*. How long would it take to get used to that? She spun as Mark approached with a lantern from the direction of the barn where the wedding had been held. Still clad in his Sunday clothes, he was more handsome than ever.

Priscilla suddenly remembered the surprise she'd planned for him. She turned to her mother. "Did you leave the package on the counter in the kitchen?"

"Just as you asked." *Mamm* nodded.

"*Danki,*" Priscilla said before turning back toward Mark.

"I was looking for you." Mark waved at her mother. "Are you and Yonnie heading in?"

"*Ya,* we'll finish cleaning up tomorrow." *Mamm* winked at her. "*Gut nacht.*"

Priscilla swallowed a gasp as her mother turned and left.

"Well, I guess we'll turn in." Mark made a sweeping gesture toward the path leading to the *daadihaus*.

Priscilla fell into step beside him as she searched for something to say.

"I meant to tell you earlier that you look beautiful," he said.

She looked up at him.

He laughed. "Why do you look so stunned? You know red is my favorite color on you."

"*Danki.*" She fingered her dress. "Your family was a tremendous help at cleaning up."

"You mean *our* family." He bumped her with his elbow. "They're your family too now."

"I know, but it will take me awhile to get used to that." They headed up the porch steps, and he reached around her to open the door. She stilled as his arm brushed hers, sending shivers dancing up her arm to her shoulder.

He wrenched open the door, and she stepped through. She

pressed her lips together as he closed and locked both the storm door and front door.

"It was a lovely day," she said.

"*Ya*, it was." He turned to face her. "I have a surprise for you."

"Really?" she asked. "I have one for you."

"Okay." He laughed. "You go first."

She crossed to the kitchen counter, picked up the package, and handed it to him.

"What's this?" He turned it over in his hands.

"It's a wedding gift." She shrugged. "It's not much. Just a little something."

"Wow. I never expected this." He opened the package, and then he blew out a puff of air as he stared at the case that held a twelve-piece wood carving chisel set. "Priscilla. You shouldn't have."

"I wanted to get you something, and you mentioned that you'd lost a few of your *daadi*'s chisels." She bit her lower lip. "I hope you like it."

"I love it." He met her gaze and smiled. *"Danki."*

"Gern gschehne." As she looked into his eyes, something unspoken seemed to pass between them. She sucked in a breath as her body tingled. Did Mark feel it too?

"Your gift." He made a sweeping gesture toward the hearth. "I hope you like it."

She spun, and then she cupped her hand to her mouth again as she took in a beautiful rocking chair sitting by the sofa. "Mark!"

She crossed the room and ran her fingers over the smooth wood. Happy tears filled her eyes.

"Where did you get this?" she asked.

"One of Jamie's firefighter *freinden* makes and repairs furniture, and his *dat* has a store. His name is Leon. I went to town one day to the hardware store, and I stopped in to see him. He had this chair there, and I thought it would be perfect for you to sit by the fire when it gets cold."

"*Danki.*"

"Try it out." He sat on the sofa and gestured toward the rocker.

She sank into it and pushed it into motion. Leaning back, she smiled. "It's perfect. I love it."

"I'm so glad."

They stared at each other as awkwardness permeated the air around them.

Finally, he patted the arm of the sofa. "I'll sleep here. Just let me get my clothes out of the bedroom." He stood and started toward the larger bedroom.

"No." She jumped up from the chair, trailed after him, and pulled him back. "Let me get my clothes, and I'll sleep with Ethan, like we've already discussed."

"Priscilla, I don't feel right letting you sleep with Ethan. It's better if I just sleep on the sofa until we have a bigger *haus.*"

"There's no discussion." She grabbed a lantern from the kitchen counter and headed into the bedroom, where she retrieved her nightgown, slippers, and robe. When she walked back out to the family room, she saw Mark had remained in the same spot as if his shoes were glued to the floor.

She walked over to him and smiled. *"Gut nacht."*

His expression clouded with something that looked like intensity, and her heart hammered. He reached over and cupped his hand to her cheek, and her breath stalled in her lungs. Was he going to kiss her? Her mouth dried.

"I just want you to know," he began, his voice low and husky, sending an unfamiliar tremor through her, "that I'm in this marriage one hundred percent. I'm grateful you're allowing me to adopt Ethan and give him my name. I'll take care of you and Ethan, and I'll do my best to be the husband you deserve."

"Danki." She nodded and held her breath, waiting for his kiss.

"You don't have to thank me." He let his hand drop to his side. *"Gut nacht,* Priscilla." Then he moved past her into the bedroom, the door clicking shut behind him.

Priscilla worked to catch her breath. Her cheeks heated as she covered her forehead with her hand. She'd been certain he was going to kiss her, and she'd wanted him to!

Was this wrong? They weren't in love. Kissing would turn into more, and her heart wasn't prepared to give itself to Mark. How could she when she didn't love him and he didn't love her? Allowing herself to become attached to him would only lead to disaster and heartache.

Forcing herself to push away her confusing feelings, she headed into the bathroom to get ready for bed.

After changing into her nightgown, she gathered her things and tiptoed into Ethan's room before carefully climbing into bed. Ethan rolled onto his stomach, and his soft snores sounded through the darkness.

She moved onto her side and tried to ignore a sudden yearning for her husband.

TWENTY-SIX

PRISCILLA SANK ONTO THE BACKLESS BENCH BETWEEN Laura and Kayla on Sunday morning. Today's service was held at the King family's farm, and Priscilla glanced around at the married women in her section. It felt surreal to sit with these other women when only a couple of weeks ago she had been with Cindy, Sarah Jane, and the rest of the unmarried women.

"So how's married life?" Laura bumped Priscilla's arm with her shoulder. "You seem *froh*. Is everything going well?"

"*Ya*." Priscilla shrugged. "It's fine."

Laura and Kayla shared a look.

"What?" Priscilla asked.

"You just look really *froh*." Kayla smiled. "I'm glad for you. Mark is a *gut* man, and he'll take *gut* care of you and Ethan."

Priscilla turned toward the rows of married men and found Mark sitting between Ethan and Jamie. She took in his serene face. The past couple of days had been comfortable as they settled into a routine. Mark seemed satisfied with her cooking, and he'd been patient with Ethan, helping him get ready for school Friday morning and allowing him to help with chores when he arrived home and yesterday.

So far her new life had been just fine—better than she'd

expected. But still, something was missing, something she and Mark would never have: a true marriage with love and affection at its core.

Priscilla studied Mark as he turned his attention to his brother beside him. He was even more attractive than usual dressed in his Sunday clothes. Priscilla admitted to herself that she could watch him from afar for hours, but she pulled her attention away and looked down at her apron. She had to find a way to remove these thoughts from her mind.

"*Was iss letz?*" Laura whispered in her ear.

"Nothing." Priscilla sat up straight and lifted the hymnal beside her from the bench. "I'm just preparing my mind for worship."

"Is everything *really* going okay?" Laura asked.

Priscilla glanced to her right. Kayla was speaking to a woman beside her.

"*Ya*, of course." How could she possibly reveal to Mark's twin that she longed for intimacy with him? This was too personal and embarrassing to say out loud.

"I'll listen if you ever need someone to talk to, okay?" Laura said, her blue eyes full of concern.

"I appreciate that. *Danki*." Priscilla fingered her hymnal and then glanced down at Laura's belly. "How are you feeling?"

"Oh, okay." Laura smiled. "I'm just really tired all the time." She nodded toward Kayla. "I can't believe we're both due in a couple of months. It's gone so quickly. Right, Kayla?"

Kayla laughed and shook her head. "No, it feels like I've been pregnant for three years."

They all chuckled.

"It's almost over." Laura smiled. "And then I'll have mine too." She rubbed her belly.

"Have you discussed names?" Priscilla asked.

"*Ya*, we have."

As Laura shared their top choices for names, Priscilla settled into her seat. She was ready to worship God and allow her worries to dissolve.

The service began with a hymn, and Priscilla redirected her thoughts to the present. She joined in as the congregation slowly sang the opening hymn. During the last verse of the second hymn, Priscilla's gaze moved to the back of the barn just as the ministers returned from choosing who would preach. They placed their hats on two hay bales, indicating that the service was about to begin.

As the chosen minister began the first sermon, Priscilla folded her hands in her lap and studied them, but her thoughts turned to Mark and their new life together. She tried her best to keep her focus on the minister, but her stare moved toward the men across the aisle. Mark sat with his head bowed, looking at his lap.

Was he thinking about their first couple of days as husband and wife? Did he already regret his decision to marry her?

Or did he feel the same invisible magnet she felt pulling her to him, causing her to long for a true marriage?

While the minister continued to talk in German, Priscilla lost herself in thoughts of the past couple of months. She'd gone from being shunned to being engaged at lightning speed. Now she was a married woman, joined to a man she'd never considered as a husband. How had her life become so out of control? But she'd never again be in control of her own decisions. Now her husband would make all the decisions for her and her son.

She looked at Kayla's belly and felt a sudden tug. Would she ever have another child? Would she ever give Ethan a brother or sister?

Stop torturing yourself! You told Mark you wanted a marriage without intimacy, and he seems more okay with that than ever.

Priscilla redirected her thoughts to the sermon, taking in the message and concentrating on God. She wondered what God had in store for her, despite what she and Mark currently felt. Did he want her and Mark to have a real marriage? Should she initiate intimacy? No, of course not! If Mark ever wanted to kiss her, he would. It was up to him to initiate any intimacy between them.

The first sermon ended, and Priscilla knelt in silent prayer between her sisters-in-law. She needed God to guide her heart and give her strength. Closing her eyes, she began to pray.

God, I'm still confused. I felt you leading me toward this marriage with Mark, but it still doesn't feel right. Are we supposed to live like two freinden, *instead of husband and* fraa? *I thought we were, but if that's true, why do I feel like something is missing in our marriage? I can't make Mark love me, but I find myself longing for him to kiss me and tell me he loves me. Who am I supposed to be? Am I supposed to be truly his* fraa, *or am I supposed to be married to him in name only? Please show me what my role should be as Priscilla Riehl.*

After the prayers, the deacon read from the Scriptures, and then the hour-long main sermon began. Priscilla looked at Mark once again and found him watching her, his gorgeous blue eyes intense. He nodded, and she smiled in response. She hoped her growing feelings for him weren't written on her face. She couldn't allow him to know if her feelings weren't reciprocated. The rejection would be too painful to endure.

Relief flooded Priscilla when the fifteen-minute kneeling prayer was over. The congregation stood for the benediction and sang the closing hymn. While she sang, her eyes moved to Mark again. She wondered if he could feel her watching him.

Laura touched Priscilla's and Kayla's hands. "I'm ready to serve if you are."

"*Ya,* I am," Kayla said.

With one more glance toward Mark, who was now talking

to Jamie and Ethan, Priscilla followed her sisters-in-law out of the barn.

As she walked up the path to the house, she heard someone call her name. She turned and stopped as Franey hurried after her. Jealousy bubbled up in her throat.

"Could I please talk to you for a moment?" Franey wrung her hands. Was she nervous?

"Of course." Priscilla nodded toward a nearby tree, her curiosity piqued.

"I didn't get a chance to congratulate you at the wedding." Franey gestured toward her. "So congratulations on your marriage."

"Danki." Priscilla folded her arms over her middle and studied her. "What did you really want to say to me?"

Franey cleared her throat and glanced toward the barn before meeting her gaze again. She *was* nervous, and Priscilla almost smiled. How the tables had turned!

"I owe you an apology."

"An apology for what?"

"I said some terrible things when I found out Mark had proposed to you, and I'm embarrassed now. I was jealous, and jealousy is a sin."

Surprised, Priscilla tamped down her own jealousy. "What did you say?"

"It was the day Mark came to the store to buy supplies for you. I was angry. I had thought for years that Mark cared about me, so I was upset when he decided to marry you." Franey swallowed and her eyes gleamed with tears. "After I'd waited patiently for five years, I thought it wouldn't be much longer before he asked me to marry him." She paused and cleared her throat.

"When Sadie Liz came to the back of the store to say Mark was there, we talked about you. Sadie Liz said she didn't know why

Mark had asked you to marry him, and I said that you already had a *kind*, so maybe you were expecting one together." She looked away as her cheeks grew pink.

Priscilla felt her eyes narrow. "How could you make an assumption like that?"

Franey wiped at her eyes as she turned to look at her. "I never should have said that. It was cruel and heartless. And Mark overheard it. He defended you and made me realize I was terrible to say that about you. And I'm very sorry. I hope you can forgive me."

"Mark defended me?"

Franey nodded. *"Ya."*

"How?"

Franey shook her head. "After he paid for your supplies, he told me it was a sin to spread rumors, so I knew he'd heard me." She wiped away a tear. "I'm so sorry. I was terrible. Mark chose you, and I'm *froh* for you both. I really am."

Priscilla nodded as Franey's words soaked through her. Mark had defended her? No one had *ever* defended her until Mark did when her father and John Smucker accused her of inappropriate behavior. And now she was learning Mark had defended her again.

Appreciation swirled through her.

"Do you forgive me?" Franey asked.

"*Ya*, of course I do. *Danki* for being honest."

"*Gern gschehne.*" Franey gave her an awkward hug and then scurried to the house.

As Priscilla glanced toward the barn, she smiled. Maybe Mark did truly care about her. Maybe they did have the seeds of a real marriage.

Her heart soared. She couldn't wait to thank him later.

Priscilla stood on the porch of the *daadihaus* later that afternoon. She rested her hand on the railing as she watched Mark and her father exit the barn together after stowing the buggies.

As Mark came up the path toward her, he smiled and waved. She took in his attractive face and bright, intelligent eyes as Franey's words from earlier filtered through her mind. How did she manage to marry such a good man?

It's a marriage of convenience.

Her smile faded away like ashes on the wind as the words taunted her.

"What's on your mind?" Mark jogged up the steps and came to stand beside her.

"Franey told me something earlier."

"Oh?" His eyebrows rose. "What did she say?"

"She told me what you said to her in the fabric store."

"What do you mean?" He leaned back against the porch railing.

She repeated the conversation as his eyes widened. "You defended me. No one had ever done that for me until you did that day in the barn with my father and the bishop, and now you've done it again."

"Of course I defended you." He stood up straight. "You're *mei fraa*, and I'll always defend you. I hope you'll do the same for me."

"*Danki.*"

His smile returned. He crossed the porch and opened the storm door. "Is any of the chocolate *kuche* left?"

"Only if you haven't finished it."

"Let's have a piece. I'll put on some *kaffi*." He disappeared into the house.

A pang of guilt flashed through Priscilla as she stood on the porch. She didn't deserve a husband as good as Mark, but someday soon he'd realize he needed more than he'd ever want from her.

TWENTY-SEVEN

"Come on, Ethan," Mark called from the porch. "You're going to be late for school."

Ethan grabbed his lunch box and dashed out the front door.

Mark glanced past him at Priscilla, who smiled and shook her head. She was beautiful today, just as beautiful as every day since they'd married exactly a month ago. There was something in her eyes too. Maybe he was imagining it, but she seemed more at ease this morning and less timid with him.

"Let's go!" Ethan called as he hurried down the path toward the driveway. "*Mei freinden* will be waiting for me, and they don't like it when I'm late."

Mark took longer strides to catch up with him as the cool October breeze wafted over them. "How do you like school these days?"

"It's *gut*." Ethan nodded. "*Mei freinden* and the teacher are nice."

"*Gut*. What's your favorite subject?" Mark asked.

"Math."

"Really?"

"*Ya*." They hurried down the driveway to where his group of friends always met him so they could walk together to school.

When the group of children came into view, Ethan quickened his steps.

"Hey, wait a minute," Mark said.

Ethan stopped and spun.

"Where's my high five?" Mark asked.

"Oh! Sorry!" Ethan giggled as he gave Mark a high five. Then he ran off.

"Have a *gut* day," Mark called after him.

"Thanks, *Dat*!" Ethan tossed over his shoulder with a little wave.

Mark's smile widened at the name. He enjoyed it when Ethan called him *Dat*. He relished being someone's father.

Mark walked back up the driveway and breathed in the crisp air. He smiled as the *daadihaus* came into view.

The past month had been better than he'd expected as he, Priscilla, and Ethan settled into a routine. He enjoyed walking Ethan to meet his friends in the morning and then working with Yonnie during the day. He ate lunch with Priscilla and then returned to chores in the afternoon. Ethan joined him after he returned from school, and then they worked together until supper.

Everything was comfortable—until they went to bed at night. Priscilla continued to sleep in Ethan's room. This shouldn't have surprised Mark since she'd made it clear the day they met with the bishop to schedule the wedding that she wasn't going to consider this a real marriage. He'd had second thoughts on their wedding day when he realized he'd love to have a child with Priscilla, but then he'd accepted her decision. Hadn't he?

So why did it still bother him so much?

He dismissed the question and jogged up the porch steps. He smiled at the fall flowers Priscilla had planted in front of their little house. Just as she'd told him, it was apparent that she loved to work in a garden.

When he stepped into the kitchen, he found Priscilla setting clean dishes into a cabinet.

She looked over her shoulder at him. "Did Ethan make it in time to meet his *freinden*?"

"*Ya*, he did." Mark leaned his hip against the counter beside her. "He told me his favorite subject is math."

She smiled. "That's great."

"I know. He's *schmaert*, like his *mamm*."

She shook her head.

"What?" Mark said. "You were brilliant when you married me."

She groaned and rolled her eyes as he laughed.

"Let's do something fun today," he said.

"Like what?"

"I don't know." He clapped his hands as an idea filled his mind. "Why don't we go on a picnic?"

"A picnic? On a Thursday?" She studied him as if he were crazy. "I have a pile of laundry waiting for me, and you have chores to do. We don't have time for a picnic."

"Come on." He spun her toward him and rested his hands on her shoulders as she peered up at him. "Let's forget our chores for one day."

"What makes you think *mei dat* will let you take a day off?"

"I don't know. Let's just do it." He stared down at her, his eyes locking with hers. His heart kicked as he ran his finger down her soft cheek.

Her eyes widened as she stared up at him. Something unspoken passed between them, and the air around them felt electrified. He was certain to the very depth of his marrow that she felt the attraction too.

This was it. He was going to kiss his wife.

"Priscilla," he whispered as he leaned down.

She sucked in a breath and then stepped away from him. "I need to get started on the laundry."

"What?" He shook himself.

She swiveled away from him and hurriedly disappeared into the utility room.

Mark leaned against the counter and held his breath while working to slow his racing heartbeat. He'd almost kissed her. He had been so close, but then she'd run off.

Face it. She really doesn't want to be more than freinden.

He closed his eyes and took deep breaths until his pulse slowed to a normal rate. Then he headed out the front door, disappointment weighing down his strides as he hurried off to complete his chores.

Priscilla leaned against the utility room door as she drew shallow breaths to slow her racing heart. When Mark spun her to face him and rested his hands on her shoulders, she was certain she was dreaming. But then he'd run his finger down her cheek and whispered her name, and she knew exactly what he was doing. He was going to kiss her.

At first, she'd wanted it. In fact, she'd craved his touch. But then she remembered that Mark wasn't in love with her, and she wasn't the woman he'd wanted. She couldn't allow him to worm his way into her heart only to reject her later when he realized he was disappointed in her. They needed to keep living as friends before they made a mistake they'd both regret.

When Priscilla thought about Mark and Ethan, she admitted the past month had been wonderful. She'd enjoyed witnessing how their relationship was growing as the adoption process progressed. Ethan had started calling Mark *Dat*, and it was obvious Mark enjoyed it because of the smile he wore every time Ethan said it.

Priscilla couldn't jeopardize that by allowing Mark to take their relationship to a deeper level. She had to keep it platonic, no matter how difficult that was.

When she heard the front door click shut, indicating that Mark had gone outside, Priscilla retrieved a laundry basket from the shelf in the utility room and then stepped into the bathroom to gather dirty laundry from the hamper.

Soon she was running clothes through the wringer washer, and her thoughts wandered as she worked. She was grateful Ethan had not only made an easy transition to an Amish school shortly after they'd arrived, but now to living in the *daadihaus*. He had also accepted that Priscilla wanted to sleep in his room until the new house was built. She explained she and Mark preferred sleeping in separate bedrooms, and Ethan never asked any questions, not even when she told him that fact should be just between them. She and Mark didn't need the world to know their marriage wasn't . . . traditional.

As she washed a pair of Mark's trousers, she thought about how her heart had raced when he touched her. She didn't recall feeling that kind of excitement when Trent touched her or kissed her. Did that mean her feelings were deeper for Mark than they'd been in the beginning with Trent?

She dismissed the thought. She couldn't allow herself to fall for Mark. It would never work. Remaining friends was the best solution.

If only she could convince her heart to believe that too.

"How's it going?"

Mark turned toward the barn entrance and found his older brother standing in the doorway. A van he hadn't heard coming sat in the driveway.

"What are you doing here?" Mark leaned the pitchfork against the stall wall and wiped his hands down his trousers.

"Well that's a nice hello." Jamie grinned. "I was out picking up supplies and thought I'd stop by."

Mark shook his hand. "It's *gut* to see you."

"You too." Jamie seemed to study him. "Is something on your mind?"

"No." Mark shook his head and tried to smile, despite the disappointment still eating at him. He'd spent all morning doing hard labor to try to dispel the frustration his wife's rejection had caused him, but it still clung to him like a scratchy wool sweater. "How's Kayla?"

"She's doing well." Jamie's face lit up. "She had a doctor's appointment yesterday, and the due date in a few weeks still seems right."

"Aren't babies early sometimes?" Mark waved him off. "You should be at home."

"It's fine." Jamie shook his head. "Calvin was a week later than expected, and my driver has a cell phone handy. Kayla will call me if she needs me, and I can be there quickly." He leaned back against the barn wall. "How are things with you? How's married life?"

Mark snorted and kicked a stone with the toe of his shoe.

"Uh-oh." Jamie's smile drooped. "What's going on?"

Mark hesitated. Should he be honest with his brother? He longed to keep his confusing feelings to himself, but maybe Jamie could offer some helpful advice. "I was hoping that somehow Priscilla and I could have a real marriage instead of just a marriage in name only. But it's impossible."

"I don't understand." Jamie's brow furrowed.

Mark shared how Priscilla had made it clear long before their wedding that they would never have a real marriage, and how she slept in Ethan's room and shied away from any affection he tried to give her. He ended with telling him what happened earlier.

"She won't even let you kiss her?" Jamie asked.

"No, but I know she cares about me, and I feel like she wants me to kiss her." Mark swallowed as the reality hit him. "I thought I could be okay with this, but it's starting to get to me. I adore Ethan, and I wouldn't mind having a few more *kinner* running around. In fact, I'd love to have more *kinner*, but we'll never have them. This is more difficult than I thought it would be when I agreed to live only as *freinden*."

Jamie folded his arms over his wide chest and pressed his lips together.

"What are you thinking?" Mark asked, hoping his brother held the answers.

"You've never had this problem before, have you?"

Mark rolled his eyes. "That's all you have to say? You want to rub my nose in my failure?"

"No, no. It's not that. I'm just surprised." Jamie grinned. "You're asking me for advice after all those years you taunted me and told me to get married. How does that feel?"

"Forget it." Mark walked over to the stall and picked up the pitchfork. "*Danki* for stopping by."

"Hold on." Jamie followed him. "I'm sorry."

Mark glared at him.

"I'm just a little stunned." Jamie paused. "I think you should give her time. Don't give up on her. Let her come to you. I have a feeling she will."

Mark nodded as hope lit within him. "Okay." He set the pitchfork against the barn wall. "So let her kiss me first, then?"

Jamie shrugged. "Or at least let her give you the cues that she's ready. You'll know when it's time."

"That makes sense." Mark smiled. "*Danki.* Would you like some lunch?"

"Do you think Priscilla will mind?"

"No, but will Kayla worry about you if you're gone too long?"

"She'll be fine."

"All right," Mark said, teasing. "But I don't want to hear about it if you get into trouble."

Priscilla climbed out of the shower and dried off before dressing in her warmest nightgown. Now that it was November, the temperature had dropped, and she shivered as she pulled on her pink terrycloth robe. She stared at her reflection in the bright-yellow light of the lantern and then combed her waist-length, dark-brown hair.

After brushing her teeth she opened the bathroom door and was greeted by the pop and hiss of the fire in the fireplace. Her eyes adjusted in the dark, and she spotted Mark sitting on the sofa, staring into the flames.

Regret settled over her as she recalled the two weeks since she'd rejected Mark when he'd tried to kiss her. He seemed to be pulling away from her ever since that day, and she had longed to go back in time and replay that event with a different ending. But the thought of allowing Mark to kiss her also frightened her. What if a kiss wasn't all she'd imagined? What if a kiss turned into more and she wasn't ready for it? Would he have stopped if she'd asked him to slow down?

"Come sit by me." Mark had seen her, and his voice was gentle. "There's a seat by the hearth for you."

"Okay." She crossed the room, and instead of sitting in the rocking chair, she sat down on the sofa beside him. She stared into the fire as its heat surrounded her like a soft blanket.

"I see why your *mammi* wanted a fireplace." Mark shifted on the sofa, moving away from her. "It's not only warm but soothing after a long day."

"It is." She looked toward Ethan's bedroom door.

"He's asleep," Mark said as if reading her thoughts. "I checked on him while you were in the shower."

"I can't believe Thanksgiving is in three weeks."

"I know." Mark rested his elbow on the sofa arm. "Florence wants to know if we're coming over for a meal."

"Do you want to?" She turned toward him. His handsome face was lit by the glow of the fire, making his chiseled features, coupled with his sprouting light-brown beard, even more striking.

"It's up to you." Mark shrugged. "Your parents could come too. Florence loves being surrounded by family."

"I'll ask *mei mamm* if she and *Dat* would like to have Thanksgiving dinner at your *dat*'s *haus*."

"Okay."

A hush fell over the room, and Priscilla felt a tug on her scalp. When she turned, she was surprised to see Mark fiddling with a strand of her hair.

"What are you doing?" she asked, trying not to laugh.

"Sorry." He grinned. "I just wanted to touch your hair. It seemed to be taunting me when it hit my hand."

She suddenly felt the wall around her heart crumbling as she looked into her husband's kind eyes. She longed to let him in and tell him everything about her past. She *needed* to let him in. Was it time to trust him?

"Are you all right?" He anchored a tendril of hair behind her ear.

"*Ya.*" She nodded. "I want to tell you something."

"Okay."

"It's about Trent."

A muscle tensed in his jaw. "Go on."

"I didn't tell you everything when we were in the barn that day," she said, her voice trembling. "When Trent lost his job, he changed. He became angry and agitated." She took a ragged breath.

"Take your time." Mark moved his fingers across her back and over her shoulder, and his touch gave her the strength to go on.

"I kept working. In fact, I took double shifts and filled in for my coworkers to try to keep food on our table and pay our rent. One night I came home and found Ethan sleeping on the sofa. I think he was about three years old. Trent was drunk and sitting in his recliner. There were dirty dishes in the sink and the trash was overflowing."

Her voice sounded foreign to her own ears, too shaky and high-pitched. "I was furious, and I told him I was tired of both working and taking care of the *haus*. I said it was time for him to do his part. That was the first time he hit me. He smacked me so hard I fell backward and hit my head on the wall. I'd never been so afraid in my life."

Mark blew out a deep breath and then pinched the bridge of his nose. "How dare he hurt you like that." He pulled her against his chest, and she rested her head on his shoulder.

"He was volatile, and I never knew what would set him off. I felt like I was walking on eggshells every time I walked into the room."

Mark kissed the top of her head. "I'm so sorry."

She stared into the fire as she spoke. "Trent never hit Ethan, but he used to yell at him. The day I realized I had to get Ethan away from him was the day I came home from work and found

Ethan alone. Trent had gone out drinking with his buddies. He'd chosen alcohol over our *sohn's* safety."

Her lower lip quivered. "I couldn't believe he had done that. That was when I decided I had to leave. I couldn't stay there and give him the chance to hurt Ethan."

She took a trembling breath. "I knew if I stayed, not only was Trent likely to endanger Ethan again, but he could turn his violence on him too. I couldn't put *mei sohn* in danger. It's my job to protect him. I can take it, but I can't let someone hurt *mei kind*. If I had been a better *mutter*, I would have escaped with Ethan before I finally snuck out one day when Trent was out with his buddies. But I was afraid. I should have been stronger and left sooner.

"That was when I came home and found you here." Tears splattered down her cheeks as sobs racked her body.

"Shh. It's okay." Mark pulled her against him, and she cried onto his shoulder, soaking his white T-shirt. "You're safe now. You and Ethan never have to deal with Trent again. I'll never let anyone hurt you. I promise you. I'll protect you and Ethan for the rest of my life."

She sniffed as she rested her cheek against his shoulder. "*Danki.*"

"Why are you thanking me?" He looked down at her. "I haven't done anything."

"You're wrong. You've done everything. You've given Ethan and me a safe home."

"I'm *froh* to do it." He released her from the hug, and she remained beside him.

They stared at each other, and her breath hitched. She suddenly felt closer to him than she'd felt to anyone in her life. Mark had become important to her. He had become her closest confidant.

"I should get to bed." He stood and then gestured toward the fire. "I put a big log on it, and it should last awhile. I'll set my alarm and check on it in the middle of the night so we don't freeze." He started toward his bedroom. When he reached the door, he turned and faced her. *"Gut nacht."*

"Gut nacht," she said before he disappeared into his bedroom, leaving her alone by the hearth.

TWENTY-EIGHT

MARK HUMMED TO HIMSELF AS HE FINISHED FEED-
ing the horses. He thought about how Priscilla had seemed to
warm up to him in the month since she told him about leaving
Trent. Jamie's plan of allowing her to come to him seemed to be
working.

Last week Priscilla, Ethan, her parents, and Mark had eaten
Thanksgiving dinner at his father's house with the rest of his
family. Priscilla had seemed to enjoy being there, and she'd
smiled and laughed as the Riehl siblings told stories about their
childhood.

She had also taken his hand when they walked to his buggy,
and after they arrived home and put Ethan to bed, they had sat in
front of the hearth and talked until late into the night.

They still hadn't kissed, but they were slowly getting closer
and acting more like a couple.

If only she'd allow him to kiss her, but he was determined to
let her come to him first.

When Mark heard Yonnie's phone ring, he jogged into the
office and picked up the receiver.

"Allgyer's Belgian and Dutch Harness Horses," Mark said.
"This is Mark."

"Mark!" His stepmother's voice was loud in his ear. "It's Florence."

"*Mamm*," Mark said as alarm gripped him. "*Was iss letz?*"

"Kayla is having her *boppli*," Florence gushed. "The midwife is at their *haus* now."

"Really?" Mark realized he was grinning. "That's *wunderbaar*. Would you please call me after the *boppli* is born?"

"Of course."

"*Danki*." Mark hung up the phone and jogged to the house to tell Priscilla the news.

"Priscilla!"

"*Ya?*" Priscilla looked up from her sewing machine when she heard someone running toward her former bedroom. Her mother had been happy to let her use it until she had her own sewing room in her new house.

Mark burst through the doorway, leaned against the wall, and panted to catch his breath. "Kayla is having her *boppli*."

"Really?" She jumped up and closed the distance between them. "She's in labor right now?"

"*Ya*. Florence is going to call back after the *boppli* is born." He gave a little chuckle. "*Mei bruder* is going to have two *kinner* before the day is over." He scrubbed his hand over his short beard. "I can't believe how much life has changed this year. I'm married now, and *mei bruder* is going to have his second *kind*. It seems like just yesterday that Jamie and I were kids, fishing together at the pond."

She studied him, admiring how his beard made him look even more handsome and mature. What would it be like to have a child with him?

That will never happen. Let that dream go, Priscilla! Just because you and Mark are getting closer as friends doesn't mean he'll ever love you.

She looked away and cleared her throat. "Let me know when Florence calls you back."

"I will. We can go visit them in a few days after things settle down."

"That sounds *gut*." She went back to work as Mark disappeared into the hallway.

As Priscilla, Mark, and Ethan climbed Jamie's porch steps three days later, Priscilla held a gift bag containing diapers and the pink baby blanket she'd made for her new niece. Despite a cold breeze, Jamie sat out on the porch with his father, Roy, and Allen.

"Congratulations." Mark shook Jamie's gloved hand. "How does it feel to have two *kinner*?"

"I'm not sure yet." Jamie's eyes widened. "Ask me in another month."

Everyone laughed.

"Congratulations." Priscilla shook his hand, and Ethan followed suit.

"Is Mollie here?" Ethan asked.

"*Ya*." Allen pointed toward the front door. "She's playing in the *schtupp* with Calvin. Cindy, Sarah Jane, and her *mammi* are there too. You should go join them."

Ethan looked up at Priscilla. "Is it okay?"

"Of course," Priscilla told him.

"Laura is upstairs with Kayla," Allen said.

"*Danki*." Priscilla looked at Mark. "I'm going to go see them."

"I'll be out here," Mark told her before sitting in a rocking chair next to his older brother.

Priscilla climbed the stairs and found her way to the nursery, where Laura sat in a rocker feeding the newborn a bottle.

"Hi," Kayla said as Priscilla stepped into the room.

"Congratulations." Priscilla handed her the bag. "I brought you a little something."

Kayla opened the bag and pulled out the pack of diapers and pink blanket. "Oh, *danki*." She hugged Priscilla.

"*Gern gschehne.*"

"Give me your coat," Kayla said, and Priscilla slipped it off. Kayla set it on the changing table.

"How is she?" Priscilla asked, leaning down to see the baby's little face and shock of golden-blond hair, just like Kayla's and Calvin's.

"She's precious." Laura held her up. "This is Alice Dorothy."

Priscilla smiled as she looked between Laura and Kayla. "Dorothy after your *mamm*?" she asked Laura.

"*Ya.*" Laura eyes grew bright with tears.

"That's beautiful." Priscilla's eyes stung with her own threatening tears.

"Would you like to hold her?" Laura held up the baby.

"I'd love to." Priscilla took the baby and the bottle as Laura stood.

"Sit." Laura gestured toward the chair.

"*Danki.*" Priscilla sat down, and Laura slipped a burp cloth onto Priscilla's shoulder. As she fed Alice, the baby made little grunting noises and stared up at her.

An overwhelming sense of longing and regret swallowed Priscilla whole as the reality of her pretend marriage gripped her. She would never experience having a baby with Mark. She'd never pick out names with him or see his reaction as he held his child in his arms for the first time. They would never watch their child learn to walk or speak or give them hugs.

She craved those things and more. She wanted to have all of them with Mark, and only Mark. She couldn't imagine being another man's wife. She enjoyed sharing a home with him and eating her meals with him. She cherished his smile, his laugh, his sense of humor. She loved how he interacted with Ethan. He was a good man, a wonderful father, and a fantastic husband.

He had become important to her. He was her first thought in the morning and her last thought before she fell asleep.

And then it hit her. She'd fallen in love with Mark. She truly loved him to the depth of her soul.

An ache opened in her chest and spread until she had what felt like a gaping hole in her heart. Tears, hot and swift, flowed down her cheeks.

"Priscilla." Laura touched her arm. "Are you okay?"

"*Was iss letz?*" Kayla asked.

Priscilla tried to catch her breath.

"It's okay." Kayla's voice was caring. "You'll have one soon. Sometimes it takes time to get pregnant."

"That's right." Laura smiled. "I've had two miscarriages since Allen and I got married, but everything has turned out fine so far with this one." She touched her protruding belly. "I'm due in the next few weeks. You'll be next. Just pray about it."

"No, no, I won't be." Priscilla held Alice out toward Kayla. "Please take her. I'm sorry."

Kayla took her baby, and Priscilla started for the door. Her hurt ran so deep that she feared she might drown in it.

"Wait." Laura took her arm and stopped her. "Talk to us."

"What's going on?" Kayla asked, her blue eyes wide.

"She doesn't know?" Priscilla asked Laura.

Laura shook her head. "I never told her."

"What don't I know?" A thread of annoyance sounded in Kayla's voice.

"My marriage is a sham. We got married to avoid being shunned." Priscilla quickly shared the events that led to her marriage to Mark, and Kayla listened with her eyes wide. "We don't live as a married couple. We've never even kissed, and I stay in Ethan's room at night." She pointed to Alice. "I'll never have the joy of having a *boppli* with Mark."

"This is all a joke, right?" Kayla's gaze bounced between Laura and Priscilla.

"Why would I joke about this?" Priscilla asked before wiping her eyes and blowing her nose with a tissue.

"Because Mark adopted Ethan, and you two are obviously in love." Kayla sank into the rocking chair. "I can see it when you're together."

"What?" Priscilla asked.

"Just last week at Thanksgiving dinner, I noticed how you and Mark smile at each other, and I saw you holding hands when you walked out to his buggy together." Kayla lifted Alice to her shoulder and rubbed her back. "You love each other."

Priscilla shook her head. "We're just *freinden* who got married. He married me so he wouldn't be shunned. And he wanted half of *mei dat*'s business and a *haus* too."

"That's not true." Laura's expression was serious. "He wanted to save your reputation. When he told me he was going to marry you, he never mentioned his own needs or wants. He talked only about doing what was right for you."

Priscilla shook her head as irritation overtook her. "I can't believe that."

"It's true," Laura said, insisting.

"No. Mark told me he wasn't ready to get married. He puts on a show in front of your family so he can convince you he's *froh*."

"No, Kayla is right," Laura said. "*Mei bruder* never would have asked to adopt Ethan if he didn't love both of you. He *is* in love with you. He's just too dense to realize it and tell you how he truly feels."

Priscilla shook her head as her eyes filled with fresh tears. "He doesn't love me. Except for gaining land and a business, his life is ruined. I ruined it by trapping him."

"Priscilla, listen to me." Laura placed her hands on Priscilla's biceps. "Mark loves you. He's never acted this way about any other *maedel*, and he's had a group of them following him since he was sixteen. *Mei bruder* would lay down his life for you and Ethan. His feelings are real." She touched her collarbone. "I can tell because we're twins. We feel things for each other."

Priscilla cleared her throat and mopped her face. "I'm sorry. I didn't mean to get so emotional."

"It's okay." Laura released her arms and smiled. "Trust me. Everything will be fine."

Priscilla wanted to believe her, but she couldn't. Yet she knew one thing for certain—she couldn't stand another day in a loveless marriage. She had to find a way out before she suffocated from her growing loneliness and disappointment.

"Where's my new niece?" Mark asked as he stepped into the nursery.

"She's right here." Laura walked over and held up the baby.

"Aww." Mark touched her little head. "Look at you." He glanced at Priscilla as she stood in the corner with Kayla. Her eyes looked red and puffy. Had she been crying? His shoulders tightened at the thought.

"Do you want to hold her?" Laura held her toward Mark.

"No, no." Mark shook his head.

"You won't break her." Kayla chuckled. "You held Calvin."

"*Ya*, but Calvin is a *bu*. I might break a *maedel*."

Laura rolled her eyes. "Just take her."

"All right." Mark held out his arms, and Laura situated the baby in them. He gazed down at her, taking in her little pink nose and pretty blue eyes. When he heard a sniff, he looked across the room and found Priscilla wiping her eyes. "Are you okay?"

"*Ya*." Priscilla gave him a watery smile. "*Bopplin* make me cry." She ripped a tissue out of a nearby box and blotted her eyes.

"Would you like to come downstairs with me?" Kayla asked Priscilla. "I have a *kuche* to share, and we can make *kaffi* too."

"*Ya*." Priscilla seemed to jump at the chance to leave the room. She followed Kayla into the hallway without giving Mark a second look.

Something was wrong. He could feel it in his bones.

Once they were gone, he looked at Laura. "What's going on?"

Laura's expression clouded. "You need to ask your *fraa*."

Laura's eerie warning haunted Mark throughout the evening as they visited with Jamie, Kayla, and the rest of their family. Priscilla seemed to avoid Mark's gaze as they ate cake and drank coffee in the kitchen. While she spoke to the women at the table, she gave him those same one-word responses to any questions he asked her. He couldn't fathom what he'd done wrong, but he had to find out before the worry ate him from the inside out.

When they finally climbed into the buggy to go home, he was determined to get her to talk to him.

She shivered and covered herself with a quilt as Mark guided the buggy toward the road.

"Are you okay?" Mark asked, lowering his voice as he gave her a quick glance. He didn't want Ethan to worry about her too.

"*Ya.*"

"You don't look okay," Mark continued. "You've been quiet all evening."

"I'm just tired."

"It seems like more than that," he said, prodding her.

"It's not." She kept her gaze fixed on the road ahead.

Frustration coursed through him. She was upset about something, and he needed to know what it was so he could fix it. Ethan started chatting about one of Mollie's toys, but an awkward silence remained between Mark and Priscilla.

When they entered the house, he set to building a fire while Priscilla got Ethan ready for bed. When Ethan was down for the night, she disappeared into the bathroom for a while. She emerged a while later dressed in her nightgown and robe with a scarf shielding her beautiful, thick, dark hair.

"Did you have a *gut* time tonight?" Mark walked over to her.

"*Ya,* I did." She looked down at her slippers. "Did you?"

"Look at me." He slipped his finger under her chin and lifted her face so she had to gaze into his eyes. "Talk to me. Something is bothering you. I can feel it."

"I'm fine." Her voice was hoarse, as if she'd screamed for hours. "I'm just really tired, okay? Please let me go to bed."

The desperation in her voice nearly sliced him in two.

"Okay." He studied her eyes, finding pain there. "You know you can talk to me, right?"

She nodded, but she didn't look convinced.

"I'll always listen, no matter how painful it is for me to hear."

Her lower lip trembled, and she pulled away from him. "*Gut nacht.*" She slipped through Ethan's bedroom door and closed it behind her.

Mark sank onto the sofa and stared at the fire. He turned toward her bedroom door and considered going in and demanding that she speak to him. But he didn't want to frighten her or Ethan. He couldn't lose her trust or risk her thinking he would become abusive like Trent.

Still, he longed to know what was in her heart. He wanted to help her.

Deep in his soul he feared she was building a new wall to keep him away, even after they'd come so far.

TWENTY-NINE

Priscilla stared up at the ceiling as Ethan's soft snores filled the room. She tried to sleep, but her thoughts roared through her mind like a cyclone. Laura and Kayla were so wrong, and she couldn't live like this anymore. She had to leave. She had to give Mark his freedom. But how? Where would she go?

She had some money saved. If her mother loaned her more, she could find a place to live and a job. She could work as a waitress or a seamstress to support herself and Ethan, and then she could pay her mother back.

Anticipation buzzed like wings of hummingbirds. That might work. She just had to talk to her mother.

She turned toward Ethan. He was fast asleep. She could sneak out now and see if her mother was awake. Some nights her mother couldn't sleep and sat in the family room to read for a while. She prayed that was the case tonight.

She grabbed the lantern off the nightstand and slowly cracked the door. When she found the sofa empty, she pushed the door open, slipped on her boots, pulled on her coat, and set out into the cold night air.

She spotted a light on in her mother's kitchen and walked faster. She climbed the porch steps and knocked on the door.

When the door opened, her mother's eyes widened as she pushed open the storm door. "What are you doing here?"

"I need to talk to you. May I come in?"

"*Ya.*" *Mamm* waved her in, and they sat down at the kitchen table together. "What's going on?"

"I was wondering if I could borrow some money from you."

"Why?" *Mamm* eyed her with suspicion.

"I can't live a lie anymore. My marriage is a sham. There's no love and no intimacy. Today I met Kayla's new *boppli*, and I realized that this pretend marriage is slowly killing me." When her eyes filled with tears, Priscilla grabbed a paper napkin from the holder in the center of the table. "I can't stay with Mark without being his *fraa* for real. I know you have money saved up from your seamstress jobs. May I please borrow it so I can take Ethan somewhere and give him a stable home?"

"You want to take Ethan away from us and Mark?" *Mamm's* eyes filled with tears.

"We can visit you." Priscilla reached across the table and touched her mother's arm. The pain in her eyes stabbed at her heart. "We won't leave forever. I could never do that to you again. I just can't stand to be here. It hurts me every day to live with Mark in a fake marriage."

"You love him," *Mamm* said.

"*Ya.*" Priscilla nodded as tears sprinkled down her cheeks. "I do, but he doesn't love me, and it's breaking me in two."

"Why do you think leaving him will make it better?"

"If I leave, he can have the life he wants. He never wanted to marry, but he can have his *haus* and his business, and I won't be in his way," Priscilla said. "I don't belong here. I have to go. Will you help me?"

"So that's it, Priscilla?" *Dat's* voice boomed from the doorway. "You're just going to leave again?"

Mark heard the front door click shut, and he rolled over in bed. Was he dreaming, or had someone just walked into his house?

He sat up and rubbed his eyes. He turned on the lantern on his nightstand and pulled on a long-sleeved shirt and a pair of trousers. He stepped out into the family room and stilled. Only the pop and crackle of the fire in the fireplace filled the little house. He walked to the second bedroom door and pushed it open. He held up the lantern. Only one person was lying in the bed.

Priscilla is gone!

Panic gripped him as he slipped his feet into a pair of boots and hurried out the door and up the path. Cold air smacked his cheeks. Lights on in Edna's kitchen alerted him that someone was awake. He hoped Priscilla was there and that she hadn't left him to go back to Trent.

There it was. The fear he'd tried to forget but never could.

Mark climbed the back steps and opened the door. Yonnie's angry voice filled Mark's ears as he stepped into the house.

"So that's it, Priscilla?" Yonnie bellowed. "You're going to just leave again? You're going to walk out on your husband, and you're going to break your *mamm*'s heart again, and be shunned again?"

Mark stepped through the mudroom to the kitchen doorway as his pulse pounded in his ears. All his nightmares were coming true. Priscilla was going to leave him. She didn't love him. How could she even care about him at all if she was willing to leave him for a man who'd hurt her and endangered Ethan? Maybe he didn't know her as well as he'd thought. His heart splintered into a million painful shards.

"You want to know what you are, Priscilla?" Yonnie continued, circling the kitchen table so his back was to Mark. "You're nothing but a harlot."

"Yonnie, stop! That's not true!" Edna yelled. "You need to stop treating her this way! She's our *dochder*. Don't push her away. I can't lose her again!"

Mark's blood boiled as he walked up behind Yonnie.

"You're going to lose the best thing that has ever happened to you," Yonnie said. "You don't deserve Mark. You're blessed to be here with us. You're fortunate that he even agreed to marry you after what you did."

"I don't deserve to be treated this way," Priscilla said, seething as she stood. "You have no right to talk to me like this, and I won't stand for it any longer. I came here looking for help, not more criticism."

Then the truth hit Mark between the eyes. Priscilla had two abusers in her life—Trent and her father. This was why she left the community eight years ago. She'd gone to escape this verbal abuse, which was worse than he'd ever heard or imagined. She told him that day in the barn that she'd fallen for Trent because she was desperate for someone to love her. But he hadn't realized that desperation came not just from a lack of love from her father, but from how horribly Yonnie had treated her.

Mark had to put a stop to this now! He had to be the one man who treated Priscilla with respect and cherished her. He had to save her from this endless cycle of abuse. He had to get her out of this toxic environment for good.

"Stop it!" Mark yelled as his red, burning hot anger erupted like a volcano.

Yonnie spun and faced him, his face twisted into a scowl. But he took a step back as Mark came into the kitchen.

Mark's body quaked as he shook his finger at Yonnie. "You have no right to treat her that way. She's not a harlot. She's your *dochder*, Ethan's *mamm*, and *mei fraa*. She's not fortunate that I married her." He jammed the finger into his own chest. "I'm fortunate that she agreed to marry *me*. I don't deserve a woman as kind, sweet, and lovely as she is. And you don't deserve to even call her your *dochder*."

He pushed past Yonnie and made his way to Priscilla. She wiped tears from her face as she stared at him.

"Let's go, Priscilla." Mark motioned for her to follow him.

She hesitated. "Where are we going?"

"I'm getting you out of here for *gut*," Mark said. "He's never going to treat you this badly again."

"Just wait a minute," Yonnie said. "I was talking to her. You have no right—"

"Actually, Yonnie, I do have a right to take her from here." Mark walked over to him. "I'm her husband, and I will not allow you to abuse her any longer."

Priscilla went to Mark, and he threaded his fingers in hers. They started toward the mudroom, and then he stopped and turned toward Yonnie, who stared after them, wide-eyed.

"Oh, one more thing, Yonnie," Mark said. "I do remember that you own this farm and you're my employer. Consider this my resignation. We're leaving tonight, and we're not coming back."

Priscilla felt as if her head was spinning as Mark held on to her hand and pulled her down her parents' back porch steps.

"Wait." She stopped and yanked him back to her. "Where are we going?"

"I was thinking of taking you to Jamie's, but they have a new *boppli*. We'll go to Laura's. She has room for us." He started down the path. "We'll pack enough clothes for overnight and come back for more in the daylight."

She opened her mouth to protest, but then she closed it again.

When they arrived at the *daadihaus,* she quickly dressed and then filled a bag with clothes for all of them while Mark gathered Ethan in his arms and covered him with a quilt. Then they hurried through the cold to the stable.

Mark hitched up the horse and buggy, and they started on their journey to Laura's house.

They rode in silence for several minutes as Priscilla stared out the window. Only Ethan's breathing filled the buggy as her father's cruel words echoed in her mind and tears filled her eyes once again.

"I'm sorry he did that to you." Mark's voice was compassionate. "He's always talked to you that way?"

"*Ya.*" She swiped her hand over her eyes.

"Is that why you left years ago?"

"*Ya.*" She shivered as her memories turned to the night that had driven her away from her childhood home. "I had been out with the youth, and we stayed out past our usual ten o'clock. When I got home it was after eleven, and he was waiting for me at the door. He accused me of being out all night, drinking and being promiscuous, which wasn't true. We had gone to spend the day at Cascade Lake and stopped at a restaurant on the way home. We were having so much fun talking and laughing that we lost track of time."

"I remember that trip," Mark said. "We all got home late that night."

"Exactly." She took a tissue from her coat pocket. "I tried to explain to him that we had just lost track of time, but he was convinced I was out misbehaving, and he said I would bring shame on him with my actions. I tried to explain that I'd done nothing but swim and spend time with *mei freinden* all day. He refused to believe me, and it was the last straw. I couldn't take the accusations and the criticism anymore, and it pushed me over the edge. I packed up my things and left after my parents went to bed that night."

"So for your whole life, he's made you think you're not worthy of his love. Or anyone's."

She nodded and tried to clear her throat past a swelling lump of anguish.

Mark halted the horse at a red light and turned toward her. "Were you really going to leave me?"

She nodded.

"Why?" The pain in his eyes was like a splinter in her heart.

"I can't live a lie anymore." Her voice was thin. "I can't stay in a pretend marriage. It's tearing me apart. You can have the *haus* and the business. I know besides not wanting to be shunned, they're the reason you married me."

After a moment he said, "Someone once told me there's more to life than owning a *haus*."

"Mark, I don't want to ruin your life anymore."

"You'd ruin my life if you and Ethan left me."

She bit back a sob as she stared at him. He turned toward the windshield and guided the horse through the intersection. Then they turned on the road that led to Laura's house.

When they reached the top of Laura's driveway, Allen came outside.

"Is everything all right?" he asked as he jogged down the steps.

Mark climbed out of the buggy. "Could we stay here tonight? I'll explain everything later, but we had to get out of the *daadihaus*."

"*Ya*, of course." Allen looked between them. "Let me help you with your horse and buggy."

Laura appeared on the porch, hugging a shawl to her middle. "What's going on?"

"They need a place to stay," Allen explained.

Laura waved them in. "Come inside out of the cold."

Priscilla leaned over the back of the buggy and nudged Ethan. "Ethan. Ethan, honey. I need you to wake up. You need to walk into *Aenti* Laura's *haus*, okay?"

Ethan rubbed his eyes as he sat up.

Priscilla grabbed the bag of clothes, and then she and Ethan climbed the steps and into Laura's house.

"I can't stay there," Mark said to his brother-in-law after telling him what Yonnie said to Priscilla. "It's too toxic for Priscilla and Ethan." He rubbed at the knots of tension in his neck. "I've never been so furious in my life."

"I can't believe how Yonnie talks to her." Allen shook his head as they stood in the office of his carriage business. "I would never speak to *mei dochder* that way."

"I know." Mark held up his hands. "I'm sorry to impose on you like this, but Jamie has a new *boppli*, and *mei dat* doesn't have room for us. Could we stay here until I find a *haus* to rent? I'll start looking tomorrow, and I'll see if I can work for *mei dat*. We'll be out of here before your new *boppli* is born."

"It's no problem." Allen shook his head. "You can stay here as long as you'd like." He pointed toward his shop, where he repaired and rebuilt buggies. "You can even work for me if you want to. My business is booming, and I can hardly keep up anymore."

"*Danki.*" Mark started pacing as Yonnie's cruel tirade rang again in his mind. "I just can't get over the words he used toward her. Priscilla is *wunderbaar,* and she doesn't deserve to be spoken to like that." He stopped pacing and looked at Allen. "She said she wanted to leave me because she's ruining my life. I don't understand it. Why would she think that?"

"Did you ask her why?" Allen sat down on a stool.

Mark began to pace again. He felt as if his insides were tied up in knots. He shook his head, and then it hit him like a bolt of lightning. "I'm in love with her. The idea of her leaving me makes me physically ill."

Allen smiled. "It's been obvious to all of us that you two are in love. In fact, Laura and I were just discussing that on our way home from Jamie's *haus* tonight. I know the truth about why you married her. Laura told me."

"She did?"

"*Ya*. She was really upset when we left Jamie's *haus* earlier, and she needed someone to talk to. She told me everything during the ride home since Mollie was asleep in the back of the buggy. It really upset her when Priscilla cried while she held Alice. She said she hoped you and Priscilla would realize how much you love each other and work it out. I'm glad you finally realize you love Priscilla." Allen pointed toward the house. "Now you need to go tell her how you feel, and she'll realize that she doesn't need to leave you. In fact, she'll want to stay."

"*Danki* for letting us stay here," Priscilla said as she closed the door to the sewing room where Ethan was asleep on the sofa. "I appreciate it."

"Of course." Laura hugged her. "I'm so sorry your *dat* was cruel to you."

"*Danki*." Priscilla took a deep breath. "I thought leaving Mark was the best solution, but Mark was the one who saved me. He got me away from *mei dat*."

"So that's why you left when we were eighteen." Laura shook

her head. "Why didn't you tell Savilla and me what you were going through at home?"

Priscilla shrugged. "I guess I was embarrassed. I didn't want you to know since you and Savilla both had loving and supportive fathers."

Laura took Priscilla's hand and steered her to the spare room. "I set this room up for Cindy. She borrows Roy's horse and buggy to come visit me, and sometimes we talk late into the night. I ask her to stay instead of going home in the dark. This room will be perfect for you and Mark."

"*Danki.*" Priscilla stared at the double bed, and her heart seemed to stutter before dropping to the pit of her stomach. There wasn't room on Ethan's sofa for her tonight. She and Mark would have to stay together for the first time since they were married.

Laura squeezed Priscilla's arm. "We'll talk more tomorrow, okay? You just get some rest." She started for the door and then turned and faced her. "*Mei bruder* loves you. Just give him a chance to tell you how he feels, okay?"

"Okay," Priscilla said, making a promise. She had to know if her friend was right.

Laura slipped out the door, and Priscilla sank onto the corner of the bed. She was confused but also relieved that Mark had taken her away from her father. Now she had to figure out what would happen next.

Soon after, she heard footsteps on the stairs and muffled voices in the hallway. Then a soft knock sounded on the door.

"Come in," she said as she stood.

Mark stepped into the room and closed the door behind him. He walked over to her, and his blue eyes glistened in the warm glow of the lantern on the dresser. "Can we talk?"

"*Ya.*" The muscles in her shoulders tensed.

"Where were you going to go tonight?"

She shrugged. "I don't know. I went to see *mei mamm* to ask if I could borrow money from her. I wanted to find a little apartment to rent for Ethan and me. I thought I could get a job working as a waitress or seamstress and then I'd pay her back."

"What did I do to push you away?"

"You didn't push me away. You've been nothing but kind and supportive to Ethan and me." Her voice thinned. "But you deserve so much better than me. I'm damaged."

"No, you're not."

"I am." Fresh tears formed in her eyes. "And then when I held Alice tonight, I realized I can't stand to live in a loveless marriage. If I can't have a true marriage with you, then I'd rather be alone. It's torture to be with you but not have all of you, not have your whole heart."

"That's just it, Priscilla." He cupped her cheeks with his hands. "You do have my whole heart. I love you. I've loved you for months, but I didn't realize it right away. I didn't know what love was until I had a chance to get to know you."

The tears escaped down her cheeks.

"I love you too," she whispered. "I didn't know what love could be like before you. When I met Trent, I was looking for someone to love me, but that wasn't love. You make me feel strong and protected."

"Please don't leave me. I can't stand the idea of losing you and Ethan after all we've been through." His eyes searched hers. "I'll make things right. We'll find a *haus* to rent until I can build you one on *mei dat*'s farm. I'll work for *mei dat*. We'll make a life somehow. Give me a chance to show you."

"But what about *mei dat*'s land and his business?"

Mark shook his head. "None of that matters without you. I don't care where we live. I just want to be with you and Ethan. I want to be a family. God chose you for me, and God never makes mistakes. You're my life. You're my future."

He leaned down, and as his lips brushed hers, what felt like an electric current roared through her veins. She closed her eyes, and as she allowed his lips to explore hers, her entire body relaxed. He wrapped his arms around her, and she lost herself in the feel of his touch. This was what true love felt like.

When he pulled away, he rested his forehead against hers and looked into her eyes. "I've been dying to do that for months."

"For months?" she asked.

"*Ya*." He grinned. "Ever since you said I had eager *maed* who followed me around."

They both laughed.

"Will you give me a chance to show you I can be a real husband?" he asked, his eyes pleading with hers.

"*Ya*," she said. "I'm so grateful God sent me back here. I've been begging him to show me where I belonged, and he led me straight to you. I thought I had to leave this community to find happiness, but now I realize my heart has always been here. I'm supposed to be a member of the church, and I'm supposed to be your *fraa*. It doesn't matter where we live. I just want to be with you."

Mark wrapped his arms around her waist, and Priscilla's breath hitched in her lungs as his lips met hers again. She looped her arms around his neck and pulled him in closer. He deepened the kiss, and it lit a fire inside her, turning her bones to ash. She closed her eyes and savored the feel of his mouth against hers.

Yes. This is where I belong—here with Mark. This is my true home.

THIRTY

THE NEXT MORNING PRISCILLA CARRIED A PLAT-
ter to Laura's kitchen table and then sat down beside Mark. She
smiled at Ethan. He was sitting beside Mollie on the other side of
the table.

"I think that's everything," Laura said. "Let's pray."

They bowed their heads in silent prayer and then began filling their plates with eggs, bacon, home fried potatoes, and rolls.

"Have you given my idea any thought?" Allen asked Mark.

"What idea?" Laura divided a look between them.

"I asked Mark if he wanted to come work for me. You know
my business has been growing, and I could use a partner."

"Really?" Priscilla turned to Mark. "Are you going to do it?"

"I'll think about it." Mark picked up a piece of bacon. "I appreciate the offer, but right now I need to find a *haus*."

"No, you don't." Laura shook her head. "We have plenty of
room here. We'll put a twin-size bed in the sewing room for Ethan.
Mollie has her own room, and we have room for the *boppli*."

"*Mei schweschder.*" Mollie sat up straight and lifted her chin.
"I know she's a girl."

Priscilla grinned as she turned to Laura. "Are you having
a girl?"

317

"I don't know." Laura shrugged. "I guess we'll see."

A knock sounded on the back door, and Allen rose. "Are you expecting anyone?"

"No." Laura shook her head.

Allen disappeared into the mudroom while everyone continued to eat. He returned a few moments later with Priscilla's father walking behind him.

Priscilla swallowed a gasp. She looked at Mark, whose face had transformed into a deep frown.

"Yonnie," Mark said as he stood. "What are you doing here?"

"I want to talk to you and Priscilla. Please." *Dat* held up his hand. "I'm here to apologize."

Laura gestured toward the family room. "Why don't you go in there so you have some privacy?"

Mark looked at Priscilla as if asking permission, and she nodded. "Okay."

Priscilla stood, and Mark threaded his fingers with hers. The simple gesture of affection filled her with strength as she walked with Mark into the family room.

"What do you want to say?" Mark stood in front of her father with his head held high.

"I want to apologize . . . for everything."

Priscilla blinked and then shook her head. This was too good to be true.

"Why the sudden change in your demeanor?" Mark asked.

Dat's expression clouded. "After you left last night, I remembered a Scripture verse the bishop gave a sermon on recently. It's Colossians 3:12. 'Therefore, as God's chosen people, holy and dearly loved, clothe yourselves with compassion, kindness, humility, gentleness and patience.' I couldn't get it out of my head last night."

Priscilla's eyes watered as Mark gave her hand a gentle squeeze.

"Edna made me realize how terrible I've been all these years. She's been trying to tell me since Priscilla was a little girl, but I never listened." His dark eyes filled with tears. "*Mei dat* was tough on *mei bruders* and me. I always resented how he treated me, but I realize now I've become just as terrible as he was—if not worse."

He turned toward Priscilla. "You told me you thought I was disappointed in you because you weren't a *bu*. And now you might think I was hard on you because *mei daed* was hard on me. But the truth is when we learned your mother and I couldn't have more *kinner*, I was hard on you for one reason: to prove I could raise my only *kind* to be the model community member *mei daed* never thought I was. In the end, I was wrong, so very wrong."

He peered into Priscilla's eyes with a look of contrition she'd never seen.

"I've always been too tough on you, Priscilla. I realize now that I wasn't loving. I never guided you. I only criticized you. I wasn't the *daed* you needed or deserved, and I'm so very truly sorry. If only I could go back in time and fix everything, but I know I can't. I'm sorry. I was wrong. I pushed you away eight years ago, and last night I did it again. I was wrong to call you that cruel name. Please forgive me and come back to the farm. You belong there, and you've earned my horse business. I want to give it to family, and you're my only family."

"I forgive you," she said, her voice stronger than she'd hoped. "But it's too late for you to apologize. I can't go back there. I've moved on, and you should too. Mark and I have decided to find a *haus* to rent, or we might stay here. He's thinking about working with Allen."

With one hand still entwined with Mark's, she placed her other hand on his forearm. Her husband's strength gave her courage and kept her from breaking apart.

"Please." *Dat* looked between them. "I want you to come back. I will do better. I will be the *daed* you deserve and the *daadi* Ethan deserves."

"You say that now," Mark began, "but how do we know you won't lose your temper and begin to call Priscilla cruel names again? The name you called her should never be used to describe someone's *dochder*. It was inexcusable. Priscilla doesn't deserve to be treated that way, and you're not the example I want for Ethan."

"You're right." *Dat* nodded, his expression forlorn. "But I promise I'll do better. I will think before I speak."

Mark turned to Priscilla. "What do you want?"

"I don't want to go back there, but I want you to be *froh*," she said. "Do you want my father's business? Do you want to live on the farm?"

"I've already told you I don't care where we live as long as I have you and Ethan with me."

"Let's stick with our plan." She gave his hand a gentle squeeze.

"Fine." Mark looked over at *Dat*. "I can't take the chance of your verbally abusing Priscilla any longer. We're going to stay here."

Dat's eyes misted over. "You won't come back home?"

Mark shook his head and then nodded toward the doorway. "I think you should leave now."

Dat hesitated and then gave a curt nod before walking out of the house.

Priscilla looked up at Mark as panic stirred in her belly. "What did we just do?"

The look in Mark's eyes comforted her as he touched her cheek. "We stood up for what was right. When I married you, I promised to protect you and Ethan, and that's just what I plan to do." He leaned down and brushed his lips against hers. "Let's go finish our breakfast, and then I'll talk to Allen about working for him."

As Mark steered her back into the kitchen, a calmness settled over Priscilla. She suddenly knew to the very depth of her being that somehow everything would turn out just fine as long as she and Ethan had Mark by their side.

⎯∽⎯

"*Mamm!*" Priscilla hurried over to her mother a week later as she gathered with the other women in the Bontrager family's kitchen before the church service. "How are you?"

"I'm fine." *Mamm's* eyes sparkled with tears as she pulled her into her arms for a hug. "How are you?"

"We're doing okay." Priscilla nodded. "Mark is working for Allen, and we'll look for a *haus* to rent unless we decide to stay at Laura and Allen's for now."

"How are things between you and Mark?"

Priscilla tried in vain to suppress a smile. "Really *gut*. I've never been so *froh* in my life. He loves me, and he's such a *gut* father to Ethan."

"I'm so glad. I knew it would work out between you two. I could see how much he loved you before you realized it." *Mamm* dabbed her eyes with a tissue she took from her apron. "How's Ethan?"

Priscilla shrugged. "He's doing well. He and Mollie get along great, but he misses you and *Dat*."

"We miss all three of you. Our home feels so empty and incomplete without you and your family. I keep expecting Ethan to walk into the kitchen and tell me about his day at school." *Mamm* wiped away an errant tear, and an intense sympathy for her mother caught Priscilla off guard. She hadn't realized just how much the result of *Dat*'s hateful words had changed her world.

"Your *dat* feels terrible about what he said. I've been telling him for years that he was too critical of you, and that he said things that were cruel. He finally realizes how wrong he was."

Mamm cleared her throat. "Would you consider coming home? Your *dat* and I want you and Ethan to come back. We miss you so much." She folded her hands as if she were praying. "Your *dat* has promised me that if you come back, he'll do his best to make you feel welcome. He'll show you that he regrets all the years he hurt you. He'll make up for it."

Priscilla swallowed back a knot of emotion that threatened to choke her. "I appreciate all you said to him and how you finally made him realize how wrong he was. But Mark won't take the chance that *Dat* will hurt me again. He also doesn't want Ethan to hear *Dat*'s cruel words."

"I understand." *Mamm* paused. "But we also need you. Your *dat* is getting older, and he can't handle the work on his own. He wants to hire someone, but he'd rather have Mark. He really admires Mark, and he wants to leave the farm to Ethan and the rest of your *kinner* if you and Mark have more."

"I don't know what to say." Priscilla shook her head. "Mark doesn't want to come back."

"Why don't you think about it?" *Mamm* touched Priscilla's arm. "Tell Mark your *dat* needs his help, and he's willing to do whatever it takes to get all of you back home with us on the farm."

"All right. I'll talk to Mark tonight," Priscilla said, willing to make the promise.

Later that evening Priscilla climbed into bed beside Mark. She snuggled down under the covers, and Mark wrapped his arms around her and pulled her close.

"Are you going to tell me what's been on your mind all afternoon? Or do I have to guess?" Mark's voice in her ear sent a shiver dancing down her back.

"Why don't you guess?" She grinned.

"Let's see," he began. "You're wondering how you managed to snag yourself such a handsome husband."

She laughed. "Not even close."

"Okay. You're trying to figure out the best gift to get me for Christmas."

She chuckled. "Nope. That's not it either."

"All right. I give up." He released her, and she turned toward him. The soft yellow glow of the lantern complemented his chiseled face.

"It's actually serious."

"Uh-oh." His smile faded. "What is it?"

"I talked to *mei mamm* today before church. She wants us to come back to the farm."

His handsome face clouded. "No."

"Just listen for a minute." She sat up, leaning her back against the headboard. "She said *mei dat* wants us back. He needs your help with the farm. He also wants to leave the farm to Ethan and any *kinner* we might have in the future."

Mark propped himself up with a pillow. "What do you want to do?"

She shook her head as confusion filled her. "I don't know. Part of me wants to go back. Laura is going to have her *boppli* anytime now, and they don't need extra people in their *haus*."

"We're not homeless, Priscilla, and we're not destitute. I'll eventually find us another place to live. I have money in the bank. I've been saving for years."

"I know that." She touched his cheek, enjoying the scratchy feel of his beard. "What do you want?"

Mark looked across the room as if the dresser held all the answers. "I like working with Allen, but I do miss the horses."

"Really?"

He nodded as he faced her once again. "I enjoyed the work. I never knew how much I could enjoy training horses until I went to work with your *dat*."

"So you like working there more than you like working for Allen?"

"*Ya*, I do." His expression became fierce. "But I won't allow him to hurt you ever again."

"I know that." She touched his cheek again as affection overwhelmed her. "But what if we went back on our terms?"

"What do you mean?"

"What if we told him we'll come back only on certain conditions?"

"I'm listening."

"We just need to decide what we want." She touched his shoulder. "What will it take to get you back there?"

Mark rubbed his beard. "I would want to earn a salary, and then I'll build our *haus* when we're ready. It will be our *haus*, and I'll pay for it. I don't want your *dat* to foot the bill, and I don't want him to have a hold on us. I'll earn my way on that farm. I'm not going there to get anything for free."

"I understand."

"And your *dat* has to prove to me that he can treat you with respect. If he says one thing out of turn, we're gone." He snapped his fingers. "Does that sound *gut*?"

"*Ya.*" She rubbed his shoulder. "Do you want to talk to my parents tomorrow while Ethan is in school?"

"If that's what you want, then *ya.*"

"Okay. It's settled, then." She smiled.

"*Gut.*" Mark grabbed her by the waist, and she squealed as he pulled her over to him. "Come here, *mei fraa.*" He grinned before kissing her.

She relaxed against him as she lost herself in the feel of his lips, and bliss bubbled through her veins.

Priscilla stood beside Mark on her parents' front porch the following morning. The door opened, and her mother gave a little squeal as she opened it wide.

"Priscilla. Mark." *Mamm* gestured for them to come in. "I'm so *froh* to see you."

"It's nice to see you too," Mark said as they stepped inside the house. "Is Yonnie home?"

"*Ya,* we were just having *kaffi* in the kitchen," *Mamm* said. "Hang up your coats and come join us."

Priscilla looked up at Mark, and he gave her a reassuring smile as they hung their coats on the pegs by the front door. Then they followed *Mamm* into the kitchen.

"Priscilla." *Dat*'s expression brightened as he looked up at her. "Mark. *Wie geht's?*"

"We were wondering if we could talk to you," Mark said.

"Please have a seat." *Dat* gestured to the chairs across from him.

"Would you like some *kaffi?*" *Mamm* offered.

"*Ya,* please," Mark said. "*Danki.*"

"I'll help you serve it." Priscilla took mugs from the cabinet and set them on the table. Mark sat down across from Dat.

"What do you want to discuss?" Dat's expression seemed hopeful.

"Edna told Priscilla you still want us to move back to the farm," Mark began. "She said you want me to work for you, and you want to leave the farm to Ethan and any *kinner* we might have."

"That's true." Dat fingered his beard. "I really need your help. I can't run this farm by myself, and you're the best farmhand I've ever had. Besides that, you're family now." He looked up at Priscilla. "And I miss all of you. I especially miss having *mei gross-sohn* around."

Priscilla's hands trembled as she poured coffee into Mark's mug. Why did her father always know how to get right to her heart, no matter how much he'd hurt her in the past?

When she handed Mark his mug, he touched her arm and gave her a tender smile. The simple gesture calmed her, and her hands stopped shaking.

Crossing to the counter again, Priscilla filled a mug for herself and then sat down beside Mark. Her mother sat down across from her.

"What do you say?" Dat asked Mark. "Will you come back?"

"We will." Mark looked at Priscilla once again. "But only under certain conditions."

"Okay." Dat's expression brightened. "What are your conditions?"

"I want to earn a salary," Mark said. "We'll live in the *daadihaus* until I have enough money to build a *haus*."

"No, I can build you one," Dat said. "I have plenty of money."

"No." Mark's voice was even but firm. "I want to earn our *haus* and build it with my own money. I don't want anything for free. I'll save enough to build the *haus* Priscilla wants." He glanced at her. "I want *mei fraa* to be *froh*."

Priscilla gave him a little smile, and then she and her mother shared a smile.

Mark faced her father again. "And you have to treat Priscilla with respect. I won't allow you to hurt her anymore, and I want you to be a *gut* role model for Ethan. You have to earn back our trust. I won't permit you to insult or criticize Priscilla at all. If you do, we'll leave again. I'll find a *haus* to rent and go back to working for Allen or *mei dat*."

Dat nodded. "I understand, and I'll prove myself to you. I'll do anything to have you come back. I don't want to lose my family again. You're all important to me."

Mark looked at Priscilla. "Does that all sound *gut* to you?"

Priscilla nodded. *"Ya."*

Dat met her gaze, and his eyes glimmered with tears. *"Danki* for forgiving me and giving me another chance. I won't let you down."

Tears stung her own eyes as she silently asked God to guide her father's heart toward her.

Mark looped his arm around Priscilla's shoulders and gave her a little squeeze before looking at her father again. "When do you want us to come back?"

"How about today?" *Dat* asked.

Mamm clapped. "I'm so *froh*. I'll have my family back together."

Priscilla smiled. "Ethan is going to be so excited." She squeezed Mark's hand.

While she knew her relationship with her father would never be perfect after the way he'd treated her, for the first time in a long time, her heart was filled with hope.

⁓

"So Mollie was right," Priscilla said as she held her newborn niece against her chest a week later. She moved the rocking chair in Florence's family room back and forth. "She knew she was going to have a baby *schweschder*."

"I know." Laura laughed. "She predicted I would have a girl, and I did."

Cindy smiled as she touched Catherine's little fingers. "I can't get over how tiny she is."

"She looks like an angel," Sarah Jane chimed in.

"I know." Priscilla looked down at her. "That little nose and that thick, dark-brown hair. She's so *schee*, and I love her name. Catherine Savilla Lambert is beautiful."

Laura smiled. "Mollie insisted we name her after her other *mamm*, as she calls Savilla. It seemed fitting that we remember Savilla this way."

"*Ya*, I agree." Happy tears gathered in Priscilla's eyes. "She's just perfect."

"You'll be next," Laura said with a smile. "I can feel it."

"I hope so." Priscilla bit her lower lip as heat infused her cheeks. Her marriage had been just about perfect the past couple of weeks, and she couldn't have been any happier. Their relationship had grown deeper and more meaningful since they'd stayed at Laura's house. Priscilla could feel Mark's love surrounding her and making her more courageous every day. She had the marriage she'd always wanted. God had truly blessed her the day she became Mark's wife.

They'd also settled into a comfortable routine on her father's farm during the past week. *Dat* had been respectful and kind to her, and they'd had a few meaningful talks. She was hesitant to trust him after the lifetime of hurt he'd subjected her to, but she allowed herself to remain hopeful that someday she and her father could grow closer.

She touched Catherine's little fingers, and her heart fluttered. She and Mark had so much to look forward to as a couple. She looked forward to the day she and Mark would have a child together. She was certain it would happen in God's perfect timing.

"May I have a turn to hold her?" Cindy held up her arms.

"Of course." Priscilla passed the baby over to Cindy and then stood so she could take the rocking chair.

"Are you ready to go?" Mark appeared in the doorway with Ethan by his side. "It's getting late."

"*Ya.*" Priscilla stood, and she and Mark both said good night to the sisters. She followed Mark and Ethan into the kitchen, where they said good-bye to the rest of the family. Then she walked with Mark and Ethan out into the cold so they could start their journey home.

"This is perfect," Mark said as Priscilla snuggled up next to him in front of the fire in the *daadihaus* later that evening. "Hot chocolate, a warm fire, and *mei schee fraa.*"

"You say that to all the *maed.*" Priscilla looked up at him and pulled the quilt over her lap. Then she smiled at the hearth, admiring the pinecones, evergreen branches, and candles she'd used to decorate it for Christmas.

"Are you calling me a user again?" he said, grinning.

"Well, you know what they say. If the shoe fits . . ." She laughed, and then she took a sip of hot chocolate before setting her mug on the coffee table and snuggling closer to Mark. "I can't believe how adorable our two new nieces are. Do you think we'll have a girl someday?"

"We can hope." He kissed her forehead. "How many *kinner* do you want?"

"I don't know. Maybe six?"

"Six?" He cringed, and she laughed. "How about two more?"

"Or three." She touched his bearded chin. "You have three biological siblings."

"*Ya*, I sure do." He pulled her closer and wrapped his arms around her shoulders. "I don't care how many we have as long as I'm with you."

"I feel the same way." She leaned against him and relished the sound of his heartbeat.

"I have something for you. I know it's not Christmas yet, but I can't wait to give it to you." He reached under the sofa, pulling up a large piece of flat wood. "I've been working on this for a while. I used to tinker with it before we moved in with Laura and Allen, before going to sleep." He handed it to her. "Here."

"Oh my goodness!" Priscilla gaped as she ran her fingers over the carving that was a perfect representation of their little house. He'd even included her small garden with the happy flowers. Tears filled her eyes at the love and tenderness he'd carved into the wood for her. "Mark. This is exquisite."

"You think so?" He frowned. "It's not perfect, but I'll get better as I work on more carvings." He smiled at her. "I wanted to use the tools you gave me to make you something special. We'll always have this as a memory of our first *haus*."

"I love it." She touched his cheek. *"Danki."*

"Gern gschehne." He threaded his fingers with hers. "This way you'll always remember where we started out."

"I love our little *haus*. I just want to stay here in front of the hearth with you." She looked up at him. "Do you think we should build a hearth in our new *haus*?"

"Why not? It's going to be our *haus*, right? We should have what we want."

"That's true."

"Like I said before, I just want to make *mei fraa froh. Ich liebe dich*," Mark whispered against her hair.

"I love you too."

Mark brushed his lips against hers, sending happiness buzzing through her like a honeybee. She smiled against his mouth and silently thanked God for giving her true love and happiness. Her most fervent prayers had been answered. She could hardly wait to see what tomorrow would bring.

DISCUSSION QUESTIONS

1. When Priscilla left the community eight years earlier, she believed she'd never go back. By the end of the book, she realizes the Amish community is her true home. What do you think caused her to change her point of view throughout the story?

2. Franey is jealous when she learns Mark is going to marry Priscilla. She's so upset that she says cruel things about Priscilla. Have you ever been jealous of a friend? If so, did that jealousy cause you to say things that weren't true? Did you regret what you said, and did you ask for forgiveness? Share this with the group.

3. Laura confides in Priscilla that she experienced miscarriages early in her marriage. She also shares with Mark that she is nervous about her pregnancy because of her past losses. Could you relate to Laura and her experience? Share this with the group.

4. Priscilla believes she's damaged and unworthy of love. Think of a time when you felt lost and alone. Where did you find your strength? What Bible verses helped?

5. At the start of the book, Mark doesn't believe he'll ever want to get married and have children. His dream of owning his own home on his father's farm is enough for him. However,

he changes as the story progresses. What do you think caused him to change his point of view about his future?

6. Yonnie has always been hard on Priscilla, believing his tough parenting style was permissible. He discovers the error of his ways at the end of the story. What made him realize he'd been wrong and ask for forgiveness? How have you felt convicted of a wrongdoing?

7. By the end of the book, Mark realizes he's fallen in love with Priscilla. What do you think helped him realize how strong his feelings for her were?

8. Which character can you identify with the most? Which character seemed to carry the most emotional stake in the story? Was it Priscilla, Ethan, Mark, or someone else?

9. What role did Ethan play in Mark and Priscilla's relationship? Did he help strengthen their marriage?

10. What did you know about the Amish before reading this book? What did you learn?

ACKNOWLEDGMENTS

As always, I'm thankful for my loving family, including my mother, Lola Goebelbecker; my husband, Joe; and my sons, Zac and Matt. I'm blessed to have such an awesome and amazing family who puts up with me when I'm stressed out on a book deadline.

Special thanks to my mother and my dear friend Becky Biddy, who graciously read the draft of this book to check for typos. Becky—I'm sure you ran out of a few dispensers of tape flags on this one! Also, thank you, Becky, for your daily notes of encouragement. Your friendship is a blessing!

I'm also grateful to my special Amish friend, who patiently answers my endless stream of questions.

Thank you to my wonderful church family at Morning Star Lutheran in Matthews, North Carolina, for your encouragement, prayers, love, and friendship. You all mean so much to my family and me.

Thank you to Zac Weikal and the fabulous members of my Bakery Bunch! I'm so thankful for your friendship and your excitement about my books. You all are amazing!

To my agent, Natasha Kern—I can't thank you enough for your guidance, advice, and friendship. You are a tremendous blessing in my life.

Thank you to my amazing editor, Jocelyn Bailey, for your friendship and guidance. I appreciate how you push me to dig deeper with each book and improve my writing. I've learned so much from you, and I look forward to our future projects together. I also cherish our fun emails and text messages. You are a delight!

I'm grateful to editor Jean Bloom, who helped me polish and refine the story. Jean, you are a master at connecting the dots and filling in the gaps. I'm so thankful that we can continue to work together!

Thank you to Janet Jeter for help with the twin research. You're so blessed to not only have a twin brother but also another set of twins in your family! Thank you for giving me pointers on Laura and Mark's connection. I'm so grateful to have you as one of my work buddies.

I also would like to thank Kristen Golden for tirelessly working to promote my books. I'm grateful to each and every person at HarperCollins Christian Publishing who helped make this book a reality.

To my readers—thank you for choosing my novels. My books are a blessing in my life for many reasons, including the special friendships I've formed with my readers. Thank you for your email messages, Facebook notes, and letters.

Thank you most of all to God—for giving me the inspiration and the words to glorify You. I'm grateful and humbled You've chosen this path for me.

THE AMISH HOMESTEAD SERIES

AMY CLIPSTON

A PLACE AT OUR
TABLE
— AN AMISH —
HOMESTEAD NOVEL

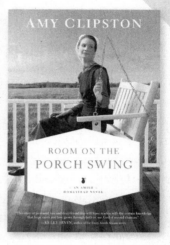

AMY CLIPSTON

ROOM ON THE
PORCH SWING
— AN AMISH —
HOMESTEAD NOVEL

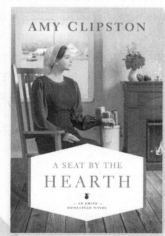

AMY CLIPSTON

A SEAT BY THE
HEARTH
— AN AMISH —
HOMESTEAD NOVEL

BESTSELLING AUTHOR
AMY CLIPSTON

A WELCOME AT
OUR DOOR
AN AMISH
HOMESTEAD NOVEL

AVAILABLE IN PRINT AND E-BOOK

ABOUT THE AUTHOR

Dan Davis Photography

AMY CLIPSTON IS THE AWARD-WINNING and bestselling author of the Kauffman Amish Bakery, Hearts of Lancaster Grand Hotel, Amish Heirloom, Amish Homestead, and Amish Marketplace series. Her novels have hit multiple bestseller lists including CBD, CBA, and ECPA. Amy holds a degree in communication from Virginia Wesleyan University and works full-time for the City of Charlotte, NC. Amy lives in North Carolina with her husband, two sons, and six spoiled-rotten cats.

Visit her online at amyclipston.com
Facebook: @AmyClipstonBooks
Twitter: @AmyClipston
Instagram: @amy_clipston